THE BURNING ROC

Gus Wilson and Kitty Cochrane, tw
chemists, are called to look into a po
natural gas reservoir beneath the e
of Bernard Morris. They discover t
Morris is indeed sitting on a mounta
of untapped gas, but gas which is so
volatile that any disturbance could trigger a huge explosion. Morris is determined to drill. When Kitty is equally determined to stop him, she finds her life in danger. It becomes a race to see if Morris can be stopped from causing a disaster the scale of Chernobyl...

THE BURNING ROCKS

THE BURNING ROCKS

by

Max Marlow

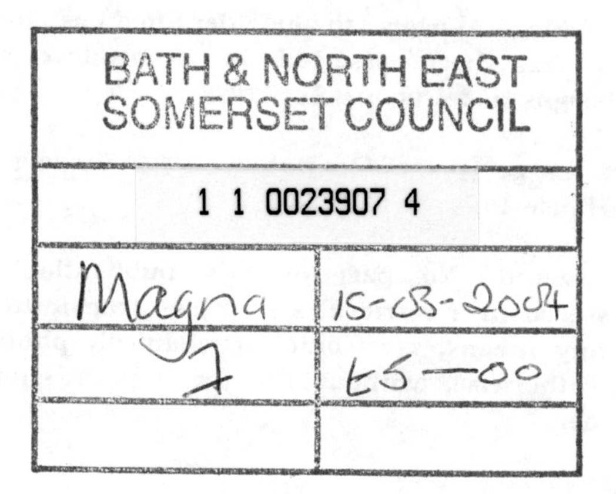

Magna Large Print Books
Long Preston, North Yorkshire,
England.

British Library Cataloguing in Publication Data.

Marlow, Max
The burning rocks.

A catalogue record for this book is available from the British Library

ISBN 0-7505-1048-X

First published in Great Britain by Severn House Publishers Ltd., 1995

Published in Large Print December, 1996 by arrangement with Severn House Publishers Ltd.

Magna Large Print is an imprint of
Library Magna Books Ltd.
Printed and bound in Great Britain by
T.J. Press (Padstow) Ltd., Cornwall, PL28 8RW.

'What the sage poets taught by th' heavenly
Muse,
Storied of old in high immortal verse,
Of dire chimeras and enchanted isles,
And rifted rocks whose entrance leads
to Hell.'

Comus.
John Milton

This is a work of fiction. The characters and places are not intended to depict real people or places. The events have not yet happened.

CONTENTS

PROLOGUE

'Hey, wait a minute. How much farther are we going?' Karen looked up at the jagged rocks looming above them, and shivered. 'Not up there? It's going to be terrible cold.' She pulled her woolly tam-o'-shanter down over her ears, trying to make it meet the collar of her anorak; when she had agreed to get out of the car and go for a walk she hadn't realized how cold it was.

Vincent paused, studying the possibilities of a good snogging spot; he had wanted to leave the car simply because the little Ford Fiesta was old and dirty, and too cramped for comfort. 'We could sit down here a wee while. It's quite sheltered from the wind.' An optimistic assessment. Though the winter snow and ice had melted, the cold March wind, whistling down into the valley from the Scottish Grampians, easily penetrated their several layers of protective clothing. But Vincent was desperate: Karen was an attractive girl, very popular with the local lads, to none of whom had she yet granted the time of day. This was an opportunity not to be missed, though he doubted he'd get the chance to penetrate as deep as the wind through her quilted coat.

'Well not for long. It's nearly dark now, and it's awful smelly round here.' Karen liked Vincent. He wasn't pushy like some of the boys and he was certainly the most attractive. Her friend Fiona had been after him for weeks. Wow, weren't her eyes going to turn green when she heard... With feigned reluctance she slid down close beside him, and waited. At least the ground was dry, which was something, but the smell! Like something had died nearby! Ugh, and if he thought she was going to unzip her coat and let that wind inside...

Vincent put his arm round her and started the kissing—to which Karen soon responded with enthusiasm as his after-shave overcame the stench. This was hopeful! He took off his gloves and started to caress her neck, and when she didn't stop him his fingers sought the top of the zip at her throat. She grunted and tried to shake her head...which he ignored. The anorak burst open and immediately his hand was stroking the thick sweater inside. Suddenly Karen gave him a great shove, screwed up her face and let out a huge sneeze. 'Oh drat!' she swore, 'It's freezing. And I haven't got a hankie. Have you?'

Vincent thought of a string of swear

words as he watched the zip ride up again to her neck. 'Here,' he said, trying to tug a handkerchief out of his pocket. It was obstinate but finally shot out, flying in the wind like a banner, and something else with it—which landed yards away with a metallic clink.

'What was that?' Karen asked, as she grabbed the handkerchief just in time for the next sneeze.

Vincent frowned in annoyance as his hand felt over the outside of his pocket. 'Ma bloody car keys!' He leapt up and over the rocks in front of them. 'They went down here, somewhere...oh damn!'

'What? What's the matter?' Karen scrambled after him.

'There's a great gap in the rock, here, and I think they've gone through.'

'Oh no, surely not. Let's search around here, first.' On hands and knees they peered through the tangled growth together.

'It's no use. This was the direction they came, I'm certain. I'll have to search in there.'

'If ye put your hand inside, can ye not reach them?'

He tried. 'No. But I think I could wriggle in after them. Trouble is the stink in there is something else!'

'Maybe an animal got trapped in there and died.'

'Well if that's the case at least it won't be able to chew ma leg off as I go in. Let me just try to get some of this heather away.' Heather was growing all around them, three or more feet high, the tough old roots winding down through the rocky ground defying Vincent's efforts to move any of it, though he was able to snap the short trunk of the bush nearest the gap, so that the growth lay back out of his way as he squeezed through, cautiously, into the dark hollow beyond.

'Can ye see anything at all in there?' Karen shouted.

'Not even ma hand before ma face. I can just make out the entrance.'

'Can ye no feel around on the floor?'

There was a pause, then he shouted up, 'No, it's too rough. Ugh! I can't breathe it's so thick in here.'

Karen swallowed. It was getting very dark; it was going to be difficult returning to the car anyway, but if they had to walk all the way back down the track before even reaching the road, and without a torch... It had been a stupid idea to come anyway, just for a wee kiss and a cuddle... 'What are ye going to do, then?' she demanded.

'I've seen ye smoking down at the disco...is there a chance ye'd have a match or lighter on ye?'

'Probably, but ye'll have to wait while I find it.' The girl removed her gloves, undid her zip and sought an inner pocket. 'Aye, here ye are.' She held the lighter at arm's length through the gap and waited for his fingers to take it. 'Hurry up then, Vin. That stench is choking me! How can ye stick it?'

Vincent's choking cough was the only reply followed by two rasps of the lighter...and a huge roar as the earth trembled under her feet.

Chapter 1

GAS

'Good-morning, Margaret.' Bernard Morris bent to give his wife a brief peck on the forehead as he passed her chair.

'Good-morning, dear.' Margaret's smiling acknowledgement failed to conceal her anxiety as she studied his back as he moved away. His mood at breakfast time usually foretold how the rest of the day would shape up. She was about to breathe a sigh of relief when he stopped near the head of the table, and frowned.

'The papers! Where the hell are the

papers? Guthrie!' he roared. Bernard Morris was a big man, a successful entrepreneur with a large stomach and florid complexion to prove it. At fifty-five he was proud of his thick crop of dark, wavy hair, which he kept well-greased above ever-watchful, pale blue eyes. Famous for the bonhomie with which he welcomed his guests, and for the self-opinionated arrogance with which he handled his business associates, he had a legendary appetite in *all* things, as Margaret knew only too well.

Since purchasing Abergannan, a minor Scottish castle with an estate of several thousand acres in the foothills of the Grampians, Bernard had worked hard to combine the life of London businessman, to which he had become accustomed since leaving the semi-detached in Milton Keynes, with the life of a Scottish laird, to which few of his acquaintances reckoned he ever *would* become accustomed, his visualization of such being at considerable variance from reality. For a start, the lairds who lived in more remote castles accepted that the daily papers were to be read during the hour before luncheon was served. Bernard wanted them waiting on his breakfast table and one of his estate employees was detailed to fetch them from the nearest town, many miles distant, at seven-thirty each morning. 'Where the hell is Guthrie?'

Margaret's face set itself into martyr mode. She was a pale woman in her mid-fifties, tall, too thin, with light blonde hair, and eyebrows and lashes so fair that her face remained featureless until her daily mascara had been applied. 'I haven't seen him yet, this morning. Unusual for him but I'm sure there must be a good reason. Anyway, he must have heard you call. He'll be along in a minute,' she said, hopefully. As Scottish castles go this was not large, and Bernard had a voice like a trumpet. 'Would you like me to pour your coffee?'

'Yes,' Bernard snapped. He operated on a short fuse at the best of times, and this wasn't one of them. But as he was aware of having been particularly critical of Margaret yesterday—he had snapped her head off twice before lunch—he had resolved to go easier on her today. She seldom, if ever, shouted back, but her quiet methods of taking reprisals could sometimes make life uncomfortable. Now his good resolution had been blown out of the window.

The door opened and a tall, bald, middle-aged man came in, looking unusually flustered. 'Ye called, I believe, sir.'

'You're damned right I called! Where

the hell have you been? And where are the papers?'

Guthrie drew himself up to prove his superior height, and looked pained. He had served the noble owners of Abergannan all his life and, with the sale of the estate, had passed into the employ of this...this Sassenach. A fact he much regretted, but at his age saw little chance of correcting. 'Wilkie has not arrived yet this morning, sir.'

'Wilkie? Oh, you mean the fellow who fetches them. Well, why not? Where is he?'

Guthrie stared into the middle distance over his employer's shoulder. 'I have no idea, sir. But it is possible that his absence has something to do with the heathfire last night.'

'Heathfire?' A high, feminine voice spoke from behind him. 'I thought I saw a glow last night from my window.' Rebecca Morris crossed the parquet floor to the sideboard and began lifting covers. 'Ooh, lovely. Some of Mrs MacBain's scramblers. But I think I'll have some porridge first,' she said, reaching for the ladle. She was a large young woman, big boned but definitely overweight, with long, dark hair which failed to look glamorous, hanging loose round her blotchy face.

'Yes, Miss. Nobody knows, yet, where or

exactly what it was.' Guthrie favoured her with a fleeting nod. She was undoubtedly the best of the bunch, in his opinion. He welcomed her weekend visits during which she invariably spent time chatting with him, seemingly keen to learn about the Scottish Highlands...and he was only too happy to impart his knowledge. And he felt sorry for her—she didn't look healthy. Maybe she was overworked in her job with the Ministry of the Environment. She was a serious lass, far too young for such an important-sounding job.

Guthrie heard voices approaching on the stairs—and frowned. That would be Tara and Niall: well the lad wasn't too bad, but the hoighty toighty blonde miss should have been put over her pa's knee years ago. And obviously never was.

'Morning Daddy, Morning, Mummy,' Tara floated into the room without acknowledging the butler but saying, over her shoulder, 'I'll have coffee. Black.'

Guthrie's lips puckered as he poured. Of course no one could deny that this child was beautiful...the most beautiful creature he had ever seen. Those eyes, the soft flawless skin, the bone-structure of her face framed by a cascade of golden hair which swept the shoulders of her tan suede suit, but dammit, the beauty was only skin deep. There was nothing beautiful underneath. He returned the coffee pot to the sideboard.

'Mornin', Dad, Ma, Guthrie. Say, did any of you see a glow in the sky last night, over towards Cock Cairn?' Niall Morris was referring to the two and a half thousand foot peak southwest of them. Niall was twenty-four, very tall, with yellow hair and blue eyes. He always made Guthrie think of an overgrown puppy, but apparently he had been to university and had a degree in something or other.

'I was just saying I thought I saw something, from my bedroom window, while I was undressing for bed,' Rebecca said. 'Just before eleven. It had just started to rain.'

'Imagination,' Bernard grunted.

'Begging your pardon, Mr Guthrie,' Mary the housemaid entered the breakfast room and spoke in a hoarse whisper, 'but Cook says would you please go to the kitchen immediately. Mr Brown is at the back door wishing to speak with you.'

'Just a minute...this is no time for the staff to be receiving social calls...' Bernard began.

'Mr Morris! If Mr Brown comes all the way up here from the village at this time of day it will not be for the making of social calls!' Mary, like Guthrie, had been in service at the castle all her life. Bony and angular, grey hair scraped back into a tiny knot below her morning-cap, she was known locally, despite her spinsterhood, as a much respected matron of the kirk. Chin held high in righteous indignation, she stood over her employer and went on, 'Mr Brown is most distressed. His boy has been missing all night along with Rabbie Wilkie's lass, and they're wanting all the help they can get searching for them.'

Bernard snorted. 'Ha! What's all the fuss about? A couple of youngsters rolling in the hay overnight...'

Mary's big knuckles grasped the back of a chair as she glared at him. 'I'm hoping, Mr Morris, that ye are not suggesting that yon London morals could be contagious.' Her eyes swept over the people seated round the table. 'I'll have ye know that young Vincent Brown and Karen Wilkie are respected members of our kirk and have been in the Band of Hope since they could walk. If they are missing it's because something has happened. Mr Brown is of the opinion they will have to be looked for.'

'Well, what were they doing on my land, anyway?' Bernard grumbled.

'Abergannan is the girl's home. D'ye not know that?'

Bernard cleared his throat, loudly.

'And Mr Brown is of the opinion it'd

not be right to call out the polis, as yet.'

'You're damned right,' Bernard snapped. 'I'm not having dirty great bluebottles crawling all over Abergannon.'

'Then ye'll help look for the young ones?'

'I'll go and get the Land Rover out of the garage,' Niall announced enthusiastically.

'We'll all come, of course,' Rebecca pushed back her chair.

'Of course,' her mother agreed.

Tara sniffed, and went on with her breakfast.

Bernard threw his napkin onto the table, angered by Mary's affrontery. 'Well, if you think it will help...'

'Indeed it will, sir,' Mary nodded. 'Won't it, Mr Guthrie?'

'Oh yes, indeed,' Guthrie nodded grimly. He wasn't at all pleased at the way the housemaid, with all that she had been at Abergannan nearly as long as himself, had put the master in his place and taken over the situation. She had done it before, more than once. She'd always been a bossy woman.

I see you've brought all the new folk out from the castle.' James MacEwan was standing beside a mud-spattered jeep containing two eager sheepdogs.

George Guthrie, his thin frame and bald

head enveloped in a thick duffel coat, nodded. 'Aye. All saving one and she'd be of no use.'

'Too elderly?'

'No! Too worried about mussing up her hair or muddying her boots. A useless baggage.'

James smiled to himself. Guthrie's dour comments were legendary in these parts. The search party was assembling at a layby on the main road beneath the foothills, if a narrow country lane could be so described.

Bernard strode up. 'We must organize ourselves into a proper search grid,' he said. 'Now you...' he pointed at James, 'I don't know your name...'

'MacEwan. And I'm afraid that the grid system would be a waste of time at this stage. First we must find the car. If they are not with it, then we will fan out from there.'

An angry flush climbed out of Bernard's collar and the muscles worked overtime in his jaw as he studied the young Scotsman. The fact that MacEwan was several inches taller than himself did nothing to endear him, neither did the heavy leather Army boots, the thick duffel coat or the sandy hair ruffled by the icy wind, nor the grey-green eyes and square cut, determined jaw. As owner of Abergannan, Bernard considered he should be in charge of this operation. 'Car?' the new laird demanded.

'I lent them mine, ye see, Mr Morris,' Brown explained. 'To go for a drive, ye ken.' He was the postmaster, an equally large man who had climbed out of a red Post Office van with several other people. 'Ah, good. I see ye've met our Jimmy, Mr Morris. He'll know how to go about this. Army training, ye ken. How do ye want us to set about it, Jimmy?'

'Now look here...' Bernard was silenced by a nudge from his wife.

'We'll split up,' James said, ignoring Bernard's expression. 'Best we have some-one familiar with the locality in each vehicle.'

'Definitely,' Guthrie commented.

Bernard drove off in his Land Rover directed by one of Wilkie's sons, with Margaret and Rebecca behind and Mrs MacBain and her son Barry on the rear seat. Niall climbed in the back of Wilkie's truck, closely followed by Beatrice, the kitchen maid from the castle, one of the missing boy's brothers, a sister and three other men. Having discussed with the locals their separate directions, James swung his jeep up a nearby track, Wilkie beside him, the sheepdogs sniffling at his collar. 'When did you last see your Karen?' James asked.

'Her mother says Vincent Brown came for her in his father's car while she was feeding the hens. It will have been around four-thirty they went off.' Rabbie Wilkie's voice was thick and his head shook miserably as he spoke; he sounded as exhausted and distraught as he looked. 'I've been up all night, inquiring around the village, but no one seems to have seen them.'

'Had they been going together for long? I mean, what sort of terms were they on?'

'They'd known each other at school, ye ken. They were only friends, I believe, him being a couple of years older than Karen, but she had told her sister she was quite taken with the lad. So they'd ha' been looking for some place to walk...and maybe just stop for a wee kiss only, if that's what ye're wanting to know?'

'Aye. Well it helps to have an idea what sort of place to look for. Reckon I know all the courting spots meself, hereabouts,' James grinned. Then hearing Wilkie's sigh, said, 'No need to go worrying yourself yet, man. Probably the car broke down some distance away.'

The gillie, unusually small and thin for a Highlander, was silent for a while as the jeep lurched up the hillside, then said, 'Ye're looking to come back for good, I'm told.'

'You'll have been told more than that, too,' James added drily. It wasn't that the locals were gossips, but everyone just happened to know everyone else's business.

'Aye. Since retiring from the Army ye've applied for old Stirling's job at the castle.' Wilkie made no attempt to conceal the fact he knew all about it.

'What do you reckon?' asked James.

'That Morris, he's a blowhard,' was the blunt reply, 'too puffed up wi' self-importance. Always telling Stirling off about something or other, he was. The poor man couldna stick it. Well, it surely is the bailiff's job ta make decisions: no' some Londoner who does'na ken awt of the highlands. Fancy wanting ta read the papers wi' his breakfast! When I remember the old laird...' he sighed.

'Aye, he was a good man,' James prompted, trying to keep Wilkie's mind off his missing daughter. 'Why did they sell?'

'When the laird dropped dead, what wi' the death duties an' all, the family had na choice. Ye reckon ye could work for such a man as this Morris? I'd certainly welcome it from ma point of view.'

James shrugged as he negotiated some protruding rocks. 'Abergannan is the only estate around here looking for a bailiff. And the Army hasn't prepared me for much else.'

'Ye were a major in the Royal Engineers, right?' Wilkie asked.

'Was,' James nodded.

'Pity ye don't use the title. Well, let me gi'e you a small piece of advice, James MacEwan: yon blowhard didn't exactly take to ye, back there, so when ye go up for the interview, having been a major will be your most important asset. Use it. It'll puff him up to tell his friends his bailiff was an army major.'

'You could be right.' James sniffed the air. 'Tell me, what's this talk about there having been a fire out here last night?'

Wilkie shrugged. 'There was a glow, to be sure. Way up at the foot of Gannan Hill, I'd say. Saw it maself when I was hunting for ma girl. Heck, ye don't suppose...'

'No,' James said. There was no point in alarming the poor fellow further, but it had occurred to him that the boy and his girlfriend might have started it. Inadvertently, of course.

'But ye're coming this way,' Wilkie realized aloud. 'Man, it's too early in the year for serious fires.' James did not reply. Now he was sure he could detect a faint smell of smoke. Then he saw something glinting through the bushes, up ahead. Metal. 'There!' Wilkie shouted. 'David Brown's car!'

James braked. To their left, against the

distant backdrop of Cock Cairn, the land rose steeply to the top of Gannan Hill before descending into the valley in a series of hummocks and outcroppings to the busy, bubbling waters of the Gannan river. Being a local man, which was why he had returned to Aberdeen in his initial search for a job after being retired at thirty-seven-years-old in the latest round of military cuts made by the government. James knew that there was some doubt whether Gannan Hill was actually part of the Abergannan Estate, or just formed the southern boundary. There could be no doubt about the ownership of the valley, however. There a flock of the famous Abergannan sheep were grazing huddled together: clearly something had disturbed them in the night.

Wilkie was already out of the jeep and hurrying down a sloping sheep track towards the battered Ford Fiesta, muttering entreaties to his Maker that he'd find his daughter there, safe. 'It's over on the other track, but it'll be quicker to go across to it on foot,' he called back. James whistled the two dogs to follow with him. 'Empty,' Wilkie said, shoulders drooping. 'It doesn'a appear to be damaged, though I scarcely think David would be pleased they drove it up here over this awful track.' He tried the driver's door. 'It's not locked, either. Why d'ye think they left her?'

'It must have broken down, and they went off looking for help,' James suggested.

'Now that's a possibility. But the car is no so far from home. No more than a couple of hours on foot, so it scarcely seems likely. Pity the key's are no here: we could try it out.'

'I wasn't in the engineers for nothing,' James told him. 'Just release the bonnet and I'll see if she'll turn over.'

Moments later the two men were staring at each other in consternation. The engine had fired immediately. 'They musta wandered off for a walk and never came back to the car!' Karen's father whispered. 'So where on earth are they?'

'That's what we're here to find out. We'll get the others up here and start the search.' He cupped his hands round his mouth and bellowed 'Up he...e...ere!!' and waved his arms till he heard responding hooters. He walked in front of the car to look for tracks but the heavy rain in the night, which had fortunately put out the heathfire, had obliterated any footmarks. The dogs were not trackers so he doubted they'd be much help.

Below them, Morris's Land Rover was climbing slowly up the uneven track, Wilkie's truck with his son at the wheel grinding impatiently behind, and, well back, the engine of the Post Office van complaining loudly. 'That Brown's car, Wilkie?' Bernard shouted as he braked beside them.

'Oh, aye, that it is, Mr Morris,' Wilkie replied.

Everyone clambered out of the vehicles, chattering, surrounding the abandoned car. David Brown peered inside, frowning. 'Well?' Morris inquired of James. 'Where are they?'

'Somewhere up there.' James pointed into the mist. 'This is as high as they could bring the car. I imagine they decided to follow the track on foot...in that direction.' He pointed.

'Hiding, are they?'

'If they were close I'd say they have to be, or they'd hear us. But there would be no reason to hide; it's more likely they're hurt, and of course we don't know how far they walked before stopping.'

'Hurt, ye say?' Brown nodded. 'Yes. I fear that may be.'

'Aye, David. Maybe.' James didn't add that if it wasn't too serious the youngsters would have called out on hearing the racket their rescuers were making.

'Hurt,' Wilkie muttered.

'Shall we send back for the ambulance, d'ye think?' Guthrie asked.

'Surely we have to find them first,'

Rebecca Morris suggested.

'Yes,' James agreed, giving a quick smile to the daughter of his possible future employer. 'I think we should all fan out, now, and head up parallel with the track.' He went southwest through the rocks and heather, accompanied by the dogs. That the car had been left where it was, at the last possible place where it could be turned, albeit with a good deal of shunting, suggested that Vincent knew the area fairly well.

He looked around at the others. Morris was behind him, and Wilkie, Brown and another of Wilkie's sons, were some yards apart to the left and right of him. And the young woman Rebecca. He had a sudden instinctive wish that she hadn't come along. 'What's that stench?' Bernard asked, catching up with him.

'Gas, most likely. Methane.'

'Eh? Gas? Methane? You mean, swamp gas?'

'Tha's what some call it. But...' James sniffed. 'It's not just methane. Could be there's a dead sheep decomposing in one of these gullies.' He glanced at Rebecca. But she was too far away to hear what he said.

'And there's your fire,' Bernard said, pointing.

In front of them, beyond a high outcrop

of rock and heather, stretched an area of scorched earth roughly thirty yards in diameter reaching down into a deep gully. 'Looks more like an explosion,' James muttered: in the army he'd seen this effect many times.

'Karen!' Wilkie shouted, starting down the slope. James ran behind him, losing his footing and sliding through the blackened dirt to arrive at the bottom alongside the gillie. 'Oh, God!' Wilkie gasped. 'Oh, ma poor bairn!'

'Easy,' James said, holding his arm as he would have gone forward. He himself dropped to his knees beside the girl's body, and swallowed. She had very little hair left on one side of her head except where the remains of her tam-o'-shanter had offered scant protection. One arm of her jacket had disintegrated into black wisps, all adhering to exposed, raw tissue and crisp patches of skin. One side of her face was raw. 'Karen?' he said, softly. 'Can you hear me?' She gave an almost inaudible moan. 'She's alive!' he told her father.

'Karen's alive!' the call went back up the slope and along the track. Tears were running down Wilkie's face as one of his sons put an arm round his shoulders.

'We'll need that ambulance,' James said. 'Fast.'

'I'll call on the phone in the Rover,'

Margaret volunteered, desperate to feel useful. 'Coming, Rebecca?'

Rebecca shook her head, staring at the girl, who was now twisting in agony as consciousness began to return. 'You mean she's been there all night?'

'Yes.' James had taken off his duffel coat and was wrapping it round the uninjured portions of the girl's body, carefully avoiding touching any burned flesh.

'Guthrie, get back up to the car and fetch my flask of brandy for her,' Bernard ordered.

'Brandy could do more harm than good,' James said. 'She needs warmth. If you've any rugs...there are some in my jeep. We'll hold them round her to form a windbreak.' He pushed the dogs away as they came snuffling up.

Not for the first time that morning Bernard glared in impotent embarrassment. 'Well, go on, Guthrie,' he ordered. 'Do as the man says.' Guthrie followed Margaret into the mist.

'Oh, ma poor bairn!' Wilkie knelt beside his daughter.

'Careful! You must resist the temptation to hold her,' James warned, 'except, look, her left hand is OK. Hold that.' He let the shocked and shaking gillie take the icy hand. 'And thank the Lord the wind took the blaze away from her.'

'What could have happened?' Bernard asked.

'But Vincent,' Brown was groaning. 'Where's ma boy?'

'He must've gone for help, after the explosion,' someone suggested.

'I canna see that. If this was the fire folk say they saw, then it started just after dark last night. Now it's ten of the morning. Where's my boy?' Brown's voice became a roar.

'He must have fallen and hurt himself,' James decided. 'We'll have to spread out and make a proper search.'

'That'd be a waste of time,' Bernard said. 'As that chap just said...the boy must have gone for help.'

'Mr Morris, I don't know yet what has happened here, but I agree with his father. And surely if young Brown had gone for help he'd have used the car.'

Morris indulged in another glare. 'Then where is he, as you know so much, Mr...what did you say your name was?'

'MacEwan. And if I could tell you where he is I wouldn't be suggesting we search.'

Bernard looked down at Wilkie, expecting his employee to back him. But Wilkie was nodding, 'Oh, aye, *Major* MacEwan is right. He'd have used the car. You all go and search. I'll stay wi' ma girl.'

Major MacEwan? Wasn't that the name... Bernard frowned.

Karen was now whimpering loudly, and James cursed the inadequate First Aid kit strapped under the seat of his jeep. If only it was a full army medical kit... 'Ye poor sweet thing,' her father muttered, rubbing her frozen hand. 'Oh, my, whatever will her mother say?' He looked up at her brother. 'She was all het up at her being out through night as it is.'

'The ambulance will soon be here, Rabbie,' James said reassuringly. 'Now, we must find young Vincent.'

'What about here?' Niall called. Both he and the dogs had wandered a short distance away to an area of blackened rock beneath a ledge near the path. 'Heather's all burnt up,' Niall pointed out, 'and it looks as though there's a hole blown out in the rock. There are freshly broken pieces, look!' He held up a large chunk, half blackened but cleanly broken on the other side.

'You're right.' James strode towards him. 'Look, you can see they're all over the place. As you say, they seem to have come from this area, here,' he leaned forward, his head almost into the hole in the rocks. But he backed away, quickly, gasping 'Wow! What a stench!' There could be no doubt that the smell was coming out of there, and it certainly wasn't that of rotting flesh: he'd experienced tribal genocide in Africa and the stench of decaying bodies was not something he'd ever forget.

Niall had been regarding the big ex-soldier's bulk. 'I think I could get through,' he volunteered.

James shook his head. 'If what we smell is methane...' But if Vincent Brown had wriggled through, for whatever reason...

'No way. Absolutely not.' Niall's father had joined them. 'Anyway, you'd be suffocated.'

'D'ye reckon Vinny could be in there?' David Brown was clearly terrified at the thought, his voice shaking.

James held his breath as he peered into the blackened crevice. This was where the explosion had happened, all right. For whatever reason, there must have been a build-up of gas in the cavity beyond. But methane gas, he knew, although certainly highly inflammable, was not often explosively so, save where it had been trapped for ages, as in some deep coal mines; this crevice was open to the air. Yet if the boy had been in there... 'We will have to go in,' he decided. 'But we'll need flashlights and breathing apparatus.'

'That'll take hours!' Vincent's sister cried, clutching her father's arm.

James licked his lips. 'David,' he said.

'If your Vinny has been in there since six o'clock last night, quite apart from the explosion, I'd say from the smell out here the inside must be literally a gas chamber.'

The postmaster stared at him for a moment, then sat, heavily. His legs just seemed to give way under his weight. His daughter screwed up her face and subsided against him in tears. 'Rebecca,' Bernard hissed, 'get back up to the car and fetch that flask of brandy.'

'And ask your mother to get on to the police and tell them we need breathing apparatus. Better say I said so,' James added.

Rebecca scrambled up the slope.

'What a bloody awful mess,' the missing boy's brother groaned, lodging a cigarette between his lips and fishing a box of matches out of the pocket of his anorak. 'Hey!'

James had struck the box from his hand. 'There's already been one explosion. We don't want to risk another, do we?'

'I suppose Major MacEwan is right,' Bernard grunted, suddenly looking alarmed. 'We'd better get back up the slope. Come on, Niall.' The Morris family retreated.

James took David Brown's arm and pulled him to his feet. 'Come along. You're only poisoning yourself here.'

'But Vinny...'

'If he's in there, we'll find him. When we've got the gear. But we wouldn't want to go risking other people's lives, would we, specially if the boy wasna in there, anyway?'

Bernard Morris threw the *curriculum vitae* onto his desk and chewed fiercely on his cigar. It was the third time he'd read the thing...and now his cigar had gone out. MacEwan! Why did that know-all major, who had got right up his nose when they were hunting for those kids in the hills this morning, have to be the only applicant for the vacancy left by Stirling's hasty departure? Of course reading this thing, there was no doubt MacEwan was ideal for the job of bailiff; he was certainly qualified. Just a pity it had to be this particular man. On the other hand, it wouldn't be a bad thing to have an ex-Army officer in one's employ; worth it to see the expression on old Appleforth's face when one mentioned it, casually, in the bar at the club. He was still smiling at the idea when Guthrie opened the door moments later and announced, 'Major MacEwan is here, sir.'

James had changed into a tweed suit and a green woollen tie. He stood his vast frame in front of the desk while Bernard went through his customary routine of busily examining papers on his desk before looking up. It didn't bother James: he'd met this proof of character weakness many times in the Army hierarchy.

'Ah! MacEwan. Sit down, man. Any news from up the hill, yet?' The older man leaned back in his carved, red leather chair, wishing the fellow wasn't so large.

James sat opposite him. 'Yes. I've just come up from the Post Office, now. Very sad for the Brown family; the body was in the cave, you know, virtually blown to bits as well as being very badly burned. They've taken it on down to Aboyne for a *post mortem* examination before the inquest.'

'What about Wilkie's daughter?'

'She's in hospital in Aberdeen. Rabbie and his wife are there with her but there's been no news of her condition, yet. Obviously she's suffering as much from exposure as from burns.'

'Yes, yes. She looked terrible. It'll be a miracle if she survives. Let's hope we found her in time. Now...' The Londoner tapped the neatly clipped papers in front of him, 'I haven't had time to study this thing in detail, but it seems to me you might be able to do the job I need you for.'

'I thought you were looking for a bailiff, Mr Morris,' James said stiffly.

Bernard frowned. 'That's right. But I

haven't explained your duties...'

'I beg your pardon, but I assure you I do know the duties and responsibilities required of a bailiff. Naturally, if there are any particular differences between this and the norm, we would need to discuss them. And should we suit each other we would have to spend time going over such details as livestock and crops. What percentage of acreage do you keep for grazing?'

Bernard Morris hadn't the faintest idea; nor did he like being questioned about it, having the initiative of interviewing taken out of his hands. It was just so damnably unfortunate that he was not in the position, at the moment, to kick this arrogant beggar out. 'It's all in the books Stirling kept in the estate office attached to the bailiff's house, the other side of the stable block. We can go over there, now. I presume that, er, if we suit, as you put it, you'll wish to move in straight away.' He stood up.

James followed him to the door. 'I'm in no hurry. I have a little place of my own just outside Aboyne.'

Stepping into the Great Hall he was confronted by a dazzlingly beautiful creature who smiled at Bernard and said, 'Daddy, I need to get down to Aberdeen. Can I borrow Wilkie to drive me?' She didn't glance in James' direction.

'But I thought you knew! Wilkie's daughter is in hospital with terrible injuries,' Bernard frowned. 'He's down there with her, now.'

'Oh damn! When will he be back?' The exquisite mouth pouted in irritation. James moved away to the vast fireplace, leaving Morris to sort out his daughter.

When Bernard returned to his study, Margaret was waiting for him. 'Well? What have you decided?'

'I offered him the job.'

'And did he accept?'

'He's asking twice what I was paying Stirling.'

'Can't say I'm surprised. Did you agree?'

'No.' Bernard slumped into his chair. 'The staff wage bill here is astronomic as it is. We agreed to split the difference.' He decided against adding that buying this place, plus the refurbishing bills, combined with his current business problems, was currently causing him an enormous cash-flow crisis: he had never discussed money matters with his wife—he clung to the idea that women did not understand the ramifications of high finance.

Seeing his mood, Margaret thought perhaps now wasn't the best time to ask him about the kitchen...but she had been waiting for days for the right moment, which never seemed to present itself. Maybe if she just mentioned it casually... 'Darling,' she began gently. Bernard's eyes narrowed as he stared up at her. He knew that cajoling tone of old. 'I'm worried about the kitchens. There are definitely mice nesting behind all those wretched old cupboards...'

'No, Margaret. You will not be having a new kitchen here this year.' His voice was adamant.

'But that's what you said last year!'

'True. And instead you went ahead and spent thousands on new panelling and carpets and God knows what, in other parts of the castle. After I'd told you to wait.'

'But you said that when that Middle East deal went through we could...'

'There were complications. It didn't turn out the way I'd planned.' He had never told her how disastrous the whole project had been. 'Look, sweetheart. I have some work to do before dinner. Do you mind if I get on with it, please?'

It was a polite dismissal. 'All right, dear. I'll leave you in peace.' Again, she thought bitterly as she closed the door behind her. What was the point in buying a fabulous old castle like this if one couldn't make it habitable? It wasn't as though they weren't rolling in money, now. Lovingly she caressed her Yves St Laurent suit, fingered the diamonds in her ears. Being married to a man who was always so busy making money had to have its compensations. But why had he suddenly got so penny-pinching over the kitchen?

'I'm afraid I'll need to leave for London after lunch,' Bernard announced while Mary was serving the soup.

'Oh Daddy! I thought you were staying for the rest of the week,' Rebecca complained. 'I've taken time off specially to be with you.' Which wasn't true. She had just endured a stormy finale to her on-off relationship with Giles, so she'd phoned into the office, sick, and flown up to the Highlands in the hopes of washing her tears away in Daddy's champagne.

Bernard was mildly touched by her words: he never concerned himself with his family's personal problems so he accepted her statement without question. 'Sorry, my sweet. Had a call this morning from Susan, my new Girl Friday. The Minister of Defence wants a meeting in the morning.' Another lie, to conceal the fact that he had to find enough cash within the next week to cover the growing commitment in his latest arms deal.

Margaret's expression was sad. It often was, for a variety of reasons. Like the fact that this latest Girl Friday would undoubtedly have been hand-picked by her husband for other than her secretarial skills. But at this moment her expression reflected her disappointment that all her family except Niall lied to each other, so much. She always knew when they were lying, even if she didn't always know the reasons. Today it was easy enough to guess Rebecca's problem...but Bernard's? His current mood ruled out any desire to hare off in the direction of Susan's bed. So what was he up to now?

'Can I come with you, Daddy?' Tara begged. 'It's so dreadfully boring, here. Absolutely nothing to do.' Especially now she couldn't get down to Aberdeen.

'Boring!' Niall exploded. 'After all the drama of last night and this morning? If you'd only pulled a finger out you could have been out there with us.'

'Whatever for? There was absolutely nothing I could do to help.'

Niall glanced at his younger sister's painted nails, immaculate make-up and designer suit. 'No. Actually for once in your life you're right. You'd only have been a nuisance. But you know, Dad,' he went on, turning to his father, 'I went back up there with that seriously nice army bloke when the rescue team arrived. They did a tremendous job with all the latest equipment.'

'I thought I told you it was dangerous up there...' Bernard snapped.

'Oh, it was all right, they lent me a mask. And I didn't actually go inside the cavern. It was all terribly interesting. They had some kind of gadget for measuring the gas and they were saying, afterwards, that there could be a huge gas reservoir under the hills.' He tore into a crusty chunk of bread and pasted it with butter before tucking into his soup.

Bernard's soup spoon remained poised halfway between the plate and its destination. His eyes narrowed, mind racing. Natural gas? On Abergannan!

'Look what you're doing, darling,' Margaret said, 'You're splashing soup all down your front.'

There was a tap on the door. Bernard scowled, said, 'Just one moment,' clapped his hand over the mouthpiece of the phone and called 'Come in!'

It was Tara. 'When are you leaving, Daddy?'

'Don't know.' He jerked his head at her in a dismissive gesture. 'Later.'

'But you said you were leaving straight after lunch...' she complained.

'Well, as you see. I am not. I'm busy. Please run along.' And removing his hand said into the phone 'Well where are they? What? Back in Aberdeen?' He pressed the receiver against his jacket and said 'Damn!' with a grimace, then asked the person on the other end of the line, 'Can you tell me where they are based? Do you have a phone number?' He scrawled the answer on a large pad. 'Thanks. Goodbye.' When he emerged from his study Tara was standing at the foot of the stairs looking petulant. 'Forget London. I'm going out.'

The petulance became a scowl. 'Oh really, Daddy...'

But he was gone. While the Land Rover raced down into the valley towards the village, the business brain was in overdrive. The possibilities were mind-boggling! If he could catch that fellow, Barker, they said might have remained in Aboyne to speak to the coroner... The heavy vehicle nearly slewed into the ditch as Bernard stood on the brakes. He'd suddenly seen MacEwan in the garden of a cottage... He reversed, weaving back up the lane until drawing level with the major. 'Good-afternoon.'

James had watched the manoeuvre with some amusement, wondering what the devil the man was up to. 'Good-afternoon, sir.'

'Do you happen to know a fellow by the

name of Barker? I believe he was involved in the rescue attempt this morning.'

'No. 'Fraid I didn't get their names.'

'I'm told he was using some instruments to measure the strength of the gas.'

'Oh, him! Yes. I gave him a lift down to Aboyne when it was all over.'

'How long was he staying there, do you know? Wondered if I might catch him before he goes back to Aberdeen.'

James shook his head. 'I doubt it. Said he was going straight into the coroner's office to file his report and then getting a lift down to the coast.'

'Damn,' Bernard muttered, and switched off the engine.

'Anything I can help with?' the appointed bailiff asked.

Bernard scratched his head. 'Don't know. I wanted to pick his brains a bit about the gas field up there.'

James raised an eyebrow, warning bells jangling in his brain. 'Gas field? Well yes, there could be some gas up there. Wouldn't care to bet on there being a field, though. Were you meaning to seal off the cavern to avoid another tragedy?'

'On the contrary. I want to investigate the possibility of getting the stuff out.'

James opened and shut his mouth, not wanting to believe what he was hearing... 'You mean extracting it, resourcing it commercially?' Visions of drillings and derricks and devastated hillsides were creating a ball of lead in the pit of his stomach.

'Yes, yes, man. Why not, if it's just lying there waiting to be taken?'

'Er...' where to begin? 'Well, for a start I doubt if the Scottish Environmental Office would consider issuing a licence...'

'Rubbish!' Bernard said, loudly. 'What the hell would it have to do with them anyway. It's under my land.'

'I grant you it could be,' James hedged, 'But the necessary licences would have to be granted and I...'

'Don't worry about that!' Bernard laughed. 'I'd soon sort those people out. If the gas is there and worth taking. You know anything about natural gas?'

'Only that there's a lot of it about.'

'Absolutely. And just out there...' Morris flung out his arm to point to the east, 'offshore, is the Frigg Field. Isn't that one of the largest gas fields in the world? Makes sense that there'd be an offshoot up here. Could be worth millions.'

'I'd say the first thing to do is find out if there is anything worth the outlay,' James suggested, crossing his mental fingers.

'There is. I'm sure of that.' He gunned his engine enthusiastically. James watched his new employer making a ten-point turn in the narrow lane before roaring off, back to his castle. He wondered if it was possible to work for someone one heartily disliked.

'Dad! You can't!' Niall was appalled.

'It'd ruin the estate,' Rebecca said. She didn't usually oppose her father in anything, but working at the Department of the Environment had given her a point of view.

'Bugger the estate,' Morris said. And glanced a trifle anxiously at the door. He had summoned the family into his study after lunch because he didn't want the servants to know what he had in mind. It had been stupid of him to mention the matter to MacEwan. But he had been so wound up at the thought of getting this damned financial tiger off his back...now it had to be kept as quiet as possible until he knew for sure he was on to something. 'What you don't understand,' he told his daughter, 'is that if there is a gas field of any size under here, then you'll be laughing all the way round the world in a private jet!'

'Or buying an island in the Caribbean?' Tara asked dreamily.

'Why, yes, if that's what you want,' Bernard said, anxious to have an ally at any cost.

'Well, I think the idea is crazy,' Margaret announced, also seeking allies and feeling she had two in Rebecca and Niall. 'We have a lovely place here...or it could...it will, be lovely, when we've fixed it up properly. Why would we want to go buying a tropical island? All sandflies, mosquitoes and inoperable loos.' She sighed. 'Really, we have no need of that sort of money.'

Bernard gave her a pitying glance, which was lost on everyone except Niall. 'It's been good to have your opinions,' he remarked. 'Now let me get on with making the decisions.' They understood they had been dismissed, and got up. 'And I do not want this discussed in front of the servants,' Bernard said. 'Or in front of anyone, as a matter of fact. That goes for your pals at work, Rebecca.'

Rebecca raised her eyebrows. 'Will you be going to London, Daddy?' Tara asked.

'I don't know. I'll have to see.'

The women filed out, but Niall remained behind, and closed the door behind them. '*Do* we need the money, Dad?'

Morris glared at him for several seconds, then his shoulders slumped; he so wanted to share the burden with someone, and Niall had a degree in Business Studies. 'I'm afraid we do.'

'But...' Niall looked left and right at the opulent splendour of the study.

'This place has cost me a fortune,' Bernard explained. 'And is going to cost me another fortune if your mother has her way. I could wear all of that, but this Middle Eastern deal has gone dead sour.'

Niall sat down. 'What exactly is it?'

'Supplying arms to one of those goddamed wog governments. It was, is, worth millions. But the Ministry of Defence has got word of it—the bastards have spies everywhere—and now they've vetoed it. After I have spent a quarter of a million greasing palms. Makes you sick.'

'So you've lost a deal. You've lost deals before. What's so big about this one?'

Bernard sighed. 'This is not to go any further.'

'It won't,' Niall promised.

'Things have been pretty rough the last few years,' Bernard told him. 'It's all because of this holier-than-thou attitude adopted by the government since that Iraqi foul-up. So I've lost several deals. Last year my bankers were a little upset. But I told them I had this big Arab deal coming off, and they gave me another year's credit. Well, these sheikhs put up a lot of money, and I used most of it to bring down the OD.'

Niall was aghast. 'You mean you didn't buy the goods?'

'Wasn't necessary,' Bernard said. 'That stuff was all out of date surplus material anyway. I was getting it for less than half of what I was selling it for. I mean, are we going to lose any sleep if some wog fires off a cannon and the whole thing blows up in his face?'

Niall scratched his head. He had never realized that his father was quite such a sharp practitioner.

'So, I was buying the goods on tick,' Bernard went on. 'And the second half of the payment, the delivery payment, would have comfortably covered it.'

'But if the deal is off, then your friends are going to want their down payment back,' Niall said thoughtfully.

'Talk about being up shit creek without a paddle,' Bernard said. 'I was going down to meet with the banks tomorrow, to try to get them to release that money and extend my credit. But I have to tell you I wasn't too hopeful. But now, this...if I can tell them I am sitting on top of millions worth of natural gas...we're in a whole new ball game.'

'But you can't tell them that,' Niall said. 'You don't know. Surely they'll want proof?'

'Proof is what I am going to get,' Bernard promised him, and reached for his phone.

Chapter 2

ENVIRONMENT

Kitty's smile was relaxed, peaceful. With the seat back at its lowest position she lay mesmerized by the motorway lights penetrating her closed lids and by the final strains of Elgar's Cello Concerto. The car cassette player clicked noisily at the end of the tape. 'You asleep?' Gus asked.

'No.'

'Funny thing. You're the only person I know who relaxes like that in the car. Gillian always insists on driving.'

Sensible wife, Kitty reckoned, not letting on that the only way she could survive with Gus at the wheel was by working on the principle that if the eye could not see, the mind could not disintegrate into abject terror... But apart from the fact that Gus was her boss, she didn't want to hurt his feelings. So she changed the subject. 'I know I'm a complete Philistine in the classical music world, but nobody could help but drift away with that particular piece. What was the soloist's name again?'

'Jacqueline du Pre. And,' the car lurched

round a massive transporter while Kitty held her breath, 'enough of this Philistine rubbish. Music is like wine. You listen to or drink what you like and forget the poseurs, the self-professed experts who try to dazzle us with their preposterous opinions.'

'I bet Gillian doesn't say that,' Kitty remarked, referring to the kindly woman and dedicated cellist Gus had married twenty years ago, and had left behind in Oxford this morning with the kids, dogs and stacks of musical instruments which were such an integral part of their lives. Kitty watched him staring vacantly at the road ahead, a funny, remarkable man, scruffy in appearance with his curly red hair thinning on top but spreading out over his collar and tangling with the beard jutting at the windscreen. A man with two ill-matched obsessions: geo-chemistry and music.

'She passed it on to me, having heard it from her music master at university. Many moons ago.' He scratched his scalp. 'Hey, you did pack that new pressure gauge, didn't you?'

'It's in the back there.' Somewhere. Amongst the torn bits of computer prints-out and miscellaneous chunks of stone accumulated over the car's lifetime...plus all the other gadgetry he had decided to bring at the last minute. Plus their respective bags. Thank heavens she was able to keep the lab tidy, but then Dr Augustus Wilson was too obsessed with his experiments and investigations to notice. Maybe, one day, she'd be able to get her hands on this smelly old wagon and give it a good clean out. He probably wouldn't notice, and neither would Gillian.

'Have you got the map handy?'

'Yes. You wanting the turn-off south of Durham?'

'Yes. Pity we left home so late, but I know a nice little B and B in the city. We can eat out tonight.'

She peered into the darkness. 'Shame we are too late for a view of the cathedral.'

'You'll see it as we cross the river, all illuminated. We should have Gillian with us. She loves Durham. She'd point out all the ancient buildings and tell you their history.' He wasn't constantly aware of loving his wife, only of the fact that when she wasn't around, he missed her. Never mind, at least he had young Kitty for company. Nice girl. He was lucky to have such a dynamic and enthusiastic assistant.

'What do you think?' Gus asked over dinner.

They'd left Oxford in a hurry, and

although he had several times endeavoured to discuss the project on the drive, she had refused with great determination; she needed him to keep his mind on the road. But now that they had both had baths and a drink, they could relax. 'I'd hate to think we're travelling all this way for nothing,' Kitty remarked. 'But there could be something in it. Going by the map, this chap's estate is virtually on the same parallel of latitude as the Frigg Field, and that's one of the largest natural gas fields in the world.'

'It may be the same latitude, but we're talking about a couple of hundred miles,' Gus argued. He enjoyed debating with Kitty; he found her invigoratingly combative. She was, in fact, an attractive little thing, little being the operative word: she was even shorter than himself. Only five feet four inches tall, and slightly built, she was by no means pretty, but the intensity of her personality made her interesting, and she had splendid hair, dark brown to match her eyes, worn straight and shoulder length.

Anyone less like a geo-chemist would be hard to imagine, but she had been a brilliant student and had a string of initials after her name; that she had elected to work for Turnbull & Heath, a private research laboratory, rather than the government or one of the big oil companies, indicated that her heart was in her job rather than the money to be made from it. Gus respected her opinions.

'That's nearly all granite,' Kitty pointed out. 'Porous.'

'Granted. But we have to suppose this stuff is shallow, and therefore organic. That would be methane and nitrogen. No hydrogen sulphide.'

'The man didn't say anything about hydrogen sulphide.'

'He mentioned a hell of a pong.'

'That could just be the methane. Anyway, Gus, it doesn't have to be a shallow reservoir.'

'Yes, it does,' Gus insisted. 'Going by what this fellow said. It's a cavern with an opening. Yet it was filled with gas. The gas had to be escaping into the open air, and yet there was enough of a build-up to explode. That surely means a shallow source.' He grinned and drank some wine. 'Probably a leaking gas main nobody knows is down there.'

'Or a deep reservoir so full of gas that although it's leaking up to the surface there's always a lot left,' Kitty spoke quietly, but very seriously.

'In which case,' Gus said, equally quietly, 'this chap Morris is sitting either on a fortune or a bomb.'

They gazed at each other for several seconds, then Kitty drained her coffee and stood up. 'I'm for bed. We may have a long day tomorrow.'

It was blowing a hooley, rain slashing at the windscreen, as the Peugeot nosed northeast. The original plan had been to leave the main road from Dundee and cut directly north over the mountains through Bridge of Dye, bearing west to Aboyne, but the weather was so atrocious, and Gus's mountain motoring so terrifying, Kitty voted to stay on the easier road till the turnoff at Stonehaven.

'Maybe the rain will ease up by the time we cross the hills to join the Aberdeen to Braemar route,' she had added, hopefully. But it didn't. What should have been spectacularly beautiful views were frustratingly obscured.

'Don't let it faze you,' Gus commented as she mopped at the misted windows. 'We're probably going to be up here for the best part of a week. There'll be plenty chances to see it all.'

'Look, there's the signpost to Aboyne... and that valley must be the River Dee, ahead. Now to find the Duke of Montrose. It's to be hoped the laird's man is still at the pub. We're over half an hour late.'

James had finished a second lager and had decided to give up waiting when the travellers walked into the bar. He had no difficulty in recognizing the weird little fellow in need of a barber and the young woman in jeans and quilted anorak. Leaving his barstool he approached them, hand outstretched. 'Dr Wilson? I'm James MacEwan.' Kitty watched as the huge Scot shook Gus's hand, noting a distinct lack of warmth in the gesture, and in turn had her own hand swallowed up in his grip. 'Miss Cochrane, did you say? A Scottish name.'

'Yes, so my father tells me. But I've never been to Scotland before.'

'Hope you enjoy your first visit,' the major smiled politely. 'Have you had lunch?'

'No, the weather was so appalling we just kept going. Didn't want to keep you waiting longer than necessary,' Gus explained.

'Perhaps we could get a sandwich here?' Kitty's stomach had gone vocal.

'Aye. Jock'll find you something. You can eat en route and save time. Mr Morris is waiting,' the Scotsman added, ominously.

Munching cheese and pickle sandwiches, they followed the jeep through the rain, pulling up when it stopped outside a cottage situated just outside the town.

'When do we reach Abergannan?' Kitty called through the window.

'Not for a while yet. The estate's a few miles away up the glen. I just need to collect some gear.' James hurried to his front door and disappeared, to return minutes later and load two boxes into the jeep before heading off again.

'Offhand sort of bloke, don't you think?' Gus remarked.

'Very. Almost rude.' Kitty watched the rear of the jeep bouncing up the lane ahead. 'I wonder why?'

She couldn't help being impressed: fancy owning an estate this size with an ancient castle, just for weekends! Not that they'd seen much of either, yet; the cars had stopped before she realized they had arrived, and in the bustle to carry their bags in, out of the rain, there had been little opportunity to study the long, low, stone-faced building, only briefly glimpsing the crenellated turrets, dark against the wet sky.

Kitty stretched a hand out for the huge towel draped over a cork-topped stool beside the antique bath and stood up. This must once have been a dressing room, she supposed, stepping out onto a towelling mat and nearly over-balancing on the slatted wooden grid underneath.

It thumped on the polished floor, while she for the first time noticed the iron bars on the windows, relics of a stormy history. The bath was on lion feet, tall brass taps standing like guardsmen at one end with an equally antique-looking hand shower wound round them. She had tried to use it to rinse the soap out of her hair, without total success.

The dress she had crammed into her bag before leaving was of one of those man-made materials that travel well without creasing, but a search of every drawer and cupboard in her vast bedroom having failed to produce a hair-dryer, she had to drag her thick hair back into a ponytail, hiding the rubber band under a wide tortoiseshell clasp. Her only lipstick was the wrong colour. She grimaced at the mirror and hurried downstairs.

'Mr Morris will see you in his study, Miss Cochrane,' Guthrie told her, leading the way.

'Pull up a chair,' Morris ordered, without getting up. 'So, as I was saying, we must ascertain just exactly the nature, quality and possible quantity we have here before proceeding any further. Er...would you like something to drink?'

It seemed a very long time since the pub sandwich. 'I would love a cup of tea, please,' Kitty murmured.

'Yes, please. Same here,' Gus agreed.

Bernard's eyebrows lifted. Not what he'd had in mind, but he tugged the bell pull behind his chair. 'Guthrie. Tea for our visitors, and...' he glanced at his watch, 'a gin and tonic for me.' Kitty studied the florid complexion and decided their host made a habit of starting too early. 'So, can you do this by measuring the gas escaping to the surface?'

'Yes,' Gus said.

'Splendid. Well, tell me what you want to do first.'

'Obviously, we need to get to the site,' Gus said. 'When can we do that?'

'It's pretty late now,' Morris said. 'Tomorrow would be best.'

'We'll probably need breathing apparatus.'

Morris nodded. 'We can supply that. What do you think the chances are of there being a sizeable deposit, or whatever you call it, down there?'

'We would call it a reservoir, if there is gas there in any marketable quantity,' Gus said. 'However, I must tell you, Mr Morris, that we cannot be very hopeful, at this stage. Of finding gas in marketable quantities, I mean.'

'Dammit, man, there was enough to blow up that lad, wasn't there?'

'Apparently, sir. But of course there

would be sufficient gas in a kitchen where a tap had been left on, to do that. Do you know anything about natural gas?'

'Not a damn thing. Save that it burns.'

'Well...' Gus turned to Kitty. 'Would you like to take over.'

'The main source of natural gas, Mr Morris,' Kitty said, 'is from organic matter, of various kinds. Principally this is derived from the fossilization of the higher plants. That is, the coal-bearing strata, from which we also obtain oil. This gas is marked by the presence of carbon dioxide and of course methane. Methane is the main part of all natural gas; it composes on average over three quarters of the volume, varying within a few per cent. This gives the gas its distinctive odour, except where there may be some hydrogen sulphide present.'

'Hydrogen sulphide,' Morris said, vaguely recalling chemistry classes in his youth. 'Would that be H2S? Rotten eggs?'

'It has an unpleasant smell, yes.'

'There was some talk of an unpleasant smell,' Morris replied.

'Did you smell it yourself?' Gus asked.

'Well, no.'

'But you were there?'

'The next morning.'

'Yes, but if the gas contained H2S and was still escaping the smell would still have been present the next day.'

'Hm. See what you mean. So what are you driving at?' Morris asked.

'Hydrogen sulphide is not usually found in North Sea gas, which is the nearest source to your estate.'

'So, is having it good?'

Gus took over. 'It could be bad. That is one of the first things we are going to have to find out. Most gas is, as we have explained, obtained from fossilized carbon, that is, prehistoric fossils. The normal development of this source is oil, usually contained in water-bearing rocks, and on the top of the oil, a reservoir of natural gas forms.'

'You mean there could be oil down there as well?'

'There could be. However, that is an outline of the anticlinal structure. And such a structure, we must point out, occurs at considerable depths. We could be talking of a thousand metres and more.'

'So, we drill,' Morris replied.

'If it is there in sufficient quantity to make drilling economically viable. The point we are making is that it is very rare for such gas to find its way to the surface. We think it is more likely the result of a fault.'

'You mean an earthquake? We don't have earthquakes around here,' Morris snapped.

'This would have happened a very long time ago. We're talking in hundreds of thousand of years. Thus we would have a fault reservoir, that is, one in which all the oil has been lost, but a considerable amount of gas remains trapped.'

'And this gas would be much nearer the surface,' Morris said, eagerly.

'Not necessarily,' Gus said. 'In any event, it would hardly be sufficiently near the surface to be leaking out over several hundred thousand years and still have any left.'

'Look, just what are you trying to tell me?' Morris demanded. 'The lad was in the cave, he flicked his lighter and he went up. So did all the bracken and heather round about. It was a gas explosion. But for the heavy rain later that night it could have been a serious heath fire. I want to know how the gas got there. That's what I'm paying you for, dammit.'

Gus gave one of his equable smiles. 'We shall be able to tell that, Mr Morris, when we have been to the site, tomorrow.'

'My wife,' Bernard said as he led them into the drawing room. 'My daughter, Rebecca, and my son Niall.'

While they went through the handshaking routine Kitty found herself wondering about these people: they didn't seem to fit. Not with each other, nor with the castle and especially not with the servants. Bernard Morris obviously saw himself as the big time businessman, playing the laird for amusement when he wasn't doing something more important. But he obviously hadn't the right background, what her mother would have called *breeding,* to match. His manners were coarse, particularly towards his wife, the pair of them sidling round each other with thinly veiled antagonism. Mrs Morris had probably been quite a good looker, ten or twenty years ago; her bone-structure was strong and her eyes a beautiful shade of green, but her blonde hair was fading and the lines around her mouth betrayed her dissatisfaction—resentment, maybe. And married to this ghastly man, who could blame her?

'What made you choose geo-chemistry for a career?' Rebecca asked.

Kitty grinned. 'I didn't. It chose me. I went in the direction of sciences rather than art long before A-levels, and one thing just led to another. When I got my degree I applied for a list of jobs and took the first one I was offered.'

'With Doctor Wilson?'

'Not exactly. But in the same laboratories in Oxford: Turnbull & Heath. I became his assistant last year. What about you? You're in the Ministry of the Environment, aren't you? Do you enjoy it?'

'Variously. Some of the files I deal with are very exciting. So vitally important to us all. But on the other hand very frustrating at times when one sees terrible things happening in our country and we are powerless to stop them...you know, pollution of our rivers and coasts, for instance.'

'I thought these things were well monitored nowadays?' Kitty asked.

'Huh! Like hell. So they catch some factory owner dumping chemicals illicitly; by the time the case gets to court and he's got himself a good lawyer—paid for by Legal Aid, no doubt—the arguments and waffling go on for years and eventually he's fined a couple of thou. Makes a nonsense of the whole thing and the case has cost the revenue hundreds of thou. Which they can never recoup.'

Margaret, meanwhile, was trying to make conversation with Gus. 'So glad you finally got here. Have you been to Scotland before, Mr...I mean Dr Wilson?'

'Do you mind using my Christian name, please. Makes life much easier.'

'Er...certainly, Augustus.

'Gus. Yes. So sorry we were unable to come up sooner. There was a seminar on in Birmingham... And yes, I have visited Scotland before. We came up to Braemar for the games two years ago. A very beautiful country, and the games are marvellous, aren't they?'

'Er...I'm afraid I've never been.' She knew how feeble that sounded, considering Braemar was only about thirty miles up the road from Aboyne. But Bernard wasn't interested and she didn't want to go alone. 'You said we...?'

'My wife, Gillian, and I. And the kids, of course. How many children have you, Mrs Morris?'

'Er... Three. And you'd better call me Margaret.' She prayed Bernard wouldn't blow her up for that, later. 'Here is Tara, now. Our youngest.'

Kitty was horribly aware of her polyester shirtwaister, as a gorgeously beautiful creature snaked into the room, a sheath of black velvet accentuating her long, slim elegance. The loose blonde curls cascading over her shoulders were perfect. Her blue eyes were enormous, the red lips a big, soft bow against flawless ivory skin. Kitty's eyes fell to the slender knees and calves cased in the finest imaginable nylons ending in dainty little black shoes with very high, gold heels: and she prayed no one would notice her fifteen denier tights and flat heels bought in a hurry in the January sales. Poor overweight Rebecca! What a disaster having to compete with a sister like this! 'Ah! There you are, Tara,' Bernard advanced on his favourite child. 'Come and meet our guests.'

The prospect did not enthrall his daughter. The big blue eyes took one glance at the man, a funny little creature with awful hair, a corduroy jacket and crumpled shirt, and were quickly averted while her limp white hand was shaken. Then her eyes moved to the female, swept over the damp hair and awful frock hanging over lusty shoulders and a saggy bra, took in the muscular legs cased in sacking and dared to meet the lively dark eyes as once again her hand was grasped. 'How do you do,' she murmured, with an obligatory smile.

'Better now that I've had a bath, thanks. Ghastly drive up, I'm afraid,' Kitty told her. 'I'm hoping this front will pass over by tomorrow. I'm dying for a chance to see the mountains.'

'Really? Why?'

'Don't tell me you're not blown away by the scenery?' Kitty's eyes widened in surprise.

'Oh, don't talk about it! Everyone raves about it...it gets so terribly boring. I mean, one cannot spend all day gaping out of windows or traipsing about in macks. Two days up here and I can't wait to get back to civilization.'

'Depends on one's idea of what is or is not civilized, I suppose,' Kitty responded, looking into the heavenly features for some indication that the girl was only leg-pulling.

'London,' Tara cooed, mascara'd lashes sweeping her cheeks. 'Where one can have such fun with the chummies. And wear decent clothes.'

'I love your dress,' Kitty said, truthfully.

'Bond Street. The only place to shop, don't you agree?' As she spoke the china blue eyes slid over Kitty's green and white polyester with ill-disguised amusement.

Irritated, Kitty smiled sweetly. 'I'd rather give my money to charity. Actually, I can highly recommend the Oxfam shop in Oxford.' Tara's exquisite make-up couldn't conceal her flush of annoyance, but before she could frame a really good come back, Guthrie announced dinner.

Niall was a welcome relief. Attentive, natural and an easy conversationalist, he and Kitty were soon exchanging anecdotes about their respective seats of learning. She watched his eyes behind their heavy spectacles—a deeper blue than his sister's—sparkling with enthusiasm about innumerable subjects, while his straight blond hair flopped over his forehead. She wondered what age he might be. Twenty-two at most, she decided.

Bernard, at the head of the table and on Kitty's left, waited till Guthrie had poured wine for everyone before raising his glass. 'May I offer a welcome to our geo-chemists and wish them a very fruitful visit...for the benefit of us all.'

'A fruitful visit!' Niall touched Kitty's glass with his own, a big, genuine smile revealing very even, white teeth.

'For all our sakes!' Tara smiled graciously at the visitors.

'Welcome!' Rebecca nodded, but the greeting lacked conviction.

'Yes, indeed,' her mother agreed.

Kitty looked to see if Gus had noted the differing responses, but seeing his vacant expression guessed he hadn't even heard the toast. She wondered whether his head was currently filled with music or with natural gas?

Later when they went upstairs and she went to his room to fetch her notebooks, she asked what he thought of the Morris family. He scratched his scalp in a familiar gesture and shrugged. 'Funny lot. None of them seem to match. Without the introductions I wouldn't have guessed they were even related.'

Kitty removed the clasp and rubber band from her hair, shaking it loose over her shoulders. 'Tara and Niall both have their mother's colouring...'

'Tara? Which one was that?'

Kitty laughed out loud, then clapped her hand over her mouth, worried they'd be heard. 'The beautiful one with gorgeous blonde hair, of course.'

Gus stared at her in surprise. 'You don't mean the anorexic beanpole with the vapid expression? Would you call her beautiful?'

'Jeepers! Wouldn't you?'

'Liked the fat one more. At least she seems to have a bit of gumption. She doesn't appear too sure about this project, though. Does she?'

Kitty shook her head. 'Nor does her mother, I suspect.'

'What about the boy?'

'The ink is scarcely dry on his degree in business studies. He can't wait to transform all our findings into figures, statistics and commercial analyses.'

'Have any of them the least aesthetic interest in Scotland, do you reckon?' Gus bent over his canvas holdall, churning the contents into even worse chaos.

'Crumbs, yes. You should have heard Niall holding forth on Scottish Nationalism, Scottish history starting with the Picts, and as for football! I've learned the names of more Scottish Premier League clubs tonight than I ever knew existed. Niall, by the way, is a Dundee United supporter and if it's your toothpaste you're after, it's just fallen into that tennis shoe on the floor, on top of your shirts.'

'Ta.' He picked up the shoe and shook it, deftly catching the screwed-up tube as it fell out. 'The big girl...'

'Rebecca...'

'Yes. Well she was eulogizing about the Cairngorms. Wants to take us sightseeing if there's a chance before she goes back to London.'

'Great. Only hope the weather soon clears. She was here at the time of the accident, wasn't she? I wish I'd had more time to talk to her before dinner.'

'Yes. Apparently she went up with the search party and was there when they found the girl.'

'I asked Mr Morris how the kid is getting on but he didn't seem to know.'

'Somehow I doubt if he is interested.'

Kitty was surprised by Gus's observation. Amazing what he did notice about people, sometimes. 'I'll ask Mr Guthrie or Mary in the morning. Anyway, I'll say good-night. See you at breakfast.'

'I'd like to speak to the injured girl, first, before going up to the site,' Gus told Bernard next morning.

Bernard munched his toast, frowning. 'Better to get straight to work, I'd say. We've already waited long enough to get started. Anyway, I don't know if she's well enough to see visitors, yet.' He took another large bite, scattering crumbs over the table.

Kitty waited. Gus might lack physical weight but she'd seen him take on far bigger men than Bernard Morris. 'I don't agree,' the bearded visitor said. 'It is always better to accumulate all available information surrounding an investigation before rushing off with a pick-axe...'

Bernard's frown became a scowl. 'Is that so...' he began.

'...and what's more, I am assured by your man Guthrie that the girl is recovering well and has already made a full statement to the police.'

'Then surely that's enough!'

'Not at all,' Gus persisted, totally unruffled. 'There are many questions I need to ask her which will not have been in their brief.' Margaret sat at the other end of the table, holding her breath. Niall wisely kept quiet. 'Perhaps you could spare Major MacEwan to take us into Aberdeen,' Gus continued, apparently unaware of the electric atmosphere. 'I will also need to visit the local Environmental Officer, or whatever he may call himself. Protocol, you know.'

Bernard grunted and picked up his Cellnet from beside his plate. 'Very well.

I'll tell MacEwan to come and pick you up. Ten minutes?'

James collected them in a white Volvo Estate, one of several vehicles kept on Abergannan for the convenience of the family and their friends. Gus sat in front beside him, Kitty behind with Mary, who also wanted to see Karen Wilkie. 'This is the first time I've been to Aberdeen,' Kitty confessed. 'Is it a big place?'

'Oh, aye,' Mary said. 'And getting bigger.'

'It's been ruined, by finding oil,' James remarked. 'Quite apart from the terminals, there's been all this building, with pressure on services...fair makes you sick to think about.'

'But surely the oil has brought a great increase in prosperity?' Kitty asked.

'There's prosperity and prosperity, Miss Cochrane,' James pointed out.

'Tell us about it,' Gus invited to defuse the incipient antagonism. 'Why do they call it the Granite City?'

'Because it's built on granite. And most of the buildings are of granite, too. It actually began as two cities, what they called Old Aberdeen, consisting of the cathedral and the university complex, on the River Don, and New Aberdeen, the commercial town, on the Dee. But of course they grew towards each other.'

'And how old is Old Aberdeen?' Kitty asked.

'They say it was founded back in 580, by St Machar. He was a disciple of St Columba.'

'And the cathedral is that old? I should love to visit it.'

'It's not there, any more, Miss Cochrane. The English came along in 1336 and burned it down. The new one dates back to a hundred years later.'

'There's the English for you,' Gus said equably. 'Didn't Byron go to school here?'

'Oh, aye, that he did. Just over there is the Bridge of Balgounie. He wrote one of his earliest poems about that.'

James smiled as he chatted and Kitty thought he was much nicer than her first impression, though there still seemed to be a certain coolness in his attitude. Not so with Mary. When Kitty said she hoped she and Gus were not making too much extra work, the stiff, middle-aged spinster shook her head vigorously. 'Very nice to have you visiting, Miss. It is always a pleasure to welcome people with such an interest in the Highlands. And as for extra work! Well, you are the first person to stay at the castle I can recall, who has made her own bed.'

'Afraid I didn't,' Gus said over his shoulder.

'I should hope not,' James laughed. 'Woman's work.'

'Do I detect a trace of male chauvinism rearing its ugly head?' Kitty demanded. 'Now tell me all about Karen. How is she connected with Abergannan?'

'Ye mean ye don't know! The family havna told ye? Why, she's Rabbie Wilkie's youngest. The gillie's daughter. And a vary sweet child, too. Regular at the kirk, she is...and that cannot be said for all the young these days. And young Vincent, too, God rest his soul.' Mary's thin white lips quivered, and were pressed tight together so they didn't lose control. 'Worst tragedy suffered in these parts since the avalanche in the forties, when I was a wee girl.' Mary enjoyed the trip to Aberdeen, pleased with the opportunity of conversation with this young scientist. A nice, well-brought-up girl, obviously from a good home. The pity was that not all young English girls were so natural.

It was decided that Mary should go in first to see Karen, and tell her about her other visitors. When she rejoined James, Gus and Kitty later outside in the hot corridor that smelled of fresh paint and carbolic, Rabbie's wife Sheena was with her.

'How is she?' Kitty asked, still worried about tiring the girl.

'A lot better in herself.' Mrs Wilkie looked weary, with dark purple rings round her eyes. 'Her breathing is improving. Her lungs were damaged by the heat and smoke, they say. But Ah must warn ye...' she bowed her head for a moment. 'She looks terrible. Half her poor wee face is in a kinda clear plastic bag to prevent infection and keep anything from touching it. So ye will see all the burns.' She took a deep, shuddering breath then said, 'Come. Ah'll take ye to her.'

'I'll be off to my shopping, now.' Mary smiled and left.

Having expected to find the patient swathed in bandages, Kitty realized that modern medicine had better ideas. 'They don't let anything stick in the open wounds, nowadays,' Karen explained. 'I hope the sight doesn't make ye want to throw up.'

'I'll ask you to ring for a bedpan if I get the urge,' Kitty grinned.

'Uh, uh!' Karen held up her undamaged hand. 'Please don't make me laugh. It hurts my face.'

Which made Kitty want to weep at the girl's bravery. 'Here. We brought you these.' She stood a woven basket of arranged flowers on the bedside table. 'I hope you've retained your sense of smell along with your sense of humour.'

'And your sense of taste, too,' Gus added, with his offering of chocolates.

Sheena arranged chairs round the bed and when they were settled said, 'Dr Wilson and Miss Cochrane would like to know what you can remember about that night.'

'Only if you feel like talking, my dear,' Gus leaned towards the bed, worried. 'We don't want to upset or tire you.'

'I'm not too bad, most of the time, now. But then the thought of poor Vinny...and things. The cold up there...it all comes over me again in waves.' She closed her good eye. The other, in the bag, was lost in a hideously swollen mess of raw flesh.

'The nurses say the cold up there may have saved her life,' Sheena told them. 'And the rain. Really poured it did, that night. It stopped the burning. But why she didna die of pneumonia Ah'll never know.'

'Do you know what set the whole thing off?' Gus asked.

'It was when Vinny borrowed my lighter.'

'But I thought Vincent wasna a smoker?' Sheena asked.

'He wasna lighting a cigarette. He was in that cave place, looking for the car keys.'

'Wasn't there a bad smell round that

part?' Gus wanted to know.

'Terrible. Like rotten eggs. He said he could scarce breathe for the stench. We wondered if maybe a sheep had died in there.'

They were silent, while Gus nodded, thinking, and Karen closed her eye again.

'I think we should go,' Kitty declared, getting up.

'Yes, yes,' Gus agreed. There were a lot of other questions he would have liked to ask this young woman, but he could tell that trying to remember that night was traumatic for her. 'Very good of you to see us, Karen.'

'Thank you, Mrs Wilkie. Don't worry,' Kitty pushed the older woman down into her chair again, 'We can find our way out.'

James had not gone in with them. Now he asked, 'Did you learn anything of interest?'

'As a matter of fact, yes,' Gus said. 'Although some of it doesn't fit my theories. Anyway, we're progressing. Now, will you please drive us to the local Office of the Environment?'

James led them back to the jeep. 'What do you hope to learn from them?'

'They might have information on recent findings in the area. But chiefly, I must make my number with them before starting any investigations. Protocol.'

James drove out of the hospital yard. 'So you want to find natural gas in the Highlands?'

'Didn't you know?' Kitty asked.

'I was told you were coming to tell us if there is any danger down there. If it might explode again.' There was a note of sarcasm in his voice. He glanced at Kitty who was now sitting beside him, Gus having got into the back.

'Well, that's part of our job, certainly,' Kitty acknowledged. 'But your boss also wants to find out if there is enough gas down there to be worth developing.'

James nodded. 'I had imagined so.' He negotiated a series of narrow streets.

'Oh, this is so quaint,' Kitty said. 'Where are we?'

'Castlegate. Used to be a market. Not any more though.' He stopped at the traffic lights on to Union Street, then eased forward. 'And if there is?' he asked. 'Gas down there, I mean.'

'Well, I imagine Mr Morris will be interested in developing it. Natural gas is big money.'

'I'd have thought he had enough big money,' the Scot muttered. 'What exactly would development mean?'

Gus didn't reply, so Kitty did. 'It would

mean boring to reach the reservoir. You must have seen photos of oil fields.'

'Jesus Christ,' James muttered, and gave her another glance. 'But this isn't oil.'

'It's the same principle. You have to have derricks to house the drills.'

'Derricks. You mean towers? Across the hills and valleys?'

'I'm afraid so.' She had never seen the Highlands except in pictures, but she could well imagine the effect on the scenery.

'And then, the gas would have to be delivered to plant,' Gus took over again. 'Natural gas is never usable when it first comes out of the ground; it has to be refined. So pipelines would have to be laid, and...' his head jerked as the jeep swung to the right and stopped.

'And the countryside?' James demanded.

'I know. It's not a very pleasant thought. But I guess you have to put it down to progress.'

'Which is why we need to be sure the area hasn't been designated green or of outstanding natural beauty,' Gus explained. 'By the Office of the Environment. Would you please take us there?'

James jerked his thumb at the building before which he had parked. 'You're there,' he said. 'Like me to come in with you?'

Kitty looked at Gus, who was already out of the jeep.

'I don't think so, Major MacEwan.' Gus gave one of his charming smiles. 'I think we'd have to rate you as an anti before we even begin.'

'Gas? On Abergannon?' demanded Mr Coultrain, filling his pipe. 'That's a daft idea.'

Gus regarded the Environment Officer with a tolerance he did not feel. 'Then what do you suppose blew up that boy?'

'Ah, well, I'm not saying there wasna some gas in that cave. Had to be. But a reservoir...'

Kitty was beginning to feel irritated. 'There's gas out there.' She pointed at the window, through which the white-grey rollers of the North Sea could just be seen.

'Ah, well, some miles away, to be sure.'

'We're all entitled to our opinions, Mr Coultrain,' Gus said. 'What we wish to know is your position, supposing we do find a worthwhile reservoir down there?'

'Ye mean ye'd want to bring it up?'

'That's one way of putting it,' Kitty muttered.

'Man, that'd be a big job,' Coultrain said. 'A big job.'

'But an ordinary job, which is being carried out all over the world, every day,' Gus said. 'And in fact it will be an easier job on Abergannan than almost anywhere else, because you have all the facilities right here.'

'Well, that's true, I suppose. But ye'd still have to pipe it.'

'We know that, Mr Coultrain. What we would like you to tell us is that there are no legal impediments to drilling in that neighourhood.'

'Ye mean at the cave where the boy was burned?'

'There for starters. But we could be talking of several miles in every direction around there.'

'Well, that's a big job,' Coultrain said again. 'Yes, sir, it's...'

'A big job,' Kitty said. 'Is there an impediment? Is it an area of outstanding natural beauty?'

'Ye've not been up there?'

'Not yet. We're going up this afternoon.'

'Aye, well, then ye'll see for yourself. It sairtainly is an area of outstanding natural beauty.'

Kitty had a strong urge to seize her hair and start tearing it out.

As Gus could tell. 'What Miss Cochrane means,' he said, 'and what we would both like to know, is whether or not there is any restriction, parish, county or national, on developing that site. With all of the necessary construction that would be involved.'

'Ah,' Coultrain said. 'Now that I cannot say. Without looking it up, ye ken.'

'We do understand that. Would you be so kind as to look it up?'

'I shall do that,' Coultrain agreed, but made no immediate sign of either moving from his desk or using the computer on it. 'It's private property, ye ken.'

'We do ken, if that is the right word,' Gus acknowledged.

'Belongs to a man named Morris,' Coultrain said, disparagingly. 'A sassenach. And a right bas...a difficult man, if ye ken what I mean.'

'We do indeed.'

'He'll no give ye permission to dig on his land, anyway.

'It is Mr Morris who has sent for us. He is employing us to "dig" on his land, as may be necessary,' Gus said.

'Ye don't say. Well, well.'

'So will you look up that information, please?'

'Oh, aye. I will do that. Where can I reach ye.'

'You mean you can't do it now?' Kitty asked.

'Well... I have a lot to do, ye see.'

'You can reach us at Abergannan Castle,' Gus said, before she could explode.

'Oh, aye? Staying at the castle, are ye?'

'Yes. But you do understand, I'm sure,

that we are only here for a matter of days. We do need the information as quickly as possible. May we expect to hear from you by the end of the afternoon?' Gus asked.

Mr Coultrain was not the sort to succumb to pressure. 'I'll call ye when I have the information ye require. Good-day to ye.'

Gus closed the door behind them.

'Bureaucracy!' Kitty remarked.

'He has to fill his day. And...well, I can't help being on his side.'

'Filling his day?' Kitty asked.

'Being concerned about the countryside. How do you feel about it?'

Kitty led the way down the stairs. 'I think it stinks. Putting up pylons in the desert is bad. Putting them up here, and then laying miles of pipelines across the mountains has got to be the pits. But...'

'... But people need the earth's resources, and if we don't find it, someone else will.'

'Granted. But where it isn't really necessary and is only going to be done to line the pockets of some fat toad...'

'Steady on. He happens to be our employer, for the moment.'

'Yes,' Kitty growled. She was almost obsessive about her job, found nothing more exciting than being involved in an investigation, the tests, experiments and occasional field work entailed in tracking down substances, gases and chemicals, known and unknown. Sometimes a few rigs and buildings did have to be erected, discreetly screened where possible, of course. It was only a matter of convincing the objectors—and there were always plenty of those about—of the advantages. But in this case...there would be no way to conceal the monstrosities. And the one thing she disliked even more about this latest assignment was Morris himself.

They ate in a low-beamed dining-room beyond the public bar in an ancient building down a side alley. James was apparently a regular, welcomed by the landlord with a gruff roar in an unintelligible Scottish accent and after handshakes all round they had leaned on the polished rail of the bar with their drinks, to choose from the menu.

'Simple fare, but good and ribsticking,' James assured them. 'Did you get on all right at the Environment office?'

'The man we spoke to, Coultrain, said he'd phone us. We only pray he does so pretty promptly,' Gus said despondently.

'I imagine that if we don't get a call within half an hour of our return, our Mr Morris will be...' Kitty stopped herself and blushed.

‘...gnawing chunks out of his Cellnet?’ James suggested.

Kitty stuck her tongue in her cheek, trying not to laugh.

Gus raised an eyebrow.

‘Don’t worry,’ James said. ‘Mr Morris and I understand each other perfectly. He made little effort to disguise the fact that he disliked me on sight. And I believe he is quite well aware that I can’t stick the best bone in his body. But he needed a bailiff and I needed a job. His was the only vacancy and I was the only applicant. We agreed that I would do the job to the very best of my ability provided that he gave me a free hand with the management of the estate and a reasonable salary...which he certainly did not give my predecessor.’

‘Funny. Till now I had thought it was Yorkshiremen who were best noted for their bluntness,’ Kitty remarked, casually.

James grinned, but was prevented from answering by the arrival of steaming plates of braised beef, carrots, onions and potatoes in a thick brown gravy. ‘Thanks, Maisie,’ he said to the freckled waitress. ‘And do you think we could have some mustard with it?’

‘You born round here, Major?’ Gus asked.

‘In Aberdeen? No. Up the valley not far from Abergannan.’

'Then you must love the mountains,' Kitty said.

'Yes.'

'And naturally don't like the idea of foreigners raping your countryside,' Gus said.

'No.'

'That's a bit over the top, isn't it?' Kitty suggested.

'No,' James said again.

The three ate in silence for a few minutes. Then Gus wiped his mouth on his paper napkin, 'This is seriously good. Delicious. I should try to get the recipe for Gillian.'

'They probably don't have one,' Kitty took a swig of beer. 'It tastes like one of those dishes that depend entirely on the cook's instinct for success.'

'True,' James nodded. 'I order the same thing nearly every time I come and every time it tastes different.' He put his knife and fork down on his empty plate with a sigh of regret. Then asked, 'Do you enjoy what you do?'

Kitty's head came up with a jerk. 'You mean research? Why yes, I love it.'

But Gus saw that James wasn't smiling. 'We don't enjoy scarring people's landscapes, if that's what you're asking?'

'Yet you do it.'

'It's a point of view, isn't it?' Kitty

bridled. 'Somebody may have thought Edinburgh Castle was a blot on their landscape when it was first built. And Balmoral...and even the castle on Abergannan.'

James stared at her pensively for a moment, then smiled. 'And almost certainly the Eiffel Tower. As you say, a point of view. However, the fact doesn't make the idea of rigs, pipes and pylons, and whatever else may be involved, any more appealing. Especially across the Highlands.'

'I hope you understand that we do appreciate your concern.' Gus spoke gravely with a solemn expression. 'On the one hand one cannot stand in the way of progress, but on the other we have to consider aesthetic as well as environmental factors. In our work we do endeavour to weigh all the pros and cons.' He drained his beer and pushed his chair back from the table. 'That was one excellent meal. Thank you, Major, for bringing us here.'

The Scotsman stood up. 'And I hope you understand that it is not so easy for me to sit on the fence...as you obviously do. Now, as we will be seeing quite a good deal of each other in the next few days, can we strike a bargain?'

Kitty and Gus, dwarfed by the man's height, stared up at him, wondering what was coming.

'If I promise not to call you Professor, will you promise not to call me Major?'

The visitors were laughing and relaxed as James led them back to the car; rather more relaxed than James himself. He accepted that they were a couple of nice, reasonable people with a job of work to do...he just wished they weren't planning to do it in his backyard. Gus was a bit weird with his wild red hair and untrimmed beard, and the way he would suddenly drift away, his mind a million miles away from the current conversation. But he was easy-going, natural and sincere. There was something very attractive about the girl, too, in a different way. He couldn't imagine her mind drifting off: she was too alert, lively. Her eyes sparkled with joy or intense interest in a subject...and flashed with anger on occasion. She could be good company if she chose, but needed watching. There was no doubt she could be a tough cookie when roused. It was going to be an interesting week.

She smiled at him, as he gunned the engine. 'So, the site?'

As she spoke there was a crack of thunder and an enormous downpour of rain, which gave no indication of being about to stop.

'Bloody weather,' James muttered. 'Would ye believe it, save for a couple of weeks a month ago, we've had rain all winter—and not a drop of snow. Looks like we may have to postpone your field trip until tomorrow.'

Chapter 3

THE CAVERN

'Yes,' Bernard snapped in response to the knock on his study door. When he looked up and saw James MacEwan he added, 'Oh, it's you. Well?'

'I thought you might be interested to know that at the resumed hearing yesterday afternoon the coroner gave a verdict on the boy Kevin Brown of death by misadventure, due to inhalation of toxic gas following injuries caused by explosion.'

'Hmm. Fairly obvious, I'd have thought. Anyway, thanks for letting me know.' He returned his attention to the papers on his desk.

'The professor and Miss Cochrane will be going up to the site this morning,' James went on. 'Did you wish to accompany them?'

'What the hell for? Nothing I can do up there.'

James wondered how long he could stick this uncouth cretin. 'I thought you might have wanted to be there on their first visit.' And as sure as God made little apples, if it wasn't mentioned you'd raise hell about not being told.

Bernard lifted his phone and began dialling. 'No thanks. Now if you'll excuse me... Hello?'

James left the room to assemble the climbers.

Niall was at the breakfast table on his second helping of bacon and sausages, his rate of consumption being hampered by his need to question Kitty about her work—which was really only a ruse to detain her. The young man was fascinated by the female geo-chemist. He wondered how such a bubbly character had become involved in such an extraordinarily unfeminine subject. 'So tell me about natural gas,' he suggested. 'I suppose you know all about it.'

'A little,' Kitty agreed, in between mouthfuls of cereal.

'Been around a long time? The gas, I mean, not you.' He grinned at her.

'For a few million years,' she said. 'They were burning natural gas in what we now call Iran several thousand years before the birth of Christ. But those were natural emissions. Could be rather like what happened up here.'

'But you don't think that's likely?'

Beatrice, the young housemaid, in cap and apron, listened surreptitiously from the sideboard. She hadn't a clue what they were talking about, but she loved watching this really dishy guy and the way his hair flopped over his forehead while he was talking. And the way he brushed it away when he wasn't. He was just ace, far the best of the family. He was the only one who seemed to know she existed. One evening, when he was a bit tipsy, he had actually put an arm round her shoulders and given her a hug. She'd relived that moment every day since.

'No,' Kitty was saying. 'Nowadays one has to drill to get at it, as a rule. Do you know they were actually drilling for gas in China a thousand years ago? Not very efficiently, as they had to use bamboo tubes.'

'Whereas now we just stick a steel pipe in the ground and bull's eye, we got it... Once we know where to put it. Right?'

'It's not quite as simple as that,' Kitty pointed out. 'In most cases natural gas cannot be used industrially or domestically without treatment, to remove things like carbon dioxide or hydrogen sulphide.'

'Hydrogen sulphide is the one that smells

like rotten eggs, isn't it?'

Kitty had just helped herself to a boiled egg, which she now regarded with suspicion. 'I think we should continue this conversation some other time.'

'I'm sorry. I didn't aim to nauseate you. But we could smell that out at the cave.'

'So we've been told. But as rule it's not explosive. Anyway, that's one of the things we're here to find out.'

'You mean, if there is gas down there, but it contains hydrogen sulphide, it won't be worth anything?'

'Not at all. The H2S will have to be removed at a processing plant before the gas is used commercially, that's all.'

'Sounds a complicated business. And expensive.'

'It is,' Kitty said, 'on both counts. But it'll pay the costs, if it's there in sufficient quantity. Do you know how much natural gas is currently being used every year in the world? Something around two plus twelve zeros cubic metres. That is to say, two million million, roughly twenty per cent of the total energy consumption.'

Niall whistled. 'And it's not about to run out?'

'Not so far as I know. And certainly so long as we keep finding new fields.' She finished her egg and her coffee. 'There are several things I must pack to take with us this morning. Are you coming?' She folded her napkin and got up.

'Sure thing! I wouldn't miss it. Anything I can do to help?' Even in her over-long woolly jumper and faded jeans she looked good enough to eat.

'I'll tell you if something crops up. See you later.'

To Beatrice's disappointment Niall immediately abandoned the bacon and sausages and followed the visitor out of the room.

'I've put picks and shovels, crowbars and a sledgehammer into my jeep. Anything else I can bring?' James asked.

'A groundsheet? Always useful for spreading out our gear,' Gus suggested. 'We've got all the breathing apparatus.'

'And another for covering it over if it rains,' Kitty added.

'We don't need too much equipment at this stage,' Gus said. 'If we find it worth investigating further, at depth, then we will have to call in the heavy stuff.' James nodded but said nothing. Just prayed that it wouldn't happen.

'Can I come too?' Rebecca appeared at the top of the stairs, obviously dressed for the occasion.

'Yes, of course,' Kitty smiled, hoping she sounded more welcoming than she felt.

Going on one of these field trips with a party of scientists was one thing, but taking along a load of hangers-on was something else. Yet she liked Rebecca and didn't wish to offend her. And Gus wouldn't mind. No, the difficult one was going to be Niall. Again, a nice boy, intelligent and keen, but she realized that unfortunately he had already developed a crush on her which meant she'd be tripping over him every time she turned round.

'I'll lead the way in the jeep and can we have a volunteer to drive the Volvo?' The car keys were dangling from James' finger. 'I've asked Andrew to come along, too. He does much of the hefty work on the farm. I thought he might be useful with the crowbar. He can go in the Volvo.'

'I'll drive it.' Niall took the keys and headed for the door. 'Coming?' he invited Kitty.

Gus took James' passenger seat and Rebecca sat with Andrew in the back of the Volvo as they drove up the valley into the hills. The cloud cover was breaking up in parts, revealing flashes of blue sky, but continuing to cling to the mountain tops...like the warm woolly hats the girls were wearing.

The cars followed a narrow road winding alongside the burn—a wide and shallow stream, bubbling noisily over rocks and pebbles, forming islets where trees and bushes had survived the winter torrents. A number of cattle were grazing on the far banks, still wearing their thick winter coats, while on the steeper slopes above the road, sheep climbed rocky paths through the trees.

'There is so much more colour than I imagined,' Kitty remarked, peering out in every direction, ducking her head to see as high as possible up the hillsides. 'And many more trees. I thought the mountains would be quite bare.'

'The vegetation becomes more sparse as we climb,' Rebecca told her. 'The temperature variation between the sheltered valleys and the higher mountains is roughly equivalent to the difference between London and the south of Spain. Some of the gardens in the lower altitudes have subtropical trees and shrubs, you know.'

'There,' Niall shouted. 'There's Cock Cairn away over on your left.' Maintaining some semblance of control of the steering wheel with his right hand, he leaned across Kitty to point out the highest peak of the range to the south.

'Look out, you clot!' his sister shouted as they took yet another bend on the wrong side.

'The jeep is out of sight,' Kitty said. Not that she was too bothered: the view was so spectacular, constantly changing, she couldn't drink in enough of it. She was livid that she had forgotten to bring her camera.

'No problem. I know the way.'

James and Gus were unloading the jeep when the Volvo braked beside them. Kitty had difficulty concentrating on the job in hand: she only wanted to stand looking, taking deep breaths as though she might draw it all into her soul. The view back down the valley was fantastic—real picture postcard stuff, she thought—but above her, the towering cliffs and granite outcrops were awesome.

Rebecca watched Kitty's reaction and smiled. Whatever happened, whatever these scientists found, this one would surely be on her side, respecting the beauty and grandeur of the Highlands and doubtless unwilling to endanger it.

'Are you coming, or what?' Gus nudged his assistant into action. 'Here's your pack. Let's get going.'

Kitty laughed as she swung the haversack onto her back. 'I think you will regret not bringing an elephant goad, before the day is out. You're going to need it!'

'Hey! Let me take that for you.' Niall grabbed at her load.

Short of staging a tug of war Kitty felt

obliged to release it. 'Thanks,' she nodded, briefly.

Near the cave entrance they spread a groundsheet over the scorched earth and laid out the equipment. Kitty knelt to unpack her bag, re-distributing the notebooks, pencils, gauges and storage phials she would need while Gus and James double-checked the gas masks and the miners' lamps attached to their helmets.

'Andrew,' James called. 'Will you start by widening the entrance, here? It's awkward getting in and out with the equipment.'

'How did the rescuers get Vincent out?' Kitty asked.

'With great difficulty. He was strapped to a narrow stretcher frame down in there and eased out. Of course the fact that he was obviously dead made it slightly easier. However, if we can get in and out freely we are less likely to damage our gear.'

Andrew, dark and stocky with the shoulders of a professional weight lifter, tackled the looser rocks with the crowbar, hacked at knotted roots with an axe and finally grasped the handle of the sledgehammer and swung it mightily at a large piece of granite jutting into the entranceway. The watchers stood well back, but Andrew knew what he was doing. A great lump was cleaved clean off the rockface and fell at his feet. 'That do ye, Major?'

'Aye. Well enough. Now how's the smell today?'

'Doesn't seem as bad as the day of the explosion,' Niall remarked.

Gus stood at the rockface and held a gauge into the enlarged aperture. 'Mmm. Not too bad. Definitely methane, though. Tell me about these mountains, James.'

'The Grampians? Or the area?'

'Both, if they're relevant.'

'Grampian itself is the entire area around Aberdeen. They say it was named after Mons Graupius, which was the name used by Tacitus as the site of the battle in which the Roman general Agricola defeated the Picts in AD 84, this being the furthest north the Romans ever fought a battle. No one has ever actually pinpointed the site.'

'And the mountains?'

'Named after the battle, I suppose. They stretch clear across the Highlands, peaking at Ben Nevis just above Fort William. That's the highest in Britain. But there're a few other big ones, such as Cairn Gorm or Ben Macdui, just over there; you can see them from here on a clear day. I'm afraid beside those fellows, our Cock Cairn is just a hill, and Gannon Hill, at the foot of which we're standing now, is a pimple.'

'I thought the Cairngorms were a

separate range,' Kitty remarked.

'They are so regarded,' James acknowledged. 'But they're all part of the Grampian Range.'

'It's their age, I'm after,' Gus said.

'They've been around a long time. We could be talking of five hundred million years. Does that make a difference?'

'Very much so. Gas is as much a fossil fuel as is oil. In fact more often than not it forms out of oil. The great forests, which were later fossilized as coal and oil and gas, were in existence only three hundred million years ago. They were followed by a huge series of upheavals which buried them, and which, incidentally, threw up another series of mountain-building eras.'

'I take your point,' James replied. 'Then I must have it wrong. These must come from that later period.'

'Don't get me wrong. There are some fossil fuels which date back before the carboniferous era, but in their case we are talking about enormous depths. Some of them, anyway.'

'So what exactly are we looking for?'

'First of all we must establish the physical quality of the gas. As we explained, there are two types, organic and inorganic. We have been acting on the theory that this pocket is organic, but the presence of hydrogen sulphide has rather blown a hole in that. However, we still have to check that out. Gas, as I say, is a fossil fuel, an offshoot of coal and oil. It rises from oil. The usual process is for a reservoir of oil to form. This will rise above the water content in the rocks, because oil has a lower specific gravity. But the gas given off by the oil has an even lower specific gravity, thus we have an unchangeable pattern reading from the bottom:—water, oil, gas.'

'Which presumably makes the gas more accessible?' James asked.

'Up to a point, yes.'

'And does that mean there could also be oil down there? You are going to make old man Morris's day.'

'There could be. On the other hand, it is also possible for there to have been a fault line in these hills, indeed, there could still be a fault line, which has allowed the oil to drain away while leaving the gas trapped in a pocket.'

'So what we're looking for is a gas pocket?'

'Right. But when I use the word pocket, I actually mean a reservoir. To be commercially viable it would have to be fairly large. And this one, if it is there, will have some very peculiar qualities.'

'In what way?' James asked.

'The gas reservoir can only form where it is sealed by rock above it. Here we have gas escaping. It obviously is not a great deal, or we wouldn't be able to approach this cave at all, without breathing apparatus. But, if the gas is escaping from a vent in the reservoir, it could have been escaping for a couple of million years, so there shouldn't be anything left, unless we happen to be standing on one of the greatest reservoirs of natural gas in the world.'

'You think that's possible?' James' throat went dry.

'No.'

'Well, then...you must have a theory?' He held his breath.

'Oh, I believe there is a reservoir down there. But I also believe that somehow or other, and quite recently, it was opened, very briefly, allowing some of the gas to escape, and was then blocked again. The gas gathered in the cave, rather like a room in which the gas tap has been left on. Most would have filtered out, but enough remained to cause an explosion when that boy flicked his lighter.'

'You're talking about some kind of earth movement? And it would have had to be quite recent? There's been nothing like that around here within living memory.'

'It may not necessarily have been caused by an earth movement,' Gus said. 'The most likely possibility is water erosion.'

James frowned. 'That stream we passed?'

'No, one underground, eating away at the rock, and finally eroding enough to uncover a gas vent.'

'An underground stream? I've never heard of one in these parts.'

'That doesn't mean there aren't any. We'll just have to find out.' He returned to the apparatus. 'OK. Let's get kitted up, shall we?'

James picked up a long coil of nylon rope. 'Andrew. We'll tie one end of this to that tree stump and take the other end in with us. You keep a hand on it and we can signal with pulls. One pull means all's well. Two pulls and we're having minor problems. Three, and you'd better run like hell for help!'

'There are only four gas masks,' Rebecca pointed out, 'so I'll stay here with Andrew.' Wanting to be useful she tried to help Kitty strap on her back-pack, but was pushed aside by her brother, so she went to Gus's aid instead. Trust little bruv to get the hots for the first female into his orbit this holiday, she smiled to herself.

Gus adjusted his helmet and switched on the lamp. The others followed his example, Kitty tucking back her hair and adjusting the black nylon straps for Niall's gas mask who, never having done this before, was feeling somewhat self-conscious as he took off his glasses and stowed them in his breast pocket—Kitty wondered how well he could see without them. Then he saw that she was again humping the largest pack, and touched her on the arm, making gestures to indicate that he was willing to relieve her of the load, but she shook her head; she wasn't handing her precious gear to anyone when actually working.

Gus glanced around to make sure that everyone was ready, and gave the thumbs-up sign. Then he lowered himself easily through the opening enlarged by Andrew. The floor of the cave was loose shale and stones sloping away into the darkness, but as he followed the beam of his light he saw that it was surprisingly small, with fresh scars and blackened streaks on the rock face.

He trod carefully down the slope to the far end, Kitty following, Niall behind her, and James bringing up the rear with the rope. Gus quickly found what he was looking for, a narrow fissure down through the rock. Obviously the gas had come up that, at some time in the past. The question was, firstly, could it still be coming up, and secondly, could they, or at least, James, who was the biggest, descend through it.

He touched Kitty on the arm, and she immediately put down her haversack and took out her gauges. Niall watched with close interest as she made notes, which she held up in front of Gus's lamp. 'Methane level four per cent in air.'

Gus raised his eyebrows; he knew as well as she, that the methane level had to be considerably higher than that to be explosive. Thus he had been right in his original contention, that this gas pocket had been cut off from its source for some time, and was being diluted all the time as it mingled with air coming in the entrance. In which case the methane reading at the time of the accident must have been abnormally, and dangerously, high.

Kitty now took a large, plastic syringe from her pack and withdrew the plunger, sucking in some of the gas and air which she immediately transferred into a small numbered jar which she sealed. Niall watched her make notes on her pad against the matching number.

Gus pointed at the fissure, and began working his way through. There was just enough width for a man in the narrow passageway beyond. Kitty followed and Niall, after a brief hesitation, reflecting on what would happen to them if there was an earth tremor while they were down there, followed her.

Once they were in the passageway they waited for James, by far the largest of the four, to get through. They directed their lamps up and to either side, but the rock was smooth apart from minor fissures and veins of marble and patches of dead vegetable matter which tended to confirm Gus's theory that the gas escape had been a recent one, or the fungi would never have grown at all. Here the roof was higher, some ten feet up, and the floor rough.

They descended another hundred feet, Gus still leading. Now and then the passage flattened out, sometimes it even rose again, before resuming its descent. In three places it almost closed, and they had to edge sideways. It was exhausting, and although it had been cold on the mountainside, they were soon panting and breathing hard. On the other hand, the methane readings had been dropping all the time, and were now virtually nonexistent.

When Gus held up his hand at the bottom of a particularly steep descent which they had made mostly sitting down, Kitty took off her mask. The others stared at her in amazement. 'There's practically no gas here,' she said.

Gus removed his mask as well, and after a moment James did the same. Niall was last, anxiously sniffing the air as he did so.

'I don't get it,' James said.

'I do,' Gus said. 'It's as I thought. Listen.'

Now they could all hear a distant rushing sound.

'Water!' Niall's voice rose with excitement. 'Just so long as we're not caught in a flash flood...'

'It's well below us,' Gus said.

'I wonder how much is down there. Could be a vast underground lake,' Niall said, no doubt thinking of some science fiction movie he had seen.

'There sounds a lot of it,' James agreed, anxiously. No experienced caver, he wanted to avoid unnecessary danger.

'And that explains what's been happening,' Gus continued.

'To you, maybe.' Niall pushed his hair back.

'What we are listening to is an underground stream, fed by surface water. That water has probably been rushing through there for centuries, perhaps hundreds of centuries. Water erodes. It has been eating away at the rock for all of those eons of time, until at last it uncovered a gas vent.'

'But there's no gas here now.'

'There's a simple explanation for that. When was your last prolonged dry spell?'

'A month ago. We had no rain for three weeks.'

'Right. That's when the water level dropped far enough for gas to escape. Then you had rain?'

'Why, yes,' James said, thoughtfully. 'On the night of the explosion, it was very wet, and for a couple of days after. That's why only the heather immediately against the cavern burned.'

'Well, you see, that heavy rain meant that the stream was in full spate, and high. That means it crossed the point where the gas is escaping, and blocked it off.'

'But didn't flow down it?' Niall's tone was sceptical.

'Oh, indeed, some of it would have flowed down. But we are talking about a very small fissure indeed, a matter of inches, or less. With the water flowing by at that great rate, only a trickle is going to go down that hole. But its sheer volume prevents any gas from escaping. Then, when there is dry spell, and the water level in the stream falls, the gas vent is exposed, gas escapes and gathers in these passageways, slowly finding its way up to the cave. This is what must have happened just before the accident. The gas which was escaping during the dry spell was gathered in the gullies and fissures, and the cavern. And young Vincent was just unlucky to flick his lighter when the accumulation was at its strongest. Since then the vent has been cut off by the rising water, and as gas is lighter than air, it has been rising, and diffusing in the air, with the result that down here is quite clear.'

'How can you know all that, just from the sound of water?' Niall, at twenty-four, liked to challenge any statement.

'Simply because it's the only explanation that fits the facts.'

'So what you're saying is,' James nodded as he spoke, 'that the gas reservoir is flooded with water every time we have heavy rain up here, which is roughly eight months of the year. So it'll hardly be worth drilling.' Was there hope? he wondered.

'I suspect the level of the stream is high enough to block the gas vent for a lot more than eight months of the year,' Gus said. 'But as for diluting the gas in the reservoir, it won't have affected that at all, except in passing. To begin with, the reservoir, if it's there, is a long way away. You won't find natural gas at much above a thousand metres from the surface, and as I have suggested, it may be a lot deeper than that. We have come down maybe fifty metres, not more. While, again as I explained up top, water has a heavier specific gravity than either gas or oil. Any water dribbling down a thousand metres from this height is probably only a small fraction of the total water, from a variety of sources including condensation, getting in there. Water entering the gas reservoir would immediately sink to the bottom, and it would go on sinking through any oil deposit that might be there, as well. Therefore the gas itself would only be slightly, contaminated shall we say, at any given time. All natural gas reservoirs have some water vapour in them, which has to be extracted before it can be used commercially. Its intrinsic value remains unchanged. Kitty?'

Kitty hesitated. What Gus was saying made absolute sense. More importantly, it tied in with her gauge read-outs. He had not, however, mentioned the most important factor of all, no doubt deliberately: where water had uncovered a vent, air would also have entered. Now they could indeed be sitting on a bomb...but it was unlikely to go off as long as the water level in the stream remained high enough to prevent any more methane from escaping, and she didn't want to alarm anyone. 'I entirely agree with that,' she said. 'But...you say there was a wet period just after the accident, James? Has it been raining since then? It's not raining now.'

'It hasn't rained for the past four days, until yesterday afternoon,' James said.

'And that was only for a few hours. It

hasn't rained at all today.' She looked at Gus.

'I take your point. If the water level is dropping again, there may be some more leaking in the immediate future. But there's no gas about now.'

'So what do we do?' Niall asked. 'Go back up and wait for the water level to fall sufficiently to uncover the vent or crack or whatever? That could be weeks away, or even months, if we have a wet spring and summer. And we still don't know if there is anything worth exploiting down there. Dad isn't going to be very happy about that.'

'Rome wasn't built in a day,' Gus said, as equably as ever. 'I would say, from what we have already deduced, that there must indeed be a gas reservoir somewhere below us, and that it could be very sizeable. I don't think we should pack it in right now. I think we should find that stream, and learn as much about it as we can.'

They continued their descent for another twenty feet, and found their passageway widening, and then bifurcating. The sound of the water was still beneath them.

'Hm,' Gus said. 'Good thing there are four of us. We'll have to split up. One pair go right, the other left. We'll meet back here in half an hour. How about you taking Niall, Kitty, and the right hand passage? I'll keep James.'

Kitty knew that he had sensed the incipient antagonism between herself and the big Scot, and was anxious to avoid any clashes of opinion.

'Who takes the rope?' Niall asked.

'You will.'

Kitty had been surveying the two bifurcations, and she did not enjoy being placed entirely in the position of junior partner. 'I think you and James should keep it,' she said. 'The left hand bifurcation appears to be much the steeper and more difficult. Ours looks pretty straightforward. If we do branch off again I'll mark the rock with chalk. Let's go, Niall.'

'Well,' James objected. 'I don't think...'

But Niall, buoyed with enthusiasm, was already leading the way. Now that the fear of gas poisoning had passed and they didn't have to wear the stifling masks, he felt more confident. It was all rather exciting, especially the thought that they could find themselves owning a veritable gold mine. Poor old Dad had been looking a bit fraught lately, after that Middle East deal went sour: finding natural gas here should improve his temper. And the whole idea appealed enormously from a more personal angle, too. He'd had a couple of temporary jobs in the city since leaving university, but nothing that made use of the past four years of business studies. He hadn't got past stamp licking yet, and there were a great many other graduates like him, trying to make it through the jungle into the executive strata. Hell, if this worked out Dad would make sure he was on the executive of their own business; he could wind up in charge of the Morris Scottish Interests. Great stuff!

'Hey! Wait for me,' Kitty's voice reached him from way back. 'Remember, I have to stop for readings and samples every few yards.'

'Sorry. Come on,' but after a few moments he was off again before she caught up. He didn't want her to get ahead—it pleased him to be leading the attractive little scientist. He found her hugely appealing, but the fact that she was senior to him in both years as well as knowledge of this subject, tended to make him feel kind of one down. Very inhibiting when one was dying to start making a play for a girl. He was grinning, thinking about having her down here all to himself, when he received an almighty blow to the head. 'Ow!' he yelled, falling to the floor.

'What? What's the matter? Are you all right?' Kitty stumbled forward. 'I can't see you.'

'Here. I'm here. I think the roof level

suddenly dipped and I walked into it. My light has gone out. I guess I must have smashed it.'

'Are you hurt?'

'No. Not at all.' He picked himself up, reaching a hand above his head to test the roof level. 'Perfectly OK. But the roof is much lower here.' Then he added, reluctantly, 'I guess you'll have to lead, now.'

'Yes.' Now perhaps, she could keep his youthful enthusiasm in check. 'I hope you made sure there were no side turnings as we came down. I've been following your light.'

'Don't worry. I know what I'm doing.' He felt pretty sure he had checked.

A few minutes later they stopped for a breather. There was an upward slope which made the going harder.

Kitty took a sample and stowed it in her pack.

'How far do you reckon we've come?' Niall asked, 'Half a mile?'

'Lord, no. A hundred yards, more like. You'd be amazed how slowly one moves in these conditions.'

'No sign of water yet. How much further shall we go?'

Kitty looked at her watch. 'About another twenty minutes, I'd say. Then we'll go back.'

'What, the same way?'

'Of course. Otherwise we could get lost.' Leading on, even she was having to duck. 'You all right?'

Niall laughed. 'Fine. But I reckon I'll soon be on hands and knees.'

'That's what caving is all about.'

Niall was happy enough; he was alone with this super girl, following her voice and the glow from her torch, appreciating the trail of perfume she exuded. Maybe, before returning, they might pause for a real rest... 'Ooops! We're on a steep down slope, now,' Kitty called over her shoulder. 'I'm going to take it on my backside, just to play safe. You'd better do the same.' It wasn't easy, half lying on her back, and still trying to focus the beam of her helmet torch on the way ahead, but when she reached the bottom she held her breath, 'Listen!'

'Sounds like someone left a tap running.'

'Yes. Exactly.' She turned her head, slowly, so the beam of light made the full three hundred and sixty degrees circuit. 'This is quite a big chamber. Must be about twelve feet in diameter, though the roof is pretty low.'

'The sound of dripping water is coming from this direction,' Niall said. 'Let's go down here.' He crossed the rocks and boulders on hands and knees to an opening roughly at right angles to their point of entry.

'Wait, not so fast.'

'It's OK. I've remembered I have a small pocket torch. I can see where I'm going.'

'That's not the point. We have to mark where we have been.' She paused, pulled off a glove with her teeth and ferreted in her pockets for the piece of chalk she knew she had brought. As her fingers withdrew it she stood up, hit her head...and the chalk fell. 'Damn! Wait, Niall, I've got to find the chalk.' She bent her head to aim the beam on to the rocky floor and said 'Damn!' again. Beneath her feet, the floor was crisscrossed with narrow fissures...and there was no sign of the chalk, anywhere. It had to have fallen down one of the gaps. 'Niall! We'll have to pack it in,' she called, and waited. There was no reply. 'Niall! Niall, do you hear me? We'll have to head back.'

The noise of running water was quite loud now, but of Niall there was no sound. Hell. She'd have to go on and find him... Amateurs! But she couldn't really be cross with him. The poor boy was only suffering from over-enthusiasm which nowadays, with so many young graduates totally lacking any sense of direction and hipped only on pops and pot, was quite refreshing. 'Niall! Where are you? Can you hear me?'

Moments later, as she rounded a bend in the rocks, she heard her name echoing through the caves. 'Kitty! Are you coming?'

'Yes,' she called back.

Five minutes later they stumbled into each other. Niall held her tightly against his side, mentally cursing the gas mask dangling by its strap before her chest. 'Blimey! I thought I'd lost you!'

'You went tearing off ahead!'

'I thought you were right behind me! Come and see, I've found the water.'

'I think we should go back; I'm worried about getting lost. Unfortunately I dropped the marker chalk.'

'OK. But come and see the waterfall first. It's only a few yards...' He was feeling very chuffed with himself, finding it.

'We'll come and see it tomorrow. We'll get to it quite quickly now we know the way.' She shrugged his arm off her shoulders. 'Now stick close to me, this time, and don't go wandering off. Up here.' Laboriously they climbed back up the steeply sloping passageway to the next level. 'Now,' Kitty said, 'we bear to the right.'

'I thought we came in from the left.'

'The right,' Kitty said firmly. Five

minutes later they came to another bifurcation. 'I don't remember this one,' Kitty said.

'That's because we came down it.'

'Did we? If we did, then I don't remember *that* one.'

'We take this one,' Niall said confidently.

Kitty was prepared to go along with that. But when another five minutes later they found themselves back at the top of the sloping passageway, she realized her warnings were too late. They were lost.

Half an hour passed before they gave up. 'This is pointless,' Kitty said. 'We've gone round in circles twice and finished up here in the big chamber. I think we'd better wait until the others come and find us. They'll have the rope with them and be able to lead us out.' She was feeling extremely annoyed. Stupid. It was the first time she had ever become lost, and she knew it was her fault for not keeping Niall under control.

On the other hand, Niall wasn't at all bothered. 'OK, what do we do now? Find somewhere to sit and make ourselves comfortable?' Far from fazing him, the prospect of sitting with an arm round Kitty and keeping her warm for an hour was well worth the aggro they'd face when they were eventually found.

Kitty's answer was a heavy sigh. Her head torch revealed a low ledge against the rock wall, so she went and sat on it. It was incredible that this chamber should be the confluence of so many tunnels. And every tunnel seemed to have several bifurcations. They had set off up half a dozen of them, two leading to dead ends, two taking them in a continuous circle, and the others being abandoned when it quickly became obvious that they had not negotiated such huge blocks of granite on their way down.

Niall sat beside her. 'Pity we didn't think of bringing a pack of cards. I suppose we can try *I Spy*.'

'We'll have to turn off our torches to save the batteries, and I'm not good at spying anything in the dark.' Her fingers strayed over her helmet till she found the switch.

'Are you cold?'

'Yes.'

He put an arm round her. He couldn't see anything of her at all, but he was still aware of her perfume and heard the variations in her breathing as he pressed her head against his shoulder.

Wondering what the time was now, and how long it might take Gus and James to locate them, Kitty pulled back the sleeve of her anorak to expose her watch and in feeling for the button to contact the light emitting diode turned her head, brushing her forehead on his chin. Hopefully interpreting the movement as an invitation to action, Niall bent his head, found her mouth with his and before she could back off his tongue was circling hers.

Oh bloody hell, this is all I need! Kitty felt like shoving him into the middle of next week, but she realized her movements had been misunderstood. She didn't want to offend him and even felt slightly flattered that at her age she could turn the kid on, but Phew! she had to get him off. She worked her hands up between them and pushed. 'Er...er... I'm going to sneeze... Aaagh!' She hoped the faked effort was good enough. 'And again... Aaaagh! Oh hell, where's my hankie...'

Well, at least he'd broken the ice. And she hadn't objected so she must have liked it. Sitting in the darkness while she fiddled about with a paper tissue, he was aware of something different. 'Listen!'

They sat in silence for a moment. 'You're right. It's the water. It's stopped.'

'Good! I can't think of a worse fate than being trapped down here in a flood.'

'Mmm. I wonder how long ago it stopped.'

'Now you mention it, I don't remember

hearing it since we came back here from that last tunnel...or was it the one before.'

'May I borrow your little torch a minute? It's easier to switch on to see my gauge.' She peered at the instrument in the pale yellow light, then switched off and handed it back. 'Thanks.' She didn't feel it necessary to tell him there was a slight gas reading...yet. And he didn't ask.

He felt her stiffen and edge away when he put his arm round her again, and cursed her attack of sneezing. 'Aren't you feeling cold?'

'Yes. Very. But not that cold, thanks.'

'Can we huddle up together if I promise not to kiss you?'

'So long as you understand it's not an open invitation.' She leaned against him and his arm was replaced. But only for a few minutes.

'What's that?' he sniffed.

'What?' As if she didn't know. She pulled the gauge out of her pocket. 'Let's have the torch again.' A glance was enough. 'Hell. Well that's it. Seems as if Gus was one hundred per cent right. He usually is. On with the our masks again.'

'Ugh! Why, what's happened?'

'My guess is that the water level has dropped sufficiently to uncover that gas vent. Or maybe another one. Get your mask on.'

'Oh, shit. I can't!'

'Why?'

'I put mine down...'

'You did what? Where?'

'Way back, when we rested before finding this chamber the first time. It's up the passage we can't find.'

Damnation! Why the hell did she allow herself to get saddled with this kid? But there was no point in ticking him off, or scaring him. For a moment she considered taking one of the passageways up, but she didn't know where any of them led, and if they found themselves in a dead end, with gas rising about them, and James and Gus unable to find them... 'Then we will have to share mine. Work a system of buddy breathing like when scuba diving.'

'But...these aren't the sort of regulators used for diving. These are masks. How can we share...' his voice rose an octave with fear.

'Easy,' she said, trying to convince herself. She had been taught the technique years ago when training for underground work, but never had to do it for real. 'Get your arms out of your jacket sleeves and I'll knot each end. Then you pull it up over your head and I shove the mask up inside.'

'What about you?' his voice called from inside the coat.

'I'm doing the same, and you pass the mask back to me. That way, if you hold your jacket real tight, when you haven't got the mask, and if you can't hold your breath till you get it back, you won't be breathing pure gas.' Suddenly she visualized his frustration, with this perfect opportunity to put his hand up her jumper but thwarted by the more important necessity to survive...and had a ridiculous desire to giggle. Or weep.

The left-hand fork led steeply downwards for some distance, and Gus and James spent most of their time sliding on their backsides. When they finally came to rest they paused for breath. 'I hope the other two will be all right,' James muttered. 'Young Niall is a good enough lad but a bit headstrong.'

'Kitty knows her stuff,' Gus said. 'I think we're quite close now. You ready?'

'Just a mo.' The rope had given a little twitch. 'I think Andrew is becoming anxious.' He gave it a single, vigorous tug. 'That should keep him happy.' There was a single tug in response.

Gus was already following the passage down; the sound of water was very loud, and a few minutes later they found themselves in a wide gully through the mountainside, on the edge of a fast running stream some three feet across. Opposite him was a wall of rock.

'I wonder how deep this is,' Gus remarked. For reply, James took a plastic bag out of his pocket, dropped a couple of pebbles into it, tied it securely with the rope and slowly lowered it into the water. 'That's resourceful of you,' Gus commented as they both watched the white plastic pulled away down the stream.

'It's not going to fall perpendicular I'm afraid,' James complained.

'Not to worry, it gives us some idea of the strength of the current.'

James pulled the bag out and removed the pebbles and water while Gus in turn took off his pack and got a tubular metal yard rule out of his pocket, expanded it and then lay down on the ledge, pushed his sleeve up past his elbow, and thrust his hand into the water, as far as it would go. 'It's pretty deep,' he commented as he straightened. 'And bloody cold.' He buttoned his sleeve again.

'No bottom?' James asked. Gus shook his head. 'So what do we do? Call the whole thing off?'

'There's gas down there, James.' His voice was incredulous that this Scotsman was prepared to give up. 'There has to be. And there could be a lot of it. Kitty's samples will give us an idea. But if they give us what we're looking for, I'm going to recommend to Morris that he get a drilling rig up here and put down a trial bore. It'll be expensive, and if I'm wrong and there's nothing there, he'll be out of pocket. But if I'm right, and I'm sure I am, he's sitting on top of a goldmine.'

'When you talk about drilling, you mean pylons, right?'

'I'm afraid so. Boring through a few thousand feet of granite can't be done with a brace and bit.'

'Grim,' James said. 'And if they do find gas...'

'Your lovely hillside and valley are going to become a bit of a mess, I'm afraid. Progress, James.'

'Yeah,' James said, more grimly yet. 'Well he turned to face the climb back up, and checked. 'With respect, Professor, but have you...er, backfired?'

'Ah...you're right,' Gus said. 'Gas. Coming down from the right. The water level must be dropping. There, you can see it.' He directed the beam of his lamp at the far wall, where there was a distinct damp mark above the actual level of the stream. 'Well, we knew it was soon going to happen, after that dry spell. Masks, and up.'

'What about Kitty and Niall? That gas is coming from the direction they went.'

Gus nodded. 'I imagine they'll be back at the bifurcation, waiting for us.'

They put on their masks and began the climb up, but it was a laborious business and took them a good ten minutes. When they finally reached the next level, Gus lifted his mask for a moment to sniff, as Kitty had the gauges, and realized that the gas was becoming quite thick, certainly toxic. Of course, the masks would cope with anything they were likely to meet down here, so there was no real danger. Still, they couldn't hang about. He touched James on the arm and made forward movements, tapping his watch as he did so.

James got the message, and they followed the rope upwards, snaking through the various passageways until they arrived at the original bifurcation—where there was no sign of Kitty and Niall. Now James took off his mask and inhaled. 'Seems a lot clearer up here.'

Gus took off his mask as well. 'We've climbed above it, for the moment. But it'll catch us up. Where the hell is Kitty?'

'Still looking for the water, I would say,' James suggested.

'She must have smelt the gas by now, and be on their way back.'

It was the first time James had noticed any urgency in anything Gus said or did.

'Let's give them a shout,' he recommended, and cupped his hands, facing the passageway along which the others had gone. 'Hullo!' he bellowed. 'Kitty! Niall!' The sound reverberated above them and to either side. Almost the entire mountain seemed to tremble.

'Steady on,' Gus recommended. 'You'll start a rockfall. Where did you learn to shout like that?'

'On the parade ground,' James said. 'Well, we'd better make sure they are safely up top. Otherwise we are going to have to get after them.'

'Kitty agreed to meet us here, she won't have gone on up without us. They must still be down there. You'd better let Andrew know.'

James tugged on the rope and waited till he felt Andrew's answering pull before setting off down the right hand bifurcation. Gus followed. Neither had put on their masks, as the air at this level only faintly smelt of the stench of hydrogen sulphide. 'You said there wouldn't be any of this rotten egg stuff, Professor,' James remarked over his shoulder.

'Two corrections. One, I said there *shouldn't* be any, if my theory is right. But my theory is obviously wrong. I won't be able to tell you why until I get all our readings back to the lab. Presuming Kitty hasn't lost them. And two, I can't take any more of this professor stuff; it was your idea we call each other by our first names.'

They came to another bifurcation. 'What do we do now?' James asked.

'Try the left. There. She doesn't appear to have marked either way with her chalk.'

'Shall I try another shout?' James asked again.

'No. Give me that knife you're wearing.'

James drew his sheath knife from its scabbard and handed it over. Gus used it to strike his steel yard rule several times. The clang echoed through the fissures, penetratingly but nowhere as violently as James' shout. Then they waited, but there was no reply.

'You know something, Gus,' James said, 'I don't like this at all. Do you think something's gone wrong. Shall I give three tugs to warn Andrew?'

'If something has happened to Kitty and Niall, no outside help is going to get down here in time,' Gus said. 'Let's go.

He took a step forward, and James touched him on the arm. 'That stink is back.' They put on their masks.

For the first few minutes, holding one's breath while the other used the mask beneath his or her jacket and inhaled for several seconds, was entirely mind-consuming. But after some ten minutes it became almost routine, and Niall was becoming affectionate again. Kitty let him get on with it; she was starting to worry. Holding their breaths for a minute and then breathing for a minute was exhausting, and the gas was getting thicker all the time.

What to do? On the one hand she was desperate to get out of here, climb the slope again...and surely this time find the way back to the separation point, where Gus and James were no doubt waiting for them. But on the other hand, common sense was telling her that would be to panic, that their exertion would exhaust them long before they could reach clear air...and that James and Gus were surely looking for them by now.

But if she was wrong, then they were both going to die! She wondered if this crazy youth who had created the potential disaster, was aware of it. And if indeed she should tell him. And then watch him go spare with terror, and bring about catastrophe even quicker than seemed probable?

There were so many things to think about, when staring death in the face...most of them totally irrelevant to the situation. She'd promised to phone Mum on Saturday about her holiday dates...and Mrs

Cummings, who owned the house where she had a flat, and was expecting her back for the weekend... And the dry cleaners had phoned twice to say her coat was waiting to be collected... She put her face in her hands and swore, vehemently.

Niall was passing her the mask, trying to squeeze her hand as she took it. She managed to stop herself pulling away: he was probably needing someone to hang on to right now. It really wasn't his fault that he was so young and high-spirited...and silly. She pressed the mask against her nose, and inhaled precious air. God, to know what to do! Then she heard a distant clang.

Niall heard it too and forgetting the toxic gas shoved his head out of his anorak to let out a yell. 'The others! Here. We're down here!' Then he gasped, and his face suffused. Desperately, although her own needs had not been satisfied, Kitty thrust the mask back at him. Frantic, she got his head and the mask under his coat, while her brain spun as her lungs demanded air she did not dare take. Her chest was agony, feeling it would burst, when he returned the mask. But now the clanging was closer. And now Niall was kneeling against her, striking his helmet with his little flashlight to set up an answering clang.

Creeping along the narrowing passageways, pausing at every tunnel and fissure leading off to listen and clang his cylinder, James trod on something spongy; instinctively he kicked at it, and listened to a faint clang. He dropped to his hands and knees to see what it was, but his sudden disappearance from Gus's line of vision caused Gus to trip and land on top of him. James pushed himself up, fumbling in the darkness, and held up a discarded gas mask.

The two men stared at each other in horror, then James quickened his advance, clanging his knife against Gus's rule with ever-increasing urgency. When he held up his hand Gus listened and heard a responding clang, echoing in the distance. He nodded his helmet light and gave a thumbs-up sign. They started forward again, reached the top of the slope and slid down rapidly into the wide chamber. James turned his head to swing the light in an arc, until it picked up the two bodies on a low ledge of rock, one hardly moving.

He and Gus realized that the two were sharing a single mask. James was alongside Kitty in two strides, unzipped her coat and thrust the mask over her face, leaving Niall to use the original mask without interruption. It took several minutes for the filtered air to restore sufficient strength to the younger pairs' muscles for them to move. James' two sharp emergency tugs on the rope brought a similar reply from Andrew as he and Gus started up the slope, pushing and pulling Kitty and Niall between them.

Gus had serious doubts that they could all get to the top alive. He had been on innumerable similar expeditions himself, often in far more hazardous conditions, his light, muscular physique ideally suited to the work. Far better suited than that of the others, who were all clearly exhausted, even the big Scotsman. Then ahead of him Kitty stopped, and held her gauge up in front of him showing the level of toxic gas had dropped dramatically. Cautiously he sniffed, then smiled and nodded. 'Thank God!'

Kitty tried to pull the mask strap away from her face but her arms were too limp. Gus did it for her.

James saw the scientists breathing normally and swayed heavily against the rockface, while Niall, suddenly deprived of his support, stumbled and fell face down on the floor.

'What's happening down there, then?' Andrew's voice ricochetted through the tunnels. 'Are ye OK or do I fetch help?' His bulk appeared in the dwindling glow of Gus's lamp. He didn't hesitate. A powerful hand grasped the back of Niall's anorak and the boy was virtually tucked under his arm and carried away. Minutes later and the champion shot-putter was back to collect Kitty.

James and Gus staggered after him.

Chapter 4

REFLECTIONS

Mary drew back the heavy, brocade curtains allowing sunlight to angle into the bedroom. 'Good-morning, Miss Cochrane,' she said. 'Ah've brought ye a wee bowl of porridge and some toast for yer breakfast. Are ye ready to sit yerself up an' take it?'

Kitty yawned, stretched...and winced. Every bone and muscle in her body was on fire. And she still had a headache. But she managed a wry smile at the tall thin figure standing over her. 'You are very kind, Mary. What time is it?'

'Going on ten o'clock, Miss.'

'Good grief! I must have slept the clock round!' Kitty sat up with a start. 'Ooh! My head!'

'Ah've taken the liberty o' putting some soluble aspirin on yer tray, thinking maybe ye might be needing it.'

Kitty nodded, very gently. 'Yes. I'm afraid I breathed in a lot more gas than was good for me. Tell me, how is Niall?'

'Eating a second plateful o' bacon and eggs and asking when he could come up and speak wi' ye. I'm believing he's more than a wee bit worried about ye, saying it was all his fault...which Ah can well imagine,' the maid added, her frown and tight lips expressing extreme disapproval of her young master.

He wasn't exactly flavour of the month with Kitty herself. His idiotic behaviour in losing his gas mask and wandering on ahead without checking the route was bad enough, but the memory of his passionate embrace and kisses, especially in the circumstances, made her redden in anger. Mary noted the reaction but said nothing as she arranged Kitty's pillows and placed the tray on her knee. The young scientist sighed. 'You can tell him I'll see him later when I come down, thank you.'

'Do ye not think a wee bit more rest in yer bed would be best this morning?'

'No. I've been here since we got back at lunchtime, yesterday, that's long enough. Anyway, I always reckon that the sooner one exercises the sooner the muscles will ease, and it rids the blood of any poisonous residue. I'll bathe and dress when I've tackled this feast.'

Mary smiled. 'Ye're probably right, Miss.' Even though these people were here investigating the possibility of destroying the countryside with their paraphernalia, it had to be said that in herself, this lassie was a comparatively nice, sensible girl. Compared, that was, to some she could mention. 'I'll tell Mr Niall you will see him downstairs.' She paused at the door. 'Ye'll ring if there is anything more ye require?'

'I can see you've already thought of everything.' Kitty poured a cup of tea from the rose-painted porcelain teapot and sipped cautiously, feeling the warmth spread through her body, remembering the intense cold of the cave and how she had wondered if she would ever feel warm again.

Over the hour of waiting for rescue, panting for breath, the grip of damp coldness increasing by the minute till they were both shivering uncontrollably, her fear had deepened. A fear far greater than anything she had ever experienced before.

Huddled together inside Niall's anorak taking turns with her mask, Niall had made no further attempt to kiss or grope her. They had clung together not as lovers but as fellow humans fighting for survival. And in the end it was Niall who had first responded to James hammering on the yard rule, very nearly at the cost of his life. Which had somewhat redeemed him in her eyes...though not in the eyes of their rescuers.

As they drove back, Gus had gone into orbit with fury about the abandoned breathing gear, and through a haze of faintness and nausea she had had to calm him down.

Unsmiling, James had carried her down to the car while Andrew threw Niall over his shoulder with a marked disregard for the boy's condition. And Gus had followed, shouting questions, complaining when their feeble replies failed to reach him. Rebecca had been terribly embarrassed by the behaviour of her brother. Kitty imagined that there was only one person in the castle at present who was totally happy, and that was the monster Morris himself.

There was a heavy, old-fashioned dark oak dressing-table in the bedroom allocated to Augustus Wilson on which he had spread a high scale contour map of the region, a calculator and slide rule, as well as all the notes taken from Kitty's readings.

While she ate breakfast, he was sitting on the tapestry dressing-stool in his room covering a quarto pad with ballpoint figures, pausing only occasionally to tap the keys on his calculator. He laid down the pen, removed his spectacles and scratched his scalp, his mind switching back to yesterday's near disaster.

He was still angry, but more with himself than with anyone else. He was the leader of the expedition and he should never have allowed Kitty to go off with that young thickhead—especially without a guide rope. Well, perhaps the kid wasn't exactly thick, but he was impulsive, hotheaded—entirely the wrong type for underground work. And being leader, he should have recognized the fact, not left Kitty with the task of keeping the boy under control.

Replacing his glasses he read through his figures again. Yes. This Morris character should be pretty pleased with the findings so far.

James was in his office in the stable block when Guthrie tapped on the open door. 'Hi, come on in,' he smiled at the older man.

He'd never met him before coming here but, inevitably, they had several mutual acquaintances in the area who had described each to the other in considerable detail, revealing that both were of one mind in their wish to prevent the Highlands being decorated with drilling-rigs.

George Guthrie wasn't quite sure how

he stood with the major in the matter of estate staff protocol. He had been on the best of casual terms with Stirling, but this man was not merely the bailiff, he was an ex-army officer. So he approached with caution. 'Good day to ye, Major,' he said, his back straight as a ramrod. 'Ah hope Ah'm not by way o' disturbing ye.'

'Of course not. Sit yourself down, man. Tell me, is this a social call, or would there be something you're wishing to discuss.'

'We...well, Ah suppose ye'd call it a bit o' both.' He sat on the chair opposite the desk and leaned back. 'Ah'm hoping ye're quite over yer nasty experience of yesterday?'

'Fortunately for me I was not one of the pair who got into trouble. It was tiring getting them out, a bit of a strain at the time, but that is what one's army training is all about, isn't it?' James said, wondering what the old man had on his mind.

'Aye, that's true. Mebbe such a training would benefit young Mr Niall?'

James grinned at him. 'Reckon you're right there.'

'And would ye reckon the Sassenachs have found what the...er...the laird was wanting?'

'You mean natural gas?' Ah, so that's what the old devil wanted to know.

Guthrie stared James straight in the eye.

'Aye. That's what Ah'm meaning.'

'Yes. They did.' The major stared back, waiting.

'In sufficient quantity to have him tear up the mountains wi' bulldozers and the like?'

'That I can't tell you, Mr Guthrie. None of them knows yet. But this I can say. I sincerely hope that between them they quickly establish that it is not a viable proposition. And if you're wondering where I stand in all this I'll tell you. I was born just over that range of hills in Ballater,' James tilted his head to the east. 'This is my country and my home and I want no part in the destruction of it.' Guthrie shook his head grimly. 'However, I can do no good by opening my mouth and blathering opinions which will only serve to get me fired. I hope I can do more good staying right here.'

Guthrie stood up and stretched his hand out across the desk. 'Aye, Major. Ah knew we could count on your support and Ah said so to Rabbie Wilkie when he came wi' the...the laird's papers this morning.'

When the old man had gone, James sat motionless, a wry smile on his face thinking how Guthrie would never accept a man like Morris as a true laird.

Meanwhile, the man who had bought the

title was sitting at his vast desk, fat fingers strumming the tooled leather top impatiently. He had spent over an hour so far this morning, stalling a Libyan arms dealer, a Middle Eastern potentate and a pompous little bugger of a bank manager, all of whom had nothing in mind but amassing more money.

For the umpteenth time he turned his wrist to look at his watch...which was quite unnecessary as a small gold digital clock sat on his desk with the information he sought clearly displayed, and a large gilded sunburst with Roman numerals was looking down on him from above the door. Where the hell were they with their information? He rang the bell and waited for Guthrie to appear. But it was Mary who answered. 'Ye rang, sir?'

Morris frowned at the awe-inspiring spinster. 'Oh! It's you. Well, can you tell me where everyone is?'

'Mrs Morris is in the kitchen discussing menus wi' Mrs MacBain. Miss Rebecca is breakfasting with Mr Niall. The Professor breakfasted more than an hour ago and said he'd return to his room to work. Miss Cochrane is finishing her breakfast in her room and says she will be down shortly,' adding after a brief pause, 'and of course nothing has been heard yet of Miss Tara.'

Bernard's fingers continued their drum roll. He didn't like ugly women around him at the best of times, and this old bag was nothing short of damned insolent, to boot. But it wasn't easy replacing staff...

'Will that be all, sir?' she asked.

'Yes, thank you, Mary. And thank you for being so helpful.'

His sarcasm was not lost on the maid, but he would have been furious had he known how much it amused her.

'Well?' he demanded, when Gus and Kitty finally appeared. And had the grace to add, 'How are you feeling, Miss Cochrane?'

'Still a little woozy, I'm afraid.' Kitty sank, uninvited, into one of the chairs before his desk. 'Probably mostly delayed shock. I gather Niall is quite all right.'

'Seems to be. I hope you have some good news for me, seeing as how this business has already nearly cost me my son.'

Gus, just sitting down himself, instantly bridled. 'Cost you your son? It was all the young fool's fault. Kitty risked her life to save him. We could have lost them both.'

The two men glared at each other, and Kitty hastened to defuse the antagonism. 'He was just over-enthusiastic, which is quite understandable.'

Morris glared at her in turn, then asked. 'Is there gas down there or not?'

'I would say there is,' Gus said.

'Well, then...'

Gus ignored the interruption and continued, scanning the paper attached to his clipboard as he did so. 'These are preliminary readings, of course, but as far as we can determine at this stage, the indications are that there is a gas reservoir beneath Gannan Hill. The samples we have taken, however, indicate some unusual aspects to this reservoir, and the gas that has escaped from it, principally the high methane level, and the presence of hydrogen sulphide.'

Morris's eyes were wide as his face was blank. 'What's all this jargon supposed to mean? Is the stuff marketable or not?'

'The composition of the gas,' Gus went on, 'with the rather important exception of the hydrogen sulphide, is approximately the same as that obtained from the North Sea gas fields, which is as one would expect, as this reservoir is in roughly the same vicinity. As I say, the main component, methane, is above the average, and we suspect that the other principal component, nitrogen, is below the average, but there are always considerable fluctuations.'

'So you are saying we have a viable gas reservoir down there,' Morris said.

'We are saying that you *may* have a viable gas reservoir down there,' Gus agreed, cautiously. 'But it lies at quite a depth. The gas field with the breakdown which is closest to yours is that of Groningen in Holland. Again, this would be reasonable, But we must advise you that the Groningen field lies at a depth of two thousand eight hundred metres. That can be converted to just over nine thousand feet,' he added helpfully.

'But Groningen is being worked, right? So nine thousand feet is not a problem,' Morris pointed out.

'No, indeed. Although of course the initial capital outlay becomes greater the greater the depths. However, there remains the unusual presence of what appears to be a relatively large concentration of H2S. That is, hydrogen sulphide.' Gus looked at Kitty for confirmation.

'What's unusual about that?' Morris asked.

'It's a matter of both depths and composition,' Kitty said. 'You see, most of the gas found in this area is composed, in the main, of methane, carbon dioxide and nitrogen, and is what we call a dry gas. This gas normally arises from fossilized coal, and from the oil that has formed above it.'

'You mean I may have an oil field as well?'

‘It’s possible,’ Kitty said, as cautiously as Gus.

‘So what’s the catch?’

‘The catch is the hydrogen sulphide.’

‘I’m still waiting to be told what that means.’

‘It can mean any number of things. The other fields, off the coast, do not have a significant H2S factor. The Groningen field to which we were just referring, has no H2S at all. And it lies at more than nine thousand feet. To find H2S one would normally expect to locate the gas at an even greater depths, and it would be wet gas. Dry gas containing H2S is only found at extreme depths.’

Morris stroked his chin. ‘Put that in figures.’

‘Well, we’re getting into the four thousand metre plus depths.’

‘Expensive, eh?’

‘I’m afraid so. But also—’

Morris interrupted her. ‘In my business, we deal with the bottom line. What is the greatest depths we might have to go?’

Kitty glanced at Gus. ‘The greatest depths at which you could possibly find gas would be five thousand metres,’ Gus said. ‘That is something over sixteen thousand feet. But then you’d be down into kerogen.’

‘Kerogen? What the hell is kerogen? You

mean kerosene, right? Then why not call it paraffin?'

'The reason I am not calling it paraffin is that we are not talking about kerosene, or paraffin, call it what you will. Kerogen is a substance found very deep in the earth that is sometimes known as oil shales. It is a solid matter which is not soluble in water. The name in fact arose in Scotland when oil shales were first discovered here.' He paused, as if to indicate that Morris should have known that.

'OK,' Morris said. 'So it's possible that my gas arises in this kerogen stuff, right?'

'If it does, Mr Morris, you had better forget it,' Kitty said. 'As we said, at that depths it's solid, and you won't get it up through a borehole. Now, as to this other matter...'

'Listen,' Morris said, leaning forward, elbows on the desk. 'I am getting fed up with this double talk. You are telling me that I have gas down there, but that the presence of this hydrogen sulphide means that it may be at greater depths than other fields. Right?'

'Well,' Gus said. 'In a manner...'

'For Jesus' sake,' Morris shouted. 'I am paying you good money to tell me whether the gas down there can be commercially viable or not, and all I can get out of you is buts. What the hell is going on?'

'We have to be patient,' Gus recommended. 'This is gas of an unusual composition. That hydrogen sulphide is one problem. As we said, you would only find this, in normal circumstances, at great depths. Now your gas reservoir may be situated at such a depth, but frankly, we don't think it is. Also, there is gas leaking out of it. This leak is of comparatively recent origin, and has been caused, I estimate, by water erosion. But this erosion is within something like a hundred feet of the surface. And below that it would seem that your mountain is a mass of vents and fissures, all filled with gas. Now, this would seem to indicate a comparatively shallow reservoir. But if that is the case, why does it contain such a high percentage of hydrogen sulphide, normally only found at great depths? Because if it is a deep reservoir, and gas is escaping, or has escaped, upwards to such an extent, well...these are questions which need to be answered. Do you follow me, Mr Morris?'

Morris gave a very heavy sigh. 'So what is your considered and professional opinion?' He looked from one to the other.

'We cannot give you one until we have taken our samples back to London and analysed them.'

'Jesus Christ!' Morris thumped his fist on the desk making the digital clock tip over. 'Will you answer three simple questions?'

'If we can.'

'Is there gas down there in viable quantities?'

'We think so.'

'Is it commercially viable gas?'

'It could be, when the various impurities have been taken out. This applies to all natural gas.'

'Right. Now for the big one: is there any reason why I should not start drilling. Now.'

'You mean as soon as you get the necessary permission,' Kitty suggested.

'That's my problem. Answer my question.'

'There is only one reason why you should wait for a further analysis of the samples we have obtained,' Gus said.

'And that is?'

'It is possible that there may be a volatile element in this reservoir.'

'Meaning what?'

'That it could be explosive. You must remember, Mr Morris, that the gas is subjected to enormous pressure down there. Now, because of some erosion of the retaining rock—I mean erosion of the rock retaining the reservoir itself, not the erosion close to the surface which caused your fire and the death of that poor boy—it is being forced upwards through every passageway it can find in that rock. It is therefore possible that the pressure is even greater than normal, and of course, the deeper the reservoir the greater the pressure. Thus drilling could be attended by certain dangers. Give us time to complete our analysis, and we should be able to give you a clearer picture of what is down there and, incidentally, at what depths.'

'How much time?'

'Well...initially not more than three weeks.'

'Three weeks?' Morris bellowed. 'Look, if there is any risk involved in extracting that gas, it's my business, right? Not yours.'

'No doubt it is, Mr Morris, but you have also to consider the people living on Abergannan, and any visitors you may have. I've been told there are quite a few tourists here in the summer, and that's not very far off.'

'Tourists have no business on my land,' Morris declared.

'I'm sure they do not. But I'm also sure that they do come on it. Now here is a recommendation we can make without having to do any analysis: you should fence off that cavern at the foot of Gannan Hill. In fact, you should fence off the entire hill. On the evidence of what we saw, every time there is a dry spell, of even a few days, the water level in that underground stream is going to drop far enough to uncover those gas vents, and every time that happens, gas is going to escape and there is a risk that it may gather, as happened in the cave, and explode if exposed to a naked light. You could then have another death on your hands. Or more than one.'

'*My* hands?' Morris shouted.

'It's your land, Mr Morris. We'll put that recommendation in our report, but I suggest you act on it now.'

'If you think that's going to stop my developing that field, forget it,' Morris said. 'I'm used to taking risks, even if you're not. I'll bid you good-day!' He picked up his phone.

'I had hoped this episode would put you off the whole idea,' Rebecca was saying to her brother between mouthfuls of muesli.

'Hell no!' Niall reached for another slice of toast. 'Don't you realize what this could mean?'

'Too damn right I do!' she stormed. 'It could mean wrecking these fabulous mountains and the lives of all the people who live here.'

'Bullshit!' Niall abandoned his toast to wave the butter knife at her. 'It would benefit the whole community. Everyone would profit from it, the traders in particular.'

'You mean Mr Brown would sell more stamps in his post office, I suppose...'

'Don't be petty. Think of all the extra mouths to be fed and watered—'

'—By some bloody great chain store opening up a supermarket to put all the locals out of business. Grow up, little brother. Be real. All Dad is interested in is megabucks. And when the hills are raped and laid bare can you imagine him wasting money replacing and replanting? Dammit, Niall, the Scottish Highlands are a precious part of British heritage...'

Niall pushed back his chair and stood up. 'Christ! Can't even eat my bloody breakfast without a bloody environmental lecture. Your bloody job is turning you into a bloody boring banner-waver.' He stuffed a piece of toast into his mouth and walked out of the dining-room.

'That was only four bloodys in one breath!' She called after him. 'Come on, Niall! You can do better than that.'

'Oh, Daddy it all sounds too good to be

true!' Tara stood at her father's study window, watching water dribble down the panes.

One couldn't see any view through the thick mist, even if one wanted to. Which she didn't. She would never have stayed so long up here in this beastly wilderness if she hadn't already overspent her monthly allowance.

It was unfortunate that liberated women were expected to chip in their cut of expenses nowadays, which sometimes got terribly out of hand. Dinner at The Pendulum had cost her eighty pounds last month, and when one took into account the cost of hairdos, facials and a decent wardrobe so that one wasn't forced to wear the same outfit twice with the same crowd, London got awfully, awfully expensive. Even Daddy didn't realize how difficult it was to survive. But...! If he really was sitting on top of all that gas... Wow! All her problems would be blown away!

'Yes, Babydoll. It does sound almost unbelievably good. However, we mustn't count all our millions till we've piped them up out of the ground.'

'But didn't our weirdo visitors guarantee it was there?' The china blue eyes widened in alarm.

'They guarantee there is gas there but they can't tell the quantity or quality until they've gone back to their laboratory and analysed all their findings. Even if they come up trumps I'll still have to spend a hell of a lot of hard cash on heavy gear to probe the few thousand feet to the source.'

'Oh!' Damn! Then this was not a good time, perhaps, to ask him to up the ante. In which case she would have to stick it out here at least till the twenty-fifth of next month.

Margaret was staring at the white elephant at the far end of the drawing-room. She often did. It was the ultimate monstrosity, *the* all-time white elephant, a monument to Bernard's nouveau riche bad taste.

In fact there were two white elephants, carved in white marble, each standing on a massive gilded plinth ornate with scrolls and vine leaves, to form pedestals supporting a heavy sheet of plate glass which served as a table top. Quite obviously designed to grace the foyer of an oriental hotel, the piece had defeated her every attempt to blend it into its new surroundings.

She had known it would be impossible from the moment the men unloaded it from the pantechnichon. She had stood on the gravel at the foot of the front terrace praying they would drop it, all of it, preferably from the top of the steps. And when the Lord failed her and the men left, she had asked Guthrie to help her push a sofa in front of it. Bernard had been furious.

It didn't matter when he wasn't here: she simply draped it in a tapestry throw rug with long tassles which completely hid the golden vines. Unfortunately he had been in almost constant residence now for the past fortnight, which meant leaving the beastly thing exposed. When she thought of all the architectural digests and glossies on interior design she had studied before furnishing this room in a style and period suited to Scottish castles...

'Oh there you are, Mummy!' Rebecca bounced into the room. 'What's the matter? You look so depressed. Is it this dreadful gas threat?'

Margaret stared at her firstborn. 'Gas threat? I'm not with you. No, I'm afraid I always feel miserable when I look at that ghastly acquisition of your father's.'

Rebecca frowned. 'You mean his elephant table? Oh Mummy, how can you say that when poor Daddy loves it so?'

'Because Mummy has better taste,' Tara said from the doorway. 'The thing is positively obscene.'

'Well, obscene or not, I don't know how you can even think about it when there is such an appalling threat hanging over us at this minute,' Rebecca said crossly.

'Threat? What are you ratting on about, Sis?'

'The environment. The hills and valleys, mountains and moors that our beloved father is, at this very moment, planning to destroy.' The elder girl's voice rose as she worked herself up.

'Oh really, Becca. Which hat are you wearing today, for heaven's sake? Your Ministry one, or have you actually joined Greenpeace?'

While her daughters squabbled, Margaret became aware of a growing sense of unease under her Cardin jacket. What were they saying? That Bernard would destroy the hills and valleys with this project? But how could that be...? One thing was certain. The girls were doing nothing to lift her depression.

'The laird,' Mary said with a tight grimace, 'seems to be well pleased wi' himself.' She was stacking lunch plates above the stove to warm.

Mrs MacBain drove a fat fist into a ball of floury dough on the old wooden table and sniffed. 'No more a laird than ma giddy aunt,' she muttered, picking up the dough and slapping it down onto the flour again causing a white cloud to rise and coat the surrounding utensils.

'Ye'd better not let Guthrie hear ye.'

'Och, Ah know he's a stickler for conventional titles, but Ah'll assure ye he no more thinks o' that one up there as a laird than he'll fly to the moon.' The dough was put in the waiting bowl and covered with a cloth. 'Ha' ye room enough for this wi' yon plates, Mary?'

'Aye.' The gaunt maid took the bowl from the castle cook. 'Ah'm fearing that his plaisure means he's found a source o' more money.'

'Ye're imagining things, Mary Mackintosh. What'll he be needing more money for?'

'Hmm. Well, Ah've ma eyes and ma ears. He's got his problems like the rest o' us. Not surprising,' she added with a grim smile, 'if he goes spending good money on such as that terrible affair he's put in the drawing-room.'

'Ah've not seen it.'

'No, you wouldna have,' Mary said. Cooks had no place in the reception rooms. 'The man has no taste and the mistress knows it.'

'Ye're not discussing the laird, I hope,' Guthrie had appeared at the door.

Mary turned from the stove. 'Aye, Mr Guthrie, we are and all. And don't you try telling me ye're filled wi' joy at what he's planning to do to fill his pockets.'

Guthrie had had a running feud with Mary for years, both battling for superiority at the kirk, as well as in the castle. But for once he had to agree with her. He shook his head and sat on a scrubbed wood chair at the far end of the table. 'Aye. Well it's a terrible prospect, but what's to do about it?'

'Not just sit yerself down on that floury chair for a start,' Mrs MacBain scolded. 'Do ye not know one o' the clerks at the town hall down in Aberdeen?'

'Hamish Hamilton? Aye, but what can he do?'

'Put a girt big flea in the ear o' one o' his superiors. Tell him this useless Sassenach plans to rape the Highlands,' the cook waved a floured fist in his face. 'That'll do for a start.'

Mary nodded in agreement. Guthrie stroked his chin.

'What do you reckon?' Kitty asked, as she and Gus returned to his room with their notes.

'That he's going to go ahead.'

'If that gas really is at ten thousand feet or more it will cost a fortune.'

'Well, presumably he has the money. Anyway, to exploit it, he'll have to go in with one of the big boys. He's probably arranging that now.'

Kitty stood at the window, looking out. 'Fair makes you sick.'

'It's the job, dear girl.'

'OK, and there's no problem when it happens in the middle of an ocean or a desert. Even a rain forest is vaguely acceptable, because there's so much of it. But this magnificent countryside...aren't they setting up some kind of conservation policy just over there in the Cairngorms?'

Gus got up to join her, pulling aside the heavy curtain to improve his view. 'If he hadn't employed us, he'd have employed someone else. It's a fact of life. Desecrating the countryside is a concomitant of our job. When it's countryside which doesn't matter, we're on a bonus. The rest of the time we just do our job, right?'

Kitty did not immediately reply, and after a moment he returned to the table to pack up his instruments and papers. 'I don't suppose you really feel like driving a few hundred miles at the moment,' he remarked. 'And I imagine his nibs will let us stay over until tomorrow. We'll make an early start, right?'

Kitty turned, arms folded. 'You told Morris there could be an element of volatility down there. What did you mean?'

He shrugged. 'There always is, with any mine.'

'You had something specific in mind?'

Gus sat down, 'If I did, it'll have to wait until we can make a more thorough analysis of these findings.'

'Tell me what it is you're brooding on.'

'Well...' Gus considered. 'The presence of H2S in really quite a substantial quantity indicates that the reservoir is at maximum depths, right?'

'Right.'

'But I don't think it is situated at that depths. It doesn't go with the other locations in this area. Eight or nine thousand feet, maybe. Twelve thousand or more, no way.'

'So, where is the H2S coming from?' Kitty asked slowly.

'There could be a perfectly natural explanation for it,' Gus pointed out. 'All we know at the moment is that the gas has an unusual composition. Thus it could well be unstable. Certainly the way in which a small pocket of it blew up at the ignition of a lighter suggests that. Then there are those seepages. We found one at the surface, but as I said to Morris, there could be many more fissures and caves, not yet open to the air, filled with gas. The whole hill could be a form of gas reservoir, all reaching down several thousand feet. That could cause real problems to any drillers, especially if that methane level remains high.'

'So we work on that,' Kitty said, once more enthusiastic, 'and prove to Morris that he can't touch the stuff.'

'Kitty,' Gus said, with as close to severity as was possible with so relaxed a man. 'We go back to London and we analyse what we have. If we should discover a volatile element in that gas, or anything else which could truly be classed as dangerous, we will inform Morris and let him make his decision on the basis of our analysis. But we do not conduct our analysis on the basis that we are *looking* for an unstable element. We are scientists, and our business is fact, as derived from the evidence presented to us. I do wish you to remember that.'

Kitty managed to avoid Niall till Guthrie struck the lunch gong. He pounced as they entered the dining-room and took a chair beside her. 'So, where have you been all morning? I've been waiting to speak to you.'

'Had a lazy lie in, then a long soak in the bath, then a business meeting with your father, followed by a technical discussion with my boss.' She didn't actually say 'does that answer your question'—but it obviously did.

'Oh. I see. Only there seems a lot of apologizing I should be doing.' He looked like an overgrown golden retriever puppy who'd been scolded, hanging his head to one side, fingers twisting.

'Forget it. Just one of those things. No harm done, luckily. Oh, doesn't that look marvellous!' She gasped at the magnificent poached Scottish salmon lying whole, eyeing her from a sea of garnish on the white oval ashet set in front of Bernard.

'But I feel so guilty...' he covered her hand on the white damask between them.

'Well, please don't.'

He wondered if she was referring to his remorse or his hand.

Her hand was withdrawn on the excuse of shaking out her napkin and laying it across her lap.

'Are you quite recovered, Kitty?' her hostess asked while spooning steamy potatoes on to the plate Mary was holding.

'I think so, thank you. Just a little tired.' She eyed the heap of vegetables. 'If that's intended for me it's more than I can handle, I'm afraid.'

'I'll have that one,' Rebecca offered. 'Did you catch this fellow, Daddy?'

Bernard, making a pig's ear of the job of serving the fish, admitted he had not, and his loyal wife omitted to mention buying it from a fishmonger in Aberdeen.

His elder daughter returned her attention

to Gus, listening attentively as he eulogized on Lesley Howard's latest CD recording of Liszt's transcription for piano of a Tchaichovsky symphony. She had no idea Liszt had ever done such a thing—but didn't let on.

She felt she did know something about music: an ex-boyfriend had been an aspiring concert pianist, working in a nightclub for months on end to buy the bread till the next engagement. He had spent his weekends playing passionately and alternately on her and the baby grand that also served as desk and dinner table in the living room because there wasn't room for any other furniture.

'When are you returning to town?' Bernard asked the family beauty. 'I thought you wanted to get back last week.'

'I'm enjoying being up here with you,' Tara lied smoothly. 'Do you mind if I stay on a little longer?' Enormous lashes swept her cheeks, working their enchantment as usual.

'This is your second home, sweetheart. You are free to use it whenever you want and for as long as you want. You know, if you miss your cronies you could always ask them up here for a weekend.'

'Oh Daddy! You are a darling!' That was a seriously good idea...if she could think how to entertain them when they weren't consuming her father's booze, or bed swapping. If only he wouldn't call them cronies...

The salmon was delicious, but Kitty's mind was too pre-occupied, both with Gus's lecture and with schemes for avoiding young Niall after lunch really to appreciate it. It took her till halfway through Mrs MacBain's fabulous apple crumble to solve the second problem. She would set him a task, mapping out on paper his entire recollection of their tour through the tunnels. And when he was out of the way she could slip out through the side door in the flower room to explore a bit of the wild country alone. It might be a long while before she was up here again.

The rain had passed, and though there was no blue in the sky the cloud cover was high, exposing pompous mountain peaks Kitty hadn't seen before. It was impossible to bring them into perspective: were they huge and distant or small and close? Either way, it wasn't the heights that impressed her so much as the sheer, wild beauty of barren cliffs and rocky promontories rearing out of the green-skirted foothills.

Avoiding the direction of the dreaded cave, the geo-chemist headed for the sloping fields beyond the stables, due south instead of westerly. Following a narrow stream she was led through a pine wood where deep beds of needles made the going soft and heavy.

Beyond the trees she found a little waterfall, spilling over into a gully from a wide pool formed among jagged rocks and boulders above. It was almost sickeningly beautiful.

Hitching her behind on a rock, she dropped her fingers into the crystal water...and quickly withdrew them. It was icy. The air was chill, her breath forming vapour clouds, but it felt good and clean in her lungs after yesterday's trauma. Which made her think of Niall and a wavelet of guilt washed the edges of her mind, at the way she had dodged him today. He was really a rather attractive boy; she found enthusiastic people stimulating, regardless of their subject, until they became obsessive and consequently dreadfully boring. He was an amusing dinner companion...such a pity he had apparently got the hots for her.

It wasn't as though she had given him any encouragement, he was far too young—mentally, of course. It was amazing to think he was actually only three years her junior. Unlike James MacEwan. She had no idea of the major's age; it was difficult to judge as he always seemed so serious, frowning and...unfriendly? A pity really, as she felt he could be a very attractive man.

Half an hour later, legs heavy as lead, she was trying to resist the urge to go on over the next hillock, round the next outcrop of rock, seek a new vantage point for a wider panorama.

On a sheep track which wound daintily through dead grass and bracken long flattened by winter snows, she was bending almost double against the steep rise, when she looked up...and stifled a scream. 'Crikey, you made me jump!'

James MacEwan was standing astride the path, hefty ankle boots laced over the thick socks which encased his corded breeches from the knees down. He was hatless, and under each arm of his padded jacket he carried a lamb. 'Hello! I'd have thought you'd seen enough of our hill country to last you a lifetime!'

'Could one ever see enough of it, even in a million years?'

'You're out of breath. Were you planning to go much farther?'

'I certainly wouldn't mind taking a breather. What's over that hill you've just come from?'

'Sheep. Hundreds of them, every one sillier than the last.'

'How can you say those little cuties are silly?'

'They're not, yet. But their mother was.'

'Was?'

'Got herself stuck in the stream higher up and drowned herself. Hence the orphans.'

Kitty stroked one of them who promptly tried to suckle her finger. 'Starving, are we?'

'Very definitely. I doubt if they'd have survived the night. I'm taking them down for hand rearing.'

'Well, as these things usually go in threes, have you any idea who you'll be rescuing tomorrow?'

James laughed. 'You again I reckon, if you keep heading on. We're going to be blanketed in cloud within the hour.' He shifted one of the lambs across to join its sibling under the same arm.

'I suppose I'd better turn back. Would you like me to carry one?'

'That would help.' He towered over her as he handed over the sleepier one. 'You go ahead, I'll follow.'

He watched the back of her anorak, topped by a woolly hat pulled down over her ears and obviously well stuffed with hair, with mixed feelings. Very mixed. He had found her undeniably appealing from the moment he set eyes on her in the bar in Aboyne: he was always more interested in women who didn't plaster themselves in make-up because it was easier to read them. Even the very young, fine lines betrayed a way of thinking—open and loving, sour and resentful, cheerful or determinedly depressed. Only a creature like Tara Morris didn't have lines...presumably because the place nature had reserved for her mind was permanently vacant.

This scientist, with her huge, lively brown eyes and over large mouth could not be classified as a beauty but very definitely interesting...if it wasn't for her involvement in this natural gas project. Unfortunately his almost overwhelming desire to seek her company was overridden by the intense antagonism he felt every time he pictured the destruction threatening his homeland.

When they arrived back at the stables Wilkie appeared in the door of the tack room. 'Got some more then, Major. Gi' them here. Ah'll put them in some warm straw wi' the bitch. She likes to have a batch for mothering each year.'

'You've plenty bottles and teats?' James asked, off-loading his burden.

'Sure. But no milk.' Rabbie put the tiny bleater in the crook of his arm. 'Come on then, ma wee one. We'll soon ha' ye a drappie o' drink.' Adding, 'And yer wee brother too,' as he relieved Kitty of her burden.

'I'll phone for young Beatrice to bring some out from the kitchen,' James said. Then without thinking he turned to Kitty, adding, 'The kettle's hot on my stove.

Would you care for a mug of tea?'

She nearly reeled with surprise, but for some inexplicable reason felt terribly pleased. 'Yes. Love it.'

James had seen her eyebrows shoot up under her woolly hat and wondered if she had previously been aware of his antagonism.

Waiting for the tea to cool, they sat at his kitchen table munching chocolate biscuits out of a plastic container...which helped fill the silence.

'What made you...' they both spoke at once.

James grinned. 'You go first.'

'I just wondered how long you have been at Abergannan. You were in the army before, weren't you?' Kitty's question was purely a conversation opener.

'Yes. They made me redundant at the end of last year, so you see I haven't been back long. I was born in these parts, but I've been away a considerable time.'

She took her hat off and shook out her hair, which did nothing for James's equilibrium. 'So now you're the new boy on the farm! Think you'll enjoy it?'

He couldn't lie. 'No. In fact I wonder every day how long I'll stick it.' Pensively he stirred sugar into his tea.

Kitty liked his openness. 'What? The job

or the boss?' she ventured.

James's mouth widened into a laughing smile, displaying to her for the first time his big, even teeth. 'The job's no problem. In fact it's something I'd always planned to do when I left the service. Does that answer your question?'

'Absolutely. And may I dare to add that I sympathize?' Then she frowned. 'Why, then, do you work for him?'

'Why do you?' he countered.

'I don't. I work for my boss, Gus. Who works for a firm of geo-physical consultants.'

James sat sipping his tea in silence. Kitty stared at the shelf of pans behind his head, at last understanding that his offhandedness was because he hated her for her work, her contribution towards possibly turning Abergannan into a gas field! She felt a wave of disappointment.

'Do you enjoy your work?' he asked, examining the marbling effect in the Formica table top.

'Yes.' Suddenly she was angry with him. 'I love it. I feel I am making a serious contribution to the advancement of our society.'

James's head jerked up, his eyes flashing green fire. 'Whose society? That of the fat, get-rich-quick merchants who'd sell their souls for a fast buck? Or are you thinking of the people who used to live in a magnificently green and beautiful country who are to benefit from a tidal wave of incomers anxious to buy up their homes and businesses and...'

Kitty stood up. 'You forgot the bit about raping the countryside and polluting the environment,' she retorted, pulling her hat back on.

James's head hurt. He leapt up and grabbed her arm. 'No, no, I'm sorry. I apologize. Please sit down.'

She scowled up into the green eyes...and believed he meant it. 'Apology accepted,' she mumbled, 'Providing I can have some more tea.' But she still wasn't smiling as she sat down.

James, slightly relieved, continued to look miserable as he put another teabag in her mug and waited for the kettle to re-boil. When he put her mug in front of her he said, 'Please will you take off your hat again? It's a shame to cover up your hair.' Her mouth fell open, but she did as he asked. 'Would you like to tell me more about your work?' he opened.

'Are you sure you want to hear about it?' she asked, still feeling prickly.

'Yes. I want you to unbias my attitude.'

'Well, I'm willing to try,' she responded, smiling at last. 'But that may be difficult. I'm afraid it is our business to find all the earth's resources, pinpoint them, and tell the development companies where to look and whether it's worth looking.'

'*Your* business?'

'If you mean, mine, personally, yes, in the smallest possible manner. My contribution is only the size of a pin head in a forest in ratio to the total work involved. There are facts one has to face, James. Our society needs power and energy above anything else. More even than food and drink, when you come down to it, because on this over-populated globe of vast oceans, and deserts of sand and permafrost, it is only the power and the energy to deliver food and water that keeps us going. Take away all power-driven transportation and millions would die in weeks.'

'It's a point of view.'

'So we have to use the natural resources of the earth. Like, it was a geo-physicist who discovered there was oil in Alaska. Now you may not like the idea of a huge pipeline crossing the snow, but that oil is playing a vital part in keeping our civilization going.'

'So you'd say, tear the entire surface off the globe, if it would uncover more resources,' James exclaimed, anger making him savage.

'No, I'm not saying that.' Kitty spoke

as evenly as she could. 'I don't believe natural resources should be exploited just for gain. But it is important to pinpoint where they are available. As in this case. I don't believe Mr Morris should exploit his gas field. There is an enormous amount of gas being pumped out of the North Sea, and I have no doubt at all that more fields will be discovered over the next few years. So maybe there won't ever be a need for the Abergannan field. That doesn't argue against the necessity to know that it's there, just in case it's ever needed.'

'And you seriously suppose that to a man like Morris such a pious hope will cut any ice beside the possibility of making a million?' He ground his teeth, adding, 'I shouldn't have said that.'

Kitty drained her mug. 'You have every right to voice an opinion on a matter about which you feel so strongly. I just wanted you to understand our involvement in the matter. And if it's any consolation to you, Gus and I entirely understand and appreciate what is bound to be local concern.'

And I, at least, will attempt to prevent it happening, she thought. But it would be professionally unethical to say that.

Gus sat on a window seat in the drawing-room, wondering where Kitty was. At least she seemed to have recovered well from yesterday's ordeal, which meant they could leave for home first thing in the morning.

He would be glad to get away from this place. Beautiful as the setting might be, the Morris family were a pretty odd lot and he couldn't wait to get back to Gillian, the kids, the dogs and the music. And to the laboratory.

It was going to be very interesting indeed, examining their findings in depth. There were a number of factors involved which were entirely new to him in these particular combinations and circumstances.

He picked up a magazine, glossy with pictures of tarty looking females described as stars, bouncing their fatherless children on long, brown thighs like the unearned medals on the chests of Third World self-promoted generals.

'Can't think why my mother buys such trashy mags,' Rebecca said as she plonked herself beside him.

'To amuse her house guests?' Gus suggested.

'Some. Others may prefer this.' She palmed a small remote control from the pocket of her voluminous, ankle-length skirt and aimed it at a mahogany cabinet. Moments later Mendelssohn's Scottish Symphony filtered through the room from concealed speakers, like mist from the mountain tops.

Gus gazed out of the window, senses of sight and sound winging together across the valley to the forest of Glen Tanar.

Rebecca silently congratulated herself. She had put considerable thought into this attempt to please him. Augustus intrigued her (she always thought of him by his proper name, it suited his size and his beard so well): he was so different from the men in her orbit, making no effort to attract or impress anyone, so extraordinarily asexual. Which was in itself a challenge...so much so that she had washed her hair and raided Tara's make-up drawer, being ever so careful to apply only the minimum needed to obliterate her zits. Augustus didn't seem the type to approve of make-up.

'Which recording is this?' Gus asked.

The question brought her back to earth. 'Er...' What the deuce did it say on the disc case? 'Isn't this the Andre Previn?' A wild guess.

'No. He is toneless compared with this. I think it must be a re-recording of the Berlin Philharmonic under Otto Klemperer.'

'Oh, of course, you're absolutely right.' She remembered seeing the name, now. She knew it was something foreign.

At the end of the first movement she pressed the pause control. 'Augustus, you wouldn't really let Daddy wreck these mountains, would you?'

He hated being called Augustus; it was the name Gillian used when she was angry about something—which was rare, but violent. 'Nothing to do with me. I'm just a chemist employed to deduce findings from miscellaneous information. How my employers choose to use those findings is their business.'

'You could...make your report discouraging,' she suggested smiling at him very sweetly.

'I told you, I am a scientist, not a financial whizz kid. I cannot falsify my figures to try and make a project look viable or not. Only accountants do that. Bent ones, that is.'

'Do you think there is any hope it won't be viable?'

'At the moment I'd say it's in the lap of the gods.'

'Mmm. The mountain gods or the god of Mammon?' Rebecca launched them into the second movement.

'Oh, I say! Going so soon?' Niall's face was a mask of disappointment as he watched Kitty zip up her bag again after extracting her sunglasses by the front door where the scientists' gear was stacked ready for loading into Gus's car. He had hunted for her in vain yesterday afternoon and had been jolly peeved to learn, when he cross-examined her across the dinner table last night, that she had spent the afternoon with MacEwan.

Kitty favoured him with a big smile. 'Isn't it a shame, just when the weather clears and the blue skies appear.'

'When will you come back?'

'I honestly don't know if we'll need to. That remains to be seen.' She rather hoped it would be necessary but didn't want Niall hanging around up here if it was.

'I'll get those sketches you needed,' he said, and it was several moments before she remembered the job she'd given him yesterday to keep him out of the way.

'All set?' Gus skipped down the stairs like a hairy gnome, a washbag in his hand. 'Nearly forgot this.'

'I hope you both had enough breakfast,' Margaret said, having sat at the table pressing them to second helpings of fat, creamy kippers and toast.

'Another crumb and I'll explode,' Kitty told her.

'Are you sure you wouldn't like to take some sandwiches?'

'Shut up, Margaret,' her husband snapped, emerging from the dining-room to bid obligatory farewells. 'They've already said no.'

'Much nicer to stop for a pub lunch,

Mummy,' Rebecca said, angry at her father's rudeness.

Bags were loaded into Gus's battered Peugeot. Hands were shaken and good wishes, genuine and otherwise, and good-byes exchanged. Nobody missed Tara, but as they drove off Kitty did glance around to see if James was lurking anywhere. He wasn't.

Chapter 5

THE ANALYSIS

'Thank God you've called,' Crowther said. 'I have been trying to get in touch with you for the past forty-eight hours. You're supposed to be here, Bernard. Not swanning about the Highlands. We're meeting the banks on Monday. What am I supposed to tell them?'

Morris leaned back in his chair and puffed on his cigar. 'You can relax, for a start,' he told his business partner. 'Our troubles are over.'

'Chance would be a fine thing,' Crowther remarked. 'I had lunch with Morant the other night. Everything we said was of course noncommittal, but he certainly gave me the impression that they could be about to pull the rug. Is there a good market for Scottish castles at the moment?'

Morris grinned at the phone. 'Morant is a banker, right? Bankers deal in money, right? The more they can lay their greedy little hands on the better, right?'

'Right,' Crowther agreed. 'And money is one commodity in which Morris Enterprises is sadly lacking, at this moment in time.'

'Listen,' Morris said. 'What could we do with a couple of million?'

'Eh?'

'And that could just be the tip of the iceberg,' Morris said, 'and what's more I'm sitting on it.'

Crowther was silent for several seconds. Then he said, 'Be serious, for God's sake.'

'Gas, Philip. Natural gas. Abergannan is sitting on enough natural gas to make us all millionaires.'

Another brief silence, as Crowther assimilated this. 'Who says?' he asked at last.

Briefly and unsympathetically, Morris told him the tragedy of Vincent Brown. 'So I got hold of the firm of Turnbull & Heath, Oxford. They're geo-chemists. They sent up a couple of their people to see what's going on.'

'And they say you own a natural gas reservoir?'

'Well, you know what these people are like. They won't say black is black unless they've analysed the entire spectrum. But I got them to admit that in their opinion there is one hell of a lot of gas down there. All on my land.'

Crowther gave a low whistle. 'Jesus! You *are* serious. If that could be true...'

'Of course it's true. Now listen. The first thing we need to do is bore a test hole down to the reservoir.'

'What exactly are we talking about?'

'It's going to have to be the whole hog. According to these people we could be talking about quite a depth. Now I can probably fix this up in Aberdeen. But it'll cost a bit.'

'Oh, yeah,' Crowther muttered.

'This is where you come in,' Morris told him. 'It might be an idea to get hold of Morant tonight, and put him in the picture. And be positive. Then you'll have additional muscle when you meet the rest of that crew on Monday. What we need, right now, is an extension on our loan.' He stressed *our,* thankful he'd made Crowther a shareholder. 'At least a million.'

Crowther gave another whistle. 'What am I supposed to offer for collateral?'

'Gas, you fool. Several million pounds worth of gas.'

'Suppose they want proof of that?'

'They'll have proof, as soon as I can have some test wells sunk.'

'To do which they'll have to have already given you the extended and additional credit. I think you should be here, Bernard. Address them in person.'

'Listen,' Morris hissed impatiently. 'Where the hell do you think you figure in our operation? You're the smooth talking figures man. Go do your job. If they want short term proof, have them contact Turnbull & Heath. I'll fax them now with permission to release to you the result of their analysis and projections. Just do it. I'm going ahead with arranging the drilling. I'll expect one hundred per cent, Philip. Don't let them pull the plug now.'

They hadn't spoken much over the past twenty-four hours. Maybe they had already spoken too much. Gus was aware that, for the first time in their two-year working relationship, there had been a rift. It wasn't that he didn't sympathize with the girl; a good deal of what they had to do, or at least, recommend, was environmentally unfriendly. But this was the first time he had seen it get to her with quite such an impact.

He knew the reason, of course. Kitty had never previously been exposed to the unpalatable prospect of tearing up some of the most beautiful country in the world. And additionally, she had allowed herself to become emotionally involved in the whole scenario. That was fatal. Yet it was so easy to do.

On the one side was Bernard Morris, a money-grubbing toad but a man who had every right to exploit the land he had bought, even if, when he bought it, he had had no idea it was good for anything save raising sheep and cattle—and shooting purpose-bred birds. On the other were people like James MacEwan, to whom that land was home, and part of their heritage. But who would have no share in the vast profit to be obtained from beneath their feet, even supposing they wished a share.

Kitty had definitely taken to MacEwan, even if the feeling wasn't reciprocated. Which might be another reason for her emotional involvement. As for that silly boy Niall, who had obviously fallen head over heels in love with her and very nearly cost her her life... Gus got angry every time he thought about him.

It was already dark. He glanced at her, hunched in the seat beside him. 'Only twenty miles,' he remarked.

'I can hardly wait,' she replied.

'To do what?'
'Get to work.'
'Not tonight.'
'But Gus, Morris is in a hurry.' Which was not her reason.
'Too much so. And you too. You need to get home and sleep,' Gus replied, pretending he believed her. 'He can wait a couple of days while we proceed normally. Maybe he'll see things differently by then.'
She knew she was a rotten liar. 'The only thing that is going to make him see things differently is for us to prove that it simply isn't practical to bring that gas up. OK.' She held up her hand. 'I promise to be absolutely impartial. But you can't blame me for feeling badly...'
'And I don't. What I am giving you now is professional advice. I am exhausted and I am pretty damn sure you are, too. You are also emotionally fazed at the moment. Don't take offence. Anyone who came as near to death as you did would be traumatized for a day or two unless they're thick from the neck up, and you're not that. All I am asking is that you go home and rest. It's Friday night. Spend the weekend reorientating yourself and come in to the lab on Monday morning fresh and raring to go. Is that unreasonable?'
She grinned, spreading her hands in

submission. 'That's very reasonable, Daddy, dear.'

'Oh, and we'll expect you to lunch on Sunday. But no shop: Gillian won't have it.'

Having dropped Kitty near her flat, Gus himself did not go straight home; he went into his office, as he always did when returning from a field trip, both to unload the samples and to see if there were any messages. And there was one, from Ben Heath. The boss wanted to see him, the moment he returned from Scotland. Although it was past seven, Gus went right up; he knew Ben's working habits, even on Friday nights.

'Where the hell have you been the past twenty-four hours?' Ben demanded. He was a heavy man who looked like a bulldog with a hangover—but his hangover was all work.

'Motoring down from Scotland,' Gus said with his invariable equability, sitting in the chair before the paper-strewn desk.

'Have you never heard of airplanes?'

'I do not like airplanes,' Gus explained, 'Except for very long distance travel. Travelling by airplane makes me feel like a very small child being taken on a school outing by people who doubt my intelligence. Travelling by car is not only more comfortable but it enables me to keep all my gear under my hand, as it were.'

Ben glared at him. He and Gus had crossed swords before over what he considered his senior scientist's eccentricities. 'Well,' he said. 'I have had one hell of a time while you have been enjoying the pleasures of motoring. Is there really the world's biggest gas field under the Grampians?'

Gus raised his eyebrows. 'Where on earth did you get that idea? Don't tell me Morris has been on to you?'

'I've had a call from some newspaper reporter in Aberdeen. Seems the place is buzzing with rumour. So, give.'

'There's gas,' Gus said.

'Commercial?'

'I would say so.'

'And does it all really belong to this fellow Morris?'

'Could be the case.'

'So why aren't you rubbing your hands with glee at a job well done?'

'There could be problems.'

'Speak,' Ben ordered.

Gus outlined his and Kitty's experiences of the past few days, and gave Ben a rough breakdown of their findings.

'So what's your theory?' Ben asked when he had finished.

'You don't pay me to have theories, Ben,' Gus pointed out. 'You pay me to make observations and then analyse what I have observed.'

Ben gave him another glare. 'This reporter seems pretty sure that Morris is going to exploit, and PDQ.'

'We'll have an analysis ready by the middle of next week,' Gus promised. 'Even superman Morris can't have a drilling rig in place by then. Anyway, he'll have to get permission from the local Department of the Environment,' he grinned. 'And that may not be easy. One of his daughters works for the Department in London, and she's against it.'

'Money talks,' Ben remarked. 'Much louder than feelings or prejudices, as a rule.'

'And Morris has money,' Gus said. 'So why does he need so much more?'

'Nobody ever has enough money,' Ben observed, wisely. 'I'd like to see your report, as soon as it is completed.'

'You will,' Gus said. 'Now I'm going home to bed.'

'Give Gillian my love,' Ben said, and turned back to his papers.

Kitty was still smiling at Gus's fatherly advice as she watched the old Peugeot chunt away up the main road. She really liked him and looked forward to Sunday lunch in the Wilson household. They had become her surrogate family.

She headed up the lane to the old iron gate in a high privet hedge. It was two years since she first found this gate and the old house behind it festooned with Virginia creeper, shutters and tall black chimney-pots that looked like old-fashioned pantrymaids' stockings.

Tucked sufficiently away from the noise and traffic of the city to rate as suburbia, she had fallen in love with the house on sight, and with the white-haired octogenarian widow whose income was no longer sufficient to maintain her home without letting the first floor as a separate, one-bedroomed flat. A bathroom and kitchenette had been added, still leaving plenty of space for Kitty's vast family of pot plants.

In the two years since taking the lease, Kitty had never lost the thrill of approaching her own place. Her parents couldn't understand why she wanted to move away from the family home, which was near enough to Oxford to make commuting quite practical; it wasn't as though there was any serious family aggro and there was certainly plenty of room.

She had tried to explain and her sister had backed her up. Mum had come round, first, but even now Dad looked hurt when she talked about her latest project...the new paper in her bedroom, and loose covers in the living-room.

Mrs Cummings and Kitty had liked each other immediately. The old lady was thankful that her tenant was a respectable looking girl with a proper job, and not an out-of-work guitarist with dreadlocks entertaining fellow musicians till five in the morning. Kitty fell in love with Mrs Cummings' three cats and automatically brought in the dustbins from the gate on Tuesday mornings before going for the bus.

'Binker! Binker, Binker!' Mrs Cummings was standing in the garden, calling.

'Is he lost again, Mrs C?' Kitty asked, carefully fastening the gate behind her.

'I hope not. Every time he is returned it costs me a reward. I really should have him neutered.' She went back inside saying, 'I've just made a fresh pot of tea. Like a cup?'

Kitty might only have been gone for a day at the office, instead of several days and nights. 'Love one,' she lied.

As Gus had pointed out, she was exhausted, and she knew that she was feeling pretty emotionally unstable; she longed to get upstairs and soak in the bath before supper followed by bed. However,

Mrs C was awfully lonely and very kind and thoughtful, taking in Kitty's milk each day and insisting on doing bits of shopping. She didn't crowd Kitty at all and never came upstairs unless invited.

'How was Scotland? Very cold?' Tea was poured from a china spout emerging from a woollen crinoline tea cosy.

Suddenly Scotland seemed light years away, rather than twenty-four hours. 'Very beautiful,' Kitty replied, 'but they said it was comparatively mild for the time of year. Nearly all the snow was melted except on the peaks. Have you heard from your son yet?' Colonel Cummings was a military attache in some Far Eastern country where postal services were not noted for their efficiency.

'Indeed! So exciting! He's coming back to England to take up a job in Whitehall,' the old lady beamed, going on to relay all the news she could remember. Then suddenly she stopped. 'Oh, dear. I am so sorry. You must be tired and wanting to get upstairs. Off you go, now.' She longed to keep the girl with her for company, but the young had their own lives to lead and anyway she had her own evening of reading, tapestry and a bit of TV all mapped out.

'I'll go and give Binker another shout for you, before going up,' Kitty said.

The phone was ringing as Kitty wearily trailed her bag upstairs five minutes later. She fought the key in the lock, dashed into the bedroom and lifted the receiver.

'Kitty?' the voice asked.

'Yes?'

'I'd just about given you up. Where have you been?' It was Toby, sounding annoyed.

'Travelling, mostly.' Why did it irritate so much when he asked questions?'

'Till now?'

She looked at her bedside clock which registered five to seven. 'I had a cuppa downstairs with Mrs C before coming up.'

'You over-indulge the old duck. Like to have a pub supper?'

Toby had reckoned they were an item for the past six months, but apart from two brief but notable periods, Kitty had not. He was a long, thin squash freak with a heavy jaw, amusingly mobile eyebrows, and a great deal of sex appeal which she had never fathomed...because she was the only girl at the squash club who had apparently noticed. Shower room chatter never included his name.

Unfortunately, despite her efforts at concealment, he had become aware of her stirring interest and had swanned her into restaurants, theatres and finally, after a rather late, alcoholic party, into bed. She couldn't honestly say she hadn't enjoyed the latter; he wasn't her first, but was definitely the best—so far.

The trouble was he didn't particularly interest her as a person. Tonight, however, she couldn't very well say, 'No, I don't want a meal first, just the sex and then you can go,' even if she hadn't felt too tired to be bothered. 'I'd rather take a rain check if you don't mind. I've just driven several hundred miles. I'm dead tired and getting into a bath.'

'I'll come round with a takeaway, then. Save you cooking.'

Shoot! But she couldn't raise the energy to argue. 'OK,' she sighed. 'See you soon.'

She was still in the bath when he arrived. Having left the catch up on the lock she lay listening to him wander into the kitchen, slamming cupboard doors...making himself at home. She heaved herself out of the water, dried herself and dragged on an old tracksuit and slippers, and found him in the living-room waiting for her on the sofa. To avoid the welcoming arm she went straight to her favourite wingback and sank deep into the cushions.

'Want a drink?' Toby asked.

'Not if I'm going to stay awake for

more than ten minutes. There's a coke in the fridge, I'll have that.' Then added hospitably, 'Help yourself to anything you want.' She pressed the remote control.

'Do you really want that?' Toby plonked a Coke can beside her with unnecessary force as he glowered at the screen.

'There's a programme I want to see in a minute.'

'Shit!' He returned to the sofa with a beer. Kitty gazed at the screen, seeing nothing. Why, she wondered, does this guy get up my nose so much? And tonight more than ever. Presumably because she was over-tired—and had too much on her mind.

'I brought Indian for a change,' he said.

'Good. Not too hot, I hope.'

'A Chicken Korma for you and Vindaloo for me.'

'Lovely. We'll finish our drinks first, shall we?' Kitty asked.

When the programme was over and she got up to set the table, Toby stood up too and put his arms round her. She needed human contact, liked his Boss aftershave and the soothing feel of strong arms, lifting her face quite willingly to take his kiss.

There was a bottle of cooking red in the kitchen which they polished off with the curries and—after she'd sliced off the green mouldy bits—they ate the bits of cheese she'd left in the fridge before going to Scotland, which made Kitty sleepy.

'So tell me about your trip.' Toby sat down with the coffee she'd made. 'Did you strike gold!'

'No. Gas.'

'I thought that was in the North Sea.'

'Not this lot. We were in the mountains.'

'We?'

'Gus...Professor Wilson, and I...me.'

'All alone?'

Why the cross-examination? 'No, actually,' she said irritably. 'There were four others.'

'Who?'

Kitty banged her cup down on the coffee table, spilling some in the saucer. 'What the hell is this? Why the inquisition?'

Toby's jaw lifted aggressively. 'Just wise me up on what's happening, will you? You've gone odd. Hyper.'

'I don't know what you're on about.'

'You didn't seem very eager to see me, even though you've been away.'

'It was a tiring trip.'

'Are you having it off with your professor?'

'Gus? You joke.'

'Well, who did you meet up there?'

Suddenly she'd had enough. 'OK, that's it. Thank you very much for the Chinese...

sorry, Indian takeaway. Very nice to see you, I'm sure. But I have no intention of being cross-examined...'

'I knew it. You're hiding something.' He was standing over her, looking furious.

'As a matter of fact I am hiding nothing, but because you have developed an objectionably possessive attitude you cannot seem to accept the fact.' She took a deep breath. 'I am my own person. Who I see, when I see them and what I choose to do with my life is entirely my own business and nobody else's. Up to now I have enjoyed your friendship,' which wasn't one hundred per cent true, 'but I will not put up with this invasion of my privacy.'

It was on the tip of her tongue to order him out—but she didn't. Instead she ended, saying, 'I'm sorry. I have had a very tiring week, a tiring day, and I'm not in the mood for this.'

'Bloody hell! And to think I came here with the idea we should discuss shacking up together. I thought we had something going.' He headed for the door. 'Let me tell you, I'm the one who's had enough. If you're not prepared to tell me what you've been up to, and who with, then it's obvious you're hiding something.' He opened the door, snarling, 'When you come to your senses you can call me,' and slammed it behind him.

'There wasn't anyone, you fool,' she shouted at the closed door, then smiled. Ignoring the mess all over the table she went straight to bed.

She was asleep in five minutes, dreaming of an enormous Scotsman in long, thick socks, with a full-grown sheep under each arm.

Having accepted without hesitation the extremely surprising offer of an extra thou from her suddenly benevolent father, Tara had returned to London at the same time as Rebecca...at least she could enjoy a few days of civilized society until the windfall ran out. Really, what with the funny little bearded gnome and his polyestered assistant, and Daddy in such a terribly tetchy mood, the castle had been utterly unbearable.

She had attempted to get the chummies to fly up to Aberdeen for a jolly weekend but they were all going off to the Thwaites' place in Cornwall for an engagement party...missing it was the last straw.

It was an enormous relief to get back to the flat in Chelsea; small as it was, an aura of wealth and well-being emanated from the Chinese carpets, polished chintz curtains and red enamelled dining suite...an aura suited to the friends she had chosen, not all of whom had chosen her.

'Bella, darling,' she cooed into a gilt and onyx bedside phone, 'What is everyone doing tonight?' Everyone who was anyone, that was.

'Some people haven't made it back from the West Country yet; Polly says they're nursing screaming hangovers. But Jonty's just decided to have a birthday party at The Graven Image. Coming?' Bella invited.

'Of course. But I didn't know it was his birthday.'

'It isn't, darling. But you know how Jontykins loves parties. Wigs and whiskers, by the way. I'm wearing a bald-with-fringe style and handfuls of sofa stuffing under my armpits.' The two young ladies rolled on their respective beds, laughing.

Then Tara stared in consternation at the wall of fitted wardrobe doors which couldn't close against the pressure from behind, realizing she hadn't a thing to wear.

Rebecca gazed at the double bed, still rumpled and messy as she had left it when Giles walked out. She didn't miss him, he'd turned out to be a bit of a bore, she kept telling herself. But she did ache for human company.

If only she could have made headway with Gus; there was something desperately appealing about him, little-boyish in a way, but all he could talk about, apart from his work, was his bloody wife.

Of course if she had established a relationship with him, she might have been able to change his way of thinking, influence him into thwarting Daddy's plans to wreck the moors and mountains round Abergannan.

She sighed and flicked through the TV channels with the remote control, lost interest and opened the freezer door, resisted the Black Forest Gateau with Brandy and Cream, took out a vegetarian pie instead and tossed it into the oven. Then she circled the secondhand pine dining-table she'd found in a Putney store, picking through the magazines and pamphlets which smothered it, finally settling into a tired looking bucket armchair with a pad and ballpoint.

She felt compelled to draft some sort of statement to the senior secretary at the M of E regarding a possible threat to the Scottish Highlands.

The ancient bedsprings creaked their objections, applauded by the headboard bashing against the wall, as Niall pumped up and down on the delighted Beatrice, expunging his disappointment at Kitty's departure.

It was the moment the housemaid had been waiting for, her ultimate triumph, and she couldn't wait to tell her pal Molly, down at the bakery. Not that Molly would believe her until Niall actually put an engagement ring on her finger, but that was surely only a matter of time.

Niall climaxed with his eyes closed and was almost sick with shock when he opened them to see, not the smooth dark hair and lively brown eyes of his beloved as he had been picturing, but a large, red nose and little green eyes peering up at him through a jungle thicket of frizzy yellow perm gone wrong. He rolled off her and lay on his back to recover from the disappointment.

'Oh Niall, love, tha' was beautiful,' the girl sighed, leaning across him, head on his chest.

He spat out a mouthful of hair and slid off the bed. 'Sorry old girl, but I must rush.' He hoped she wouldn't ask why—he didn't want to offend her. Running down the attic stairs he could hear his father's voice shouting from the nether regions, but only when he approached the head of the main staircase did he realize his name was being called. 'You wanting me, Dad?'

'You could say that,' Bernard grumbled as his son reached the grand newel posts guarding the bottom stair. 'I've been trying to find you for the past ten minutes. Where the hell have you been?'

'Ramming the kitchen maid in the attic,' Niall announced.

Bernard threw back his head, roaring with laughter at the idea. 'Now let's be serious. Come into my study.' He led the way. 'It's time you and I talked. I've been giving the business accountancy angle of this Scottish gas operation a lot of thought,' he said as they sat either side of the vast desk, 'and I want you be involved from its inception.'

Niall leaned forward, forgetting the girl he had just had, and the one he hadn't, in the new excitement of a career take-off. 'Yes,' he breathed eagerly.

'I can't spend all my time up here, so I want you keeping an eye on everything, representing me and our Morris financial interests.' Bernard held up his hand as Niall opened his mouth to speak. 'You have a degree in business studies, which at this stage of the game is about as much use as a snowball in hell, but we can build on that knowledge. We will have experienced accountants, computer operators, gas field managers and operatives up here, qualified and competent to run the show...'

'But what...'

'Your job will be to follow everything they do, every discussion they have, decision they make, problem they run into and keep me posted...constantly.' He sat back, watching his son's reaction.

Niall was frowning at the idea of being planted as a sort of industrial spy. 'But how will I get access to all this info, Dad?'

'You will be a director, with the authority to see and hear everything that goes on, ask any questions and demand details you think could be important if you suspect anything is being withheld.'

Well...the directorship could be a great incentive, but he wasn't to be involved in running the operation at all, and the people he would work with were bound to realize his designated purpose. Yet if he didn't do it, who would? Some guy who would not give a damn as long as the money was good... Bernard raised an eyebrow at the boy's hesitance.

Niall took a deep breath and nodded. 'Yes, Dad. Sure. Sounds great.'

'It is great. A great opportunity for you. And in due course when you have gained experience and knowledge of the business, you will gradually assume a more hands-on role.' He opened a file and drew out a sheaf of papers. 'Right. Let's get down to detail.'

Niall drew his chair nearer, determined to give this opening his best shot.

Kitty spent a restless weekend. She forced herself to stay in bed all Saturday morning, resting, instead of emptying her bag and washing her smalls. She was still suffering a little shortage of breath from time to time, but she suspected that might be more from shattered nerves than lung damage.

Although she had slept heavily on Saturday night, she had endured several nightmares after her initial pleasant dream; through the deep sleep wall which had surrounded her they had become blurred, but she knew they were mostly to do with deep, dark places where breathing was difficult. Again, she told herself, they'll soon pass off.

Dragging on a comfy old jumper and jeans, she grabbed her car keys; the antique Metro argued for some minutes before coughing into action and setting off to the rambling Wilson residence on the edge of town.

The once-gravelled drive was green with winter weeds because the owners were musicians, not gardeners. Beethoven spilled out of the front door with dogs and children and Kitty was swamped by enthusiastic barking and shouts of welcome, with young arms winding round her like coils of cooked spaghetti.

'Come and see Daddy's train set. He was given it when he was little and it's been in the attic for years,' Bobby tugged at her arm.

'Mummy says we'll have to eat in the kitchen 'cos he won't move it off the dining-room table,' his elder sister added.

'Something smells super.' Kitty sniffed appreciatively as she was dragged along the hallway over loose rugs rumpled by excited dogs.

Gillian bounced out of the kitchen, flour to the elbows. 'Lovely to see you, dear. Come, sit and talk to me while I finish the rhubarb tart. How was Scotland? Can't get a word out of Gus now he's got the train set down.'

Much as Kitty enjoyed the Wilsons and the relaxed atmosphere in their home, she was reluctant to tell Gillian about anything except the scenery, especially as Gus had forbidden it. She didn't know if he had mentioned the traumas, or if his wife had even the remotest idea how dangerous his job could be on occasion.

In the end she launched into anecdotes about the Morris family which soon had Gillian in stitches, and which drew Gus away from his trains to investigate the mirth and add a few of his own, crisp observations.

The lunch was scrumptious and boisterous and Kitty almost felt guilty afterwards that she hadn't been able to get Scotland, Abergannan and its possible impending problems off her mind. The main fact was that she was desperately anxious to get down to the lab and start tests on her samples.

As they waved her away down the weedy drive, she was even tempted to go in on her way home, but she knew that Gus would never forgive her.

He could not criticize her for going in early, though, and on Monday morning she was in the building just after seven; by then she was, as Gus had prognosticated, feeling almost one hundred per cent again.

Mrs Holding, the cleaning woman, raised her eyebrows as she spotted the diminutive figure hurrying into the lab. 'Something important, dearie?'

Kitty grinned at her as she put the kettle on for a cup of coffee. 'I just seem to have been away forever.' She settled herself, with books and notes, and did her reading before starting on any experiments.

As they had told Morris, natural gas, like oil, from which it arises in so many cases, occurs through the successive transformation of various raw materials, over millions of years, during the period when the earth's crust was still building, so that the gas and oil became trapped in reservoirs hundreds and sometimes thousands of feet beneath the earth's surface.

She agreed with Gus that there was almost certainly a gas reservoir under Abergannan; the initial question was, how deep was it, and how much gas did it contain? Because her rough analysis made in Scotland suggested that this particular reservoir might indeed possess some very unusual characteristics.

In the first place, it was a dry gas, on the evidence she so far possessed; that was to say that it appeared to be in a gaseous state in the reservoir, and had given no indication of containing any liquid deposit at surface pressure and temperature. This could indicate that it arose from an oil reservoir—but if it did, there should have been no hydrogen sulphide. Yet she was sure there was. Hydrogen sulphide would only be present if the gas arose from extreme depths, again as they had indicated to Morris. That, of course, should be simply a financial and technological matter, except for the pressure factor.

Her first test was to discover what was called the standard volume of the gas. This was always expressed as a condition of the gas at a temperature of fifteen degrees centigrade and a pressure of seven hundred and fifty millimetres of mercury.

She subjected one of her phials of gas to these conditions while working out the very complicated formula, PV=Zm/MRT, P being absolute pressure, obtained from her meter, plus one atmosphere, V being the volume at that pressure and at the absolute temperature, T, of two hundred and seventy-three degrees centigrade. Z was the compressibility factor, the two m's represented the molecular factors. Her results had to be expressed in relation to the theoretical 'perfect' gas that fulfilled the equation under all conditions.

She was still working on this, and frowning at her initial answers, when Gus came in. 'Hello,' he remarked. 'When did you start?' She waved at him, busy with her computer. He peered over her shoulder. 'Deep stuff.'

'As we thought.'

'So what's the breakdown?'

'I'm going to start work on that as soon as I complete this. But I'm not happy.'

'Lunch with me,' Gus said, and went to his office. He knew Kitty could be trusted to come up with an absolutely reliable analysis, despite her prejudices.

'Morning, Gus.' Lois was his secretary and general factotum. When she had started work for Turnbull & Heath four years earlier she had been a neat, pretty young woman who had taken great care with her appearance. But as she had very rapidly learned that no one in the laboratory ever took the slightest notice of make-up or clothes, and that she was as like as not to have some indelible or destructive substance dropped on her, she had abandoned chic for old clothes and a generally untidy air. But she was efficient. 'There's been a call and a fax.'

Gus raised his eyebrows as he sifted through the mail. 'Don't tell me: a newspaper reporter with a Scottish accent.'

'The fax is from Scotland, from your client Morris. The call was from a London accountant with an impeccable accent. Name of Crowther. He wants you to call him the moment you come in. Which is now,' she added helpfully.

Gus regarded both the name and the telephone number with suspicion. He distrusted accountants, not because he had doubts as to their honesty, but because their appearance generally meant trouble and expense for somebody. 'You'd better get him for me,' he said, and looked at the fax. Then frowned.

'Mr Crowther,' Lois said.

Gus picked up the phone. 'Wilson.'

'Professor Augustus Wilson? Philip Crowther. I understand you have just carried out a geological survey for Mr Bernard Morris, on his estate in Grampian.'

Gus continued to survey the fax, which gave him permission to answer the question. 'That is correct, Mr Crowther.'

'I am Mr Morris's accountant, and a partner in his business.'

'So I understand,' Gus said.

'Ah. Then you've heard from Mr Morris.'

'I have his fax in front of me.'

'Then may I ask when the information he requires will be available?'

'How long is a piece of string?'

'Eh?'

'We are working on the analysis now,' Gus said. 'Giving it top priority. But it is quite impossible for me to say when we will have a report available.'

'Look here, man, I need that information today,' Crowther snapped.

'I'm afraid that will not be possible. Perhaps tomorrow. More likely Wednesday.'

'Are you that incompetent?' Crowther was definitely angry.

'On the contrary, Mr Crowther,' Gus said, as equably as ever, 'it is because we regard ourselves as a competent firm that I refuse to rush into what might be premature judgements. You will have the report as soon as it is available. Good-morning to you, Mr Crowther.'

He replaced the receiver and looked at Lois, who was waggling her eyebrows.

'Would you like a small bet?' she asked.

'I'd lose,' Gus said. 'As I imagine you're going for fifteen minutes.' They were both spot on. Gus had not quite finished with his mail when the buzzer went. 'I'll be right up,' he said.

'Just what have we got ourselves into, Gus?' Ben asked.

'You tell me.'

'This fellow Crowther is pretty high-powered. He's a company accountant, and has his fingers in a lot of very lucrative pies. Not all of them are entirely savoury.' He shot his senior chemist a glance. 'That is confidential. So tell me what is so urgent about this gas field you've found? Or is Morris just a curious man?'

'Well, I'd say I'd be curious if I suspected I might be sitting on top of a fortune,' Gus said.

'So curious you'd have your accountant start tearing the air to get hold of the facts?'

'I have only ever had one meeting with

my accountant,' Gus said. 'And that was to handle an Income Tax return, many years ago. Since then, I have decided I could do it better on my own.'

Ben snorted. As he held the same opinion of Gus's driving and general lifestyle as did Kitty, he wondered how the Income Tax Department was still in business. 'And if you had a fortune already?' he asked.

'Well, as you said Friday night, Boss, no one ever has enough money. But here is a theory.' Ben raised his eyebrows; Gus didn't usually offer theories. 'I'm beginning to wonder if there *is* a fortune, already,' Gus said.

'Elaborate.'

'From what I saw and heard up in Abergannan, there has been a strong smell—if you'll pardon the expression—of over-reaction from Morris ever since he found out about the possibility of a gas field. Seems he wasn't all that interested in that boy being killed and the girl all but burned to death, until someone suggested that the gas which had caused the explosion had to come from under the ground. He certainly left Kitty and me with a sense of urgency. Now we have him faxing me instructions to let his accountant have the report as quickly as possible, and his accountant himself on the phone, as you say, tearing the air because we're not ready for him yet. Multimillionaires, which I understand is how Morris is rated in the city, don't over-react like that. People who were *once* multimillionaires but who may have dug themselves a financial hole, do.'

'Hm.' Ben Heath was a man who believed in first things first. 'Are you trying to tell me our account won't be paid?'

'I wouldn't spend the money, unless we turn up some gas.'

'But you say it's there.'

'Yes. But there are aspects of it that Kitty and I don't like.'

'The depths? I thought we agreed that was Morris's problem? If he can't raise the money to drill, well, then, he'll have to call in the big chaps. If he can, we've done a good job of work.'

'There are other factors,' Gus said. 'But I'd rather not go into them until Kitty has completed her analysis and I've had time to re-work her findings in detail. What I do recommend, however, is that you get hold of one of your financial whizz kid friends and see what you can find about about Morris.'

'Is it really any of our business, as long as he settles our account?'

'His eagerness is a factor too, Ben. Maybe it's not something we can feed into a machine. But I think it is something we need to bear in mind.'

‘So, how’s it going?’ Gus asked during lunch in a pub round the corner.

Kitty munched. ‘There is gas down there. An awful lot of it.’

‘Sounds good so far.’

‘I think there’s too much of it.’

‘I’m not with you.’

‘My samples were taken within a hundred or so feet of the surface, right? Now, what I got has found its way up through nooks and crannies in the rocks for something over ten thousand feet, if our hydrogen sulphide reading is correct. That in itself is pretty unusual.’

‘But that’s how the presence of natural gas was first known to the ancients,’ Gus pointed out. ‘By odd emissions which were perceived to burn.’

‘Granted. But just about all of those odd emissions, as you call them, came from shallow fields. Here we have the stuff coming up from an enormous depth. The psi down there must be fantastic.’

‘Figure?’

‘We’re looking at seven thousand by my calculations.’

‘Jesus Christ! I beg your pardon.’ Gus did not usually blaspheme. ‘The highest pressure around the North Sea is only about five thousand. You must have mis-keyed your calculator.’

'Treble checked it,' she replied.

'OK, so we have a reservoir so full of gas that it can't hold it in...' he frowned. 'You're not supposing it is still forming down there? That would simply not be possible.'

'I'm not suggesting that, Gus. But the pressure per square inch is there. I think there has been some shift down there, and maybe a new underground stream has formed, quite recently, perhaps as a result of unusually wet weather, with the result that the reservoir is being squeezed, as it were. This would have happened quite recently, geologically speaking. Maybe only in the last few years. But the result is that the gas has been forced to find a way out, or explode. Now, we know it hasn't exploded, because the mountain is still there. But it has forced its way up into every nook and cranny, as I say, until checked by that last wall, which has now been eaten away, so that it is leaking into the air.'

'Which has, presumably, taken off the pressure.'

'Some. God knows what it was before that hole appeared, if it's seven thousand now. Gus, I reckon that whole mountain is one enormous bomb waiting to go off. It would make Hiroshima and Nagasaki look like firework displays.'

'Well, it appears to me that the sooner we get Morris to start drilling the better. So it'll come out in a rush at the start, but those riggers will know how to deal with that, and then things will settle down.'

Kitty finished her lager and leaned across the table. 'Suppose its unstable? You suggested it could be.'

'It was just a suggestion. Have you checked the components yet?'

'I'm going to start on that this afternoon.'

'OK. Let me know the moment you complete.'

'I think it's unstable,' Kitty said.

Gus rested his hand on hers and gave it a gentle squeeze. 'You mean you want to *prove* it's unstable. That's what we're talking about: proof.'

James backed the jeep into position and began unloading the stakes and wire. Wilkie and Andrew were there to help him, together with the passengers of the second jeep, four strong young men recruited in Aboyne.

'Wire!' Wilkie remarked in disgust. 'I never thought to see wire on Abergannan.'

'Let's hope it won't be permanent.' James looked at the sky; it remained dark and threatening, but at the moment was dry. On the other hand, it had rained a good deal over the past couple of days, so that the underground stream had to be up virtually to its maximum level; certainly there was very little smell. Although it could be noticed.

'That's swamp gas,' said Andy Mearns.

'Aye,' Wilkie agreed. 'That's what we're after. Stopping people getting close enough to yon cave to get gassed. Or burned.'

'Like your lass,' agreed Brian Murdoch. 'So, Major, are we at risk here?'

'Not right now. But let's get on with it.' James was busy with compass and range finder, mapping out where he wanted the stakes placed.

'It's going to be a problem up the top,' Wilkie remarked, looking up the slopes.

'Do you seriously suppose anyone is going to come over the top of Cock Cairn?' James asked.

'Ye never can tell, once the tourists start,' Wilkie argued.

It had not occurred to James that this business would not be completed, one way or the other, before the arrival of the first tourists. But Guthrie had a point. 'We'll put up a notice board, several notice boards, up the slope to the effect that it is dangerous to proceed,' he decided.

'Aye, well, if ye think that will deter the young,' Wilkie agreed lugubriously.

James wondered what that attractive little geo-chemist was doing now? Oddly, for all her sometimes spirited defence of her work and her profession, he had had the feeling that she might just be on his side, at the end of the day. He wondered if he would ever see her again.

Having checked and re-checked her figures as regards the pressure in the gas reservoir, and becoming increasingly unhappy about it, Kitty got to work on the actual components of the gas samples she had taken. Being composed of a variety of chemical molecules, most of them very minor indeed, all aspects of natural gas itself have either to be refined for separate use or eliminated as being obstructive or even dangerous.

She began with the least important, as always, referring to existing levels at other fields, and punching her findings into her computer. 'Hexane,' she muttered. 'C6H14. Caproic acid. A hydrocarbon. Normally has a strong, goat-like smell.' But the quantity was infinitesimal, a matter of zero point zero one per cent.

'Pentane. C5H12. Another paraffin source.' But again in minute quantities, as she would have expected. Both of these substances were found in North Sea gas, although not necessarily in other parts of the world, such as Algeria.

'Butane. C4H10.' This paraffin source

was easily separated from the gasses such as methane with a lower boiling point, and was of value commercially but the percentage present, zero point zero seven, was lower than in any of the reference fields she had to hand. Kitty began to frown, even if she was already suspecting what was going to be her final analysis.

'Propane. C3H8.' Another valuable by-product, and again present in far less than its usual quantity: zero point two three per cent.

'Ethane. C2H6.' This was one of the most valuable components of natural gas, because of its use in the ethyline petrochemical industry, although a very large percentage of the ethane found in natural gas, perhaps as much as ninety per cent, was usually burned with the gas. But here again, the percentage was lower than the average, two point two one per cent.

'Carbon dioxide. C02.' This was a universal component of natural gas, and the amount present, zero point seven five per cent, although less than that normally found in North Sea Gas, was considerably higher than anything found in places like Algeria or North America.

'Oxygen. O.' Always present in minute quantities. Zero point zero two per cent.

'Nitrogen. N2.' Again, always present,

as it was present in every organism on earth. And again, the percentage, ten point one six, was down on her North Sea comparisons, but well up on North Africa or North America.

'Hydrogen Sulphide. H2S.' This was the outsider, and it was present in considerable quantity: one point two per cent, which but reinforced the depths theory.

But now she could have no doubt about what she would find as the last component. 'Methane. CH4.' A staggering eighty-five point three two per cent.

Kitty checked her findings again, with great care. But she had been right the first time. Methane is always the greatest component of natural gas, just as it is also by far the most explosive and inflammable of the components. But normally, it composes roughly seventy-five per cent of the gas. The figure, as she saw from her references, went up with regard to North Sea gas, but even there eighty per cent was about the limit. This gas contained four percentage points, one twenty-fifth, more methane than any of her references.

She sat for several seconds staring at the computer, then ran from her laboratory and along the corridor to Gus's office.

Lois was just tidying up, as much as she dared; Gus always knew when any of the pens he left scattered about his desk had been moved so much as a millimetre.

'Where is he?' Kitty demanded.

Lois looked at her watch. 'Home by now, I imagine.'

'Home?'

'It *is* half-past six, Kitty.'

Kitty looked at her own watch. She had been quite unaware of the time. 'Oh, Good Lord. I'd better get after him.'

'You'll have to hurry. He's taking Gillian to a concert at half-past seven.'

Kitty tumbled down the stairs, and broke the rule of a life time by summoning a taxi.

Fifteen minutes later she was at Gus's house in the Oxford suburbs, and banging on the door. Dogs barked, and there was general movement inside the house. Then Gus opened the door, wearing a dressing gown. 'Kitty?' He was astonished. 'Whatever is the matter?'

'It's as I thought from the beginning,' she panted. 'Morris *is* sitting on a bomb!'

Chapter 6

THE DECISION

'You'd better come inside,' Gus said. Kitty went into the sitting-room, chaotic with dogs and musical paraphernalia; the children were doing their homework but abandoned it to greet her. Gillian was just descending the stairs, her face for once unwelcoming. She was very fond of Kitty, but she was passionate about music, and scented a possible threat to the concert. 'Now be coherent,' Gus recommended.

Gillian looked at her watch. 'We leave in ten minutes.'

'Oh, shoot,' Gus said. 'I have to finish dressing. You'd better come upstairs.'

Gillian raised her eyebrows and sat down while Kitty followed Gus upstairs and stood with her back to him while he pulled on his clothes. 'It's exactly as I thought from the beginning.'

Gus zipped up his pants. 'You promised to be impartial.'

'I am being impartial. You saw my findings regarding the pressure. It's way above normal.'

'I accept that. But it won't be the first gas well with abnormal pressure. We discussed this.'

'Add that to the fact that the methane content of the gas is at least four percentage points above average? That's why that poor kid got blown up. There was something over ten per cent methane in the air he was breathing. That's explosive.'

Gus knotted his tie. 'Those are exceptional figures,' he conceded. 'If they're true.'

'What do you mean?' Kitty bridled.

'I'm not suggesting you're allowing prejudice to cloud your judgement,' Gus said placatingly. 'I'm saying that figures so dramatically adrift from the norm are going to be questioned when we present them. Therefore we have to be absolutely certain of their accuracy. I'm sorry, Kitty, but we're going to have to double-check your findings.' He knotted his tie and hunched into his jacket.

'And Morris and his people?'

'What about them?'

'Suppose he's starting to drill?'

'He won't, because he can't, until his accountant has seen our report and raised the necessary funding.'

'That's going by the book...and your theory. But Morris doesn't go by the book. I reckon he could start work on that site at any moment.' Her voice was shaky with anxiety. Urgency.

Her boss remained cool. 'So?'

'Gus, in my opinion,' she nearly said *professional* opinion, which would have sounded ludicrous compared with Gus's seniority, 'that mountain is just waiting to blow its top. One spark could set it off. I think they were damn lucky that boy and his lighter didn't do it. I suppose it had been sufficiently diluted by air in the cave. But if anyone messes about *inside* that hill where that much pressure exists and causes even the slightest spark, we are going to hear the bang down here.'

'*If* your figures are correct you *could* be absolutely right. But we cannot dash round the country ringing alarm bells and terrifying people. I must repeat, Kitty, that it is absolutely essential for you to check those figures before we release them to Morris and his associates.'

'And if I am right?'

'Then we'll fax Morris and bring him up to date; warn him not to go ahead until and unless we can issue an assurance that there is no risk.'

'Augustus! Time to go!' Gillian called up the stairs.

Gus threw his hairbrush on the bed. The concert would be ruined if they arrived late. 'Coming!'

'And do you suppose Morris is going to take any notice of our fax?' Kitty followed him on to the landing, 'Once he's got the bit between his teeth?'

Gus shrugged. 'That's up to him. We'll have done our best to warn him. Look, I have got to go, or we'll be late.'

He ran down the stairs, Kitty behind him. 'All right,' she agreed, 'I will double-check those figures. Again. Then I would like the rest of the week off.' He halted, looking over his shoulder. 'I have leave due,' she pointed out.

'And where do you propose to spend this leave?'

'Visiting a sick friend.' Karen Wilkie might not exactly be described as a friend, but she was sick. Kitty was a stickler for the truth.

When Gus walked into the office next morning he found the pile of computer prints-out waiting on his desk, together with a note: *'Checked and double-checked,'* Kitty had written. *'Now your turn. See you on Monday.'*

She must have come straight back to the office and worked all night, the crazy kid. Grinding his teeth he strode into the laboratory, to the bench where Kitty had set out the apparatus, and switched on the computer. He decided to start from scratch, working his way through each of the samples, grumbling over the calculator and striking the computer keyboard so hard that it rattled.

Two hours later he sat at his desk, a mug of cold coffee at his elbow, comparing the print-out of Kitty's findings with his own. When he had finished he was frowning. He scratched the top of his head and went upstairs. 'Ben, we have a problem.'

Ben Heath studied the figures, deep creases developing on his forehead. 'You sent these to Crowther yet?'

'No. How would you like to do it for me?'

Ben raised his eyebrows. 'If believable, this combination of figures is unusual to say the least. I've never heard of anything like it before. Would you say it is conclusive?'

'Could be. I'd like the rest of the week off.'

'To go chasing after your assistant? You don't know where she's gone.'

'Of course I know where she's gone: Abergannan. God knows what she'll get up to there, and that Morris fellow could get nasty if we cause him to hold up operations unnecessarily. The reputation of the firm could be on the line.'

'I know. Right. You go up there and get her back before she throws too much shit at the fan.' Ben jabbed the air with his ballpoint. 'Use the shuttle.'

Gus sighed. He'd have to drive down to Heathrow first. 'You going to fax Morris?'

'No. I'm going to leave the whole thing up to you.'

'But Crowther will certainly get in touch with him, the moment he gets those figures.'

Ben grinned. 'So? You did tell him they wouldn't be available until tomorrow, didn't you?' He put the report in his in-tray.

There was half a gale blowing in from the North Sea as the aircraft approached Aberdeen Airport. Kitty peered through breaks in the cloud at the city spread out below and to her right. She recognized the spire of a church James had pointed out to them the day of their visit, and watched streams of cars on a dual carriageway as the plane banked through turbulent air into the wind and careered down to the runway, bouncing three times before finally rolling unsteadily towards the terminal.

Kitty allowed herself to take a deep breath. She wasn't normally a nervous flyer but the last thirty minutes had left her stomach somewhere over Dundee. She only had a cabin bag so went directly to the Avis desk to negotiate a car.

'Your easiest route to Aboyne is via the Aberdeen ring road and turn on to the A93 to Braemar.' The girl at the desk was smart, friendly but tired, depressed by the weather. She checked Kitty's completed form, slid her Visa card through the machine and handed over the keys.

It was nearly noon, but it might have been dusk as the clouds were so low and the rain so heavy, and as Kitty edged on to the main road she was already asking herself if she wasn't a prize idiot, trying to reach Abergannan in time for lunch. Supposing after all this they didn't offer her any? The signposts were clear and finding the Braemar road was no problem. But the storm clouds had closed in long before she reached Aboyne and she reckoned her chances of finding the obscure turning to the estate in this downpour were zero.

Just as she began wondering where she could stop for a meal the rain suddenly eased off and she realized she was in the town...facing the pub where she and Gus had first met James MacEwan. The car slotted neatly into a parking bay.

'Oh, aye, 'tis a terrible day,' the landlord told her as he drew a pint for the local standing beside her at the bar.

'Could I have lunch?' Kitty asked. 'And do you have a telephone?' She hadn't wanted to call the castle at the crack of dawn before leaving London, but it would be impolite to arrive entirely unannounced.

'Aye.' The landlord seemed to be answering both questions at once. 'Phone's in the passage.' He tilted his head towards a door marked 'Lads and Lasses' at the far end of the smoky room.

Armed with the number, Kitty edged her way through the customers.

'Abergannan Castle,' a voice said.

'Ah...would that be Mr Guthrie?'

'Indeed it would. Who is speaking, please?'

'Kathryn Cochrane.' There was a brief silence, while Guthrie tried to determine who Kathryn Cochrane might be. 'I visited you last week, with Professor Wilson,' Kitty explained.

'Oh, aye. Ye're the wee scientist.'

'You've got it. Now I'd like to visit you again.'

'Oh, aye?' Guthrie's voice took on a note of caution. 'When would ye be thinking of coming, Miss?'

'This afternoon?'

Another brief silence. Then Guthrie said, 'The laird and Mrs Morris are no here at the time, ye understand.'

'Not there?'

'They're in Aberdeen, ye ken, Miss. They'll no be back before tonight. I'd have to ask them, ye understand.'

'Oh,' Kitty said.

'Mind ye, there's Mr Niall. Maybe he'd be prepared...'

'No,' Kitty said definitely. She had no desire either to be Niall Morris's guest or to find herself alone at the castle with him. 'I'll call again this evening. What time would you recommend, Mr Guthrie?'

'Aye, well, it wouldna be before seven, at the earliest, Miss Cochrane.'

'Not before seven. Thank you.'

Winding her way back to the bar counter, feeling distinctly put out that she should have come all this way in such haste to no purpose, she developed a peculiar sensation that people were watching her, whispering. She looked round at the sea of faces, but all eyes were immediately focussed on the pints and drams in hand.

She studied the hand-written menu and chose a rump steak and chips but when she ordered, along with a glass of wine, the landlord was no longer smiling. 'Ye're one o' the scientists wantin' ta take gas out o' the mountains, are ye no'?' He slammed her glass down, spilling wine on the counter.

The entire room was hushed, all eyes watching her. Kitty went puce. But her chin came up and in a loud voice she said, 'Yes and no. Yes I am a scientist, and no, I am not personally interested in drilling for gas.'

A short, thickset man with an aggressive beard came up to stand next to her. 'Ye tak' money, tho', for finding it for the wealthy Sassenachs ta come an' destroy ower environment.' His face was close to hers and she could smell the whisky on his breath.

She smiled into his angry eyes. 'I am paid for making a scientific evaluation of a great many of the earth's substances, often for the benefit of the environment.'

'Benefit!' he snarled. 'The only benefit is ta the one calling humsel' the *laird*...an' yersel' tew, nay doot.'

Kitty regretted her decision to eat here and glanced round for a path of retreat. But when she turned back to her inquisitor he was otherwise engaged, backing off from the vast bulk of Major James MacEwan.

'Aye, Jock,' James was saying. 'And wasn't it the likes of Miss Cochrane here we had to have analyse the filthy chemicals you were dumping in the Dee from your workshops and poisoning all our fish?'

Jock found himself pinned against a table full of glasses and spilled beer. 'Ah dinna ken at the tame ut was poison, or Ah wouldna ha' done ut,' he grumbled defensively.

'Wha' Jock did was only an accident,'

declared one of his supporters. 'Ut was no' deliberate.'

'Accident or no' ut was cairless at the least. Ma Sally had a turrible stomach fer weeks fra' eatin' troot reet here in thus reum,' declared a stout matron sitting on a bench by the window, clutching her port and lemon.

Jock was about to suggest that her Sally's stomach problems stemmed from an entirely different activity than eating...but thought better of it.

Kitty cast a grateful glance at her saviour who responded with a grim nod. 'You'd better come and eat over here at my table,' he invited, unsmiling.

She felt about as welcome as a boll weevil in a cotton field, as she picked up her glass and followed him through the hostile drinkers. 'This is very kind of you,' she said stiffly as she sat down. 'I don't want to be an embarrassment to you.'

A suggestion of a smile lightened his expression. 'Who's embarrassed by whom? Jock spoke way out of turn, there.'

'From which I assume Morris has made his intentions public.' She sipped her wine, heart still pounding from the confrontation.

'When you apply to a local government office for anything, here, it is automatically public knowledge.' He shook his head. 'I believe “leaked to the press” is the term used in modern speak.’

‘Ah! But is it politically correct to use modern speak in this context?’ Her facial muscles relaxed into a smile.

A girl in jeans and tartan shirt brought their plates of food. ‘I see you chose good Scottish beef,’ James commented.

‘And you’re risking the fish. Are you sure it’s safe?’

‘As safe as your steak is from BSE.’ James drained his beer. ‘Another glass of wine? That one was half empty when you got it. And perhaps you’d tell me what brings you back to our neck of the woods so soon.’

They ate and drank in silence while Kitty considered, but when the girl brought their coffees she had decided to tell him about her findings in the laboratory. She couldn’t explain, even to herself, why she was behaving in such an unprofessional manner, but for some reason she wanted this man to understand.

When she stopped talking he was smiling. ‘I reckon that’s the best news I’ve heard in weeks,’ he said, sitting back and stirring his coffee so fast the saucer was swimming.

Kitty cocked an eyebrow at him. ‘You joke!’

‘I’m dead serious. And the sooner we get this news down to the Aberdeen office the sooner the whole project can be quashed.'

'Hey! Hold about there! I hoped you were on my side...'

James dropped his spoon on the table, deep furrows forming between his eyes. 'Funny. For the past twenty minutes I thought you were with us.'

'I am!' she protested. 'But getting me fired for leaking a client's confidential information isn't going to help anyone. At least, certainly not me.'

'Point taken. But surely the risks are too great, now, for the drilling to proceed?'

'I cannot be one hundred per cent certain of that. There may be factors, methods of diminishing the dangers, that I know nothing about.'

'But your findings can surely buy us time. Enough time to organize protests, tackle our MP, perhaps even get questions asked in Parliament... Not that London ever shows much interest in us up here, other than as a source of income for the public coffers.'

Kitty grimaced at him. 'Our friend Morris getting under your skin? Or is that a genuine observation?'

'My skin has been totally undermined ever since I took this job,' he growled. 'As for the government, well,' he glanced round the room, 'if you ask anyone in here their opinion of rule from Westminster, you'd better be wearing a crash helmet and flak jacket.'

Kitty giggled.

'So why are you here, if not to go public?' James asked as she recovered.

'To warn Morris of the dangers before anyone gets killed.'

'You don't imagine he'll listen, do you? He's negotiating an order for a mass of heavy machinery already. Says it should be here by the end of the week.'

'Oh no! Shoot!' She pushed the fingers of both hands through her hair and drew it tightly back off her face. What to do? She had flown up here in a mad rush to warn Morris. She just had to go through with it whatever his reaction. Well, she'd known he would go ape anyway, hadn't she?

James studied the emerging features with interest. With her hair off her face her high cheek bones and arched brows were revealed—most attractively. Amazing how classic lines never needed make-up. Now if she ever wore a white, high-necked blouse and a tartan skirt she would look stunning. Suddenly he realized he was staring at her... And she was staring back. 'I...I was just wondering what you were planning to do now?'

'I had planned to go up to Abergannan, but I gather the Morrises aren't there, and I didn't exactly receive a prodigal daughter welcome from Guthrie.'

'Guthrie's all right, but he daren't change the cutlery without a say so from the laird.'

'He told me Morris would be back this evening. So it looks as if I have to find something to do with my afternoon. In the rain.'

James looked at his watch. 'Why not come up to my place for a final cup of coffee?'

'Right up at Abergannan? Bit far for a coffee, isn't it?'

'No, no. I've got a cottage a quarter of an hour up the road. I haven't fed the animals yet so I must go.'

Kitty looked baffled. 'I thought you lived on the estate.'

'Part of the time, yes. But I haven't moved in completely. I cannot feel I'll be with our friend Morris indefinitely.' He stood up. 'Will you come?'

She tried not to let on just how pleased she was to accept.

It was teeming with rain as they ran to the back porch. Inside the cottage was Stygian; James flicked on the light in the kitchen and immediately warmth and cats wrapped round them.

James removed his boots, so Kitty left her wet shoes with them and padded over the rugs into the little sitting-room where James immediately stooped over the open fireplace and struck a match.

'I hope you're not bothering to light that just on my account,' Kitty said.

'No. Anyway, it's no bother: I cheat with firelighters. They soon get it going. Afraid there's no Aga here, only a gas stove, so the kettle will take a while. Make yourself at home while I feed the moggies.'

All the furniture was ancient and battered, but the throw rugs and heavy curtains made the room cosy and she sank miles down into the cushions on the sofa.

'Don't sit on the sofa,' James called through the open door. 'The cats and dogs use it whenever they get a chance and it's covered in hair.'

Kitty had already discovered that, too late but she moved to a cute little old chair with tassels, and castors on wooden legs. He put the mugs of coffee on the papers and magazines strewn over the low table between them.

'Have you got family?' he asked.

'Indeed. My parents and sister live about forty miles from my flat. What about you?'

'Mine lived up here when I was a child. This is where I grew up. But they're elderly now and live with my brother near

Glasgow.' He watched her face, reading the question in her mind. 'No, I haven't ventured into marriage, yet.'

She was amused at his perception and asked, 'Deliberate policy or accident of fate?'

'Bit of both. Army quarters are not much fun. The more so with the wrong partner.' He leaned forward to jab the fire with a poker. 'What about you? Got a boyfriend?'

Kitty thought about the irritating Toby and said, 'No. I go out with various friends from time to time, but there isn't anyone special.' She felt a bit guilty, saying that. But it was true. Certainly at that moment.

Across the empty coffee mugs his hand reached out for hers. 'Do you have to go on with this gas project?'

Her hand revolved, allowing her fingers to toy, idly, With his. 'You know I must. Why do you ask?'

'Because I want us to be friends, real friends, working together on the same principles.' He was staring at her face, waiting for her to look at him.

She tried not to, knowing she could be lost once he caught her eye. 'Don't you understand yet, that we *are* on the same side? I'm not aiming to destroy the land of your childhood, only to improve the standard of living of people in general. Inevitably some folk have to make sacrifices for the benefit of the majority. There's nothing new about that.' Accidently she lifted her eyes from the fire and found herself locked onto his gaze.

'But what about this new risk you were talking about?'

'I can only warn Morris of the possibility and suggest he holds off, temporarily at least. I cannot stop him completely or irrevocably.'

'When do you plan to tackle Morris?'

'As soon as I can. Tonight.'

'Not recommended.'

'But Guthrie said he'd be back...'

'When Morris gets back from Aberdeen tonight, he is going to be full to the brim with both whisky and aggro. He always is.'

'Oh. Don't you think I should even go out there, tonight?'

'Again, not recommended. He'll certainly want to hear what you have to say, right then, and then shout you down. Tomorrow afternoon is your best bet.'

'Afternoon? Why not in the morning?'

'Because I happen to know he's arranging to meet an engineer on site tomorrow morning. Your turning up then could again spark an explosion, if you'll excuse the pun. I'm hoping that by tomorrow afternoon not only will the expert have told him how difficult drilling will be, but also how expensive, and he may be having second thoughts anyway.'

Kitty considered. What he was saying made sense; there was absolutely no point in tackling Morris if he was going to be in a totally negative mood. But to have rushed all this way and then have to kick her heels for twenty-four hours... 'So I just hang around until then?' She hoped she wasn't going to discover this delay was some excuse to make advances.

James grinned. 'I know a widowed lady who does the best B and B in Aboyne. Certainly the breakfast. Shall I give her a ring for you? And then, tomorrow, I'll meet you up in the pub. We can have lunch together, and afterwards I'll drive you out to Abergannan. If that suits you.'

'That would suit me very well. But it seems very inconvenient for you.'

'I've got to come back into town for vet supplies around twelve. Shall we meet at twelve-thirty?'

Kitty tried not to let on just how happy a prospect that was, despite their opposite stands on the situation. 'If you're sure you're not too busy?' she said, then thought it sounded a bit off hand, so added, 'That would be great. Thanks.'

He phoned the bed and breakfast lady, and an hour later he drove her down to the boarding house, which was a stone's throw from the pub. 'Mrs Logan will give you supper as well,' he said. 'I've arranged it.'

'You're looking after me as if I were a long lost relative,' she remarked.

Another of those grins. 'Relatives, Kitty, are two-a-penny.'

She wondered whether to blame the wine she'd had with lunch or her own perverse idiocy when a sense of disappointment swamped her mind as he leaned across to open the car door and let her out beside her hired car. He had made no attempt even to shake hands let alone kiss her good-night.

Next day, having spent the morning exploring Aboyne, she was sitting in a corner of the bar trying to remain unnoticed, when the door swung open. She looked up, expecting to see James' bulk blotting out incoming light...and her mouth fell open—as she found herself staring at Gus.

His surprise was equally obvious. 'What...? I thought you'd be up at the castle,' he said, walking over to her table.

'What on earth are you doing here?'

He removed his tweed cap to scratch his

head. 'I've jetted up to stop you stirring up trouble for us all.' He gazed round the room. 'What are you doing in *here?*'

'Waiting for James. And I wasn't aiming to get anyone into trouble,' she added crossly. 'I'm going up to Abergannan this afternoon to see our friend Morris.'

Gus shook his head, 'Not wise.'

'Courageous?' Kitty ventured, attempting humour she didn't feel.

'Foolhardy, perhaps. Come on. What are you drinking?'

'I'll have another tomato juice, please.'

He had a pint. 'Where are you staying?'

'Across the road in a B and B. When did you arrive?'

'An hour ago. Couldn't get a flight last night. Well, I'm damn glad you haven't seen Morris yet. Far the best idea is to tackle him together.'

'If we're going to be on the same wavelength.'

'We work for the same firm, Kitty.'

'Did you check my findings?' she asked.

'Yes, I did. They're impressive, and frightening. But not necessarily as dangerous as you think.'

'You mean you've come up here to override me, and give Morris the go-ahead.'

'I have come up here to do what I said I was going to do: put Morris exactly in the picture, pros and cons. After that, it is up to him. It is his land, and if he can obtain environmental permission to develop it as a natural gas site, despite our findings, then there is nothing we can do to stop him.'

He was not saying anything very different from what she had told James yesterday, but she knew his approach was going to be quite different when they finally got to see Morris, and that was important.

'I'm sorry, I can't go along with this,' she said. Gus raised his eyebrows. 'I don't believe,' Kitty said, 'that Bernard Morris is psychologically or temperamentally capable of making a balanced judgement in this matter. He is a go-getter and to hell with the possible consequences. This is the way I reckon he has always worked when there has been the slightest chance of a profit at the end of it. If he can pull this off, he is going to make himself one hell of a profit. Therefore nothing is going to put him off save a doomsday scenario, spelt out in language a child could understand.'

'You mean, lie to him,' he said.

'Of course not. I just mean that we state the facts and our prognostication in the most forceful, and united, manner we can.'

'And I cannot go along with *that*. You're talking about leaving the realms of science for that of instinct. Any scientist who does that is a dead duck.' They glared at each other, and then he smiled, and reached across the table to hold her hand. 'Kitty, Kitty. I thought we'd resolved this. You promised me...'

'You made me promise that I would undertake my analysis in a totally impartial frame of mind. I did that. And came up with exactly the result I had anticipated.'

'You came up with a physical analysis, Kitty. It is the interpretation of that analysis that is at issue now. You happen to believe, because of your analysis of the gas down there, that if Morris attempts to drill into that mountain, he will blow it up and probably himself and a good chunk of Scotland with him. I happen to accept that, as a result of our analysis, if he starts to drill, he may have some problems. The word is may. But neither of us can possibly be proved right, until it happens.'

'Not interrupting anything, am I?' They had been so caught up in their argument that neither Kitty nor Gus had heard James come in.

'Not at all.' Gus stood up to shake hands. 'We were having a purely professional discussion.'

'About whether or not Gannan Hill is going to blow its top, eh?' James asked.

Kitty gulped as Gus looked at her.

'Haven't said the wrong thing, have I?'

James asked, anxiously.

'Just what did she tell you?' Gus asked.

Kitty licked her lips. 'Only that we had some doubts about the stability of the gas.'

Gus sat down again, somewhat heavily.

'Would you like another drink before lunch?' James asked.

'I'd like you to sit down,' Gus said. James did so.

'I'm terribly sorry,' Kitty said. 'It sort of slipped out. I was so lonely and miserable, last night...'

Gus decided not to probe into anything else her loneliness and misery might have driven her to, last night. 'James,' he said. 'I know you are one of those who are entirely against this project. However, I must tell you that whatever Kitty told you last night, it was against all the rules of the game. It was a breach of client confidentiality.'

'I would have been bound to find out soon enough,' James protested. 'I work for the man.'

'You would have found out if and when Morris chose to inform you, and that would have been his decision. Now I must ask you to give me your most solemn word, firstly, that you will not repeat what Kitty told you, to anyone, and secondly, that the knowledge you possess will not influence you in any way, unless and until Morris himself makes it public, or at least confides in you without a reservation.'

James looked at Kitty, and she could feel her cheeks burning. 'He's right, James. I did breach a client's confidentiality.'

'And suppose I don't choose to play by your rules?' James asked Gus.

Gus shrugged. 'It will be severely damaging for our firm, and will almost certainly cost Kitty her job.'

James looked at Kitty again.

'I'm sorry,' she said in a small voice.

'But, you're now on your way to advise Morris against drilling, right?'

'No,' Gus replied. 'We're on our way to present our findings to Mr Morris. On the basis of what we have to tell him, he will no doubt make a decision.'

James snorted. 'And we all know what that will be.'

'No, we do not,' Gus said evenly.

James looked from one to the other. 'We'd better eat. Then I'll lead the way up to the castle.' He fetched the menu.

Bernard Morris stood beside Archie MacPhail at the perimeter fence around Gannan Hill. 'What do you reckon?'

'It'll no be easy.' The engineer was a short, slight man, with a deceptively laid back air. 'Ah don't reckon there's more'n six feet of flat ground any place roond here.'

'But a rig can be erected?'

'Oh, aye, we've erected rigs in stranger places than this, to be sure.' He wrinkled his nose. 'Ye know yon gas is escaping?'

'A little of it escapes from time to time,' Morris said. 'It's to do with the water level, and it hasn't rained for a couple of days before yesterday. But that's why I've fenced the area off. Now come back to the castle with me and we'll talk turkey.'

MacPhail sat beside him in the Land Rover as they bounced their way back to the castle. 'Ye've all the papers from the Department?' he asked.

'No, I have not.'

'Man, I canna start erecting a drilling rig wi'out the papers.'

'You'll have your papers,' Morris assured him. 'I have been guaranteed that. I just want to get everything together before I make formal application. Once I do that, you see, MacPhail, it'll be common, public knowledge what I propose to do.'

'Ye'd not say it's common public knowledge now, Mr Morris?'

'Right now it's rumour, MacPhail. Gossip. Nobody can do anything based on gossip, pros or cons. And there's a lot of cons.'

MacPhail nodded. 'I have noticed that, to be sure.'

'We don't want that anti-lobby crystallizing until we know we're on to something worthwhile,' Morris pointed out.

'Ye mean ye do not know yet?'

'Today's the day. I'll be hearing from my people in London today. Then we'll have the go ahead. But I'd like some facts and figures out of you, first.'

'London,' MacPhail said reflectively. 'I've never been to London.'

'Haven't you?' Morris was astounded. MacPhail was one of the best known drilling engineers in the world.

'Never had a reason,' MacPhail said. 'They do say it's a terrible strange place, London.'

'I suppose you could say that.' Morris parked in the huge forecourt and strode towards the oaken doors. 'Where the devil is MacEwan? Guthrie!' he bawled 'Guthrie!'

MacPhail followed him into the baronial hall, looking around himself in some awe.

Guthrie appeared from the pantry. 'Ye called, Mr Morris?'

'Yes, I did. Where's Major MacEwan?'

'He was here,' Guthrie acknowledged. 'Then he said he had to go into Aboyne. Said he'd be back right after lunch.'

'I often wonder whether I am paying that fellow to look after my business or his own,' Morris grumbled. 'In here,

MacPhail.' He led the way into his office, glared at the empty fax machine. What the devil was Crowther doing? 'Have a seat. Drink?'

Macphail sat, somewhat cautiously, in one of the leather armchairs before the desk. 'I'd no' refuse a dram.'

Morris strode to the door. 'Guthrie! Guthrie! The bell never works,' he said over his shoulder. 'Or he never answers it. Whisky and water...scotch I presume?'

'Aye,' MacPhail said. 'But I dinna take the water.' He sounded as if Morris had suggested he should accept a bribe.

'Oh, right ho. And a G and T,' he told Guthrie, then returned behind the desk and sat down. 'Now tell me what we're talking about.'

'A test drill? What kind of depths were ye thinking of?'

'I'll be able to tell you for certain as soon as I hear from London. But let's take twelve thousand feet as a norm.'

MacPhail gave a low whistle. 'That's deep, for gas.'

'But not impossible?' Morris was anxious.

'Oh, no, man. We've drilled for oil at twice that depths. But ye ken, it's expensive.'

'What are we we talking about?'

MacPhail looked at the ceiling. 'The last oil field developed in the North Sea cost five hundred million. Pounds, ye ken.'

'*What* did you say?'

'Aye, it's expensive. Mind ye, Mr Morris, they'll hope to take ten times that in revenue.'

Morris leaned back in his chair. Five billion. His imagination could not quite cope with a figure like that.

'But we'll no be talking of that kind of money here,' MacPhail said, reassuringly. Morris sat up again. 'Well,' MacPhail said. 'Ye're on dry land, for a start. But ye'll still have the drilling and the piping. Oh, we'd be talking about half that.'

'And what kind of return?'

'Well, that depends on both the quantity and the quality. Ye'll have to get that from your chemists.'

'That's what I'm waiting on. But supposing it was a good, big field?'

'Aye, well, we'd be talking of about ten times again, to be sure.' Two and a half billion. He'd settle for that. 'Of course,' MacPhail said. 'It'll no cost ye that much to put down a test bore. No, no. On the other hand, if we test bore and there's nought there, well, that's your loss.' He peered at Morris, not wishing there to be any doubts on that score.

'I understand. Very good, Mr MacPhail, you prepare your plans and be ready to start drilling. I'm pretty certain we'll be going ahead, but I'll confirm in a couple of days. Maybe tomorrow.'

'Ah...' MacPhail accepted his glass of whisky from Guthrie, and waited until the butler had placed Bernard's gin and tonic on the desk and withdrawn again. 'Even setting it up isn't cheap.'

'You'll get paid,' Morris snapped. 'Don't harbour any doubts about whether I have the funds available.' He looked left and right, as if suggesting MacPhail might do the same.

'I'm a drilling engineer, Mr Morris,' MacPhail said. 'I'm no in the business of estimating people's financial standing. That's what banks are for. I'll settle for a guarantee from your bank.'

Morris frowned at him. 'In what amount?'

'Let's say a hundred grand.'

'A hundred thou...just to drill one hole?'

'Well, no. It'll no cost that much. But the bank guarantee will keep everybody happy, ye ken.'

'A hundred grand,' Morris muttered.

'It's no a problem?'

'Of course it isn't a problem. I'm just amazed at the way you people do business. Right. You'll get your guarantee.'

'That'll be grand. I'll be waiting to hearing from ye.' MacPhail finished his whisky and offered to shake hands as he stood up. Morris responded reluctantly.

The moment the door was closed Bernard was on the phone to London. 'What the hell is going on? I'd expected that fax to be on my desk by now.'

'I've nothing to fax,' Crowther explained.

'What?'

'Nothing's turned up yet. I called those blasted people Turnbull & Heath. Actually spoke to the active partner, chap called Heath. Well, I'd spoken to him before. He assures me that the report has been completed and mailed to me.'

'Mailed?' Bernard's voice rose an octave.

'I know. Shitting incompetent. But these people have no sense of urgency. Well, what would you expect; they're scientists, not businessmen. I asked to speak with this character Wilson, but was told he's had to go out of town for a day or two.'

'He has an assistant,' Bernard muttered.

'Ah. Shall I get back on to them and speak with her?'

'Waste of time. Never could stand blue-stocking females. I don't imagine she's got the authority or brains, anyway. You were supposed to meet Morant and his people this morning.'

'I've put them off. Told them we have something big coming off and can they hold it till Friday. They seemed agreeable.'

'Listen. You'll have to get back to

Morant. I need a guarantee of a hundred thousand, now.'

'I'm not sure he'll go for that, Bernie. They'll carry the existing can till the end of this week, because the OD is quiet. If I start asking for another wallop...'

'For Christ's sake, what's a hundred thou when we're sitting on millions?'

'We don't know that yet.'

'Of course we do. That asshole Wilson virtually told me so. I need that guarantee to set up a trial drill. We want to get this moving just as rapidly as possible.'

'What's the rush? If you get a favourable assessment from Turnbull & Heath the bank will certainly go along with you. That gas isn't going anywhere, even if it does have a little leak.'

Bernard raised his eyes to heaven. It always confounded him the way a genius like himself had to be surrounded by, and largely dependent on, utter morons. 'The rush is because, my dear Philip, while the cave where the gas was first found is on my property, we don't know that the whole gas field, or reservoir, or whatever, is. But if it's all in one reservoir, there is no reason why we shouldn't draw it all out through wells on Abergannan, even if some of the field is underneath somebody else's land. That possibility doesn't seem to have occurred to anyone else as yet, I suppose mainly because the land climbs into the mountains beyond Gannan Hill. But it is going to occur to someone, sooner or later. By the time that happens, I want us to be in full operation, pumping gas out of there just as fast as we can.'

'See what you mean,' Crowther said thoughtfully. 'I still don't think that, in all honesty, I can go back to Morant and ask for a guarantee without having that assessment to hand.'

'Well, even if the fools have mailed it, you'll have it tomorrow. Set up a meeting for then. And fax me a copy the very moment you receive it.'

He banged the receiver down and went into lunch, clearly in such an explosive mood that neither Margaret nor Niall dared speak to him.

'Have you heard from Rebecca?' he demanded as he stirred his coffee. 'She was supposed to be in touch by now.' He had given his elder daughter the task of sounding out her superiors just to make sure they were not, at any stage, going to attempt to throw a spanner in the works.

'Why, yes, dear,' Margaret said. 'She telephoned an hour ago.'

'What? Why wasn't I told?'

'You were with that engineer. I didn't want to interrupt anything.'

'Hm. Well, what did she say?'

'That she's flying up this afternoon.'

Bernard glared. 'Coming up here? Whatever for?'

'She didn't say. Just that she should be here this evening.'

'She said nothing else?'

'No, dear. Whatever is the matter.'

'There is just one goddam thing after another,' Bernard said and left the table, to look through the window and watch in amazement as the White Volvo Estate drove into the yard followed by two identical red Ford Fiestas from which emerged, respectively, James MacEwan, Gus Wilson, and Kitty Cochrane.

Bernard was at the front door before Guthrie. 'What the hell is going on?' he demanded. 'Where's my report?'

'We have it here, Mr Morris.' Gus tapped his briefcase.

Morris glared at him. 'You were supposed to let my accountant have it, this morning. Then I was told you'd posted it.'

'We thought we should present a copy to you, in person,' Gus explained.

Morris gave him another glare. 'You'd better come inside.'

Gus looked at James, who shrugged, and went back to the car.

'How did MacEwan know where to find you?' Morris asked, as he led Gus and Kitty into his office.

'He didn't. We happened to see him when we were having lunch in Aboyne, and he offered to lead the way up here.' Gus wanted to keep things as simple as possible. He opened his briefcase and laid the document on the desk. 'It's all there.'

Morris glanced at it, then raised his head. 'This is all mumbo jumbo to me. What does it mean.'

'There are four important factors to be considered, Mr Morris,' Gus said. 'All of them are as we feared would be the case after our preliminary examination of the site.'

'Feared?' Morris snapped.

'The first is the extreme depths of the base reservoir,' Gus went on, ignoring the interruption.

'What depths?'

'We estimate four thousand metres. That is something in excess of twelve thousand feet.'

Morris snorted. 'So what's new? You suggested that figure when you were here. And I can tell you that I have taken expert advice, and drilling twelve thousand feet is no problem at all.'

Gus glanced at Kitty, who was prepared

to take up the tale. 'Of course it isn't, Mr Morris. However, to move on to the second factor, due either to some movement of the earth, or to the porous nature of the rock, there has been considerable upward seepage of the gas.'

Morris frowned. 'You trying to tell me the reservoir is empty?'

'By no means. Very little of the gas has escaped into the atmosphere, because its exit has been blocked, for thousands, perhaps millions of years. Now that blockage is being eroded, by water.'

'Once again, you're repeating yourself. So every time the water level falls a little gas escapes. That's why I want to get at the reservoir before we lose any more.'

'What we are trying to explain, Mr Morris, is that because of these eons of seepage into every last nook and cranny, Gannan Hill is itself one vast gas reservoir, if you like.'

'You mean I don't have to drill more than a few feet? Well, that's great news.'

'You will have to drill right down to the reservoir to obtain gas in any quantity,' Gus resumed. 'However, the drilling bit, and the casing, will be passing through rock which may be filled with gas.'

'And that is a problem?'

'It could be, bearing in mind the other two factors.'

'Well?'

'Factor Three is that our calculations have convinced us that the gas in the reservoir is at a very high pressure, about twice the norm.'

'You mean there's too much gas for the reservoir? Despite the seepage?' Morris asked.

'That is a possible reason, certainly. There could be others. It may be even deeper than four thousand metres. As you go deeper, the pressure increases.'

'I'll go for that one. But it still isn't a problem. As far as I'm concerned, that's terrific. Right?'

'Not necessarily,' Kitty said, 'Especially having regard to the final factor.'

'Which is?'

'The methane readings are unusually high, even at the surface or just beneath it, where we took them.'

'So?'

'Do you know anything of the quality of methane, Mr Morris?'

'I know it's called swamp gas.'

'That's true. And it is the principal component of natural gas. It is what makes it burn.'

'As you have told me already. Seventy-five per cent, right?'

'Or a little more. The methane content in Gannan Hill, again taken near the surface, is eighty-four per cent. That is very high.'

'This means,' Gus went on, 'that it could be dangerous. As I said, methane burns readily, but is normally a stable gas. That is at its normal content in air of less than five per cent. More than five per cent, and it becomes explosive, as many a coal miner has found out to his cost. And as that unfortunate girl and boy discovered. The gas in that cave was very diluted. But it still exploded. Our calculations indicate a methane percentage in the air inside Gannan Hill of thirteen per cent at the time of the accident. That is very nearly as concentrated as you will find anywhere.'

Morris looked from face to face. 'So we'll ban smoking on site.'

Gus sighed. 'It's not quite as simple as that. You are proposing to drive a bit through that mountain, and as I said, the bit will have to be protected by a casing. This all has to be metal. When you start driving metal through rock, there are certain to be sparks. If one of those sparks occurs while the drill is passing through a methane pocket, well...'

'Well, what? You mean there could be an explosion.'

'Yes.

'Right. So we have an explosion.'

'It could be quite a big one,' Gus said mildly.

'Oh, yes? So we have a big explosion. I'll warn my people of the possibility of that.'

'Mr Morris,' Kitty leaned forward. 'We are talking about a *big* explosion. You could set off a mini earthquake.'

Gus cleared his throat. Morris looked at him. 'You believe that?'

'Well...it is certainly a possibility.'

'But nothing more than that. A possibility.'

'No!' Kitty shouted. 'It is a probability. It is almost a certainty.'

Morris continued to look at Gus, whose cheeks were pink. 'There are a lot of imponderables,' Gus muttered.

'Possibility, probability...' Morris snorted. 'Let's get down to cases. What are the chances of an explosion if I start drilling for that gas?'

'Ah...' Gus looked at Kitty, who held her breath. 'I would say the possibility of some kind of explosion could be put as high as ten per cent.'

'Ten per cent,' Morris said.

'Gus!' Kitty shouted. 'You know it's more than that!'

Morris raised his eyebrows. 'What would be your estimate, Miss Cochrane?'

'I'd go as high as fifty per cent. Certainly

not less than twenty-five.'

'Now, Kitty...' Gus protested.

Morris looked from one to the other, smiling. 'Now, Professor, you say there is a one in ten chance that there could be some kind of explosion as a result of drilling. I assume you are referring to a minor event. What is the percentage risk, in your opinion, of there being a major explosion?'

'Well...' Gus hedged. 'As I said, there are a lot of imponderables, such as the amount of methane present where the explosion took place, the density of the rock in which it was situated, the depths, obviously...'

'I'd like a figure.'

'On the chances of a major explosion? I'd have to go as high as five per cent.' Kitty drew a deep breath.

'Five per cent,' Morris said with total satisfaction. 'One in twenty. Right, now let's get down to the fantasy of setting off an earthquake. Give me a figure on *that.*'

'Oh,' Gus said. 'Well...that is going it a bit.'

'I see. You don't really believe there is the slightest possibility of that, do you?'

'Well...it's never happened before.'

'That's because we've never had a situation like this before,' Kitty snapped, with a growing sense of both betrayal and desperation. 'It can happen. I believe it *will* happen. You want figures, Mr Morris? I was hedging just now. I believe that if you start drilling there *will* be an explosion. The realistic percentage is one hundred. A total certainty. OK, you might just get away with a small, local explosion, which would cost you some gear. But the odds on *that* are hardly better than five per cent. You might just get away with a big bang which would entirely destroy your drilling rig and could cost a couple of lives. There's your fifty per cent. But you could just set off the entire environs of Abergannan. And there's a better than ten per cent chance of *that*.'

'I see.' Morris continued to smile. 'This is your professional opinion, based on the information you have accrued.'

'It is my professional opinion, based on the information we have *not* been able to accrue,' Kitty retorted. 'We do know that there is gas escaping from the reservoir up various fissures inside Gannan Hill. What we do not know is whether there are other fissures or passageways through which gas is also escaping to form sub-reservoirs, but which thus far have not been eroded sufficiently to allow the gas to escape. Therefore that gas could be filling those sub-reservoirs at the same enormous pressure as obtains in the base reservoir. In those circumstances, we cannot tell how far a fire, started in say the area we explored, would spread. One thing is certain, though: it would spread very quickly and very explosively.'

Morris turned to Gus. 'You go along with this doomsday scenario?'

Gus was looking thoroughly unhappy. 'Of course it's possible, Mr Morris.'

'But you don't believe it.'

'Well...' Gus bit his lip. 'It's never happened before,' he repeated.

'Absolutely.'

'But you cannot take the risk!' Kitty thumped the desk.

'I will of course discuss what you have said with my mining engineer,' Morris said. 'However, I am bound to tell you, Miss Cochrane, that I am more inclined to take the opinion of your superior than accept your somewhat hysterical depiction of nearly impossible events. In the meantime, I wish it clearly understood that our conversation here today is strictly confidential, and is not to be repeated under any circumstances until and unless I give you permission to do so.'

'You mean that despite the risks you intend going ahead?' Kitty asked, before Gus could get a word in.

'Yes,' Morris replied.

Chapter 7

CONFLICT

'In that case,' Gus said, standing up, 'there is nothing more to be said.' Kitty opened her mouth and then shut it again. 'We have to get back to Aboyne,' Gus went on. 'I have to arrange somewhere to stay.'

'My dear fellow,' Morris said, expansively content now that he had, in his opinion, shot these two boffins down in flames. 'You'll both stay here, of course.' Also, he reckoned, it would be better to have them where he could keep an eye on them.

'I already have a place, Mr Morris,' Kitty said, trying to keep the mixture of anger and despair that was threatening to explode at any moment, under control.

'Cancel it,' Morris said. 'I'll send into Aboyne for your gear. We'll expect you for dinner.' He strode to the door and flung it open. 'Guthrie! MacEwan!'

Kitty shot a look of intense anger at Gus.

He felt himself wilting. 'We did what we had to do. There's absolutely no point losing your rag,' he hissed. 'And there is nothing either you or I could have said which would have affected the decision.'

'Ah, MacEwan,' Morris was saying. 'I'd like you to drive into Aboyne to pick up Miss Cochrane's things from wherever it is she was staying. And then perhaps you'd be good enough to go over to Aberdeen Airport and meet my daughter. She's arriving on the shuttle this afternoon.'

'Oh, I'll meet Becky, Dad,' Niall said, coming along the hall. 'Hello, Kitty. Gus. Didn't know you were here.' Which Kitty found hard to believe. 'Perhaps you'd care to drive into Aberdeen with me?' Niall asked.

'No, thanks,' Kitty said, still flushed with anger, 'I'm afraid I need to go and collect my gear myself, and pay for my lodgings, for a start.'

'Well, sort yourselves out,' Morris said. He could hear the fax machine whirring behind him and wanted to get at it. He virtually pushed Gus and Kitty through the doorway, closed the door, and hurried to the printer.

After the copy of the report, Crowther had written:

> 'I'm afraid this puts us up the creek without a paddle, and I've a meeting with Morant at five. Perhaps you'd advise me exactly what I am supposed to tell him?'

Morris sat behind his desk and picked up his phone. 'Listen,' he said. 'We're not up any creeks, except one paved with pound notes.'

'Haven't you read the report?' Crowther asked.

'I have done more than that. I have had Wilson sitting the other side of my desk going through it with me.'

'That's even worse than I thought. What am I to tell Morant?'

'Forget the negatives. You simply play up the relevant positives. What we have is a huge reservoir so stuffed with gas it is maintaining a pressure way beyond the norm, despite the fact that it is seeping out at the surface. So the methane content is also higher than the average. That means the gas is far more saleable than normal.'

He could almost see Crowther frowning as he spoke. 'Wilson tell you all this?'

'In a word, yes.' His lower left eyelid developed an involuntary twitch.

'And what about the risk of an explosion?'

'Some crazy idea of that idiot assistant of his, a stupid bimbo who's out to make a name for herself by creating waves. Wilson himself flatly opposes the idea of an explosion. He puts the figure as possibly one in twenty. No higher. He had to list every possible danger in his report, otherwise in the very remote chance that there were to be an accident involving the gas his firm could be sued for negligence.'

'That's what he said?' Crowther was still cautious.

'I am quoting his very words,' Morris lied. The twitching increased.

'Well, of course I'll put all that to Morant...'

'You can also tell Morant that I have had Archie MacPhail out here...'

'Who?'

'You've never heard of Archie MacPhail?'

'I'm afraid not. And I very much doubt that Morant has, either.'

'Well, then, you can both look him up. He is a top drilling expert. He was here and pronounced everything was to his satisfaction. He's assembling his gear now, and can start at any time. But being a true Scot he wants the cash guarantee. Don't let me down on this, Philip.'

Crowther could not help but be inspired by such ebullient confidence, especially when it was supported by an expert.

'I won't let you down,' he said.

Having talked Kitty into letting him drive her into Aboyne, James was aware of her tension as they cruised down the narrow mountain road.

He didn't know whether to be pleased or sorry: he genuinely liked both Gus and Kitty even if he didn't like the situation their work was likely to bring about. The discord between them as they left the castle separately was obvious, and he was left wondering what had happened.

'Seems to me Morris was in a surprisingly good humour,' he ventured, 'for a man just told his scheme isn't on.'

'His scheme *is* on,' Kitty snapped.

The car swerved. 'You mean he's going ahead? But didn't you tell him the facts?'

'We did, and he made his decision.'

'In spite of what you had to say?'

'*Because* of what we had to say.' There was a bitter edge to her voice. 'Why don't you ask Gus about it?'

From which James realized that Gus hadn't backed her fears as much as she'd hoped. So that was it. He concentrated on the road, drawing up outside the modest house with a Bed and Breakfast sign in the window. 'I thought you were planning to spend tonight here?' he said.

'I have been invited to spend it at the castle,' Kitty replied. 'So, as soon as I've packed my stuff and paid Mrs Logan, I propose to return there.'

He got out. 'I'll carry your bag down.'

'Thanks,' she said without smiling.

James scratched his head. 'Why are you

so upset? Was it a particularly difficult meeting?'

'Yes. For me.'

'Come again?'

'Gus and I had a difference of professional opinion. I told Morris if he touched that mountain it would explode; Gus refused to go along with me.'

James gave a little whistle. 'Will it? Explode, I mean.'

'It could.'

'Ah.'

'Don't you start,' Kitty snapped. 'OK, maybe I went over the top. But I *know* there's a real danger. And nobody is prepared to listen to me.'

'I am,' James said quietly.

She glanced at him, and allowed a thin smile to reach her eyes. She was in need of a friend. 'So what do we do? Start a day and night vigil on Gannan Hill? Lie down in front of the bulldozer and tell his drilling expert, you shall not pass, and wait to be removed by the police? I've always been against that kind of protest, not least because rent-a-mob invariably manage to muscle in and start trouble.'

'I'm with you on that,' he agreed. 'But there are other ways of making your opposition known. Like, I happen to know there's a meeting right here in Aboyne, this afternoon. To discuss the situation.'

‘Inspired by whom?’ She was immediately suspicious.

‘Not by me,’ he rounded, defensively. ‘But it’s become pretty common knowledge that Morris is planning some kind of development around Gannan Hill, and the Greens have got hold of it. They’ve been invited to send someone up to discuss the situation with concerned locals, and I believe their prospective candidate for Parliament is coming. I’ve an idea some of the local council will be there, too. If you were to turn up...’

Kitty shook her head. ‘I don’t think that would be a very good idea.’

‘Why not?’

‘Firstly, because Morris has invited me to spend the night at the castle and I have accepted, if only to monitor anything else that is said and possibly restart the discussion. I couldn’t expect to get any sort of a hearing if it was known I’d been to a meeting to raise opposition, even if only on the grounds of environmental issues.’

‘I don’t follow that. Do you have to agree with everything your client proposes? We’ve already established that you don’t agree with Morris on *anything.*’

Kitty leaned on the bonnet of the Volvo, sighed and shrugged. ‘I still foster some hope that I could influence him, if only through his family. Otherwise, I wouldn’t be going back there.' She pulled at her hair. 'If I went to this meeting, I certainly wouldn't be able to say anything against the proposed drilling without wrecking my chances with them.'

'Why? Morris knows your point of view. You can agree to differ.'

She gave a cynical laugh. 'I can. He couldn't and wouldn't. He'd make a hell of a stink.'

'And would that leave you in any worse position than you are now?'

Kitty gave up on that one. 'All right. But supposing I did go to this meeting. I wouldn't be able to reveal any of my findings; they're still confidential, and Morris has insisted that they remain so. That applies to you, too, by the way.'

'Surely you could present an anti point of view, without revealing any figures? The mere fact that you, as a geo-chemist, are against drilling should carry a lot of weight.'

The argument could go on ad infinitum. Kitty let her eyes drift towards James' face, then quickly averted them. The trouble was she liked this huge Scot too much...more than liked him, and found herself disconcertingly attracted to him. Which wasn't going to help her make a sane and logical decision. 'Are you going?' she asked.

'I will if you will.' His grey-green eyes met hers, challenging.

Which made things worse. But she grinned. 'We could both wind up getting fired.'

'Might be worth it, if we could stop Morris.'

She had never really considered anything as drastic as that.

'In any event,' he pointed out. 'It can't be a bad idea to hear what the opposition has to say, whether or not we decide to join them. Then we can go out to the castle afterwards.'

'I'll get my gear,' Kitty said.

'Guess who I have with me?' Niall asked, opening the door of his father's study.

Bernard looked up in irritation at the interruption—he had spent the last hour glaring at his fax machine, willing it to deliver what he wanted—but decided to smile as he saw not one, but both of his daughters. 'An invasion,' he remarked.

'Oh, Daddy, darling, I just had to come.' Tara swept round his desk to give him a hug and a kiss. 'I'm broke,' she whispered in his ear. Bernard gave her an affectionate squeeze. He could have wished she didn't spend money like water, but if Crowther came good it wouldn't matter.

'Surprise,' Rebecca said, remaining on

the far side of the desk. Bernard realized she was accompanied by a man, who looked far too old and withered to be a boyfriend. 'This is Mr Bartlett,' Rebecca said. 'From the Ministry.'

'Eh?' Bernard stood up.

'I was talking to Mr Bartlett about your project,' Rebecca said. 'And he said he'd like to see for himself.' She smiled sweetly at her father, which he assumed was meant to indicate that if Mr Bartlett approved, a certificate was a certainty.

Morris smoothed his hair back and hurried round the desk to shake hands. 'Welcome,' he said.

'This is a very nice place you have here,' Bartlett remarked.

'One tries to improve one's quality of life,' Bernard said expansively.

'I thought we might drive Mr Bartlett out to Gannan Hill now,' Rebecca suggested.

Bernard glanced at her. He still was not absolutely sure in his mind whether his eldest daughter was a hundred per cent for the scheme so he certainly could not risk her taking Bartlett out there on her own, and maybe prejudicing him the wrong way. 'Good idea,' he said. 'I'll just get my coat.'

By the time Bernard returned, an hour later, the fax had been busy. He tore off the print-out with trembling fingers, sat down to scan the words, and felt an enormous glow of relief spreading through his entire body. There was the guarantee, with almost a promise that all the further money necessary would be forthcoming the moment the reservoir was actually tapped.

He ran a finger round the inside of his collar and leaned back in his chair the better to savour the moment. Of course there were hurdles ahead and he didn't know for sure how high they might be. Bartlett, for one. The environmentalist had been most interested in everything he had seen, apparently impressed by the way the area had been fenced off, had uttered not a word of criticism, raised not a single objection, during his brief tour of inspection. But while he had indicated neither approval nor disapproval of the project, he had clearly also been impressed by the natural beauty of the site. Thus he could be a problem. But only a slight one, Bernard was determined.

He marched to the door. 'Guthrie!' He did not shout quite so loudly as usual.

Mary appeared. 'Mr Guthrie is not available, reet noo.'

'Very well, can you tell me where Mr Bartlett is?'

'I showed him to his room, Mr Morris.

I believe he has remained there. Nay doot he will be dressing for dinner.'

'Right. Now Mary, I wish you to get hold of my wife, and all the children, quietly, and tell them I wish to see them all in the study. Now.' The elderly maid's expression didn't alter as she went to do her employer's bidding.

Margaret was first to arrive. She hated being at Bernard's beck and call but dreaded his angry outbursts if she didn't click heels to order. She was bored. At least in London there were friends to meet up with, shopping to be enjoyed and masses of super restaurants to try. Here there was nothing. Part of the original idea of a Scottish castle had been to provide an oversized 'weekend cottage', a place for entertaining house guests on a grand scale.

However, over the past year that scenario had dwindled into a sort of glorified bolt-hole for Bernard to escape London business pressures. And where they had walked, talked and taken drives out into the Highlands together for a while, now business had followed them and Bernard spent most of his time in his study...when he wasn't eating, drinking, snoring or shouting at somebody. Which left her alone all day, every day, her only activity being an attempt to dodge the flak when something, or somebody, sparked off his increasingly volatile temper.

When she had been able to indulge her interest in interior decorating and transform each room in studied, authentic style, loneliness had never bothered her. But Bernard had put a sudden stop to all that...almost as if they'd run out of funds...

'Where are the others?' Bernard demanded impatiently.

'I have no idea,' she answered pleasantly.

'Why on earth not? Surely you know what they're doing. They are your children.'

'They were *our* children, but they are now adults and free to come and go as they please.' She smiled, speaking calmly, masking her resentment at his tone. If only he knew how sometimes she cursed him, silently. Even hated him.

The door swung open and Rebecca bounced in. Her spots had vanished, either with better diet or heavier make-up, and she appeared to have lost some weight. 'Mary says you want to see me, Daddy.'

'Yes. Sit down.' Her father didn't look up.

Rebecca raised questioning eyebrows at her mother. Margaret shrugged and spread her hands, helplessly. The silence hung in the air, oppressively. Ridiculously. As though Bernard was a headmaster and they were recalcitrant pupils. 'If you're not ready for us we can come back later, Daddy. I was in the middle of writing an article...'

'No. Just wait.' He leaned back in his chair, fingertips drumming on the desk.

Niall was next. He looked at his mother and sister and said, 'Hallo! Is this a family conference?'

And was surprised when his father answered, 'Yes.'

Bernard was looking at his watch, again, comparing it with the sunburst clock, when Tara drifted in. 'At last. Now we can begin. I want to speak to you all about my plans for developing the gas field here at Abergannan.'

'Why, Daddy? We don't have to be involved in the technicalities, do we?' Tara was examining the colour of the nail varnish she had been trying out when Mary delivered the summons.

'Will you just let me talk, please?' He gave his younger daughter an unusually severe frown. 'There is enough gas up there to make us all mega-rich for the rest of our lives...all we have to do is get it out and market it.'

Niall rubbed his palms together. 'I just can't wait to get started,' he began, but was silenced by Bernard's expression.

'Needless to say, there are always people around who will try to find fault with any new or proposed project...people who are jealous, resentful of others whose hard work makes them appear more fortunate than themselves. People who enjoy trying to put a spanner in the works, just for the hell of it.' He leaned across the desk, staring at them each in turn. 'We are going to be surrounded by these people for weeks: gutless little people whose only lift in life is belittling others' efforts. People who will invent problems where there are none. So we,' he smiled for the first time, in encouragement, 'we in this family have got to stick together. Back each other up. I want your undivided, unstinting support in the face of all and any opposition from whatever quarter.' He continued to smile. 'Understand?'

'Yes, dear.' Margaret reckoned she understood only too well. No matter what anyone else's thoughts or feelings might be on the matter, he would demand one hundred per cent support from his family while he rode rough-shod over the lot.

Following her mother's lead, Tara said, 'Yes, Daddy.' She hadn't actually heard what he'd been saying, but she had decided that this colour had a fraction too much pink in it to wear with the new Donaghue suit. The Dior varnish would be better.

Niall bounced up and down on his chair. 'Absolutely, Pa. Christ, I can't wait to begin.' He couldn't truly imagine anyone in the world opposing this fantastic development.

Bernard turned to face Rebecca, waiting. She shifted uncomfortably on her chair. 'What makes you so convinced, Daddy, that this scheme of yours is right?'

'Right? Of course it's right! What could possibly be wrong with it?' A question he immediately regretted.

'The transforming of a fantastic area of natural beauty into a scene of total devastation...' she began.

'Rubbish! We are talking about extracting gas by pipeline, not opencast coal mining.' He laughed at her childishness.

'...and bringing high-tech industry into a rural district...'

'So what? Give these local yokels a bit of work to do for a change.'

'...plus increasing the density of the population by about a thousandfold,' Rebecca continued, earning admiration from her mother but antagonism from the other three.

'Surely that will bring more business to local shops and other industries,' Niall suggested. 'I really can't see any reason...'

'Of course you can't,' his sister hissed at him. 'You are to be part of the operation.

Made to feel important. Naturally you want it all to happen, and you refuse to accept there can be any rational arguments against—'

'There aren't any, Rebecca!' Her father rounded on her. 'This is the kind of disloyalty I had hoped to avoid...'

'I can see that. What I don't see is why on earth you are so determined to destroy this community...'

Bernard jumped out of his chair. 'Will you shut up this sentimental claptrap! What you don't see would fill a book!'

Rebecca stood up to face him. 'Why, Daddy? Why? It's not as though we *need* all that money...' Her eyes suddenly narrowed. 'Is it?'

The two stood glaring at each other, but it was Bernard who dropped his eyes to his desk. His chest heaved as he sucked in a deep breath, and sat down.

He nodded at her, indicating the chair behind her, and she too, sat. 'Yes. We do. That is the crux of the matter.' He looked at the four faces in front him, over steepled fingers, wondering just how much to tell them. But only for a few moments.

It didn't take long to conclude that the news that they stood to lose all the luxuries they had accumulated over the past twenty years if this deal didn't come off, would bring their united and hundred per cent support, as he had asked. He hadn't wanted them to know the extent of his failure, but better that, ensuring their backing, than risk their opposition causing a total financial collapse.

'I'm afraid I have had a couple of very big deals go sour on me, recently, leaving several of my companies with a serious cash deficiency.' He smiled expansively, spreading his hands. 'Of course you realize that this sort of problem arises in all big businesses. The bigger the business, in fact, the bigger the problems. So you see this gas project is urgently needed to put us back on track.'

Niall was frowning, nodding wisely. Tara, having caught the drift, sat with her beautiful mouth hanging open, while her mother pursed her lips as the various inexplicable happenings of recent months fell into place.

Rebecca remained silent. There were a million things that could, should be said. But maybe with Daddy, with the whole family under financial pressure, now was not the time.

Bernard stood up again. 'Well? Do I have your support?'

One by one, reluctantly or otherwise, they nodded their agreement.

'Shall I put the kettle on?' Kitty asked.

They were back at the cottage again. With an hour to kill before the meeting, a cup of tea seemed to make sense.

'Thanks. I'll switch on the electric fire.'

In the tiny kitchen Kitty had found a tray, a pair of chipped mugs with the faces of the Prince and Princess of Wales printed on, and some Dundee cake in a tin. 'It is enchanting here,' Kitty remarked, eyes roaming over the old dresser tucked tight under the beams, and uneven wooden lintels over tiny windows. 'How old is it?'

'Depends which bit you're looking at. My mother told me that my grandfather was born here, that's on my father's side, but as to the date...I don't know. Some self-confessed expert who told me he could sell it for me any time I wanted, dated it to late seventeenth century. Not much more than one room with a thin partition across the middle, in those days.'

'And a privy out back,' Kitty added.

'That's right. Still there, built over the stream so that everything washed down the valley to the sea. Come and look.' Laughing, his guest allowed herself to be led down the mossy stone path to the tiny wooden hut at the bottom. 'See?' He swung the door open. 'You step onto the platform, select the one you want to use and remove the lid.' He lifted one of the wooden discs.

'Why are there three holes in a row?'

'Well, more than one person might get taken short at the same time,' he grinned.

'And all sat side by side!'

'Have you never visited the public loos at Ephesus?'

'You mean the ancient city? No, can't say I have.'

'Made of marble. And the wealthy would send a servant down ahead to warm a seat for him or her. Sat about twenty round the room at one time.' He closed the door as they emerged.

'Sounds revolting! But tell me, do you entertain all your visitors in the privy?'

The garden was attractively wild, only a small area of grass cut near the house. Spring bulbs were pushing their spiky leaves up through the soil, and buds were fattening on the trees.

'If you turn round and face the back of the cottage you can see the newer bits added on to the side,' James said. 'That's my bedroom, now, but when I was a kid I used to sleep in the attic. Now I wouldn't be able to get off my knees.'

'I notice you have to duck through every doorway.'

'Unfortunately I don't always remember.' He rubbed the top of his head ruefully. 'Let's go see if that kettle is boiling yet.'

Kitty didn't sit down immediately, but wandered about the little living-room, admiring some of the ornaments, reading the titles in the bookcase. 'Don't you get lonely here, all by yourself?'

'Sometimes.'

'Which times?'

'When I meet someone I imagine I'd like to share the place with.'

Kitty's head jerked up to stare at him, but he turned away.

'There's a bit of fruit cake left in the tin. Like some?'

The school hall was full, but as Kitty and James were a few minutes late they were able to slip in at the back virtually unnoticed. On the platform there was a surprisingly attractive looking middle-aged woman, smartly-dressed and clearly articulate, a local vicar, two men Kitty had never seen before...and the man, Jock, who had verbally attacked her in the pub.

She gave an involuntary jerk at the sight of him, and James squeezed her hand. 'Damn cheek his being here at all,' he whispered. 'His environmental record is zilch.'

They remained standing, as there were no chairs left.

The meeting had already been called to order, and was being addressed by the woman. 'I have not been out there myself,' she was saying, 'although I intend to visit the site tomorrow. However, I have read your newspapers, and discussed the situation with the Reverend Sangster and with Mr Petersen...' she paused to smile at Jock, 'and I can well understand your concern. This area of Scotland has already suffered a great deal of environmental damage because of North Sea oil...'

'It's had a lot o' prosperity as well,' someone declared.

Kitty raised her eyebrows. She hadn't expected to find a pro-Morris faction here.

'Prosperity can sometimes be too dearly bought,' the Green Party lady retorted. 'In any event, while North Sea gas and North Sea oil may have been of some benefit to Great Britain, I understand that this Abergannan field, which by the very nature of its situation cannot be very extensive, is the property of one man who intends to develop it to his own profit. It isn't as if there is any shortage of natural gas at this moment in time.' Kitty winced at the professional political phrase. 'There is thus no necessity to desecrate an area of such outstanding natural beauty merely, as I understand it, for the sake of lining the pockets of one man who is already a millionaire.'

'Is no the Queen, God bless her, drilling

for oil in Windsor Castle?' someone called.

Kitty looked between the rows of heads and shoulders to see who had spoken and gasped. She nudged James. 'That was Guthrie!'

James nodded, whispering back, 'I guessed he'd be here.'

'Nae in the castle itsel', ye daftie,' someone replied to Guthrie's question.

The prospective MP drank some water, and seemed prepared to reply to the dissidents when Jock Petersen suddenly stood up. 'Spies!' he bawled. The Green Party lady put down her glass with a thump, now looking distinctly alarmed. 'I see you!' Peterson shouted, pointing at James and Kitty as heads turned.

' 'Tis the wee scientist,' someone observed.

'May we ask what you are doing here?' demanded Petersen.

'We understood this was a public meeting,' James said, mildly.

'Oh, aye, Major? So ye came along to hear what was said so that ye could report back to that employer of yours.'

'My opposition to Mr Morris's plans are fairly well known,' James replied, still mildly.

'Oh, aye? And what about yon scientist? She's behind the whole thing.'

'That is rubbish,' Kitty declared. 'My

company was employed by Mr Morris to investigate the possibilities of there being a gas reservoir beneath Gannan Hill. That is all we were required to do. There *is* a gas reservoir beneath Gannan Hill, and we have reported so. That is all we have done.'

'And why are ye returned the noo?' Petersen demanded. 'Is it no' to give Morris the go ahead?'

The Green Party lady was hurriedly conferring with the men Kitty had not seen before.

'Miss Cochrane has returned to Abergannan, with her colleague Professor Wilson, to give Mr Morris her report in person,' James said. Kitty gave a warning tug on his sleeve. She didn't want him saying more than that.

The people on the platform had come to a decision. One of the men stood up. 'Would you, Miss...' he glanced at Petersen.

'The lass's name is Cochrane,' he said.

'Miss Cochrane. Would you be prepared to take questions from the floor?'

'His name is Hamish Hamilton, and he's a clerk at the Town Hall,' James whispered. 'He's also a pal of Guthrie's.'

Kitty hesitated for the briefest of moments, gave James a glance, and squared her shoulders. 'As long as I am not required to breach the terms of client confidentiality.'

'Would you join us on the platform?'

'Certainly,' Kitty responded and went forward. James followed. He did not attempt to mount the platform, but remained at the foot of the steps, leaning against the wall, but very obviously assuming a protective role. Or was it, Kitty wondered, proprietorial? Either way, she was glad he was there.

'I'm Hamish Hamilton, Miss Cochrane,' the smaller of the two men said. 'I'm chairing this meeting. 'Tis good of ye to attend.'

'Miss Cochrane, I'm Ethel Yardley, the Green Party representative.' They shook hands. 'And this is Bill Buckston, my agent.' Another handclasp. 'Now...' Ethel Yardley faced the somewhat restless assembly. 'Here we have a...' she glanced at Kitty.

'I am a geo-chemist,' Kitty said.

'A professional geo-chemist, employed by Mr Morris, to discover gas. This she has done. Does your brief, your profession indeed, Miss Cochrane, ever take environmental problems into consideration?'

'Only if we are required to do so,' Kitty said.

'But you were not required to in this case?'

'We were not.'

'But...having visited the site, and done whatever you do, and discovered that there is a gas reservoir beneath Gannan Hill, did you not find reason to stop and consider the natural beauty that would be destroyed by exploitation?'

'Yes,' Kitty said. 'We did.'

'But it made no difference to your recommendation that drilling commence.'

'It made no difference to the compiling of our report,' Kitty said carefully. 'We were employed to do a job of work, and I repeat that is what we did.' There was a murmur of condemnation around the room.

'However,' Kitty resumed, slightly raising her voice, 'although we could do nothing more, in writing, than state our findings, the reason why I returned to Abergannan, with my colleague Professor Wilson...' —Gus was going to shoot her for this, but he had brought it on himself— '...was to advise Mr Morris, verbally, that in our opinion he should not proceed with the project.'

There was a brief silence; she had taken the wind out of all their sails. Then James started to clap, and the whole hall suddenly swelled with approbation. Even Jock Petersen, after some hesitation, joined in. Ethel Yardley waited for the applause to die down. 'You are to be congratulated, Miss Cochrane, on your public spiritedness. So, may we assume that Mr Morris accepted your recommendation?'

'No, he did not,' Kitty said.

Voices were raised all round the room. 'Ah, well, then,' Ethel Yardley had to shout to make herself heard, 'there is nothing left for us to do but picket Abergannan Estate. We'll see if we can obtain support from the media, and from the sitting MP, and thus generally attempt to make Mr Morris sit up and take notice.'

'A fat lot of good that'll do,' Jock declared, 'The man's got no sensitivity at all.' No one in his audience was prepared to argue with that.

Kitty looked at James, then took a deep breath. 'I entirely agree with Mr Petersen...' she nodded in his direction and left him speechless with surprise, 'that Mr Morris is not interested in either the beauty of his property or the protection of the environment. I also agree that he is not the sort of man to be swayed by appeals, either to his personal sensitivity or to his responsibility to the people of Glen Tanar; he would say that he has no responsibility to anyone save himself, where his own property is concerned.

For that reason, appeals to your local MP, to the Department of the Environment, even a national newspaper campaign, based purely on the environment, is unlikely to do anything more than make him angry and thus more determined to go ahead with his plan. However, I do believe there is ground on which he can be fought, and perhaps successfully.'

She paused to look over the faces below her; now she had their entire attention. She gave James another glance; he had stopped leaning against the wall, was standing straight and attentive. 'The reason my colleague and I recommended to Mr Morris that he should not attempt to drill for gas on Gannan Hill had nothing to do with the environment, per se. It was, and remains, because we feel that, owing both to the disposition of the gas field and its chemical composition, drilling could be an extremely hazardous and potentially catastrophic business.'

There was a moment of silence while her listeners tried to assimilate what she had said, then everyone was muttering to their neighbour.

A young man with reporter stamped all over him, who had been sitting at the back of the hall, patently bored, suddenly came to life and began to write vigorously.

Buckston swallowed. 'Perhaps you would

care to be more specific, Miss Cochrane,' he suggested.

'I'm afraid I can't be more specific,' Kitty told him, 'because that would be to breach client confidentiality. However, knowing that a report outlining the very real dangers of drilling for gas on Abergannan exists, if you were able to bring pressure to bear, either through the media or through a question in Parliament, sufficient to cause it to be required that that report should be made public, then you might well have an answer to your problems.'

Another brief silence. 'You of course know what is in this report?' Ethel Yardley asked.

'I drew it up.'

Miss Yardley's mouth fell open in surprise. There was a rustle round the hall.

'Yet ye canna tell us what was in it,' Jock Petersen remarked.

'No, I cannot, unless I am given permission to do so by Mr Morris...'

'Fat chance of that.'

'Or I am required to divulge the contents by a court order.'

'Well,' said Miss Yardley. 'I am bound to say that this is a quite unexpected development. I am sure you will agree with me that Miss Cochrane has shown us by far the most advantageous way forward. May I suggest we now wind up this meeting. I will investigate what can be done to make this business public. However,' she went on, as people began to stand up and pull on their coats, 'I do not think we can leave without offering a vote of thanks to Miss Cochrane for her very valuable support.'

There was another round of applause, and Miss Yardley shook Kitty's hand. 'Would you care to come over to the pub with me for a drink? You and Mr er...'

'MacEwan,' James said.

'I don't think we should,' Kitty said. 'I would say I have caused enough mayhem for one evening.'

'I understand. But would you mind giving me a phone number or address? I would like to stay in touch.'

'No problem,' Kitty said, trying not to smile at the inappropriate cliche. 'Have you something I can write on?'

Ethel Yardley hurried away with two bulging cardboard files under her arm. Kitty took her coat from the back of a chair and was about to follow when she heard her name. 'Miss Cochrane,' said the reporter from the floor of the hall beneath them. 'Some questions, if you please.'

'No questions,' Kitty said.

'Well, then, a photograph...'

'Definitely not.'

'But Miss Cochrane...'

'Willie,' James said, standing above the young man, 'the lady has said no. And when this lady says no, she doesn't mean maybe.' Willie gulped, and backed off. 'I think we should get out of here,' James suggested.

Kitty nodded, and he escorted her out to the Volvo. There were still several people gathered outside the hall, all wanting to talk to her.

'How to achieve instant popularity,' James muttered, as he got her seated and started the engine.

'Are you coming up to the house for dinner?' Kitty asked.

'No chance. I'm the hired help, remember.'

'Oh. Well...will I see you again before I leave?'

'That depends when you're leaving.'

'Tomorrow morning, I suppose.'

'To drive into Aberdeen and catch the plane?' She nodded. 'Will Gus be with you?'

'That's up to him,' she replied.

'Forgive me for asking, but how do you rate your future employment with him?'

Kitty half smiled. 'We've had differences of opinion before.'

'This serious?'

'Not really. But I'm sure we'll patch it

up. About tomorrow...'

'I'm afraid I have business here in Aboyne, first thing. What plane were you hoping to catch?'

'There's a late-morning flight. I think I'll need to be there by ten-thirty.'

'Oh, right. I'll try to get up to the castle before you leave.'

'I'd like that,' Kitty said, quietly.

'I'd like that too,' James agreed.

As they drove out to the castle, Kitty kept telling herself that she really had no reason to be happy: despite what she'd said to James, it was extremely likely that her job with Turnbull & Heath was over.

It wasn't that Gus was the least vindictive or ever bore a grudge; it was simply that he hated hassle, and if he came to the conclusion that she was more trouble to work with than she was worth, as he might well do when he learned of her attendance at the meeting and what she had said, as he was bound to do...she squared her shoulders: so what the hell? At least he would have to admire her integrity. And she had met this super bloke! Trouble was, was she ever going to see him again, after tomorrow?

It was nearly dark, and the castle was a blaze of light from just about every window, she noticed as she waved goodbye to James and carried her overnight bag to the front door.

She was just wondering if there was a side entrance or if she would have to ring the bell and alert the entire household to her arrival, when the door opened for her.

'Let me carry that,' Niall said. Kitty hesitated. But she was on his territory now. She handed over the bag. 'Saw you arrive,' he said. 'Well, I was looking out for you.'

He leaned forward, clearly with a kiss in mind, so she presented her cheek; he couldn't do any manhandling with the bag in one hand.

'Your father very kindly offered me a bed for the night,' she said.

'Oh, indeed.' He ushered her into the great hall. 'But surely you'll stay more than one night?'

'I was planning to fly south tomorrow. But it depends on whether I'm asked to stay on,' she replied. She had been thinking of Gus and Bernard, but she had given him a cue.

'You'll always be welcome on Abergannan,' he said, leading her up the stairs.

'That's very nice of you,' she muttered absently, adding, 'though I'm not sure you can speak for your father.'

He turned left along the thick-carpeted

landing. 'It was quite a bust-up, I gather. But Dad is perfectly happy. He's a bit of a sadist, I suppose, and was rather amused by the sight of two eminent scientists having a serious difference of opinion. Just as long as he gets his own way in the end, of course. This is your room.' He opened the door, and stepped back to allow her to enter.

Kitty went in. It was the same room she had been given on her previous visit, which meant that Gus was probably next door. Well, if he wanted to kiss and make up, she'd be delighted; but she wasn't going to make the first move.

Niall placed her bag on the frame in the corner. 'Thank you,' she said.

'We've a guest for dinner,' he said. 'Apart from you and Wilson, of course. Name of Bartlett. He's one of Rebecca's bosses, up here to give a decision on whether or not Dad can dig.'

'Just like that?'

'Well, he can't give the permission himself, of course. But if he recommends it, then it's a fait accompli. He hasn't given an opinion yet.' Kitty raised her eyebrows. 'So…' Niall licked his lips. 'We'd all appreciate it if the meal went off without any fuss. Preferably without any reference to the gas at all. Just a nice social evening.'

'Were you by any chance deputed to coerce me?'

'Good heavens, no.' He moved towards her. 'I'm very fond of you, Kitty. I really am. And when you think what we experienced together, nearly dying in each other's arms. Well, when two people have been through that, they really do have a bond, wouldn't you say?'

'We nearly died in each other's arms because of your crass stupidity,' Kitty pointed out. She really did want to get rid of this overgrown youth so that she could think. If there was a man from the ministry actually in the house, and he had not yet given a decision...it might be possible to nip the whole looming catastrophe in the bud right here and now—and hang the consequences.

'Well,' Niall said, 'It's all very well for you to come over all hoity-toity...' he grinned. 'I still say we have the potential for a great relationship. Don't you agree?'

He put his arms round her, but she brought her fists up between them, pushing him away. 'You're being silly.'

'For wanting you? Christ, you've turned me on from the moment I saw you. And now... What's to stop us?'

'Me,' she said.

'What the hell do you mean by that?' He was beginning to look very like his father.

'Simply that the feeling is not mutual. It is not simply a matter of switching on the vibes to accommodate a bloke.'

Again he tried to hug her, and again she kept her hands, and elbows, between them. 'You think you're one hell of a bint,' he remarked, panting.

'If you don't lay off,' she warned, 'I am going to have to knee you where it'll hurt.'

They glared at each other from a range of about six inches, then he let her go, so suddenly that she almost fell over.

Niall went to the door and turned. 'You want to play hard to get? Well that's OK with me, I can wait. But I must warn you. You make waves, tonight, little Kitty, and you are going to be in deep shit. Your job will go, for a start. Dad will see to that.' His voice was patronizing, almost sympathetic.

Kitty nearly laughed out loud...but she was too irritated. Silly young bugger! For some unknown reason he'd got the hots for her: wanted to bonk her! Yet at the same time had the nerve to threaten her not to 'make waves' about his Daddy's project. He was behaving like a twelve-year-old, and she had a growing impulse to smack him... 'Go find yourself an icepack and cool off, will you?' She pushed him out of the door, slammed and locked it.

Shaking, she staggered across to the window and peered out through the bars into the darkness, past the image of her room mirrored on the glass. She wondered where James was, tried to picture him in the bailiff's quarters. In his youth, had he ever been such a crazy mixed up kid as Niall? Without the disadvantage of a father like Morris, probably not.

Kitty had to take a quick bath as it was getting late. She couldn't do much about dressing for dinner; her overnight bag only had room for a change of undies and a clean jumper with flowers printed on the front.

She refused to accept she was as shaken as she felt. It was not so much Niall's threat as the aggressive change in his personality. She had cast him down as a rather harmless son of a domineering father—as so often the case.

The fact that he had gone over the top with her was merely a thorough nuisance. But now his attitude seemed almost menacing. How does the prospect of suddenly discovering a financial windfall affect people? she asked herself. Except that neither Niall nor his father needed such a windfall. Or did they? Just how wealthy *were* the Morris family? But no matter the answer, it would not make her any the more sympathetic towards them.

Downstairs, the party had already gathered in the drawing-room. 'Miss Cochrane,' Bernard announced loudly. 'Good to see you. You'll take a glass of champagne?'

Kitty's eye caught Guthrie's for a split second as she accepted the champagne from his salver...before turning to smile at her hostess.

Gus came and stood behind her, frowning. 'I didn't know you'd got back,' he muttered. 'You and I need to talk.'

'What about?' she asked, sweetly. His frown deepened. 'I mean, is there anything left to say?' she queried.

'Miss Cochrane! Kitty! You don't mind if I call you Kitty?' She tensed. For a moment she had actually thought Bernard was going to put his arm round her waist. 'We've a guest here who's dying to meet you,' the host beamed. Kitty looked past him at a man who had to be Bartlett, standing between Rebecca and Niall. Niall was smiling, but his eyes were cold. Rebecca looked apprehensive. 'Mr Bartlett is from the Ministry of the Environment,' Bernard said. 'So you'll know why he's here, eh?'

'I'm sure I can guess,' Kitty said, as she shook hands with the civil servant, aware of Niall's threatening stare.

Then Guthrie appeared in the doorway, banging a little gong.

Conversation was general throughout the first part of the meal with, as Niall had ordered, not a mention of natural gas.

Kitty was seated between Niall on her left and Tara, obliquely opposite Bartlett, who was on Margaret's right, with Rebecca exactly opposite Kitty, and Gus on her right, next to Bernard at the top of the table.

The table itself was a huge oak refectory, large enough for twice the number of diners, so they were all fairly well spaced. As Tara seemed to have no desire to speak with her at all, Kitty found herself dependent for conversation on Niall. He was at his brilliant and witty best, with not a hint of the scene in her room, earlier, while Kitty found herself growing more and more irritated.

She could hear what was being said on the far side of the table, and when, with the dessert, Bartlett began to hold forth on the beauties of the countryside, she could not prevent herself from asking, across the table, 'Then you would be against its destruction in the name of Mammon, Mr Bartlett?'

There was a sudden silence; Kitty had spoken during a comparative lull in conversation and even Morris, at the other end of the table, had heard what she had said. Gus began to fiddle with his wine glass.

Bartlett seemed unaware of the tension. 'Destruction of the countryside is always an emotive issue, Miss Cochrane,' he said. 'Sadly it is an inescapable part of modern life, as you obviously must be aware. I can well remember, as a lad, the fuss in the years following the Second World War, when electricity pylons were being erected all over the English countryside. Many people regarded that as the ultimate desecration. But do you know, I wonder how many people today even notice they are there, much less regard them as eyesores. While everyone in the country is more dependent on electricity than any other form of energy.'

'Exactly my own feelings,' Morris said, loudly. 'No one can stand in the way of progress. Canute tried that, eh, and where did it get him?'

'Canute, Mr Morris,' Kitty said agreeably, 'tried to stand in the way of the forces of nature. And yes, he found that he could not do that. An example one should bear in mind.'

There was another brief silence broken by Bartlett, at last aware that there was at least an undercurrent of hostility present. 'Have I missed something?' he asked.

‘It is just that Miss Cochrane considers that it might be dangerous to drill for oil on Gannan Hill,’ Morris said. ‘Something to do with the pressure, I believe.’

‘And the high methane content of the gas,’ Kitty added.

‘Hm,’ Bartlett commented.

‘I think I should point out,’ Morris said, ‘that Miss Cochrane is something of a tyro in this field. Her colleague, who is her senior, does not share her pessimistic point of view. Do you, Gus?’

‘Well...’ Gus gave Kitty an anxious glance. ‘There is an element of risk, of course...’

‘But that is present in all drilling conditions, is it not, Gus?’ Niall asked.

‘Well, yes, of course.’

‘And,’ Morris went on, ‘I may say that, providing I receive the proper permission of course...’ he smiled at Bartlett. ‘I intend to employ Archie MacPhail to drill. Now, you cannot find a better, more experienced, or more careful man than that.’

‘Oh, indeed,’ Bartlett said. ‘I know MacPhail’s work. A good man. You should have no trouble with him.’

‘Well, then...’ Morris took a deep breath. He had not intended to press the matter, but since this bimbo had raised it... ‘Do you think we’ll get our permission?’

Kitty found she was holding her breath, but then, she suspected several other people round the table were doing that.

'Well...' Bartlett was clearly enjoying himself. 'I can see no reason at all why permission should not be granted, Mr Morris. After all, it's your land, and natural resources are there to be exploited, are they not?'

Another of those brief silences. 'You'll make a recommendation to that effect?' Morris asked.

'As soon as I get back to town, certainly.'

'But you can't!' Kitty flung down her napkin. Bartlett raised his eyebrows. 'Quite apart from the environment, drilling for gas on Gannan Hill could well cause a catastrophe!' she exclaimed.

Bartlett looked at Gus. 'Kitty,' Gus said severely. 'Do please stop it. This is a dinner party.'

'Dinner party, my foot,' Kitty argued. 'There can be no drilling on Gannan Hill.' She looked around at the faces surrounding her; most were angry—even Tara was looking interested. 'It may interest you to know that there is a considerable groundswell of opposition to this entire business.'

'Inspired by Greenpeace, no doubt,' Morris said contemptuously.

'Inspired by the people of Aboyne, mainly,' Kitty retorted. 'I attended a meeting there this afternoon, and questions are going to be asked in the House, concerning the safety of this project.' This time the silence was electric.

Bernard Morris leaned as far over the table towards her as his stomach allowed. Lower lip thrust out and eyes narrowed he hissed, 'You told them it was dangerous?' then glanced at Gus.

'Oh, Kitty, how could you?' Gus looked genuinely distressed.

'Because it was necessary.'

Morris's fist struck the table, rattling the cutlery. 'That report was a confidential matter between your employers and me,' he shouted.

'I did not divulge the contents of our report,' Kitty said. 'I merely told them to demand that it be divulged.'

'Kitty,' Gus said. 'Do please be quiet. And I think you owe Mr Morris an apology.'

'Apologize? To him?' Kitty stood up. 'You are so hidebound in your customer-relations thing you can't see the wood for trees. Well, I am not.'

'Kitty!' Even Gus was starting to get annoyed. 'If you persist in this I shall have to make a report to Ben Heath.'

'You can report it to whoever you like.

And to save you the trouble of firing me, I resign.' With as much dignity as she could muster, Kitty stalked out of the room.

Chapter 8

WITH MURDER IN MIND

Kitty's head was pounding. She was furious, confused. Only one thing was certain, she couldn't stay in this place tonight. The scruffy overnight bag lay open on the bed with stockings and a spare bra hanging out of it, and she was carrying her toiletries across from the bathroom when someone knocked on the door. Which of them might this be? Gus, to try talking her into some sort of public apology? Niall trying to capitalize on the upset to get a leg over? She debated whether to ignore whoever it was, but in the end she dropped the armful of gear onto the bag and opened the door.

'May I come in?' Rebecca asked.

Kitty had noted earlier that she had made quite an effort with her appearance tonight; her make-up was good and her hair brushed smooth and straight. The clothes remained shapeless, but maybe that was due to the bulges underneath.

Kitty offered a thin smile and stepped aside. 'Sure,' and closed the door behind her.

'For a start, I want you to know I'm on your side.' Rebecca flopped onto the dressing stool.

'I'm glad someone is.' Kitty returned to the bed and continued cramming gear into the bag.

'You're not packing up and going, are you?'

' 'Fraid so. No point me hanging around here. It's not as though I'm exactly flavour of the month.'

'Oh, Kitty! Please don't. I need you here.'

Kitty stared at her with raised eyebrows. 'You do? What the hell for?'

'To help fight this thing.' Rebecca came and stood the other side of the bed, facing her. 'While I was in London I wrote a report about the whole project for my boss, you know.'

'For or against?'

'Against, of course!'

'Why of course? I didn't notice you speaking up for me in the dining-room. Was that because your boss was there?'

'My boss? Oh, you mean Bartlett. Lord, no. He's not my actual boss. He is just one of the inspectors. No, I suppose I was just befuddled. I... Well, you see, it's a matter of family, and all that.'

'What is?' Kitty straightened up and stared at her, arms akimbo. 'Sorry but you've lost me.'

'Well,' Rebecca spread her hands, hesitating, then took a deep breath. 'Well, I suppose it doesn't matter if I tell you, so long as you promise to keep it to yourself...'

'Tell me what?'

'Daddy's business is...well...just about to go down the pan.' She paused to watch for Kitty's reaction but there wasn't any so she went on. 'He has had big problems recently and we, the family that is, desperately need this gas thing to take off, to save the whole shooting match.'

'Sorry to sound dim, but what are you trying to say? That although you think the project stinks you want me to back down to save your family fortunes?'

'No, no! I don't mean that. I just want you to understand why Daddy is behaving like this. He has asked us all to back him up but, to be honest, I don't like it one bit. And I think you are absolutely right. Oh shit!' She flung herself on to the bed beside Kitty's bag. 'Why is life so damn complicated? It is so difficult. I feel so sorry for them, Mummy in particular.

Poor darling doesn't like this business any more than you or I do. She has taken so much stick from Daddy for years and all this,' her hand wafted in a circle round the room indicating, Kitty presumed, the whole of Abergannan, 'is a sort of compensation. She's bloody well earned a bit of luxury.' She rolled on to her back and stared up at Kitty. 'Can't you see what I'm getting at?'

Kitty tugged her hair back with both hands. 'That you are suffering an acute case of divided loyalties? Yes. I do see that. But so what? Where do we go from here?'

'I don't honestly know. But I don't imagine it is going to help the situation if anyone, you or I, or Mummy, or anyone else, throws in the sponge. We really do have to sit it out and try to resolve the problem.'

'Are you suggesting that putting my job and livelihood on the line and shouting my case, amounts to throwing in the sponge?' Kitty demanded.

'Hell no! I thought you were marvellous. Fought your corner fantastically. No. What I'm suggesting is that it would be a shame if you walk out now. Abandon ship, as it were.'

'Come on, Rebecca,' Kitty returned once more to her task. 'Get real. There's no way

I can stay on here. Not after blowing a gasket at the dinner table.'

'I don't see why not. You simply spoke up against what you see as a very real danger. Nobody can knock you for that.'

Kitty snorted. 'Nobody? Try your father for starters.'

'Daddy has been blowing his top every few days for as long as I can remember.' Rebecca forced a laugh. 'He gets over it.'

'Well I'm not in the habit of blowing my top and when I do I don't stop shaking for weeks,' Kitty countered, but her resolve to bolt was weakening. Just a little.

Rebecca Morris looked at her watch. 'It's far too late for you to leave, anyway. You'd never find lodging for the night.' She rolled off the bed and stood up, straightening her skirt. 'Isn't there anything I can say to change your mind?'

Kitty knew the girl was right: it would be impossible to find a bed, now. And the thought of spending the night huddled in her hire car was not appealing, to say the least. 'I'll think about it,' she said.

'OK. Can't ask more than that. I'll give you some space.' Rebecca went to the door. 'Meanwhile I'll try and work on Daddy.'

'Thanks. And I promise I won't sneak off into the dark without saying goodbye.'

When the dining-room door had closed, rather violently, behind Kitty, there was a prolonged, uncomfortable silence. Then everyone tried to speak at once. 'Oh dear,' Margaret murmured. 'Er, Gus, would you like coffee?'

Gus never drank coffee in the evening because he swore it kept him awake. However, after Kitty's embarrassing departure he felt obliged to accept...for politeness' sake. 'Yes please.'

Watched by her husband and children in stony silence, Margaret poured from a silver pot and Guthrie, who had witnessed the entire episode, placed the delicate cup and saucer in front of the guest, keeping his face superbly blank. Margaret smiled nervously at her husband. 'Will you have one, dear?'

Bernard pushed back his chair and stood up. 'No. I need to make some calls.' And he strode out of the room.

'I found a heavenly little silk suit at Harrods last week, Mummy,' Tara said, toying with the rope of pearls which hung entrancingly into her cleavage. 'It's very pale blue with self-coloured embroidery on the cuffs and collar. Just perfect for Henley.'

Gus realized he was staring at the gorgeous creature: at the wide blue eyes, flawless creamy skin and platinum hair falling in loose waves round her shoulders. He was gaping in dazed wonderment, mystified at the workings of her mind...if *workings* was the correct term in her case.

'How nice, dear,' was her mother's wooden reply. 'Did you bring it with you? I'd love to see it.'

'Oh God!' Niall exclaimed. 'Excuse me, I feel a puke coming on.' He got up and left the room.

Tara watched her brother go. 'Oh dear. Do you think he has a tummy upset?'

Margaret sighed. 'I doubt it, dear.'

Rebecca also got up, and without a word left the room.

Gus continued to sit, exchanging inanities with the mother and daughter, trying to think up a reasonable excuse to escape.

Bernard stamped towards his office, and was checked by a cough. Bartlett had followed him from the dining-room. That was all he needed.

'What exactly was that young lady talking about, Mr Morris?' Bartlett asked. 'If I am not being presumptuous.'

You are being bloody presumptuous, Bernard thought. But he decided against saying it, and showed his guest into the office. 'She's drunk.'

'Ah...was she really?' Bartlett sat down.

'Still...if there is any truth in what she was saying, well...I should have to reconsider my position. And my recommendation.'

'There is absolutely no truth in what she was saying,' Bernard asserted. 'The truth is that she and her bearded friend found a slightly high methane level in the gas escaping from Gannan Hill. I am sure you know as well as I that this is not at all uncommon.'

'I do know that. But still, if an element of risk is established...'

'There is absolutely no element of risk involved,' Bernard said. 'You said you knew of Archie MacPhail?'

'Why, yes.'

'How would you rate him?'

'Well...as I said, one of the best in the business. He has, of course, received a copy of the geo-chemists' report?'

'Absolutely,' Bernard lied.

'Well, that seems satisfactory.' Bartlett frowned. 'But you do realize that if this young woman carries out her threat and goes public, it could cause some problems. At the very least there will be considerable delays in obtaining permission.'

'I told you, she was drunk. She's been here before. We all know she can't hold her liquor. Tomorrow morning, when she's sobered up, I intend to have a serious chat with her, and I can assure you that she isn't going to go public.'

'Ah. Right. Well, if you're happy with the situation. I'll say good-night.'

Bernard carefully closed the office door behind him, and then locked it. He was actually surprised at how calm he was. His brain had suddenly gone ice-cold. It was ice-cold rage. He was sitting on top of a fortune, discovered at the very moment when he was facing bankruptcy—and worse. Those bloody wogs weren't likely to forgive a man who had used their money for his own purposes and not come up with the goods. They'd have some long-knived hit man after him the moment they realized they weren't going to get their money back. Did some doe-eyed bimbo really think she was going to put him in that position?

She could do that, he knew. If he let her get away with it. There were in any event going to be enough problems with the people who considered that one should never turn over a clod of earth if it was green on one side and brown on the other—no matter that one might own the clod. He could ride that, certainly now he had the support of the Ministry. But if he lost that support...and Bartlett was clearly uneasy. Well, fuck her, he thought. If his life was on the line, then so were a hell of a lot of others. He couldn't let that happen.

He picked up the phone and punched the numbers. Thank God he had a company accountant with the right connections. 'Do you realize the time?' Crowther was not amused.

'You go to bed too early,' Bernard told him. 'We have a problem.'

'Speak.'

'This female Einstein we inadvertently employed is threatening to go public with her report.'

'You joke.'

'I do not joke where my finances are involved, Philip.'

'But if she does that, the whole thing could be blown sky high. One whiff of uncertainty and the bank will certainly pull the rug.'

'That is why I am calling you in the middle of the night. The young lady has got to be stopped.' There was a brief silence. 'You do realize it's your finances as well?' Bernard asked.

'*You* do realize what you are asking me to do? You do understand the consequences if something should go wrong?'

'As far as I am concerned, Philip, nothing can go more wrong than having this bitch spouting to the media. Can you handle it? You've always boasted you can take care of any situation.'

Another brief silence, then Crowther said. 'Where is she now?'

'In her bedroom packing, I should think.'

'Hm. I would have thought...'

'Forget it. That would be crazy. It has to be an accident. Anyway, it's not my scene. Can you handle it?'

'No. But I know someone who can. The moment she returns to Oxford. You'll have to obtain her address for me.'

'No,' Bernard said. 'We can't chance that. We have no certainty that she won't stop and talk to someone on the way. It has to be done between here and Aberdeen. Between here and Aboyne, come to think of it. Before she gets to any main roads. I can stop her telephoning from here, but once she reaches someplace like Aboyne...'

'Well,' Crowther said, 'as it happens, I do know someone in Glasgow who does this kind of work.'

'Is he reliable?'

'Absolutely. But obviously, I'll need some time.'

'How much time?'

'I'll try to set things up for tomorrow morning. What car is she driving?'

'A red Ford Fiesta. I'll need to get back to you with the registration number.'

'Fair enough. But your friend must stay put tonight.'

'She will,' Bernard promised. 'I'll take care of that.'

'And she mustn't leave too early. Not before eight.'

'Not before eight,' Bernard acknowledged.

Having invented some nonsense about sorting out papers, Gus beat a retreat from the dining-room, tripping over his own feet in his embarrassing haste. He stumbled up the stairs and into his room where he paced with uncharacteristic tension for the next half hour, debating whether or not to go and speak to Kitty.

Meanwhile, Margaret and Tara had drifted into the drawing-room, the latter continuing to ramble at length about clothes, make-up and social darlings, testing her mother's powers of concentration to the limit. This peaceful scene was abruptly terminated by Bernard. 'Margaret. In my office, please.' She ground her teeth and dutifully obeyed. 'Close the door.' She did.

He sat himself in his favourite position of power, behind the huge desk. 'Sit down.' She did. He smiled with his mouth, but his eyes remained cold. 'Amazing, isn't it, how some of today's young cannot hold their liquor.' Margaret's blank stare conveyed the fact she hadn't a clue what he was talking about. 'The Cochrane female. She was way out of her tree, tonight.'

'You think she was drunk?'

'Of course. Why else would she have shouted the odds like that.' He looked at the long, thin colourless woman in front of him and decided he had every excuse for rogering the new bint in his London office. 'Pity she blew her top like that. Sad. But we can't let her wander off tonight in her car. Dangerous.'

'Eh? How do you mean?'

'Isn't it obvious? In her condition she may well go careering off the road. Finish up upside down in the river, or something.'

'Oh!' Margaret's mouth remained open, amazed at herself that she hadn't realized Kitty was tipsy.

'Have you been up to her room?' Bernard asked.

'Er...no.'

'Well I think you should, quickly. Just make sure she doesn't try to leave before tomorrow, when she's slept it off.'

Margaret's annoyance with her husband melted away. He really could be so caring and considerate, sometimes. It never ceased to surprise her. After all, the girl had spoken very rudely to him. He would be quite justified in letting her drive herself to damnation. But... 'But what excuse do I use to stop her going, I mean, I can't very well tell her she's too drunk...'—the sort of feeble waffling that normally sparked off an exasperated explosion.

However, tonight Bernard was keeping his rag under strict control. 'Just tell her you'd be devastatingly embarrassed, as her hostess, were she to leave so abruptly.'

'What a good idea, darling,' Margaret responded with relief. 'Why didn't I think of that?'

Bernard refrained from telling her. He watched her hurry away to Kitty, then released the tense muscles round his mouth from forced smile mode.

Rebecca wasn't the only one doing mental battle with conflicting interests. Kitty was sick of the Morrises, the castle, the project. She wanted out, and the sight of her bag lying on the bed, only waiting to be zipped up and carried off to the car was very tempting. On the other hand, despite having given her phone number to the Green Party woman at the meeting, if she did go the chances of ever seeing James MacEwan again were very remote.

So what? A lot. She had to admit she had been disproportionately attracted to him from day one, though she wasn't sure why. Was it simply a great big physical lust at the sight of the handsome, sandy-haired giant...or was it more? Love, for instance.

Could one fall in love with a person one hardly knew? She hadn't a clue. She only knew there was a sickening lump forming in her stomach at the thought of a final parting.

She was saved from making a decision by a tentative tap on the door. Was Rebecca back already? She opened the door. Margaret stood in the corridor smiling nervously. 'Hello, Kitty. Er... Are you all right?'

'Yes, thanks.'

'Can you spare a minute?'

'Yes, of course. Come in. What can I do for you?'

Margaret's mouth was dry. 'I was just hoping you wouldn't think of leaving. Tonight, I mean.'

'Has Rebecca been on to you?'

Margaret looked blank. 'Rebecca...?'

Obviously not. 'I thought you'd be pleased to see the back of me.'

'Why?'

'I was very rude this evening.'

Margaret didn't think her guest looked or sounded the slightest bit drunk...nor was she suffering from alcoholic amnesia. 'Er, not at all. Everyone has a right to their own opinions.'

'But not the right to express them on social occasions and bust up dinner parties.'

'That is not the problem. Happens all the time, married to Bernard. Oops,' she clapped her hand over her mouth, appalled at her own disloyalty.

'Then what is the problem?'

'The embarrassment I should suffer, dear, if you allowed this evening to upset you so much that you wanted to leave.'

Studying the woman's face, Kitty realized she truly was embarrassed. She looked nervous and unhappy, with dark circles round her eyes. Poor thing! And poor Rebecca. If both of them were really worried about the gas drilling destroying the countryside, or simply wanted to delay commencement of operations till further investigations had been carried out, it was only their two feeble voices against the four men: Gus, Bernard, Bartlett and Niall. And neither of the women had any technical knowledge to back up their arguments.

Perhaps Rebecca was right; it would be ratting to rush off and leave them to it. Maybe if she just stayed overnight and then reassessed the situation in the morning. 'Well, if you are sure you really want me to remain till tomorrow...'

'Oh, yes! Please. Please do.' Margaret appeared genuinely relieved.

'But what about your husband? I should think he can't wait to see the back of me.'

'Oh, no. On the contrary. He is very anxious for you to stay.' Margaret backed towards the door. 'I'll go and tell him, straight away. He'll be delighted.' With a last, nervous smile she was gone.

Kitty stood frowning at the closed door. Morris *wanted* her to stay? Anxious, was the term Margaret had used. Very odd. She shook her head, went back to the bed and tipped her things out of the bag. What the hell was that devious bugger up to?

Kitty got undressed and slid gratefully between the sheets; it had been a very long day. Although she suspected she wasn't going to sleep. But in fact she was just nodding off when she was awakened by a tap on the door. She sat up and looked at her watch; twelve-fifteen! Didn't anyone ever sleep in this benighted castle? She switched on the light, pulled on a dressing gown, and opened the door. 'Oh, good lord!'

'Am I that repulsive?' Gus inquired. 'Here, I sneaked these out of his lordship's bar.' These being a bottle of brandy and two glasses. 'Thought we could both do with a nightcap,' he explained. Kitty thought that mightn't be a bad idea. She sat on the bed and accepted a goblet. 'Here's to gas,' Gus said, brushing her glass with his.

'I'm not sure that's funny.'

'It's not meant to be.' He straddled a chair, facing her. 'Kitty, you can't do it.'

'I'm very tired, Gus. Thanks ever so for the drink. I needed it. But now...'

'Kitty! If you persist it'll cost you your job. More, it'll cost you *any* job in this business. Breaking client confidentiality will mean a blackball.'

'And you think a job, any job, is worth human lives?'

'You cannot prove that will happen. There may well be some way of avoiding the problem...'

'Gus, we've been through all this a dozen times already. I'm sorry.'

He finished his drink and stood up. 'It will also cost my friendship. Or maybe that isn't important.'

'That is the most important thing of all, Gus. You're a scientist. You believe in the job, the whole job, and only the job. You believe in facts. If it isn't a fact, it can't matter. If you can't prove something, it doesn't exist. When it comes to probabilities, only the percentages matter. Believe me, I respect that point of view. Perhaps I'm sorry I don't have it.' She attempted a smile. 'I guess maybe I'm not a true scientist after all. I let my emotions get in the way of my test tubes.'

‘I want you to know,’ Gus said, ‘that I am going to be here, monitoring the drilling, and I am going to make sure that this fellow MacPhail takes every possible precaution.’

‘I never doubted that you would.’

‘But you won’t change your mind.’

‘I’m sorry.’

‘In that case, I assume you are sticking by your resignation.’

She hesitated only a moment. ‘Yes. Yes, I am.’

‘Then I would like your copy of your report.’ She stared at him with her mouth open. ‘If you no longer work for Turnbull & Heath,’ he pointed out, ‘then you no longer have a right to any material under the firm’s name.’ He held out his hand. Kitty delved into the pocket of the suitcase, took out the folded report, and handed it to him. He closed the door behind him, without another word.

He’d left the bottle, perhaps deliberately. Kitty poured herself another brandy, sipped it slowly, still sitting on the edge of the bed. She couldn’t help but wonder to herself why she was so determined to stick her neck out for these people, none of whom she really liked. But it wasn’t just the Morrises involved. There was the staff at the castle—and those she did like.

And there was James. When the drilling started, James would certainly be there. Hating her for having begun this? But no, he understood. They were on the same side. She could not endanger his life.

She fell into a deep, uneasy slumber, and was awakened again by a knock on her door. For a moment she could not remember where she was, then she sat up again and looked at her watch. It was just gone six, and as she had forgotten to draw the curtains she could see that it was broad daylight outside. She pulled on her dressing gown and opened the door. 'For God's sake! What do you want?'

'I'd hoped you might have simmered down a little, after a good night's sleep,' Niall said.

'I haven't *had* a good night's sleep, yet,' Kitty pointed out, coldly. 'So if you don't mind, I'd like to sneak in another hour's uninterrupted kip.' She made to close the door, but he pushed it open with such force she staggered backwards, and he came into the room, kicking the door shut behind him. 'Just what do you think you're doing?' she demanded, clutching the robe around herself.

'We need to talk.' He went to her dressing table. 'Drowning our sorrows, I see.'

'You can see what you like. If you don't

get out of my room this instant, I am going to ring to have you thrown out.'

He sat in the chair vacated by Gus. 'Wouldn't do you any good. Nobody will answer at this hour.'

Kitty glared at him, but she had an uneasy feeling that he might be right. She remained standing, arms folded. 'OK, talk.'

'This gas deal is very important,' Niall said. 'Not only to Dad. To all of us.'

'Rebecca mentioned something about a financial problem...'

'Financial problem?' He gave a brief laugh. 'We are bust wide open, darling.'

'That *is* rough. On the other hand, you have this vast estate to sell, and I presume a few other desirable modern residences scattered about the place. That'll still leave you a darn sight better off than most people.'

'You still don't get it, do you? When I said bust wide open, I wasn't talking about your ordinary respectable bankruptcy. I am talking about a great big black hole into which everything we own can be poured without ever resurfacing. I'm also perhaps talking about our lives. You must have heard of the Mafia.'

'Oh, don't start that old saw.'

'I'm not going to. The people Dad has been dealing with are so tough they make the roughest don in history look like a kindergarten schoolteacher.'

'You expect me to take that seriously?'

'It happens to be the truth. Dad happened to, shall we say, use some of their funds for a purpose they had not intended. If he can't replace that money, they are going to be very angry. You have to understand that.'

'And what about the lives that will be at risk when your dad starts drilling?'

'Your boss said the chances of anything going wrong are infinitesimal.'

'And I don't happen to agree with him. Likewise, perhaps you wouldn't agree with me if I suggested that the chances of this kind of terrorist-style doomsday scenario you're dreaming up ever happening to your father, are also infinitesimal.'

'You know what you need, you little bitch,' he said, getting to his feet with a lecherous smirk curling his lip.

Kitty lost her temper. She uncoiled herself and picked up a heavy wooden coathanger which lay on the oak chest at the foot of the bed. Then she reached the door in two strides and flung it open. Niall was staring at her with his mouth open. 'You get out of here,' she shouted. 'Out! Out! Or your problems come to an end, right now.'

Niall wasn't intimidated by her threats

or the coathanger—but kept well wide of her as he strode out of the door in what he fondly imagined was a dignified exit. He had no intention of waiting the arrival of the wakened household.

Kitty slammed the door violently behind him, locked it, then sat on the bed...shaking. The effect the prospect of a fortune could have on some people!

But obviously she couldn't stay here a moment longer. She had been an absolute idiot to accept all their blandishments last night, and agree to remain even until this morning. Certainly she had to go, now. Even if it meant missing James? But she had to chance that.

Hurriedly she repacked, dressed, and opened the door, half an inch...listening. Surely someone must have heard the raised voices. She waited a full minute before opening the door wide enough to look through...the corridor was empty. She tiptoed along it and down the stairs...and almost dropped the bag. Guthrie was in the front hall.

'I'm afraid breakfast will na be ready for an hour, miss,' he said. Guthrie wasn't sure whether he approved of her or not. He approved of the way she had spoken out at the meeting, yesterday, as regards digging up Gannan Hill, but in all the years he had spent as bootboy, under-footman, footman and butler, he had had it ingrained in him that scenes at table were simply not acceptable, no matter what the provocation. Even in the form of Mr Bernard Morris.

'I'm not breakfasting, Mr Guthrie,' Kitty said, and lugged her bag to the door.

'Ye're not leaving? This early?' He was scandalized.

'I'll write you all a postcard,' Kitty promised, and opened the door.

'Just where do you think you're going?' Bernard stood at the top of the stairs, wearing a flowered dressing gown, mainly reds and mauves.

'Home,' Kitty said.

'You come back here,' Morris bellowed, and ran down the stairs. 'Stop her, you fool!' he bellowed at Guthrie.

But Guthrie was not into manhandling young women, and in any event, Kitty was already down the front steps and running towards her car. Bernard ignored Guthrie, who remained standing motionless as a statue, and ran out of the door behind her. Kitty reached her car, wrenched open the door and threw her gear on to the passenger seat as she got behind the wheel. Bernard charged towards her, a really rather absurd sight: he was very obviously naked as his dressing gown streamed behind him.

'Stop!' he bellowed. 'Come back here!'

Kitty couldn't imagine what he had in mind. Vague suspicions of kidnapping flitted through her brain. In any event, she had no intention of obeying him. She gunned the engine, and when he grasped at her door, put her foot flat on the accelerator. The car surged forward, and Bernard tumbled away from it. Kitty cast a hasty glance in her rear view mirror, and saw that he appeared to be unhurt, if winded. Then she was out of the yard and on to the lane that led down to the village.

Bernard remained panting for several seconds, glaring firstly at the disappearing car and then at Guthrie, who had at last bestirred himself and come down the steps. 'Would ye be all right, Mr Morris?' he asked, solicitously.

Bernard scrambled to his feet. 'Of course I'm all right,' he snapped, pulling at the dressing gown to cover his dignity. 'But that silly little bitch has got away.'

'The young lady was in a hurry to be home, I'm thinking.'

'Young lady, hell.' Bernard stamped past him up the steps and across the hall into his study, glaring at the clock. Quarter to seven! Crowther had said his man could not be in position before eight! Damn, damn,

damn. Talk about treacherous women!

He listened to the house stirring, aroused by his shouting. What to do?

Kitty's car roared through the village, and out the other side, and then had to brake hard as she found the road filled with sheep; the engine promptly stalled.

She pushed her head out of the window, and the very young shepherd waved and grinned at her. The temptation to blast on the horn was enormous, but he was only doing his job. So she waited for some fifteen minutes while the bleating animals slowly baaed their way on to the meadow on the far side of the road. Then she turned the key; the engine growled, but did not catch. And again.

The youthful shepherd ambled up to her. 'It's flooded,' he said.

'Oh, damnation,' Kitty seethed.

'What you want to do,' the youth said. 'Is put your foot hard to the floor, and then turn it.'

Kitty glared at him. 'That'll work, will it?'

'Oh, yes. Every time. Well, nearly.'

Kitty muttered under her breath, then did as he suggested. Pressing the accelerator flat to the floor, she turned the switch, and after a brief rumble, the engine roared into life.

'Nearly every time,' the youth said.

'Thanks,' Kitty said, and pulled away.

She drove slowly; she didn't want to be in and out of Aboyne before James started his return journey. It was a magnificent spring morning, crisp and clear. Inevitably, cloud was gathering above the mountains, especially, it seemed, over Cock Cairn and Gannan Hill; the mountain of death, she thought with a shudder.

The narrow road twisted and turned as it wound its way along the valley to Aboyne. There was at least no risk of missing James. Unless he had been and returned very early, and had taken one of the side lanes—hardly more than tracks—leading off into the foothills. But there was no reason for him to do that, in view of their date—if it had been a date.

Yet, when she reckoned she was halfway between Abergannan and Aboyne, she saw an obvious four-wheel drive parked a little way up one of the side tracks. Her heart leapt, and she instinctively slowed, then realized that it wasn't James' jeep but a big Nissan.

She continued driving slowly, however, until she was parallel with the track, and waved a 'Good-morning' at the driver of the parked vehicle, who was wearing a bulky anorak with the hood tied close round his face. Why, she wondered, was he wearing sunglasses on this gloomy, overcast morning?

Then she realized that the vehicle had been parked with its engine running, and as she reached the foot of the track, where it joined the lane, it roared forward. For a moment she thought that the idiot had merely taken his foot off the brake by mistake, then she understood that he meant to hit her.

Desperately she gunned her engine, and listened to the squeal of brakes as the Nissan came out onto the road broadside on. Frantically she drove at the next corner, but it was a sharp one, and instinctively she touched the brake. The car checked its speed, and before she was round the bend the big fender on the Nissan had caught her rear right wing.

The car shot sideways, on a road which was far too narrow for such a manoeuvre. Kitty fought the wheel to bring the vehicle straight, and the Nissan hit her again, this time fair and square, just behind her driver's door. The impact threw her to the left. Her seatbelt prevented her being hurled across the car, but her Fiesta was hurled across the lane. She caught a glimpse of bushes and a sloping parapet, and was then rolling over and over down the slope, banging her arms and legs and shoulders, before coming to rest upside down, hanging from her belt, while the entire earth seemed to revolve about her.

She heard sounds, and a moment later her assailant was peering at her through the glass. 'Fucking modern cars,' he grumbled. 'They make them too well.'

He pulled open her door. Feebly she struck at him, but that only helped him to grasp her wrist with one hand while reaching past her to release her seat belt with the other. There was a blinding pain in her head as she collapsed on to the roof of the upside down car, and he pulled her clear. 'We'll bash the seat belt catch about to make it appear as if it burst,' he muttered to himself. 'So you would have been thrown clear. And hit your head...this'll do the trick.'

Still gasping for breath and dizzy with the pain in her head, Kitty was dragged to her feet and found herself facing a tree a few feet from where her car had come to rest. 'Now, then,' her assailant said, breathing beer and onions over her, 'A good hard bash, or as many as may be necessary.'

Desperately she dug in her heels and struck at him with her fists, but she did not seem to be making any impression through his heavy quilted jacket, while on the wet, slippery grass her feet were giving way to his superior strength, and the tree was coming closer... 'What the hell is going on?'

So intense had been their struggle, that neither of them had heard the jeep. Now James came sliding down the embankment towards the wrecked hired car. 'Shit!' said the man holding Kitty, glancing at James' bulk and deciding against taking him on. 'I just dragged her out of that wreck,' he gasped. 'Try to make her comfortable while I phone from my car for an ambulance.' And he dashed off up the slope to the Nissan.

'No!' Kitty tried to shout, 'Stop him!' but the word sounded more like a groan.

James lowered her on to the wet grass and knelt with her cradled against him. 'Don't try to speak, my love. Just keep still.'

She twisted in his arms, trying to sit up. 'No! You don't understand...'

'Hush.' He pushed her down again. 'Just relax and we'll soon get...help...' he stared up at the Nissan, watching in amazement as it revved up and sped away. 'What the...?'

'I keep trying to tell you,' Kitty muttered. Her teeth began to chatter and she was beginning to shake. 'James. He forced me off the road. He was trying to kill me.'

James frowned. Though she didn't appear to have any broken bones, he suspected her mind was wandering—she was obviously going into shock...but on the other hand, why did the bloke cut and run like that? He shrugged. Time to think about that later when he'd done something about Kitty. 'Come on lassie. We'll have to get you up and out of here. It's nothing short of miraculous that you seem to have escaped that car with little more than bumps and scratches.'

Kitty smiled faintly, thinking how ironic it was that after all her fantasizing, when at last she was in James' arms, she was in too much pain to appreciate it. Nevertheless it was very comforting to feel herself lifted and carried up to his jeep.

Half an hour later she was wrapped in blankets in an armchair in his cottage, watching him relight the fire. 'Can't you take this towelling off yet?' she asked.

James had grabbed an old dog towel from the floor of the jeep, folded it and wound it round her neck in place of a brace. 'I think we might replace it with a cleaner one,' he smiled, 'but you'd better keep it on until you've had a proper checkup.'

'Have I got to go to a doctor?'

'I've called Doctor Dalgleish up from Aboyne. He'll be here in a minute. How are you feeling, now?'

‘A bit sick. The room starts spinning every few minutes. Oh lord, I think I’m going to start howling.’ She tried to stop herself, but she was too weak to hold back the tears. James crouched beside the armchair and held her against him, gently stroking her hair. Which did nothing to stem the tears but did succeed in making her feel a lot better. ‘Thank God you came by,’ she sighed. ‘He was going to kill me, you know.’

James still found it hard to believe. ‘Yes, well we’ll see about that. Meantime, in waiting for the doc would you like a cup of tea? The kettle should have boiled by now.’

‘Please.’

Doctor Dalgleish was a Glaswegian, with an accent so thick Kitty needed James to interpret for her. The stout, elderly man asked to use James’ bedroom where Kitty lay flat while her bruised ribs were checked, along with reflexes and limbs. Having given her some analgesic tablets, congratulated her on surviving with nothing more than the bruises and cuts on her hands, face and shins from the shattered windscreen, the doctor departed, leaving James with instructions to keep her warm and resting for a couple of days.

‘But I can’t stay here!’ she argued,

trying to sit up and wincing with pain. She had not told the doctor what had really happened, allowed him to suppose she had merely skidded off the road. She had to convince James first before she could attempt to convince anyone else.

'Why not?' James leaned over her to arrange the pillows higher.

'I'm in your bed, for a start!'

'I promise you, you are welcome to stay in it.'

'For two days!'

'For the rest of your life, if you like.' The words were out before his brain was engaged. He sucked in his breath waiting her reaction. Knowing he had to be out of his mind.

Kitty saw his anxious expression, blinked, and then smiled. 'Don't worry. I didn't hear that.'

He lifted her hand from the coverlet and pressed it against his cheek. 'Sorry, I shouldn't have said it. But I dare say you'll hear it again when you're feeling better. I've just called the car hire people to let them know what's happened, so don't worry about that.'

She continued to feel the tingling of his stubble on her skin, long after her hand was released. 'Could I have another cup of tea, please?'

'Sure. And is there anything you want from your bag? I went back and fished it out of the car while the doc was with you.'

'Thanks. Yes, could I have my hairbrush, please?' Then she frowned. 'Have you rung to notify the police yet?'

'No. I wanted to wait till you felt up to being interviewed. You've been saying some strange things...'

'Listen to me, James,' she said crossly. 'That Nissan was parked up one of the tracks off the road with its engine running. When I came round into his view he shot down the track at me, and when I didn't go over the first time he rammed me, repeatedly, till the Fiesta was rolled over the parapet.' She saw the dubious reaction in his eyes. 'Don't you believe me?'

He rubbed his chin. 'Maybe I just cannot imagine why in the world anyone would want to... Well I mean to say, if that bloke wanted to kill you, why the hell was he trying to rescue you when I came along?'

'Rescue me? You joke! He hauled me out of the car to bash my brains out on a tree. To make it look as though I'd been thrown clear and killed on impact!'

James shook his head. 'How could you know that?'

'Because he was talking aloud to himself as he went about it. Said he'd smash the seat belt buckle to make it look as though it broke in the crash, releasing me to be thrown out.' She sank back into the pillows, eyes closed, exhausted with the effort of trying to convince him.

James didn't want to believe it; but he did want to believe Kitty. Who on God's earth could possibly want her dead, he asked himself?...and immediately knew the answer. Something else he didn't want to believe. 'What happened at the castle last night?' he asked. 'You didn't let on about the meeting, did you?'

Kitty screwed up her face. She was hurting. It hurt to move her left leg: her back ached: the bruising on her ribs hurt with every breath. Despite the solution with which the doctor had swabbed her shins, hands and face, all the little cuts were stinging. And worst of all her brain hurt. Feebly she nodded. 'Yes. I lost my rag and let fly with both barrels. But James,' she opened her eyes and turned to look at him. 'What possible connection could there be with that...and what's just happened this morning?'

James swallowed. 'I don't know. But if there was a row—if Morris got scared your theories were going to cost him a few million quid, I imagine it is quite possible there is a connection.' He sat on the edge of the bed, smothering one of her hands in his. 'Yes. The more one thinks about it the more one realizes it does all add up to more than coincidence.' Subconsciously he lifted her hand again. But this time he kissed it.

Kitty tried not to wince as the stubble on his chin scratched into her cuts. But at least she could enjoy the fact that the feeling between them was mutual. The sound of a car roaring past at speed broke the spell. 'So what do we tell the police?' Kitty asked.

'The truth. What else?'

'Will they believe me? Any more than you did?'

'We can give them a fair description of the bloke.'

'Pity I didn't get a chance to see his registration number.'

James gave a wry grin. 'If this was a deliberate set up, I imagine that Nissan was stolen. He'd hardly have been daft enough to use his own car.' He got up. 'I'd better call the station in Aboyne, now. But...we tell them what happened, nothing more. We stick to facts, not suppositions or accusations. Right?'

Kitty nodded.

Kitty hadn't a clue where she was. Slowly

her eyes began to focus on unfamiliar objects: a framed photograph of an elderly couple in a garden: a large, flowered jug and bowl on an oldfashioned washstand.

Wincing with pain she rolled her head on the pillow and stared up at a low, beamed ceiling, and over the brass footrail of the bed to where sunlight was sneaking round the edges of a heavy curtain. Then she remembered. This was James' room... James' bed! What was the time? How long had she slept?

Throwing back the bedclothes she tried to roll to a sitting position on the side of the bed...but the effort left her gasping with pain and weakness, tears threatening. She persevered, dropped her feet on to the floor and gingerly stood up, holding on to the bed for support. Slowly as she stretched each muscle, worked her shoulders, hip joints and her spine, each movement became easier. Not less painful, but definitely easier.

She staggered to the window, pulled back the curtains and looked at her watch. Ten past two? Jeepers! Those tablets the doctor had made her swallow must have knocked her cold for about four hours!

She hunted around for her shoes but gave up, opened the door and went into the sitting-room. It was empty. She found James at the kitchen table, eating. He jumped up when he saw her. 'What are you doing out of bed?' He pulled out a chair for her.

'I can't stay there. I must get home.' She flopped onto the chair and leaned on the table.

'Why?'

She stared up at him, yawning. 'I can't remember. It'll come back to me. Oops! Excuse me,' she added as her tummy gurgled.

James grinned. 'When did you last eat?'

She screwed up her face, trying to think. 'Last night, I suppose. Whatever it is you're eating smells divine.' She sniffed appreciatively.

James put down his knife and fork and went to the oven. 'Voilà, madame!' he put a plate in front of her and whipped off the cover. 'Courtesy of Mr Bird's Eye.'

She recognized the neat slices of meat and two veg. 'What would we do without freezers?' she smiled, and picked up her fork.

They ate in silence. When he was finished, James said, 'I telephoned the police in Aboyne.'

'What did you tell them.'

'Just that your car had gone off the road and you were sleeping, on the doctor's instructions.'

'Do they want to see me?'

He nodded. 'They should be here soon. They were going to examine the crash first.'

She looked at her plate. 'I'm sorry, but I don't think I can manage any more, right now. I should get ready.'

'For what?'

'To leave. I must go as soon as the police have finished with me.'

James shook his head. 'Oh, no, you don't.' He picked up the dinner plates and put them on the drainboard.

Kitty gave a brief laugh. 'And who says?'

'I do. You are in no fit state to travel. And I certainly don't want you wandering off with a homicidal maniac on your heels.'

'You don't, huh?' she challenged.

'No. And if you are wondering what the hell business it is of mine, I shall tell you. I have reached the conclusion that I've become disproportionately concerned about you. Try as I may, I cannot get you off my mind. A very annoying situation for a confirmed bachelor, I may tell you.'

Kitty's mouth opened and shut, twice. The last person to speak to her like that had been Toby and she had not merely resented it...she had been furious. So why, when James took the same authoritative tone with her, didn't she feel a similar reaction? She suppressed a smile. Heavens! She was almost enjoying it! 'I suppose I should be flattered,' she said, feigning annoyance. Then, seeing his mournful expression, wished she hadn't.

A sudden thumping on the kitchen door was followed by a voice shouting 'Are ye in there, Jamie?'

'Here they are.' James' chair scraped on the stone floor. 'Come on in, Davey,' he called, and the door was pushed open by a man as large as himself.

Police-Sergeant David Harvey had been known to get fierce on a few exceptional occasions during his long career in the force, but generally he would best be described as a gentle giant. One of the old school. He had joined the force with no burning ambition to track down criminals and bring them to justice, but simply because his father was a policeman—as was his elder brother. The years had added several inches to his girth and his round, jovial face was topped by bushy grey brows and a thick grey thatch of hair.

He walked straight to the table, reaching across to shake Kitty's hand. 'Ye'll be Miss Cochrane, then?' His companion was a very young constable introduced as Andy Searle.

'A cup of tea, Davey?' James offered.

'Aye. We could do with warming up

after spending an hour down yonder with the remains of yer car, Miss.' He spread his bulk over an inadequate bentwood chair and unbuttoned his coat.

'Is it a total write-off?' Kitty asked.

Davey gave a hearty laugh. 'Nay, lass. There's one wheel no' bent, and for some mysterious reason the rear view mirror is intact. So ye canna say it's total. An' mebbe the rest o' the twisted metal can be used for a corkscrew.' And he laughed some more. Kitty had not been looking forward to the interview, but found herself relaxing, laughing with this obvious friend of James'. 'So will ye be telling us how ye managed ta survive? Or better still, begin at the beginning an' tell us how on airth ye got yesel' doon there in the furst place.' He was smiling at her in paternal fashion, waiting. But as she recounted her story his face grew serious.

When she finished he was frowning. He turned to young Andy, asking, 'Did ye get all o' that doon in yer book?'

'Yes, Sergeant.' He handed his notebook to his superior who flicked the pages back to the start.

'Had ye ever seen this man befoor?' the sergeant queried.

'No.'

'Would ye recognize him again?'

'I doubt it. The draw string round

the hood of his anorak was tied tightly round his face, and he was wearing dark glasses.'

'Tell me again about him pulling ye from the car.'

Kitty repeated the story, and found herself beginning to shake again.

'Aye. Weel, this'll be a matter for the CID. Andy, get that infernal gadget frae yer pocket an' radio the station. Tell them we have a case here of attempted murder.'

Hours later, after darkness had fallen and they'd drawn the curtains in the sitting room and built up the fire, Kitty curled up in an armchair trying to recall just how many times she had had to repeat her story. James was busy in the kitchen, having refused her offer of help saying, 'I never could stand having a woman messing about in my kitchen,' then wondering, hopefully, if he might live to regret the words.

A selection of Gilbert and Sullivan was relayed through the CD player and Kitty found herself humming bits of *The Pirates of Penzance.*

James came in. 'Wine or whisky?'

'Wine, please.'

'Red or white? We're having a bite of Scottish beef tonight.'

'Red, then. Thanks.'

He came and sat on the floor by her chair. He'd changed his boots for a pair of leather slippers, and filled a bowl with potato crisps and they sipped and crunched in companionable silence, watching the flames and listening to the music until he jumped up, saying, 'The tatties'll be mush!' and rushed back to the kitchen.

They ate their supper on their laps in front of the fire; it was delicious, the steaks, potatoes and salad followed by chunks of cheese with biscuits and grapes. When James sat on the floor beside her again to drink his coffee, Kitty's fingers strayed subconsciously onto his shoulder. His hand reached up to cover hers and he turned his head, allowing their eyes to meet.

'You look tired,' he said.

'Yes, I am, but I don't want to move.' She gave a contented sigh. 'What time is it?'

'Nearly ten.'

'I'd better get an early night.' Reluctantly she dragged herself to her feet. 'I can sleep here on the settee...'

'Rubbish!' James sprang up. 'You'll go back into the bedroom. I'm afraid I haven't changed the sheets...'

'But where will you sleep?'

'On the settee.'

'Now who's talking rubbish? You couldn't even fit half of you on that.' She grinned at the idea of James on the cottage two seater.

'Well I'll crawl up into the attic...'

'We can share if you like,' Kitty suggested, and held her breath.

James's grey-green eyes bored into her dark, brown ones. 'I'd like, all right,' he gave a half smile. 'But whilst I might, with considerable effort, keep my actions under control while I'm awake, I can make no guarantee what might happen should I fall asleep. Which I doubt,' he added, his mouth widening into a grin.

'Well, the invitation is only for sleeping, not for a wild, sexual orgy. Apart from anything else, and not wishing to offend, of course, I don't think I'm feeling fit enough, tonight.' And suddenly she was in his arms, laughing, kissing him and hugging him as tightly as her bruised ribs would allow.

'Actually, I must confess I doubt the arrangement would serve much purpose,' he confessed into her hair. 'There is no way this disproportionate concern I mentioned earlier, will allow me to get any sleep with you lying there beside me. However,' he held up a hand when she tried to interrupt, 'I am very willing to lie awake in comfort all night.'

Chapter 9

SECOND TRY

After Kitty had driven away, Morris went back into his office, fuming and at the same time anxious. His overwhelming desire was to go after the girl and bring her back by force. But that would be absurd. There was no way he could allow himself to be involved.

He had been stupid even to try to stop her leaving, with Guthrie present; he was well aware of how much the servants disliked him. But now...she had gone off just an hour early. She could be in Aboyne before Crowther's man reached Abergannan. What to do? He sat drumming his fingers on the desk. Telephone Crowther? That wouldn't do any good. Crowther operated through agents; there would be no way he could get directly in touch with his hit man. Crowther would not even know who he was. Damn, damn, damn. He went upstairs.

'What was all the shouting about, dear?' Margaret asked.

'That stupid Cochrane female, taking off

like a bat out of hell. Tried to stop her. Ill-mannered brat...so damn rude! Thought she was going to kill herself on the bend in the drive. She probably will, if she goes on driving like that.'

'Oh, I do hope she doesn't. But how odd, for her to go off like that! Without saying goodbye. I thought she would be staying until breakfast, at any rate.'

'Modern youth,' Morris grumbled. 'Well, damned good riddance, I say. I'm going to shower.'

By breakfast, everyone knew of Kitty's departure, even those who had slept through the altercation.

'I am bound to say, Wilson,' Morris remarked, 'that your assistant has the least scientific attitude I have ever known.'

Gus looked acutely embarrassed. For all his threat, he wasn't at all sure he was going to do anything about Kitty, who he liked both as a person and a scientist. But she did seem to be operating under a head of excess steam, at the moment. 'All I can do is apologize, Mr Morris,' he said. 'I can only imagine that she is even more upset than we supposed. I'll get on back to Oxford and see if I can sort her out.'

'I think that would be a very good idea,' Morris said.

'I don't suppose *you* chased her off?'

Rebecca inquired of Niall.

'Me?' He was indignant.

'I heard you speaking in the corridor this morning, at about six.' Everyone looked at him.

Niall flushed. 'Well... I knew she was awake...'

'How?' Rebecca asked.

'Look, I knew, right? And I guessed she might be going to bolt, so I had a word with her, yes. Didn't do much good. She said she was going, and she went.'

'That's not the way it sounded to me,' Rebecca snorted.

'This is all a terrible bore,' Tara complained. 'Does it matter if she stayed or if she went? She was an awful wet.'

Gus raised his eyebrows, but he didn't feel he could intervene on Kitty's behalf.

Head tilted, Margaret said, 'Isn't that the office phone?'

Bernard virtually dropped his coffee cup as he dashed from the table, slamming the office door behind him. 'Yes?'

'We seem to have missed,' Crowther said.

'Damnation,' Bernard said. 'Yes, I guessed as much. The stupid bitch left an hour early.'

'Eh? We didn't miss in that sense. The job was all set.'

'Then how the hell...?'

'I don't know. These people operate in their private code. I've had a call from my contact in Glasgow saying that the hit failed. I don't think even he knows what actually happened yet; the operative called him on his Cellnet with a single coded word, which apparently meant he tried but missed.'

'Shit! I thought you said this set up was reliable?'

'Usually is. Something obviously went wrong, something unforseen. I've asked Glasgow to get all the particulars as soon as possible and come back to me re another attempt. I presume you still want the job carried out?'

'If it's not a case of shutting the stable door after the horse has bolted. If she ever gets to a newspaper...'

'Don't worry, we'll sort it out,' Crowther said. 'Stay cool.' He hung up.

Stay cool, Bernard thought angrily. And glared at the door as there was a knock. 'Yes?'

Gus pushed his head in. 'I'm just off.'

'You're going to catch up with that girl, I hope. And talk some sense into her. Do you know where she'll have gone?'

'Well, home, I imagine. I doubt she'll go to the lab.'

'Where's home? I have a friend in Oxford.' Another lie, but he had to know.

'She has a flat in a house owned by a Mrs Cummings. I don't remember the address. Don't worry, I'll talk to her. What I wanted to say was, I'd like to be present when the drilling commences.'

'Why?'

'Professional interest,' Gus said easily.

'Well, I have no objection to your being present. But if that's your intention, then there's no point in your returning to Oxford. I'm expecting MacPhail with his gear tomorrow, and we'll be starting drilling on Monday.'

'You've received permission?'

'It's on its way.' Morris leaned back in his chair. 'I don't believe in letting grass grow under my feet.' He grinned, 'Or gas. Now, if you'll excuse me, Professor...' He watched Gus close the door behind him, and picked up the phone. He had information for Crowther.

'Who did you say?' Bernard demanded. He had spent the past few hours waiting for a telephone call that had never come, and was feeling intensely irritable.

' 'Tis Inspector Campbell of the Aboyne constabulary,' Guthrie said. 'Says it is most important he have a word with ye.'

'Ah...right.' Bernard kept his features still with an effort. 'I'll be right out.'

Guthrie closed the door behind him, and

Bernard hastily opened the bottom drawer of his desk and took out the bottle of malt whisky he kept there for emergencies. This could be classified as an emergency. He took a deep swig, telling himself that all he needed to do was keep his head. Crowther would never let him down, and Crowther was the only person in the world could link the attempt on Kitty Cochrane's life with him. He took another swallow, corked and replaced the bottle, wiped his lips, and went to the door. 'Inspector...?'

'Campbell, sir.'

The policeman was a somewhat cadaverous looking individual; Bernard thought he'd be well-suited by a deerstalker.

'I don't think we've met.' Bernard shook hands. 'Come in, man, come in.' He held the door of his office open. 'I must confess I don't often get visits from the police.'

'Aye, well, it's a strange business, to be sure.'

'What is? Sit down, man, sit down. Would you like a drink?'

Campbell raised his eyebrows as he glanced at the clock; it was not quite five in the afternoon. 'I won't, if ye'll excuse me, Mr Morris. I'm on duty.'

'Ah, so this is not a social call?'

'I'm afraid not, sir. May I ask if ye've recently had a young lady named Cochrane staying at the castle?'

'Cochrane? Oh, yes, of course. She's one of the scientists we've had here. Because of that poor boy's tragic death, you understand? I've had some experts in to make sure Gannan Hill is safe.'

That was not what was being rumoured in Aboyne. However, the environment was not Campbell's business. 'May I ask when the young lady left the castle?'

'Early this morning. She was going to catch the shuttle out of Aberdeen.'

'I see. Well, sir, I have to tell you that shortly after leaving here she was involved in an accident. Or perhaps ye already knew that.'

'An accident? Miss Cochrane? Good heavens! No, I certainly did not know that, Where is she? Is she hurt?'

'Just a few bruises, I'm happy to say. She's presently at your bailiff's house in Aboyne. The point is, sir, that Miss Cochrane feels it wasn't really an accident. She says someone drove into her and tried to kill her.' Bernard stared at him. He actually did not know what to say. 'I can see ye're shocked,' Campbell commented. 'But you see, sir, it happened while she was still on Abergannan Estate. Now, sir, d'ye have any idea who might have done such a thing?'

'My God!' Bernard said. 'On my estate? What an outrage!'

'Ye can think of no one who might be responsible?'

'Of course I cannot. I am absolutely horrified. Does Miss Cochrane not know who tried to kill her?' He held his breath.

'Sadly, sir, no. Miss Cochrane does not think she ever saw the man before. He was in any event wearing an anorak tied across his face and dark glasses.'

'Well, I can assure you it was not one of my employees. The very idea is outrageous. Miss Cochrane made herself very popular with all my staff.'

'I am sure she did, sir. I wonder if I could have a word with them?'

'Certainly not,' Bernard snapped. 'As I say, the very idea is outrageous.'

'Well, sir...'

'Look, Inspector, if it is important to you, I will question my staff myself, and let you know if I discover anything. But I do not wish them upset by even the suspicion that any of them might have been involved.'

'That is not what I had in mind.'

Bernard stood up. 'I'm sorry, Inspector. That is my final decision. Now, I'm afraid I must bid you good-day. I'm a very busy man.' He stood in the doorway to watch the policeman drive off. He thought he'd handled that rather well. But it was something else to tell Crowther.

Kitty was suddenly wide awake, feeling remarkably relaxed. Perhaps partly due to having slept so much the previous day.

She lay still, not wanting to disturb James; he was asleep on his stomach, spread-eagled across the bed, leaving her very little room. Amazingly, he was wearing pyjamas—she didn't think anyone wore them in the nineties. Maybe it was solely as a gesture to their present celibate state. But through the striped material she could feel the comforting warmth of his body...which required her to apply enormous self-control. The urge was strong to slide her hands under the jacket, over the bare skin of his back, inviting his natural response; to feel his arms wrap round her body—and take possession. There was no doubt in her mind that he wanted this, too, but she was old-fashioned enough herself to want to wait for him to initiate their first union.

Her mouth was dry and her body stiff. She wanted a drink, and to stretch the aches from her bruised muscles. Very, very slowly she edged herself over the side of the big, high bed. James shifted in his sleep but didn't wake as she slid her arms into his bulky towelling robe from the hook behind the door, and carefully turned the handle.

In the kitchen she fielded the ritual morning greeting from Castor and Pollox—the dogs, filled the kettle and lit the gas, and fed the screaming cats before opening the back door. As the dogs spilled out with a rush, she gasped, pushed the door closed with a crash and turned the key. Heart pounding she leaned against the door, paralysed, too terrified to go near the window to check whether her imagination had been playing tricks. But if it had, why were the dogs barking so aggressively?

'What the devil was that?' James demanded, staggering into the kitchen in his pyjamas, yawning.

'Me, slamming the door,' she hissed. 'Sorry to wake you up, but...I thought I saw someone out there.'

Seeing her white face and frightened eyes, he said, 'The dogs seem to have the same idea,' and went to the window, peering left and right, before moving swiftly to the front door. He saw nothing, but the sound of a car engine reached him quite clearly from further down the road. The oak clock on the sitting-room mantlepiece showed five-thirty. Far too early for his neighbours, such as there were, to be about.

Back in the kitchen Kitty made the tea and they sat warming their hands round their mugs. Castor barked at the door and

James let them back in, still in a state of high excitement. 'Well? What do you reckon?' Kitty whispered.

'That someone wanted to know if you were here.' His face was grim.

'So, now that they know, what happens next?'

James stirred two heaped spoonfuls of sugar into his tea, thinking. 'Maybe we'd better get you out of here. But not to Oxford.'

'I really want to get to London.'

'Got any friends or relatives there you can stay with?'

'My cousin has a flat in Fulham.'

'Phone him, now. Invite yourself for a few days.'

'She's a female and she'd kill me if I phoned her at this hour.'

'I wish I could come with you...'

'You can't. What about your job?'

James drained his mug and set it back on the table. 'I don't know if I still have one, having gone AWOL yesterday.'

'And my friend Morris won't love you very much for harbouring the enemy, either,' Kitty observed.

James scratched the stubble on his face. 'Which raises some interesting questions. Does he know you are here? If so, how? Has our morning visitor reported seeing you?'

'And did he send the Nissan man to get me?'

'Who else?'

Kitty thought for a minute. 'An unemployed oil driller who'd attended the meeting, and saw me attempting to spoil his chance of a lucrative job?'

James shook his head. 'Unlikely.'

'Or some homicidal maniac imagining he is helping the Green Party cause by wiping out geo-chemists?'

James watched little laughter lines appear round her eyes as she relaxed. A vibrant expression lit her entire face, wrinkled her nose, and her mouth widened into a big grin. She looked so tiny, peering out from the folds of his bath robe. 'That's better. You're beginning to look like your old self.'

'I'd feel even more like my old self if I could soak in a hot bath for a while. Before I depart.'

'I wish you didn't have to go,' he said, solemnly.

She smiled into those compelling green eyes. 'I'd love to stay. But there are too many reasons why I must leave...as soon as possible.' She watched a frown draw his brows together. 'What's the matter?'

'Just thinking it's a pity I can't get away. But I guess it would be irresponsible to abandon the estate, particularly the livestock. I cannot leave it all to Andrew and poor old Wilkie. Would it sound crazy to say I'll miss you—after you've only been back here a couple of days?'

'Utterly ridiculous, Major,' she giggled. 'Now, lead me to my bath.' She got up and waited for him to move.

'Do you mind if we call it our bath? I want one, too. But the boiler will take a couple of hours to reheat the water, so I'll ask you to leave your water for me to use, afterwards.'

Kitty stood by his chair, looking down at his uncombed curls. 'Won't it be cold by then?'

'Yes. But you might find me a bit large to share a tub with.' He twisted in his chair to look up into her face. One eyebrow raised.

Kitty's eyes held his. 'You took up three-quarters of the bed last night, but I coped.'

'Are you telling me you see no difference between sharing a bath or a bed?' His arm slid round her, and when she didn't answer immediately he cried, 'You hussy!' and pulled her onto his knee to kiss her.

Kitty stayed in the kitchen, clearing away the mugs and putting the milk in the fridge, while James went into the bathroom to shave and run the bath.

She grinned to herself, thinking over all the emotions of the past couple of days: anger and frustration, nervousness slipping into sheer terror. And love! She had no doubt whatever that she was in love with James.

Wherever she was, whatever she did, his huge, muscular frame filled her vision...and his grey-green eyes, which filled with love and gentleness when he spoke of his parents and flashed anger at the mention of Morris, spoke silent volumes in her dreams. She wanted to believe he felt the same for her. That he really did love her and wasn't simply lusting after her...

Her smile spread wide. Hearing the bath water pouring, anticipating sharing a bath with him, she couldn't kid herself that her shivers of excitement were anything other than lust.

The sound of running water stopped. 'Your bath awaits you, ma'am!' James called. He was leaning across the bath, placing soap and a loofah on the far side. Stark naked. Her shy glance was brief, but long enough to assess that he hadn't an ounce of spare fat on him—only hard muscle. The bulging calves were coated in fine, curly hair, his thighs were thick and muscular. Tight, narrow buttocks and waist widened at the base of his huge rib cage, and thick neck muscles were supported by powerful shoulders. A veritable Goliath!

He turned his head to grin at her. 'May I take your robe, ma'am?'

She arched her neck. 'What, no bath foam?'

'Absolutely not. We don't want anything to hide your charms, do we?' He was facing her, reaching out to take the robe from her. Studiously, she kept her eyes on his face, resisting the temptation to drop her gaze. And as he hung the robe on the bathroom door she quickly jumped into the water, gasped at the heat but curling down, busily pretending to wash her face.

She had expected him to sit opposite her with his back to the taps, but instead he slid down behind her, his hard arousal pressing against her back. Trembling, she leaned against him and felt his big hands envelope each breast. He nuzzled her neck through her wet hair and she turned her face for an awkward, half-kiss.

The bathing ritual didn't last long. Wrapped in a big, white towel she was carried into the bedroom, dumped on top of the bed and completely submerged under his damp body.

Later, James said, 'What about your bruises? Afraid I forgot all about them.'

Kitty sighed and snuggled against him, pulling a blanket over his bare back. 'So did I. In fact, I can't feel them at all.'

'I feel guilty I haven't been back to visit Karen. How is she?' Kitty asked as they ate a ham and egg brunch.

'They've transferred her to a burns unit down south. She's getting on quite well, considering.'

'Tell Mr Wilkie I asked after her, will you?'

'Sure. More coffee?' James took the mugs to the coffee maker.

'What will you do now?'

'You mean after I've seen you safely on to your plane at Aberdeen?' He put her mug in front of her. 'I think I'll go and see Morris, and explain that having found you in your wrecked car and installed you down here, I couldn't leave you till you'd been checked over by the doc and interviewed by the police. Last evening.' He sat down again, adding, 'I'll say you've gone home. I won't mention London. Or what actually happened, for the time being. If he is responsible, well...'

'We want to give him room to hang himself,' Kitty replied.

'You scared? We could tell the police the truth.'

'Sure I'm scared. But we can't prove what happened, at the moment. Although... he's a blowhard, right? You might get some results if you *did* tell him what happened, making it plain that we know all about it, and see his reaction.'

'Good thinking. I might just try that. Without letting on that we suspect him, of course. So you just keep out of trouble while I do a bit of amateur detective work.'

'Thanks. In fact thanks for a lot of things.' She put down her knife and fork. 'Mmm. That was seriously good.'

James finished eating and sat back in his chair, looking at her. 'So. Where do we go from here?'

'How do you mean? Now, to the airport?'

'I mean us. You and I. Oxford and Aberdeen are a million miles apart, my darling.'

'It's hard to think ahead, at the moment. About the future and all that.' Kitty grasped her hair and tugged it back from her face. It was a gesture James loved. Bereft of hair, her face took on an elfin quality: full of life and yet so small and vulnerable. He waited, anxious to hear her say more. Her eyes were dark and sad. 'Dearest James. We will have to play the next few weeks by ear, won't we? This whole situation we're involved in will have to be sorted out before we can make any decisions about ourselves.' She grabbed fiercely at his wrist. 'Telephone me, every night, won't you?'

'If you give me a number.'

'Ah, good thinking. I'll give you Joanne's address, too.'

Neither of them could think of much to say on the drive down to Aberdeen. Kitty got a ticket on the three-thirty to Heathrow and James stayed with her until she boarded, watching the travellers milling round the terminal for any suspicious-looking characters. Feeling reasonably confident she was safe, he kissed her goodbye and watched her disappear through security.

Despite his forceful handling of the Aboyne police the previous afternoon, Bernard Morris had spent another anxious day making frantic and furious telephone calls, ripping faxes off the machine and scrawling angry replies.

Fortunately, although most of the household had been aware that Campbell had called, and he had been forced to tell them that the reason was to inform him that his ex-house guest had careered off the road but was not seriously hurt, Margaret accepted the news as proof that he had been right all along about Kitty Cochrane drinking too much.

Rebecca was the only one, apart from Wilson, of course, who had been seriously concerned, but he had been able to reassure them both that she was really quite all right. He had not told them that it might not have been an accident.

However, he was still furious that the girl had escaped. God alone knew how much damage she might do to the gas project before Crowther's contacts caught up with her. Of course, if she was still at MacEwan's...

For the third time that day he was shouting down the phone at Crowther when there was a sharp rap on the door. He smothered the mouthpiece with Crowther in mid-reply, and called 'Come in!' then said to Crowther, 'I'll call you back.' He replaced the receiver.

James entered and crossed to the desk.

'Well?' Bernard snapped.

'I've come to apologise for my absence,' James replied.

'Wondered where the devil you were,' Bernard lied. 'What was your problem?'

'That Miss Cochrane you had staying here. Her car went off the road early yesterday morning, a few miles down from here. I got her to my place and had the doctor check her over.'

'I know all about that. The police reported it. And that kept you busy for twenty-four hours?'

'She was badly shaken. Some maniac

had deliberately pushed her car over a parapet.'

Bernard snorted. 'A likely story!'

James resisted the temptation to lean across the desk and throttle the bastard. 'It could have been murder, sir. I saw the culprit myself,' he added, and had the satisfaction of seeing his boss's face turn grey. 'We have both given full statements to the police.'

'Hmm. Yes. One of them came up here to say what had happened but they don't appear to be taking it very seriously. Miss Cochrane still staying with you?' Because if she was, the problem might be solved. His mind was already working out an excuse to get MacEwan up into the hills away from the cottage while Crowther's contacts returned to finish their job. One more day should do it.

'She left at noon.'

The words took a moment or two to sink in. 'Left!' Damn. 'Where's she gone?'

James shrugged. 'Don't know. Home I suppose,' he said and watched Morris's face turn from white to puce.

'She must have given some indication where she was headed?' Morris snapped.

'I imagine she might be back at the laboratories where she works, tomorrow.'

'Pigs might fly,' Morris snorted. In fact he wasn't sure where MacEwan stood in all this. He had heard that the major had attended that damned meeting in Aboyne, but hadn't established which side of the fence he was on.

All he did know was that he disliked this man, with his clipped army accent and formal manner. He wished there had been even one other applicant for the job of bailiff; longed to sack him, but that was impossible. He needed him, at least for the present. And anyway, it would be better to have him on the payroll, beholden, where he could keep an eye on him. Always keep the enemy in your sights, eh? But doing what? He knew precious little of what happened on the estate. He played one off the cuff: 'Macphail is bringing his gear in tomorrow.'

James was surprised. 'On a Saturday?'

'The world doesn't stop because it's a weekend, MacEwan. My world, anyway. Now, there'll be a lot of activity around Gannan Hill. I think the sheep in that area should be moved.'

James and Wilkie had moved them days ago. But assessing Morris's motive he said, 'You're absolutely right, sir. I'll put that in hand immediately. But...you're starting to drill tomorrow?'

'I said the gear arrives tomorrow. We'll start drilling first thing next week. These operations take time to set up. I'll need you on hand.'

'I'll be there.' He stepped back. 'Will that be all?'

Bernard Morris congratulated himself on his clever strategy. 'Yes,' he said, strumming his fingers on the desk. 'That will do for today. But check with me tomorrow morning, will you?'

If the situation hadn't been so serious, James might have given the game away by laughing. The entire scene had been pure theatre. Morris sitting there, lying in his teeth, unaware James knew the truth. And himself playing dumb, faking innocence of Kitty's whereabouts. He could only hope the man didn't know he was lying, too. On the other hand, next week! Would that give Kitty enough time to raise the roof?

Rebecca paced her bedroom, fuming. She felt so helpless. Useless. She had been profoundly disturbed by the wanton destruction of the countryside, the wastage of the planet's natural resources and the damage to the ozone layer long before commencing work at the Ministry of the Environment. Taking the job had been a conscious commitment to doing something constructive towards righting the wrongs. And now, here she was right in the thick of it, personally involved and doing absolutely nothing to prevent her father perpetrating yet another disaster. If only Kitty hadn't run out on her... If only Gus was on their side...

She paused in midstride, distracted by her reflection in the long, wardrobe mirror. There was no doubt she was looking heaps better than she had a month ago. She'd stopped bingeing on booze and chocs for a start, and her hair had improved after a treatment and trim. It was nice to be able to tuck her blouse into her skirt without looking like an over-stuffed sofa, and the pottery Pisces sign she'd made at evening class, hung prominently on its leather thong without being lost between what had, till recently, been mountainous boobs.

She stepped closer to the mirror to examine her complexion and admire the lack of zits...and a thought occurred. Gus! She had been attracted to him from the beginning, but he had brushed aside her efforts to be friendly. And who could blame him? But now...she turned sideways to admire her profile, nodding approvingly. She really would like to be friends with him...close friends. She felt an urge to cuddle away his serious frown; mother him. And if he reciprocated, then who knew? Maybe she could get him on her side.

The opportunity for a gambit presented itself as she opened her bedroom door and saw her quarry heading up the stairs from Bernard's office. 'Gus, darling,' she cooed. 'What a very busy person you are. And I was so hoping we might have another opportunity to talk. We do have so much in common, don't we?'

Gus could think of no interest whatsoever he might have in common with this weird female, but he smiled politely, muttering through his beard, 'Yes. Perhaps we do.'

'Are you still very busy, right at this moment?' Rebecca asked in a plaintive voice.

'Er, no. I'm not, actually.' It would be useful to have the sort of brain that quickly conjured up polite excuses, but he hadn't.

'Great!' She took his arm and turned him round. 'Then now is the perfect opportunity for us to go up the burn and see the waterfall.'

He asked, 'Won't we need overcoats?' as he was propelled down the stairs to the front door.

Rebecca knew it would be chilly out there, but had no intention of relinquishing her hold. 'Not if we keep on walking. And if we stop we can keep each other warm, can't we?' she added, giving his arm an affectionate squeeze.

Gus was quite used to being mothered by Gillian: she kept his social diary, put out clean socks and personally trimmed his beard each week. So being taken in hand by Rebecca caused him no surprise or irritation. Anyway, he would quite like to take a walk up to the burn: he needed some fresh air, away from the tensions which were so evident inside the castle. Even if it meant putting up with this peculiar girl.

'I'm so glad you didn't dash off, like Kitty did,' Rebecca said, striding up the track towards the burn, hair blowing in the breeze. 'So important for you to be here as Daddy's project gets underway.'

Gus couldn't think of a suitable response, so said nothing. He paused for a moment to absorb the view, listen to the birds' spring mating calls and watch high vapour trails linking cotton wool clouds to the mountain tops.

'This is all very well,' she indicated the panorama with a sweep of her hand, 'but there's an awful lot of it and one cannot stand in the way of progress, can one?' She was working on the theory that an uninvited opinion would bring an automatic and opposite argument.

'No,' Gus agreed, not listening.

Rebecca tried again. 'Kitty really was going OTT the other night, wasn't she?'

'Eh? Sorry, what was that?'

'Over the top. Kitty...'

Gus scratched his head, stirring his hair into a frenzy. He found this girl hard to understand; having appeared to be the ultimate environmentalist, she now seemed to have gone into reverse. And anyway, what he personally thought of Kitty's attitude had nothing to do with anyone else. 'I don't think we can criticize her for a strongly held opinion, even if we don't agree with it.'

'You mean you don't think Daddy's project is any threat to this environment?'

'No...well, I mean, it depends on the angle...' He started up the track again in sharp, agitated strides. Was this girl being naive, or deliberately trying to corner him? If he said a positive 'no', she might report back to the ministry that he was an uncaring boffin. And if he said 'yes' she could tell Morris...who would kick him into touch.

Rebecca was intelligent enough to realize that her strategy wasn't working, so she reset her sights. 'We are nearly there,' she puffed, trying to keep up with him. 'Mind if I hang on?' She linked her hand into his, obliging him to tow her along. She liked the feel of his hand, it was small but strong. She was amused at how attractive she found him.

Gus was amused, too, that this young thing was seeking his company; he hadn't given much thought to her advances, but had assumed that whatever her motives she was harmless enough. And when they topped a rise and found themselves gazing down into the burn as it bubbled its way over and around dark boulders, circled tiny islets clustered with trees and fell into swirling rockpools, he was happy enough to sit on a grass bank to enjoy the scene with Rebecca slightly below him, leaning against his leg.

In fact, when he looked down in response to a question and met her dark green eyes he decided she was almost attractive. She was asking whether there were times when he needed to find such peaceful settings, as solace for his soul. 'We all need this enrichment in our lives, periodically, don't you think?'

It was typical of the phraseology he remembered from student days. A long time ago. The thought made him smile. 'Personally I'm an audio type,' he said, adopting the jargon. 'Music has always been my opt-out vehicle.'

'Oh, Gus! How wonderful. Do you know, I've a seriously fab set of classic discs for my portable CD. We simply must bring them up here for a double space out.' Her enthusiasm included holding his knee and rubbing her cheek against his thigh.

Unseen, Gus raised an eyebrow. 'Don't know that there'll be time for that. We're going to be busy, shortly.'

'Yes,' she sighed. 'I suppose we are.' Then after a brief silence she added thoughtfully, 'I do hope it isn't *all* going to be spoilt. It would be tragic.' And she sighed again.

Mating songs were exchanged between the birds each side of the burn. A small fish plopped noisily below them. 'Yes,' he nodded without thinking, 'Wouldn't it.'

'Oh, Gus!' Rebecca rolled onto her knees, sitting back on her heels. 'Do you really think we should let it happen?' She grasped both his hands and gazed into his eyes, pleading.

He smiled down at her, but the smile turned to amazement as she launched herself into his arms, held his ribs in a vice-like grip and began to sob.

He scratched his head with one hand while patting her back with the other, wondering how the hell he'd got himself into this. 'Er, look, my dear...' he tried to pull himself away but was pinned to the bank. 'I don't know if you are referring to your father's gas drilling,' though he had a nasty hunch that that was what this was all about, 'but, as you yourself remarked just now, we cannot stop the march of progress.'

He frowned. What the hell was she playing at? Was she really as innocent as she made out, or had she some ulterior motive in getting him up here? Human psychology had never been his forte, but there were times when one had to give the matter some thought. And this was one of those times.

His mind went into computer mode, flicking back over the various conversations in which she had been involved, the expression on her face when Morris was enthusing over his project, glances with her mother. Quickly his brain analysed his findings and answered his query. Yes. She was undoubtedly trying to con him into a Green stance.

But back to square one. Should he give her a sharp brush-off and risk antagonizing Morris and/or the Environment Department, or play her along? The latter option was not in his nature; he had never been a political animal. But maybe on this occasion he should play safe.

He patted her shoulder again and this time made it to his feet. 'Don't know about you,' he faked a shiver, 'but I'm getting damned cold up here. Let's go back and see if we can call up a hot cup of tea.'

'Perhaps we'd better,' Rebecca agreed

reluctantly. But she contrived to maintain a grip on his hand all the way down to the castle.

Kitty telephoned Joanne from Heathrow. 'It'd just be for a few days,' she said.

'Man trouble?' Joanne asked.

'I'll tell you when I see you. I've just got to nip out to Oxford and pick up some things. I'll be with you by eight at the latest.'

'I'll hold dinner,' Joanne said, obviously very interested in this latest development of her cousin's love life.

Kitty then telephoned her friend Bill Ashton, who was a feature writer on one of the tabloids. 'I have something which will interest you,' she said.

'Speak.'

'I can't, over the phone. But it's environmental dynamite.'

'Sounds possible. When?'

'Well...' she looked at her watch. It was just on six. 'Tonight?'

'What time?'

'Ah... Can you make it after nine?'

'Not for tomorrow's edition.'

'Well...' but one more day would surely not matter. There was no way Morris could start serious drilling before next week. 'As long as it's in on Monday.'

'That depends on what you have to give

me. Where will you be?'

'At Joanne's flat. See you at nine.'

Joanne would have to grin and bear it.

Kitty drove home slowly, glad to be back in her own car. She still wasn't at all sure of her feelings, knew she was hovering on the edge of hysterics. She had fallen in love, deeply and completely. There was an occasion for hysterical happiness. But she was also abandoning the job, and perhaps the profession, that she loved—not to mention a friend and colleague for whom she had the deepest respect. An occasion for hysterical misery.

She could of course still forget the whole thing, telephone Bill and tell him she'd changed her mind. He'd swear a bit but he'd forgive her. But then what? Commitment to James meant commitment to stopping Morris. There was no way out.

She braked, swung the wheel into the turning to Mrs Cummings' house and caught a glimpse of a strange car, parked close to the hedge farther down the lane. Well, she had no reason to object to its being there. Probably visiting a neighbour.

She parked in front of the garage beside the house, as usual, and tugged her travel bag over from the back seat. She'd just drop these dirty things, pick up some clean clothes, and be away.

Mrs Cummings would undoubtedly want her to come in for a chat, but she'd have to put her off; she couldn't tell how long the man, or men, Morris had hired to get rid of her might take to track her down here—it would have been simple enough to obtain her address, from Lois for instance, who would have had no reason to withhold it.

She was getting out of the car, dragging the bag after her over the handbrake, when she thought again of the strange car, parked in such an unusual place. Her heart did several flip-flops, as she hesitated.

Although it was still daylight, the lights were on in Mrs Cummings sitting-room; the house looked so invitingly safe. But it wasn't safe at all, if a killer was determined to get in. And she couldn't risk involving Mrs Cummings.

She turned and threw her bag back into the car, got behind the wheel. As she glanced in the rearview mirror, she saw a man dash out of the shrubbery, pointing something at her. She started the engine and engaged reverse in one synchronized movement.

There was a clump as something struck the bodywork of the car. The car shot backwards, forcing the man to leap out of the way, falling to one side. Kitty almost rolled the car as she swung the rear on to the lane, braked and ground the gear lever forward. There was another clump. Then she was turning onto the main road through Oxford and racing for the motorway to London.

'Come on, come on, you dumb bunny!' Why do some drivers lose concentration at traffic lights and sit in a daze long after the change to green? Not that her own concentration was all that brilliant at the moment, driving with one anxious eye perpetually on the rearview mirror.

Kitty's heart was pounding, her mouth dry. It occurred to her as she finally filtered on to the motorway that even if her assailants were following, did get right up behind her, she wouldn't recognize them; she hadn't had time to get a good look at their number plate and there were thousands of white cars around all the time... All this assuming that the car parked in the lane had belonged to them in the first place.

Her pulse rate quickened when she realized the car behind was crowding her. It swung out to overtake in the fast lane, driver and passenger peering at her as they passed. Their windows were down and they waved and wolf-whistled... Kitty gasped with relief.

Traffic was heavy, the rush hour at its height and she couldn't make up her mind whether that was a good thing or not. Of course although she didn't get their number, they undoubtedly had hers! There might be people watching the motorway exits... Oh hell! Now I'm getting totally paranoid, she thought.

But she was tempted to turn off and find a hire car firm...then decided that if they were behind, keeping a discreet distance, she would be playing right into their hands. Yet it would be fatal to lead them right up to Joanne's door...

Still undecided, she left the motorway at the Brentford exit and took the Chiswick High turning, off the roundabout. There was a big Parcel Post van behind her, followed by a bus and heavy transporter...so she turned the wheel left towards the supermarket, swung into the car park and found a space waiting.

The bullet holes in the rear and driver's doors convinced her. Grabbing her bag, she dodged through the park towards Turnham Green Station. They'd never find her on the Underground.

Leaving the train at Baron's Court, she took a short cut through Hammersmith cemetery, continuing to look over her shoulder, until she was able to walk sedately up Pridholme Road and ring Joanne's bell.

Joanne's sitting-room might be described as arty: the bare floorboards had been sanded and stained a pale, honey colour and were dotted with a variety of small ethnic mats and a large sheep's skin. A modern interpretation of Cyclops stared at visitors from his vantage point over the fireplace...which was filled by a misshappen pot full of dried grasses.

Not really Kitty's scene, at all, but the ancient settee, with its tasseled throw rug and cushions was comforting, like the hot mug of tea Joanne had pressed into her hand within minutes of her arrival.

'Well? Are you going to tell me about it or do I have to resort to violence?' Joanne demanded. She was perched on a black, spindly chair, her equally spindly legs encased in tight leggings, with a skinny jumper proving an almost flat chest.

Kitty replaced the mug on a mosaic-topped table and offered her an apologetic grin. 'Afraid your dull old scientist cousin has gotten herself involved in a James Bond type drama.' Despite the fact she was beginning to unwind, and although the room was centrally heated, she was shivering...or was it just shaking?

Joanne leaned forward, her black pigtail brushing her knee. 'Give!'

'Difficult to know where to start, but I

was shot at on the way here.'

'You what?!' Joanne jumped up and rushed to the window. 'Are you sure?'

'There are bullet holes in my car to prove it.'

'Where is your car?' Joanne pressed her face against the window pane.

'In a supermarket car park. I got a train from Turnham Green.' She reached for her mug and held it up. 'Look, if you get me another cuppa I'll try to put you in the picture...unless you can wait till Bill gets here.'

'Bill?' Joanne took the mug.

'Bill Ashton. I'm going public on this. He's coming here to interview me after dinner...at nine.'

'Dear Lord! That's all I need!'

Bill Ashton wore glasses and a somewhat ripe waistcoat. His hair was untidy, but his brain was razor-sharp. He had met Joanne before but clearly regarded her as one of life's irrelevancies, and settled himself with his recorder to listen to what Kitty had to say. 'Can you support all of this?' Gradually his eyes widened.

Joanne's eyes were like saucers.

'The drilling rig will be up there any time now. And there's my holey car. And James MacEwan will back me up.'

'Just a little lacking in substance.'

'For God's sake...'

'Relax. I'm on your side. But I have an editor to persuade. Tell me where your car is, and we'll have a photographer down there for the bullet holes.'

'If it hasn't been clamped or towed away by now.'

'We'll find it. What I'd really like is a copy of your report...' he paused, hopefully.

'Haven't got one.'

'You still have keys for your lab, haven't you?'

'Yes...but I don't know if I'm entitled to use them.'

'You haven't been officially fired yet, have you?'

'No. But even if I haven't, I can't hand out our confidential findings to the press.'

'Darling,' Bill said, with considerable patience. 'You called me here to do just that. All I'm asking is some proof.'

'These people may be watching the laboratory,' Joanne remarked. 'Waiting for her to return.'

'Hell, yes,' Kitty muttered. 'I'd forgotten that.'

'I'll come with you,' Bill volunteered.

'And you'll definitely publish?'

'With a copy of that report, we'll definitely publish.'

'Shot at you! For God's sake, darling, you'd be better off up here with me.'

Kitty flinched. She had never heard James so angry. 'I didn't ask them to shoot!' she complained.

'Them? However many of them are there?'

'I wish I knew. I had a feeling there was a man sitting in a car parked near the house when I arrived. And another must have been hiding in the bushes.'

'I suppose they followed you.'

'I don't honestly know. There doesn't appear to be anyone lurking outside right now. And there was no one at the lab; Bill and I got in and out without any hassle.'

'Do you want to come back here?'

Kitty frowned. 'I don't know. I haven't got a car, for a start...'

'Why not? Was it badly shot up?'

'No, no. Only a couple of bullet holes. I dumped it in case they tracked it down. But, James, I wouldn't want to return till I've spoken to the people at the Environment Office. That was my chief reason for coming to town, if you remember.'

'That's a waste of time now. Morris has got his permission, the drilling gear arrives tomorrow, and they start work on Monday.'

'Oh, my God,' she said. 'Then they can't be stopped?'

'I'm not sure about that. You say your journalist friend is definitely going to print straight away?'

'He promised. But it can't be until Monday, either. They'll have started before he can have any impact. Listen! What about Rebecca? She is definitely Environmental. Told me so herself.'

'I'm not sure I'd take bets on that,' James said. 'Andrew saw her going walkabout in the hills, hand in hand with your boss.'

'With Gus! Oh go on, what rubbish! Andrew imagined it.'

'Of all people I know, Andrew has the least imagination. Not the type, believe me.'

'Nor is Gus the type to get lecherous with a girl half his age. Or with anyone but Gillian, for that matter.' Kitty looked up and saw Joanne's amazed expression... which brought on a fit of the giggles.

'There's only one way to handle it now,' James said. 'I'm going to organize a protest march. I'll round up everyone who's opposed, in either Aberdeen or Aboyne, and get them on site. And you know what? I think the best place for you to be is right here with us, where I can keep an eye on you, where you'll be in the middle of a crowd, and where you'll be doing the most good.'

'Darling James. I really am desperately tired. Far too tired to think. Let's talk again tomorrow.'

'Of course. You try to get some sleep. I'll call you in the morning. But think over what I've said. I'll be going down to the pub and get the boys going with a mass picket, anyway.'

'Good-night then, my darling.'

'I love you, Kitty Cochrane.'

'I love you, too, James.' She replaced the receiver.

Joanne's eyebrows had shot up even further. 'Now this I have to hear about.' She disappeared into the kitchen.

Kitty listened to cupboards and drawers opening and closing. 'What are you doing?' she called.

'Opening a bottle of wine. This story is doubtless going to take some time in the telling.'

Kitty only wanted bed, but felt she owed it to her cousin to talk. At least the wine will put me to sleep, she decided, as she settled herself back on the settee. But by then her mind had been made up; she would go back to Scotland in the morning.

Chapter 10

THE CONFRONTATION

It was hardly past dawn when the villagers lined their fences, stood at their gates and peered from their windows, as the motorcade made its way slowly up the road to Abergannan.

There was hardly a soul in the Grampian region who, over the past twenty years, had not seen, or at least become aware of, drilling rigs, but few of the folks of Glen Tamar had ever seen one close to: only at sea. Not that they could see anything that looked like a rig now, merely a stream of trucks and lorries carrying pieces of equipment and lengths of metal.

'So the great day has arrived,' Wilkie remarked, joining James by his garden gate.

'I reckon.'

Wilkie gave a little cough. It really was not his place to criticize the morals of the estate bailiff, but over the past two days the village had been a buzz of gossip. 'The young lady's gone, then?' he ventured.

'Aye, she went yesterday,' James said.

'Engaged, are ye?'

James glanced at him. 'You'll have to ask her that, Rabbie.'

'Aye, well...she was hurt, they say. And there was nay room at the hospital at Aboyne, I imagine.'

'I am sure there was room in the hospital in Aboyne, Rabbie, but Miss Cochrane was not sufficiently badly hurt to need hospitalization. Just a few bruises.'

'Oh, aye?'

James grinned. 'What will you be thinking of next, Rabbie. I do intend to marry the girl.'

'Even if she's responsible for all this?'

'She isn't,' James told him.

James drove up to the castle behind the convoy, found the Morrises and all their servants gathered at the bottom of the drive to watch the trucks rumble up and come to a halt. With them was Gus Wilson. James wondered if the professor had any idea what had nearly happened to Kitty. If he had, surely he wouldn't be standing there? Or would he? It was impossible to tell which side Gus really was on. Not even Kitty seemed sure.

But any idea James might have had of having a chat with the professor disappeared when the convoy stopped and a man he recognized as Archie MacPhail got out, and was introduced to Wilson by Morris. Then the three men went back up to the house, obviously on the best of terms. He reckoned he'd have to put Gus with the Indians. And anyway, now it was time to drive to Aberdeen Airport to meet Kitty.

Archie MacPhail studied the Turnbull & Heath report, sitting beside Gus in front of Morris's desk; his battered trilby hung on his knee. It was the first time he had seen it, no matter what Morris had told Bartlett. Morris calculated that, having got his gear here, MacPhail would need a lot of putting off, now. Yet he watched him anxiously. 'What do you reckon?'

'It's a high reading,' said the drilling engineer.

'But is it dangerous, man?'

'Ye'll have to ask the professor.'

'I have already done so. Wilson?'

'There is an element of risk,' Gus said.

'How great, in your estimation?' MacPhail asked.

'You said, five per cent,' Morris reminded him.

'Well, yes. That's the best estimate.' Gus hated being pinned down. He had always regarded it as his responsibility to present figures based on his observations and calculations, and let others make the deductions and decisions. Now, once again, he was being drawn into the centre, and these were the final decisions.

'And the worst?' MacPhail surveyed his sweaty headband.

'Oh, come now,' Morris protested.

'Pays to know the facts, Mr Morris.'

'Well,' Gus said, 'my assistant put the figure much higher.'

'She's an over-excited young woman,' Morris said, choosing his words with care: he couldn't afford to antagonize Wilson, at least not at this stage, so his mouth smiled.

'Your assistant,' MacPhail said, thoughtfully. 'But you don't agree with her, Professor?'

'Well...frankly, I think she is being somewhat over-cautious. There are other factors, you see. The very high pressure and the suggestion that there may be several vents leading up from the reservoir, with the possibility of other pockets of gas, the existence of which we won't know until the drill reaches them, if you follow me.'

MacPhail nodded. 'But if we tap them, that should reduce the pressure.' He stroked his chin. 'Ye'd settle for a one in twenty chance of an explosion, Professor? Ye understand that it is common practice to use small quantities of dynamite where the drill runs into solid rock? Would ye say the chances of a gas eruption resulting from a controlled explosion are greater, or less?'

'Well, obviously greater.'

'But as regards an explosion large enough to be dangerous, would ye stick by your five per cent?'

Gus gulped. 'If I say yes...'

'We'll start drilling.'

'And if I say it could be higher than that?'

'We'd mebbe have to reconsider. How much higher will ye be going?'

'For God's sake!' Morris exploded. 'Night before last, Wilson, you said quite definitely that the chances of anything going wrong were five per cent. My entire family was there when you said that. And so was Mr Bartlett. You going to change your mind now?'

Gus sighed. 'No. I won't change my mind, Mr Morris. I'd say one in twenty is about right, Mr MacPhail. But I would advise that you proceed with the greatest caution.'

MacPhail gave a cold smile. 'I'm a cautious man, Professor.'

James was waiting in the Arrivals Lounge. Kitty had never known anything quite so comforting as being held in his arms against the muscular hardness of his chest. 'Dammit, girl,' he growled, 'I've been out of my mind with worry.'

'I reckon I have a few white hairs myself,' she agreed.

'Hungry?'

'They fed us something on the plane: not what I'd call food. Anyway, it's too early for lunch.'

'Not at Ian's pub, it isn't.'

'But...there's so much to be done! Isn't Morris starting to drill today?' And she wasn't sure she could face food.

'They have to erect the pylon first. Don't worry, I have things rolling. First, let's eat. As Napoleon said, an army marches on its stomach, right?'

'I don't agree with Napoleon on most things, but I guess he got that one right.' She nestled against him in the jeep. 'So tell me: are you still the Abergannan bailiff?'

He grinned. 'You'll have to ask me that again tomorrow. Now you tell me: any problems?'

'Not for the past twelve hours. I think I lost them when I dropped my car.'

'When I think of those bastards trying to kill you...' James muttered.

She squeezed his arm. 'They haven't made a very good job of it, so far.'

'They'll know where you are as soon as we march up to Abergannan.'

'But now I have you to protect me, haven't I?'

'And a whole lot of others,' he promised her. 'We're meeting at the pub. But what about your car? Aren't the police interested?'

'I should think they are. We—Bill Ashton and I—took a tour round by the supermarket where I'd left it, and it'd been towed away.'

'Full of bullet holes. They'll be looking for you to provide an explanation for that.'

'They have to find me first.'

'After today...'

'I know. But it won't matter, after this weekend. Bill's story is going to be out on Monday; the object is to hold Morris up till then, and then we can let everything rip. Don't worry, I telephoned Mrs Cummings to tell her I was still in Scotland but would be back in a day or two. She can tell them that when they trace the car and go to see her. No one knows anything about Joanne, save for Bill, and you.'

He braked in the pub car park, turned to her. 'You're enjoying this, you little minx.'

'Never had so much fun in my life,' she assured him. She did not add that she was scared witless.

'Let me get this straight,' Bernard Morris

said into his telephone. 'Your people missed again? I thought they were experts.'

'About as expert as anyone else in this God-forsaken country,' Crowther conceded; he was just as angry as his partner.

'So where is she now?'

'Nobody has a clue. She boarded a subway train before our people could get down to the platform, and has just disappeared into thin air.'

'What about her car?'

'Oh, the police have that. As it has a few bullet holes in it, they'll be looking for her too.'

'And when they find her, and she spills the beans...shit!'

'What beans? There is absolutely nothing to relate someone trying to kill her to us.'

'Oh, don't be bloody stupid, Philip. I'm the only person in the world who wants her silenced. Unless she's been sticking her nose into someone else's business, too. And what about this story she's carrying around? You say she's disappeared? I can tell you where she's disappeared to: some newspaper's newsroom, that's where she is.'

'Which one?'

'How the hell do I know? Well, let me tell you this, Philip: you had better find her and PDQ, or we're all up shit creek without a paddle.'

Crowther digested this. 'How close are you to starting drilling?'

'The gear goes up this afternoon. We start Monday.'

'I'd see if you can't hurry it along. It'll be that much harder to get an injunction prohibiting drilling if you've already started.'

'Well, Prof, the great day, eh?' Niall said across the breakfast table.

Gus looked out of the window at the enormous accumulation of equipment waiting to commence the last leg of its journey to Gannan Hill; the castle courtyard looked like a badly organized fairground in process of being packed up for its next show. 'Yes,' he agreed.

'Shame Kitty wouldn't stay, eh?'

'It would probably have made her sick,' Rebecca remarked.

'It's so exciting,' Tara said. 'It makes you feel as if we were in the middle of a war, or something.'

Margaret drank coffee, silently. If only they could all just go away, she thought to herself.

Mary cleared her throat from the doorway. 'Begging your pardon, Professor, but there is a telephone call for you on the house phone.'

'For me? Oh! Right.' Gus hurried

through the doorway into the hall.

'Mary?' Margaret asked. 'Where is Mr Guthrie?'

'That I dinna ken, mam. He dinna come in this morning.

'Good heavens,' Margaret remarked. 'I wonder what can be the matter?'

'Maybe he's sick,' Rebecca suggested.

Margaret wondered what Bernard, in his perpetual hyper mood of the moment, was going to say when he came out of the office.

'I didn't get you out of bed, I hope,' Ben Heath said with some sarcasm.

'I have been up for hours,' Gus explained.

'Will you tell me what's going on? You were due back here yesterday.'

'I decided to stay on. Tried to get you. They're going to begin drilling on Monday, and I felt I should be here.'

'And Kitty?'

'Ah...she left. I don't know where she is.'

'Well, I can tell you where she's been,' Heath said. 'At the lab, printing out at least one copy of her report.'

'Eh?'

'Fact. She let herself in some time last night. The security cameras picked her up, with an unidentified man, and those in the lab picked her up again, still with the same man, operating computer and printer.'

'Oh, good lord,' Gus commented.

'I agree with you entirely. You are going to have to have a serious chat with that young woman, Gus—or I am. Anyway, what did she want additional copies of the report for? Hasn't she got one there?'

'Ah, no. I relieved her of it. The fact is, Ben, that Kitty has been acting...er, off her own bat, recently. She is so certain that drilling on Gannan Hill will be dangerous that she has resigned her position...'

'She has done what?'

'Resigned,' Gus said, 'and is threatening to go public with the report.'

'She can't *do* that!'

'Exactly. Which is why I relieved her of her copy. She then stormed out of here. As I say, I don't where she went. But she must have come down to Oxford...'

'And taken additional copies,' Ben growled. 'Pity you didn't relieve her of her keys when you relieved her of that report. Well, I am going to report her to the police. Even if she retained her keys, she had no right to enter the lab once she had resigned...'

'We've nothing in writing, as yet,' Gus reminded him.

'We have your word for it. I am going to sort her out.'

'Yes,' Gus said. 'I think what we want to worry about, first, is what she is going to do with that report. If it appears in a national daily, or any other form of media, without Morris's agreement, he could sue us.'

There was a brief silence on the other end of the phone. 'Then you had better have a word with him about *that,*' Heath said. 'Oh, by the way, I've finally obtained that report *you* wanted.'

'Which report?'

'The one on Morris's financial status. This is absolutely top secret, Gus.'

'I understand that. You mean he has a problem?'

'I mean he's skint, and will be bankrupt if this deal doesn't come off. So you make bloody sure it does, Gus, or we don't get paid.' He banged the phone down on its cradle. Gus replaced the phone more thoughtfully.

Kitty blinked at the crowd of people waiting for her in Ian's pub.

'You remember Ethel Yardley,' James said.

'I'm so glad you're coming with us,' the Green Party candidate said.

'And Bill Buckston?' Kitty had her hand squeezed by the agent.

'And Jock Petersen.' For a moment Kitty

thought Jock was about to kiss her.

'And Hamish Hamilton. And Fulton Coultrain.'

Kitty goggled at the environmentalist. 'But you gave Morris permission to drill,' she said.

'Ah, well, no, I did not, Miss Cochrane,' Coultrain said. 'I did what I was asked to do, by your own good self, ye may remember, and looked up the status of the land. It may be beautiful, but it has never been designated green, if ye follow me. There is nothing to stop Mr Morris from drilling for gas on his land, providing he can obtain the permission of the Department, and I believe he has done that.'

'But you're prepared to protest against it?'

'That I am.'

'Coultrain's presence will lend us a lot of clout,' James said. 'Now, ladies and gentlemen, Miss Cochrane and I are famished. As ye know, Ian has laid on an early lunch for us all in the back. We'll leave as soon as we've eaten. And had a drink,' he added with a grin.

'But this is marvellous,' Kitty whispered as they sat down. 'There must be thirty people here.'

'You haven't seen anything yet,' James assured her.

It was mid-morning before all MacPhail's gear had arrived, and he opted for an early lunch before continuing. 'We'll have things ready by this evening,' the engineer assured an increasingly agitated Bernard.

'I was hoping you could start drilling before then,' Bernard said.

'What's your rush, man? Your gas isn't going to run away. And there's calculations to be made.'

'Well, then, why not tomorrow?

'Sunday? Man, that'll cost ye.'

'I don't give a damn about the cost. Can you start tomorrow?'

'Aye, well, we could, if everything's in order. Now, Professor, ye say ye calculate that there are several vents in yon hill into which gas has seeped from the reservoir. Is that correct?'

'That is my estimation, yes,' Gus replied.

'And ye reckon this is a big reservoir.'

'I do.'

'But ye canna say which way it runs.'

'Not until we've drilled a few holes.'

'Right. Now, Gannan Hill rises out of elevated land, am I right?'

'Well, yes.' Gus began to frown.

'Would ye have an opinion on whether there might be any *lateral* vents into which escaping gas might have seeped? Or conversely, if the field extends, say, in this direction, that there might be other, vertical vents, filled with gas, above wherever the reservoir is situated.' He grinned. 'Maybe even as far as this castle. It's only a couple of miles.'

'You mean there may be gas under where we're standing?' Even Bernard frowned at that prospect.

'It is possible,' Gus said. 'But there is absolutely no indication of it. Nor has there been any smell of methane around the castle.'

'Aye. But that could be because there has been no water erosion, down here, so no gas has reached the surface, although it may be close to it. Just speculating, ye understand. Then ye don't suppose there'd be any point in drilling on the lower ground.'

'I certainly cannot give you any scientific reason for drilling down here, Mr MacPhail.'

'Aye, well, I didna expect ye to. It's just that it would be a lot cheaper.'

'Hang the expense,' Bernard said again. 'Let's get at the gas.'

'Right ye are, Mr Morris. Ye're in the driving seat.' He went to the door, where all the women as well as Niall were gathered in anticipation. 'Take her away, MacGregor,' he shouted at his foreman.

The engines promptly started, and the trucks began to move.

'Oh, it's so exciting! I think I'm going to faint,' Tara announced. 'We can go up there, can't we, Daddy?'

'Of course,' Bernard said.

'What exactly are you going to do first, Mr MacPhail?' Niall asked.

'Well, look at the plans here.' MacPhail led the young man into his mobile office. 'First of all we erect a derrick to hold the drill. We use a rotary drill, ye see, which is by far the most effective. Years ago they used what they called a cable-tool drill, in which the drill, it was shaped like a chisel, would be raised and lowered, each time biting away at the rock. Just like pile-driving, ye could say. But that method had a lot of drawbacks. In the first place, ye had to stop every so often to remove all the broken bits of rock clogging up the hole. Then second, ye had to keep the well free of liquid, or the bit couldn't bite on rock, ye understand. But in the third place, when ye did strike oil, there wasna any means of keeping it out of the well, and so ye had what they called gushers, huge oilspouts into the air which was not only dangerous but wasteful. Why mon, ye could lose the equivalent of a year's production before ye could cap the well.

'But nowadays, ye see, we use the rotary

drill. The great thing about the rotary bit is that it keeps the well full of mud and water. Thus, ye see, by hydrostatic pressure, it keeps out all other liquids, and that includes oil, or gas, while sending up all the broken rock and mud to the surface where it can be carried away. But as the well is always full, there isna room for the gusher to cause bother.'

'Sounds tremendous. But how do you make sure the bit is going straight down?' Niall asked.

'Aye, well, it's sunk with a drill pipe, that is, heavy-walled tubing, which not only protects the bit but prevents it wandering off. Mind you, no bit lasts forever. They wear out pretty regular. Up on yon hill it'll be more regular even than that. But it's all part of the business. So, ye see...' again he indicated the plan, 'the bit goes down, churning away, and as it forces its way doon, it forces the mud back up—all the time keeping the well filled with mud, mind. The surplus mud is forced up, past the kelly, that's the square section above ground which controls the turntable, and is then sucked and pumped off by a hose into a waste basin.'

'And when you reach the gas?'

'There's no problem; it's blocked off by the mud and pulverized rock until we are ready to let it come up.'

'You keep saying mud,' remarked Rebecca, who had also come into the office. 'But there won't be any mud until you get well down, will there? Gannan Hill is solid granite.'

MacPhail grinned. 'Not so solid, according to the Professor. So maybe some gas will come up in the initial stages, but we can burn that off easily enough until we reach the reservoir. All set?'

The motorcade rolled over the track leading to the foot of Gannan Hill. The trucks were already there, and the engineers were marking their ground.

Gus was relieved to see that the water level in the Gannan Stream was quite high—it had been raining on and off heavily throughout the past few days, although it had stopped for the moment—so at least there was no gas escaping from the cavern. But the rain also meant that the ground was at its softest, and pouring the cement for the derrick's feet proved a tedious job. Much of the fencing round the cave had already been torn down out of the way.

Meanwhile the various lengths and uprights were being assembled, as was the casing for the drill; this was in thirty-foot pieces, and would be joined up as necessary.

'How deep are you expecting to go?'

Tara asked. She had bought green wellies and a matching scarf specially for the event.

'As deep as we have to, Miss,' MacPhail told her, adding, 'to a maximum of twenty-five thousand feet.' He chuckled, 'Now that's clear to the centre of the earth, that is.'

'It's going to take them *hours* to assemble all that stuff,' Bernard muttered to Gus.

'You'll be surprised how fast it'll all go up, Mr Morris,' Gus assured him. 'He'll be ready to start drilling on Monday.'

'We're starting tomorrow,' Morris said, and cocked his head. 'What the devil is that racket?'

All heads turned, including those of the engineers, as the sounds of engines drifted up the valley, overlaid by that of a brass band. Bouncing over the track were a dozen cars and trucks, and in the lead truck was the band, which was playing 'When the Saints Go marching In'. There was also a variety of flags, mostly green, with various devices.

'Looks like a protest gathering, Mr Morris,' MacPhail said.

'On my land? By God... Niall, nip down to the Land Rover and use the phone. Call the police in Aboyne and tell them we are being invaded by an army of trespassers.'

'I don't imagine they'll be able to do

anything about it, Dad, without a court order.'

'Just tell them, right.'

The colourful motorcade had come to a halt behind the cars and trucks of the Abergannan party, and were now discharging close to a hundred people.

'Your play, Mr Morris,' MacPhail remarked.

'Keep working,' Morris told him, and strode down the hillside to the crowd.

'Gosh, what do you think is going to happen?' Tara whispered to her sister.

'We'd better get down there,' Rebecca decided.

They ran down the slope, and after a moment's hesitation, Margaret followed. Gus also went down.

MacPhail watched them go, then shrugged. 'That's his business, boys. This is ours. Let's get that derrick up.'

Bernard was out of breath by the time he reached the first of the protesters. Then he paused in angry amazement. 'MacEwan?' he demanded. 'What is the meaning of this?'

'This is a deputation from the people of Abergannan, with representatives from Aboyne, Mr Morris, here to request you not to drill into Gannan Hill.'

'Not to...you work for me, MacEwan.'

'That's not to say I must agree with everything you do, sir.'

Bernard glared at him, then turned his attention to the men beside him. 'Guthrie? Are you mad, man?'

'It's come to me senses I have, Mr Morris.'

'Coultrain? By God, man, you gave me permission...'

'Nay, nay, Mr Morris. Let's keep the facts straight. I told ye, as I was bound to do, that there is no legal reason why ye shouldna drill on your own land once ye obtained permission from the ministry. Even on this land, beautiful as it is.'

'Well, then? I *have* permission from the Ministry.'

'Now I'm here with these good people to appeal to your moral sensibilities, Mr Morris.'

'My...' Bernard had been so angry he was only able to take in the members of the deputation slowly. Now his jaw dropped as his blood pressure soared. 'You!' he bellowed.

'Kitty?' Gus shouted in amazement.

'I'm here, Mr Morris,' Kitty said. 'Despite all your efforts.' Bernard was momentarily speechless.

Ethel Yardley stepped forward. 'Mr Morris? We haven't met. I am Ethel Yardley.' She did not offer to shake hands. 'I shall be standing for Parliament in the next election. Now, I may inform you that these people represent only a small proportion of the vast numbers who are irrevocably opposed to the desecration of Gannan Hill. I may also inform you that, beginning on Monday morning, there is going to be a campaign launched in a national newspaper to bring your intention to the notice of the nation at large, and to the Members of Parliament. May I therefore appeal to both your good sense and your sense of moral values to cease this business now, and send those men and their machinery away.'

There was a moment's silence while Bernard got his breath back. Then he roared, 'Get off my land!'

'My dear Mr Morris,' Ethel Yardley protested.

'You are trespassing!' Bernard shouted. 'I have already called the police to inform them of this. If you are not off my land within fifteen minutes, I am going to take all of your names and bring civil actions for trespass against you.' He glared across their faces. 'I already know most of your names, anyway.'

'My dear man,' Ethel Yardley said, clearly unused to being treated in this manner.

'Off! Out! Clear off!'

'And if we refuse to go, Mr Morris?' James asked.

'Then I'll have the police here by tomorrow morning, with a court order to move you, by force if necessary. And you...' he pointed, 'are fired.'

'Correction, Mr Morris. My resignation is in the post.'

'The same goes for you, Guthrie. And don't suppose you'll get a reference from me. As for you, young woman...'

'Are you going to fire me too, Mr Morris?' Kitty asked sweetly.

Morris turned to look at Gus. 'I think we need to have a word, Kitty,' Gus said.

'As soon as I can spare the time, Gus. Right now, I've got to help my friends put up a few tents. Because we're staying put, aren't we?' she shouted.

'You bet we are,' Ethel agreed.

Their followers began to unload the trucks; there were few tents, most being equipped only with sleeping bags and prepared to bivouac or sleep in their trucks and vans. Morris glared at them, then turned and stumped back up the hill.

'What are you going to do, dear?' Margaret asked.

'Ignore them, until I get that court order.' He went on up to the waiting oilmen. 'You'll ignore them too, MacPhail, and get your gear ready.'

'And if they come up here, Mr Morris? I've nay mind to get involved in a civil disturbance.'

'If they attack you, it's them creating the disturbance. I'll be back by this evening, with that order.'

'What do you reckon?' James asked, as the Morris family drove past on their way back to the castle. Bernard and Margaret had studiously looked straight ahead, ignoring the trespassers; Tara had laughed. Niall glared fiercely at them, and mysteriously, Rebecca had actually waved...encouragingly? Gus looked embarrassed.

'We must do nothing illegal,' Bill Buckston said.

'Aye, and there's thirty big brawny men up there, and only half of us are able-bodied,' Jock pointed out. 'And half o'them is wimmen. I'd not like to provoke a fight.'

'Of course you must not,' Ethel said. 'We will just make camp here and embarrass them.'

'You wouldn't say we were being illegal in doing that?' Kitty asked. She was feeling truly distressed at seeing Gus apparently so firmly on the far side of the fence.

'Not until we are required to move by a court order.'

'Which will be here by tomorrow,' Guthrie said gloomily.

'But the story of what Morris is doing, and the extreme danger involved, will be nationwide by Monday,' Ethel Yardley replied. 'Our business must be to delay the start of the drilling for as long as possible, then if there is sufficient public outcry we may be able to have his drilling permission rescinded. Or at least delayed pending a public inquiry.'

'I wouldn't say we're doing too much delaying at the moment,' James grumbled, looking up the hill to where MacPhail's men were hard at work, and the derrick was slowly climbing into the sky.

'The important thing is that they don't start drilling,' Ethel urged. 'Tomorrow morning we'll surround the derrick before dawn. Now, chaps, let's strike up the band while we make camp.'

'You know what, James,' Kitty confided, 'I think this woman has a good chance of being elected.'

'I am going into Aboyne, to have a word with the police, and then into Aberdeen to see my solicitor and a magistrate,' Bernard announced. 'I am going to sort that lot out, by God.'

His wife and children made no comment, even if they wondered how far he was going to get on a Saturday afternoon; familiarity with the heat of his temper, far from acclimatizing them, had taught them to be wary...in this mood he could turn on anyone.

'Anything I can do to help?' Gus ventured.

'You haven't been much help so far,' Bernard barked. 'You know as well as I do that that little witch you brought up here as your assistant is behind all this.'

'I could try having another word with her,' Gus suggested, purely as a gesture of appeasement. He knew it would be hopeless.

'You can do whatever you like,' Bernard told him. 'But I'm handling things my way, now.' Which reminded him that others to whom he had delegated duties hadn't done very well, either. So far. He stamped into his office, locked the door, and picked up the phone. 'Would it interest you to know that I have discovered where Little Miss Marvel is?' he inquired.

'She's disappeared into thin air,' Crowther complained.

'She happens to be camping on my property, out on Gannan Hill, right at this moment,' Bernard told him.

'Eh? Good God! Well, I'll get back on to my contact in Glasgow...'

'Unfortunately, camping with her are

best part of a hundred other people, led by an incipient MP.'

'Shit!'

'In any event, it's too late now,' Bernard said. 'Seems she got her story to a newspaper, and it's being published on Monday morning.'

'Shit!'

'So from here on in we are going to play it straight. I should've done that from the beginning. The drilling rig is going up now, and tomorrow morning we start.'

'On a Sunday?'

'So it's going to cost a bit extra. It'll be worth it. I have my permission, and by the time these cranks and weirdos can get an injunction I will have struck gas.'

'If that reservoir is at more than twelve thousand feet, not even MacPhail is going to get there for a couple of days.'

'Possibly. But those couple of days, legally, are going to be taken up with my court case against these people who are squatting on my land. I'm going to see to that now.'

'It's not going to go down too well with the banks, all this legal stuff. As for the adverse publicity...'

'So make yourself scarce, where they can't contact you, until we've sorted it out.'

'I could come up to Abergannan.'

'Brilliant. I have a list of documents you can bring with you. And Phil, you'll remember to call your dogs off. We can't afford to be caught out of line, now.'

'Right.'

'When can I expect you?'

'I'll pick up a shuttle...should be there tonight.'

'Good.' Bernard flicked open the folder on his desk. 'Got your pen handy? This is what I want.' When he finished, he put down the phone and hurried out. He had things to do.

Gus walked from the castle to Gannan Hill. It was a matter of nearly three miles, but he not only wanted the exercise, he needed to think. Concentrated thought was difficult with constant interruptions.

He remembered what MacPhail had said, something he simply had never taken into account—but then, until this moment, there had been no reason to take it into account: his business was to tell the experts whether or not there was a field and whether or not it was viable, not to designate its size or shape. But if the field *did* extend in this direction, and if there *were* similar vents in the rock, or indeed, if there were veins in the granite allowing the gas to seep up Gannan Hill, why shouldn't there be veins underground leading *away* from the hill.

MacPhail had been almost joking, but there was no logical reason for them not to be there. He could be walking over gas-filled veins right now. As for the castle, of course the inert gas was not flammable...or was it? Weren't there caves somewhere in middle America which had been on fire for centuries, so far as anyone knew? They were supposed to be coal seams but were obviously being fed by oxygen getting down there. Maybe simmering coal fires didn't need much oxygen to combust. But gas was far more combustible than coal. It would burn quicker, and more violently, too.

Back to the doomsday scenario outlined by Kitty. But the odds *were* twenty to one. It would have to be a most peculiar concatenation of circumstances, or carelessness, to set Gannan Hill alight.

He heard music, topped a shallow rise, and looked along the length of the valley. At the foot of Gannan Hill MacPhail's men were finishing erecting their drilling derrick; others were erecting tents—they clearly intended to sleep on site to negate any risk of the protesters tampering with their gear.

Below them were two parks of trucks and cars, their own and those of the protesters. Nearer to hand was the camp of the protesters themselves, and it was from there that the music was emanating; they were gathered round the band and a large fire, and he could smell barbecueing bangers and hamburgers. They were obviously planning an enjoyable, and noisy, night.

He left the track, walked down the grassy slope towards them, and was checked by a remark: 'Something on your mind, Professor?' It was James, who had been sitting in the shelter of some bushes, with Kitty.

'Just the people I'm looking for,' Gus said.

'I suppose Morris sent you,' Kitty suggested.

'As a matter of fact, no. He's decided that there's to be war. Well, what did you expect? I'm still hoping to negotiate a peace.'

'There are elements of which you don't know,' James said.

'Then I wish you'd explain it to me. OK, so you've spilled the beans to the media, Kitty. I'm afraid I cannot condone that. But leave the legality of it aside, for the moment. Tell me what you hope to achieve. MacPhail is starting to drill tomorrow morning. My estimate is that it will take him about three days to get down to the reservoir, supposing it's around twelve thousand feet. So your story is going to be national Monday morning. Let's say it's taken up by everyone, which is unlikely. You're not going to get an injunction to stop the drilling before next Tuesday at the earliest, and that'll be a miracle. By then Macphail will have struck gas. If it's desecration you're worried about, it will be a fait accompli. And in any event, any injunction you're likely to get, if you get one at all, can only be to delay the project while there is an inquiry.'

'And if there is an explosion?' Kitty asked, quietly.

Gus grinned. 'If there is a significant explosion, it will have happened by then. If it hasn't happened, then your claim that drilling will prove dangerous will be shown to be an exaggeration.'

'So you want us to tell these people to pack up and go home.'

'That would be the most sensible thing to do, certainly.'

'Are you aware, Professor, that Morris is employing hitmen to have Kitty killed?' James asked.

'Oh, really, MacEwan...'

'Twice,' Kitty said.

Gus stared at her.

'That car accident was no accident,' James said. 'I happened along just in time. But the bloke who was trying to stove Kitty's head in got away.'

'What bloke?' Gus was obviously incredulous.

'No one we know,' Kitty said. 'We think he was hired.'

'Then when she returned to Oxford, there was another attempt, this time with a gun,' James said.

'You expect me to believe that?'

'I have a car full of bullet holes to prove it,' Kitty said.

Gus scratched his head. 'And you imagine Morris is behind this?'

'Well, who on earth else would want me dead?'

Morris was on the verge of bankruptcy, Ben Heath had said.

Kitty was watching his expression. 'So?' she asked.

'I'm sorry, but I simply can't believe this,' Gus frowned. 'I happen to know he's strapped. But to try to bump you off... Anyway, that doesn't really give you a legal right to stop him drilling, you know.'

'Oh, for God's sake,' James said. 'The man is a thug, Gus. We can prove it. He needs money, and he is going to let nothing stop him getting at that gas. He thinks. But we are going to stop him.'

'Now you're making it personal,' Gus pointed out.

'You're damned right. When someone tries to kill the woman I'm going to marry, I take it very personally.'

'Marry?' Gus looked from one to the other.

'Yes,' Kitty said, feeling like the cat who got the cream.

'Well...congratulations. But you realize that while you may have the strongest suspicions, you have absolutely no proof against Morris?'

'It'll all come to light.' James sounded more certain than he felt.

'I think you should be careful about spreading these accusations. Supposing someone were to tell him?'

'You mean you?' Kitty challenged. 'Be my guest.'

'Oh, God, Kitty!' Gus looked totally dejected, eyes dark and confused, his hair and beard flaming red against the distant firelight. 'I think I'd better say good-night.'

He looked like a sad little gnome, Kitty thought. But she couldn't forgive him. 'Good-night,' she repeated.

Gus put his hands in his pockets and returned to the track.

'Think he'll tell Morris?' James asked.

'Gus is such a strange mixture of a conventional character,' Kitty said, 'with a singularly unconventional way of life. This whole business is a bit much for him. But I'm sure he'll try to do whatever he believes is the right thing.'

Gus went up to his room and packed. The Morrises had not yet returned from Aberdeen, but he did not feel he could stay in their house a moment longer. If his utterly civilized mind found it almost impossible to conceive of one human being seeking to kill another just to secure his finances, he was aware that these things did happen—and he also knew Kitty was not a liar. And while there was not a shred of evidence to connect Morris with the would-be hit-man, again he recognized that the entrepreneur was the only person who had a motive.

He took his bag downstairs. The house seemed strangely empty without the ever-present Guthrie, although he did observe the giggling maid, Beatrice, doing some dusting. Beatrice was not giggling this afternoon; the news of the confrontation and of Guthrie's sacking had reached the servants' hall. Gus wondered if Morris would be able to replace the old retainer?

He sat in a straight chair in the hall and waited, but only a few minutes later heard a car engine in the courtyard. He stood up, expectantly, but instead of Morris marching in, the bell rang.

Gus was wondering whether or not to answer it when Mary strode through the baize doorway, stiffly erect. 'Oh, Mr Wilson! You did gi'e me a start,' she said severely.

'Someone's at the door,' Gus said.

'Aye, I heard the bell.' Mary opened the door. 'Why,' she said, 'Mr Crowther.' She peered at his overnight bag. 'Ye've come to visit?'

'Yes,' Crowther said.

Mary hesitated. But she knew this man was a business associate of her employer; he had visited Abergannan when Morris had first bought the property. 'Then ye'd best come in,' she invited. 'The laird is no here the noo, ye ken. But he'll be back this evening.'

'He's expecting me.' Crowther entered the hall. He was a small man, with fair hair and a bristling blond moustache. He stared at Gus.

'I'm Augustus Wilson,' Gus said. 'We've spoken on the phone.'

Crowther hesitated about shaking hands; he wasn't sure which side of the fence this man was on and in any event, he had conceived a considerable dislike for him after their phone conversation. 'I remember,' he said. 'Still here, are you?'

There was no possible reply to such a non sequitur, and Gus was recalling that *he* had equally formed a dislike for *this* man after that phone conversation.

'Would you show me to my room, please?' Crowther asked Mary.

'Aye, well, I'll show ye to a room, Mr Crowther,' Mary said. 'As to whether it'll be the one, well, we'll have to wait for the mistress.'

'I just want to wash and brush up,' Crowther said. 'I've had a long journey.'

'Aye,' Mary agreed, and led him up the stairs.

Gus sat down again. He wondered what Morris's accountant was doing here? Almost certainly a legal matter to do with the injunctions he was afraid of. Then he wondered what Crowther would say if he was told that his partner was a would-be murderer? That might really put the cat amongst the pigeons. But after due consideration, he decided that it would be proper to confront Morris first.

He turned the pages of Margaret's selection of magazines suitable for castle guests until he heard the Land Rover scrunch into the gravel courtyard. Crowther had not returned downstairs, clearly reluctant to share a tête-à-tête.

Gus stood up as the door swung open. 'That was fun,' Tara said, in a bored voice.

Rebecca looked hassled, like her mother.

But Niall was grinning, and his father also looked pleased, as he waved a piece of paper at Gus. 'Court order. The police are going to be here first thing tomorrow to clear that scum off my land.'

'I don't really think you should refer to those people as scum,' Gus protested, mildly.

'In my opinion, Wilson, that is what they are.'

Gus changed the subject. 'I wonder if I could have a word with you, Mr Morris.'

'Eh?' he looked past Gus at Mary, standing at the foot of the stairs. 'Well, what is it, woman?'

The maid's face remained expressionless. 'Begging your pardon, Mr Morris,' she said, 'But that Mr Crowther is here.'

'So that's who that hired car belonged to,' Niall said.

'That was quick,' Bernard said. 'Have you shown him to his room?'

'I showed him to a room, sir, yes.' Mary looked at Margaret.

'I'd better go up and sort things out,' Margaret decided.

'Ask him to join me in the office as soon as he can,' Bernard directed.

'A word,' Gus repeated.

'Oh, yes, yes. Come in. Close the door.' Bernard sat behind his desk. 'Well, have you seen that female of yours yet? Has she anything to say for herself this time?'

Gus closed the door and sat down. Whatever his professional manner, he was not a diffident man in himself. Now he opted for a frontal attack. He drew a deep breath. 'She accused you of attempting to murder her. Or have her murdered.'

Bernard stared at him with his mouth open, mind racing. But no. There could be no possible link to himself, except circumstantially...

'I know it seems far-fetched,' Gus said. 'But it appears to be a fact that there have been two attempts on her life over the past week, and, well...you must admit you are the man who stands most to gain were she just to disappear.'

Bernard had always believed attack to be the best method of defence, so as soon as he had got his breath back he thumped his fist down on the desk and roared. 'You have the affrontery to sit there, in my own house, and accuse me of murder?'

'Attempted murder, this far,' Gus reminded him.

Bernard pointed at the door. 'Get out! Get out of my house! Get off my property. As of this minute, my contract with Turnbull and Heath is terminated. You are terminated, Wilson. Go on! Get out.'

'My dear fellow...' Gus realized he was starting to sound like the Yardley woman, but like her he was staggered by such naked aggression.

'Do you want me to throw you out?' Bernard stood up with such violence his chair crashed back against the wall.

Gus saw the menacing expression on the man's face, and felt a trickle of cold sweat in the small of his back. My God, he thought. This man is capable of...anything. But he had no intention of acting the coward. He stood up. 'I was leaving, anyway, Mr Morris. But I must warn you, in view of your attitude, naturally I will have to rethink my position in this dispute.'

'You can take whatever fucking position you choose,' Bernard told him, loudly. 'I am going to sue that girl for slander. And that goes for you, too, if you repeat those...those accusations. And let me tell you something else,' he paused to draw breath, a thick vein pulsing in his purple neck, 'only an Act of God is going to stop me bringing up that gas.' He grinned. 'And there aren't too many of those about, nowadays.'

Chapter 11

THE BURNING ROCKS

A weird noise woke Kitty at five-thirty, just as light was beginning to press against her eyelids. She sniffed a strange smell, stretched and gasped at aching joints...and then remembered. She and James were in a tent, the smell was wet canvas...and the noise was Gus, snoring. It had been so good to have him back in the fold, no matter what the eventual outcome.

She sat up, pushed hair from her eyes, and thought how wonderful it would be to soothe her aches in a hot bath. But there were more important things to do.

Outside, the protesters' camp was just beginning to stir. Several people, including James, had brought camping-gas units, and soon tea and coffee was being passed around. But there was no food until...

'Someone's coming,' Bill Buckston said. Bouncing along the track was the red post office van.

'Didn't know the postal service was this efficient in Scotland,' Gus remarked in a feeble attempt at humour.

'Thought you people might be hungry,' Ken Brown said. 'There's hot food inside.'

'What's the plan?' James asked, as they munched their hot rolls and finished their coffee.

'The Reverend Sangster has arrived. We're going to have a brief service, then we are going up to the hill to form a circle around the site,' Ethel Yardley said.

'We don't let anyone in, and we don't let anyone out. If necessary, we link arms.'

'Do we say anything?'

She shook her head. 'We don't say anything, and we don't do anything. It's a silent protest, and it stays within the law. Agreed?' They all nodded.

'And when the police come?' Coultrain inquired.

'If they do have a court order instructing us to leave Morris's property, then we have no option but to go. Hopefully, by the time that happens this will be big news.'

The telephone jangled beside Bernard's bed. He reached for it with a grunt, only half awake. 'Didna wake ye, I hope.'

'Eh? Of course you did. My God, MacPhail do you realize the time? It's barely six!'

'I thought I'd let you know we're ready to go.'

'Oh, are you? Great stuff.' Bernard sat up, carrying the covers with him and disturbing Margaret. 'Wait for me. I'll be up in fifteen minutes.'

'There's nae hurry. I'm also telephoning to let ye know that we're surrounded by these protesters.'

'Eh? Are they causing trouble?'

'Na, na. They're just standing there, staring at us. But they've formed a cordon across the road. They say they won't let anyone out, or anyone in. So unless ye have your court order in your hand...'

'I have it,' Bernard said.

'And a police escort to enforce it,' MacPhail added.

'The police are coming at eight o'clock.'

'D'ye want me to hold off the drilling till then? Or start now?'

Bernard pulled his nose. He dearly wanted to be there when the bit first sank into the rock. On the other hand, there was no possibility of its reaching the gas reservoir for at least two days, according to the experts, so he wouldn't be missing much. And his instincts told him that the sooner the work started the better; once the story broke every minute might be vital. 'You go ahead,' he told MacPhail. 'I'll be out with the police, at eight o'clock.'

'Ye have it,' MacPhail said.

'Something wrong?' Margaret asked, drowsily.

'Not a thing,' Bernard assured her. 'We're starting to drill.' That woke her up. 'You coming out?'

'What about all those people?' she asked.

'We're going to see them off,' Bernard assured her.

The sun rose out of the North Sea sending pink rays to illuminate Gannan Hill, and its surrounds; there was not a cloud in the sky...it was in fact a perfect spring day.

The derrick rose like a beacon against the hill itself, and Kitty clutched James' arm as the travelling block began to move, slowly, up to the crown and then down again, while MacPhail and his men, vivid in their yellow hard hats, exchanged short, crisp, comments and commands. Then the swivel began to spin, and the turntable beneath it, and the bit crunched into the rock. Within seconds it had sunk well in, and the engineers were fitting the protective casing, while splinters of rock began to emerge from the mud hose and sink into the sump. The noise was tremendous, overwhelming the sound of the rushing stream.

'I feel quite shattered,' Kitty muttered to James.

'And nothing has happened, yet,' he

said. 'Maybe it won't.'

She glanced at him, then stared at the derrick and the men again. *'Yet,'* she repeated, heart skipping a beat.

'Morning all.' Niall entered the breakfast room in his usual boisterous fashion. 'When do we start?'

'We've started,' his father told him.

'Without us?' he cried.

'We're waiting for the police, so we can clear away rent-a-mob,' Bernard explained. 'Mary!' he bawled.

'Ye called, Mr Morris?'

'Hasn't Wilkie brought the papers yet?'

'Ah havna seen Mr Wilkie this morning yet, sir. Nor Miss Tara. But it's terrible early,' she added with a sniff.

'There's nothing on local TV,' Niall said. 'I was watching it while I dressed.'

'Nothing *yet,*' Rebecca said grimly.

'I do hope there isn't going to be any trouble,' Margaret said.

'If there's trouble, they will have started it,' Bernard told her. 'Now eat up. I'm expecting the police at any moment. Oh, good-morning, Philip. Ready for the off?'

'Looking forward to it,' Crowther agreed. 'Morning Margaret. Morning kids.'

Rebecca snorted; she had never liked Crowther, and she did not like being referred to as a 'kid'.

'Your office phone's ringing, Dad,' Niall said.

Bernard put down his coffee cup and hurried to his desk. Crowther followed him and closed the door.

'Is that you, Mr Morris?' MacPhail asked.

Bernard raised his eyes to heaven. 'Of course it's me, MacPhail. You have called my private number. What's the problem?'

'It's no a problem, really, Mr Morris. But as I thought might be the case, we've struck some real hard rock.'

'What depths?'

'Sixty feet.'

'You're down sixty feet already? In less than two hours?'

'Man, we're working. But I just wanted to let ye know we're going to have to blast.'

'Eh?'

'It'll be just a wee explosion, ye ken. But ye might just hear it, and I didna' want ye to be alarmed.'

'Oh. Right. Are those people still there?'

'Aye, they're here,' MacPhail said. 'But your police will be arriving any moment, ye say?'

Bernard looked at his watch. 'Any minute,' he agreed.

'So I'll be blasting as soon as we can set the charge.'

'Right,' Bernard said. 'You do whatever you think best, MacPhail.'

'They've stopped drilling,' Ethel Yardley said.

'Probably an early morning tea break,' Buckston commented.

'Well, it's a break for our ears as well,' Coultrain remarked.

'Listen,' James said. 'That's a police siren.' It was a long way away, but now that the noise of the drilling had stopped they could hear it clearly.

'Well, that's that, then,' Hamish Hamilton said.

'They're not here yet,' Guthrie reminded him.

Kitty felt a lump of lead gather in the bottom of her stomach. Just to be herded away like sheep, without really having accomplished anything... 'What do you think they're doing?' she asked Gus. For the drilling crew were certainly not having tea.

Gus levelled his binoculars. 'Can't see too well but I suspect they're preparing an explosive charge.'

'Oh, my God.'

'Isn't that standard procedure, where they strike rock hard enough to damage the bit?' James asked.

'Yes, it is. And it is one of the things

we warned them against. Quite apart from the risk of igniting some of that excessive methane, there's the chance of opening up those vents, which are currently being blocked by water. And if they do that, God alone knows what will happen next!'

'Well, then, this is it.'

Kitty stared at the drillers as they prepared their charge. She had the wildest desire to run up there and throw her arms round the bit in an attempt to stop them, but she would only be carted to one side and left with nothing but humiliation. In any event, MacPhail was walking across to them.

He stopped some forty yards away. 'We are about to set off a small, controlled explosion,' he said. 'The operative word is controlled, but I canna guarantee there might not be the odd piece of rock thrown out. I'd advise ye all to withdraw another hundred yards, otherwise I canna take any responsibility for injury.'

'Don't you realize that if you set off that charge you will blow up the entire hill, and everyone on it?' Kitty shouted.

'Ah, don't be daft, woman,' MacPhail retorted. 'Ye've been warned.' He turned and went back up to the derrick.

Kitty's words might not have concerned MacPhail, but they certainly had an effect on the protesters, who immediately began to fall back to the lower ground. 'You could have said too much,' James remarked.

'Not for the first time,' Gus commented. Kitty glared at them, but they were each holding an arm and urging her back down the hill after their companions.

'The police are here, Mr Morris,' Mary said.

'And Wilkie?'

'Nay sign of him, sir.'

'I am going to fire that old fool,' Bernard growled, and walked on to the front steps as the two police cars and the van swung into the courtyard. 'Good-morning, Inspector Campbell.'

'Good day to ye, Mr Morris,' the police inspector said, stepping down. He did not look as if he really considered it a good day. 'Ye have a warrant, I understand.'

'That I have, Inspector. And I want it served immediately.'

'That it will be, sir. If ye'll give me the paper, we'll go up there now.'

Bernard gave him the warrant. 'Should I come with you?'

'Nay, sir. I do not think that would be a good idea. We want these people to leave quietly, and the sight of you might just set them off, ye ken?'

'Whose side are you on?' Bernard demanded.

'The police do not have sides, Mr Morris. They carry out the law of the land. And the law of the land says ye are entitled to evict trespassers from your property, with the law's permission,' his tone indicating that in this instance he considered the law an ass. 'So I'd be obliged if ye and your family...' he looked past Bernard at Margaret and the children, and Crowther, 'would remain indoors until we have sorted this matter out. I will report back to you on the outcome, later.'

Bernard opened his mouth and then shut it again, then turned back to his family. 'Impudent bastard,' he muttered. 'That's what's really wrong with this country today, you know. The police are as bolshie as anyone.'

'Just keep cool,' Crowther recommended. 'Let them do what they're paid to do.'

As he spoke, there was an enormous bang. Even the castle seemed to shake, and every head turned to look in the direction of Gannan Hill. But there was nothing to be seen. The policemen were speechless, their vehicles halted as they had started out of the yard. Bernard dashed inside to his office, grabbed the telephone, and punched the single button that connected him with MacPhail's mobile. 'What the hell has happened?'

'Oh, is that ye, Mr Morris?'

'For God's sake, who the hell do you think it is?' Bernard bellowed. 'What was that bang?'

'That was the explosion I was speaking of.'

'You said it would be a small one. What the hell happened?'

'Aye, well, it was a little bigger than I reckoned. I figure we must have struck a pocket of gas.'

'What's the damage?'

'Ah, well, there's some damage, to be sure,' MacPhail said. 'Ma derrick is bent and two of ma men are hurt. I don't know about the protesters. There was some rock showered down there. But I did warn them. Oh, and we've a fire.'

'A what?'

'There are flames coming out of the shaft, to be sure.'

'What? But my God...!'

'Noo, noo, there's nought to get excited about.' MacPhail might have been speaking to a small child. 'Like Ah said, we must've struck a wee pocket of gas. We're killing the fire now. What it means is there'll be a slight delay before we can resume drilling. Dinna worry, Mr Morris, we have it all under control.'

'I'm coming up,' Morris snapped, and thumped the phone down. His family and Crowther were gathered in the doorway, looking like a ghosts' convention. 'He struck some gas,' Bernard explained. 'But it's all under control. I'm going up to have a look, anyway.'

'We'll come with you,' Margaret decided.

The explosion had sent a cascade of chunks and slivers of rock, some of them quite large, flying into the air.

'Take cover!' James bawled, and everyone threw themselves to the ground, while the missiles crashed and thumped about them. Someone gave a shout of pain, and someone else gave a shout of annoyance as a lump of rock descended on his car with a loud clang followed by the sound of shattering glass.

'Who's hurt?' James was on his feet.

'I think I've a bloody broken arm,' Buckston complained. He had certainly been struck, hard; the sleeve of his anorak was torn and stained with blood.

'We'll get you to a doctor,' Ethel assured him, and glared up the hill. 'That bastard!'

'He did warn us,' Gus said, as usual seeing both sides of the argument.

Kitty stood up to stare at the derrick. She supposed they had scored a mini-triumph in that the pylon was clearly damaged; it had taken on a distinct tilt to suggest a leg had been buckled. Thus the drilling had been stopped, and could not be re-started until the rig was repaired. She knew that would not take a man like MacPhail very long, although it would have to be twenty-four hours or so. By which time the papers would have been circulated and things might be happening—save that nothing *was* happening.

She had predicted a huge, destructive explosion. She had got a loud bang and some dislodged rock. Her whole campaign was based upon the danger to human life, and instead there was one possibly broken arm and a dented car. She felt sick.

Gus put a friendly hand on her shoulder. 'The odds on something serious *were* very long. At least they have a problem.'

Kitty blinked at the site. MacPhail's men were pouring earth into the shaft. 'My guess is they've got an ignition down there,' Gus said. 'They'll have to block that shaft and wait for the fire to go out before they can commence again. We've bought some time.'

'That's not going to do us too much good,' James said. 'Here come the police.'

'But, wait a moment,' Kitty said, heart starting to pound. No one took any notice of her.

Ethel and Coultrain were binding up Buckston's arm as best they could; several of the others had gone back down to the camp site to examine the damage and make sure *their* cars hadn't been hit by the falling debris. The rest were forming up to receive the police, even Gus and James. Kitty was left staring up the hill, where MacPhail's men were hard at work filling the shaft.

Oh, my God, she thought. Oh, my *God!* She ran down the slope, caught up with Gus as the police vehicles came to a stop, and a mass of men in blue emerged. 'Gus!' she gasped.

He glanced at her. 'Looks like they mean business.'

'Gus!' She held his sleeve. 'Listen to me. You said you think there was an ignition.'

'That's most likely, for two reasons. One, they obviously set off some gas with their charge, and two, they're filling the shaft in to kill the oxygen.'

'But Gus, those vents could be open. And others. They can block up their hole, but they're not going to put out the fire by doing so.'

Gus frowned at her, then turned to look back up the hill. 'You mean that whole hill could be on fire, inside?'

'If it isn't, it soon could be.'

Just like those caves in America, Gus thought. Burning for centuries. But that fire was based on coal, which is inert when it comes to explosions. This is methane gas!

'Come along now,' the police inspector was saying.

'Sorry about this, James,' Davey Harvey said.

'We were expecting you,' James said. 'Kitty, Gus, time to go.' Ethel Yardley and her people were already getting into their truck.

'We need to go up the hill and have a word with Mr MacPhail,' Kitty told the inspector.

'I'm sorry, Miss. My instructions are to have you all off the estate, immediately.'

'You don't understand,' Gus said. 'Those men up there could be in serious danger.'

'Yes, sir. I believe that is what you have been saying all this while. Well, sir, they don't look to be in any danger to me. Now, sir, Miss, I am very sorry, but if you won't leave quietly my men are going to have to carry you.'

'You...'

Gus squeezed her arm. 'Just remember what we said,' he told the inspector, and guided Kitty down to where James was waiting with his jeep.

When they got there, Kitty turned for a last look up the hill, where there was some agitation amongst the drillers. Then... 'My God!' she shouted, 'Look.'

Every head turned, to watch a tongue of brilliant flame suddenly shoot out of the hillside. 'That's the cavern!' James shouted.

Following the flame, there came a dull rumbling roar. The watchers gazed in horrified consternation as the earth beneath the derrick gave way, to be replaced by another leap of flame, into which the derrick itself crashed, disappearing from view. With it went several men, and the rest came scrambling down the hillside as fast as they could, some with their clothes on fire.

'Up there!' Ethel Yardley shouted, jumping out of her truck and running up the slope.

'Come back here,' bawled the inspector. But James and Kitty and Gus were following her, as were most of the others. The police followed *them.* The inspector ran to his car, and reached for the phone. 'Gannan Hill,' he snapped. 'We need fire engines and ambulances. Now.'

There was a roaring of an engine, and the Morris's Land Rover scraped to a halt. 'My God!' Margaret jumped out. 'What *happened?'*

'Seems like the whole bloody hill has caught fire, begging your pardon, ma'am,' the inspector said.

'Oooh, it's like a firework display!' Tara's fresh make-up beamed from behind a silk scarf and designer shades.

'Jesus!' Niall muttered. Rebecca stood open-mouthed.

'My gas!' Bernard groaned. 'My gas!' he shouted. 'Going up in smoke! They're burning my money!'

'With respect, sir,' the inspector said. 'There are men dying up there.'

Morris started forward, but Crowther caught his arm. 'There is nothing you can do, Bernie,' he said. 'It'll burn itself out. There's millions of tonnes of gas down there. It can't all have escaped to the surface.'

'Those people, sir,' the inspector said, 'your protesters, are risking their lives to save the lives of the drilling crew. Now what I suggest you do, sir, is return to your home, and prepare space to receive the injured and burn cases. The ambulances will get here soon.'

'Yes,' Margaret said, before Bernard could reply. 'We'll do that, Inspector. You bring the injured people back to us.'

James led the rush up the track to the slopes of Gannan Hill. 'Be careful!' Gus shouted, following with Kitty, and overtaking Ethel and Coultrain.

Kitty gazed at the scene in front of her in horror. The mouth of the cavern continued to burn like a torch, and even as she watched some of the hillside above, it fell in as the fire surged through it. Even down here the heat was almost suffocating. Nearer to hand the derrick had quite disappeared, while the various equipment and piping lay scattered about, surrounded by flame; the trucks which had brought the equipment were burning fiercely and exploding.

Coming down towards them were MacPhail and all his surviving people. Those on fire were rolling in the heather in an attempt to put out the flames, screaming their pain, and being dragged on by their fellows.

James whipped off his windcheater to stifle the flames on the first man; Kitty and Gus did the same. No chance of feeling cold now—the air was like a blast furnace.

MacPhail stumbled beside Kitty and Gus. 'One in twenty,' he remarked, bitterly. Gus looked at Kitty. But now was not the time for remonstrances, as there was another rumbling roar, and another section of hill collapsed. 'That whole hill could disappear,' MacPhail observed. 'With ma drilling rig! And five of ma people!'

'We have to get the injured to safety where we can help them,' Ethel ordered.

The inspector hurried up. 'Ye'll take

them to the castle, Miss Yardley,' he instructed.

'The castle?'

'Mrs Morris is waiting for them. I've ambulances on the way, but it'll be a while before they get here.'

James half carried the first man down the hill, tenderly cradling his severely scorched arm. The man whimpered and groaned; the clothes had been burned down his right side, his hair singed. 'We need painkillers,' James said.

'Get him to the castle, James,' Harvey recommended.

The police were bringing down others with minor burns, glancing back at the hill, from which there were now sprouting several sheets of flame.

'What it must be like inside...' Coultrain said.

'Hell surfacing?' Hamish suggested.

The injured men were laid on the trucks, and they began to move out. The police went with them. James, MacPhail, Gus and Kitty found themselves alone, gazing at the hill and a man lying dead, all the skin burned off his back, James shook his head, disbelieving the horror.

'I've never seen anything like it,' MacPhail said.

'How many of your men went in?' James asked.

'Five. *Five!* My God, man, what am I going to tell their people?'

'Have you never lost a man before?' Gus asked.

'I have. In the North Sea. One man. But five!'

'We'd better get down the castle,' James suggested.

Kitty continued to stare at the hill, which was now burning like the slopes of an active volcano. Everything she had prophesied, and yet, she knew they had been enormously lucky. The hill was burning, but it had not exploded; it was imploding, if anything. There had been loss of life, but not on the scale she had envisaged. And as there was so much gas down there, no matter how much the explosion had enlarged the vent, when next it rained and pushed the water level up higher, the reservoir would probably again be sealed, and Morris would still have his billion-pound investment.

Again she felt sick, as much with herself, for having almost *wanted* something to happen to prove her point. Or merely to end Morris's dreams? She wondered if she hated him.

Of course, all his grandiose dreams might still be ended. That would depend on how long the internal fire burned; whether he would still be permitted to drill. And on whether his bankers were prepared to wait... 'Aren't you coming, Kitty?' James called. He and Gus and MacPhail had reached the jeep.

Kitty turned to look at them, and past them, at the stream. It still bubbled merrily—but there was steam rising from its surface. She gasped, and knelt. It was only nine o'clock, no heat yet in the sun. The heat was all up there, on Gannan Hill. Or was it? Slowly, hesitantly, she placed her hands flat on the earth. It was warm to the touch.

'I am not turning my house into a bloody hospital,' Bernard growled as he drove the Land Rover into the castle yard.

'I don't think you have any choice,' Margaret told him. 'The important thing is to keep the authorities on your side, and that includes the police.'

'She's right, Bernie,' Crowther said. 'You're going to get a bad press out of this.'

'Me?' Bernard roared.

'Kitty did warn you this would happen, Dad,' Rebecca said.

'She said the hill would explode,' Niall said scornfully. 'She was just guessing.'

Margaret ignored them, and looked at Mary and Beatrice who were distinctly agitated. 'We have some injured people arriving in a moment,' she said. 'I want you to bring some mattresses down from the servants' quarters and lay them on the utility floor.'

'Can we no take them upstairs to beds?' Mary asked.

'Certainly not,' Margaret said. She had no intention of having messy injuries from bleeding, muddied, and blackened men filthying up her bedrooms. 'Rebecca, Tara, give them a hand. Oh, I wish Guthrie were here.'

'Bloody blackleg,' Bernard said, and stamped into his office. 'The moment MacPhail gets here, I want to see him.'

Margaret continued to ignore her husband. 'Now, we'll probably need some brandy, at least for the rescuers. I don't think we need use the Hine Antique.'

'There's cooking brandy in the wine cellar, ma'am,' Beatrice volunteered, frizzy hair bursting out of her cap.

'Then go and fetch it. Bring a couple of extra bottles.'

'Yes, ma'am.' Beatrice glanced invitingly at Niall, who grinned.

Like everyone else, his adrenalin was in full flow. 'I'll give you a hand,' he offered, not mentioning where.

They went down the cellar stairs below the main staircase. These gave access to a small lobby, below ground, off which opened several doors. One led to the boiler room, where the oil-fired central heating was rumbling away; the oil tank was sunk into the concrete floor. This was a contravention of the building code, but it had been installed by the then laird nearly a hundred years ago, before the building code had been invented.

'That boiler needs lagging. It's far too hot down here,' Niall commented. As he opened the door to the wine cellar a blast of heat hit them.

'It's even hotter in here,' Beatrice remarked. 'Much hotter than usual.'

'Now, that's odd,' Niall said. There was only one small radiator in this cellar, designed to keep the wines at just the right temperature, but certainly not to overheat them.

'Ye should mention it to Major MacEwan,' Beatrice suggested.

'Major MacEwan has lost his job,' Niall told her. 'We'll have to get a plumber in. Now, where is this cheap brandy?'

'It's stored back here.' Beatrice led him along the row of racks to the very end. 'It's the top shelf. Can ye reach it?'

'It'll be easier if you do it,' he suggested. 'I'll give you a boost.'

'Oh, Mr Niall,' she squealed happily, as he put his arms round her thighs and lifted her from the floor. She grabbed two bottles and turned as she slid down him. 'Can we stay a minute?'

The police vehicles rolled into the castle courtyard, followed immediately by those of the protesters. The injured drillers were carried through into the utility room, where Mary and Rebecca were still laying out mattresses, while Tara came down the stairs carrying a plastic First Aid box and looking thoroughly contemptuous of the whole proceedings.

The injured were moaning, the rescuers white and shocked. 'Where on earth is Niall with that brandy?' Margaret demanded.

'It's not brandy, I'd recommend,' Coultrain said. 'What everyone needs is a lot o' hot tea. And those burns should be bathed in cold water.'

'That's an idea,' Margaret said. 'Tara, be a dear and go into the kitchen and tell Mrs MacBain we need lots of tea. Rebecca, will you and Mary fetch some bowls of water? Mr Coultrain, perhaps you could scrub up your hands and roll up your sleeves.'

Inspector Campbell was stripping off his gloves. 'I'd like a word with the laird,' he said.

'You'd better come into the office,' Crowther suggested. He opened the door, and Campbell stepped inside.

'Oh, it's you.' Bernard was sitting behind his desk, looking thoroughly disgruntled. 'Where the devil is MacPhail?'

'Making sure there's no one left on site, I'd say,' Campbell suggested. 'He'll be along. This is a nasty business, Mr Morris. Five men dead and several more badly injured.'

'Are you suggesting that it's my fault?'

'There's people out there saying ye were warned that drilling into Gannan Hill could be dangerous.'

'MacPhail made the final decision. You'll have to speak with him.'

'I will do that,' Campbell said. 'But the actual decision will have had to be yours, as ye own the land and it's your gas they're after. I'm just making the point that there will have to be an inquiry. It's best to be forewarned about these things. Now I'd better go and see how close those ambulances are.'

'Fucking little Hitler,' Bernard growled, after the policeman had left the room, and glanced at Crowther. 'They can't do anything to stop me, can they?'

'Well...if that Cochrane woman really has sold her report to the media, and they make it big...' He shrugged his shoulders. 'She is being proved right, isn't she?'

'Of course she isn't. She said the mountain would blow sky high. She was talking about earthquakes. So we've got a small gas fire. Big deal.'

'All depends what the media make of it,' Crowther said again. 'Do you find it hot in here?'

'That's what central heating is for,' Bernard pointed out.

Crowther grinned. 'And when you have your gas field working, I suppose you'll switch from oil.' He had wandered to the window. 'Talk of the devil. And she looks as if the devil is after her.'

'She always looks like that,' Bernard said. 'Just keep her out of here. I don't want to see her, much less speak with her.'

James nearly hit a police car as the jeep screamed into the castle courtyard.

'Where's the fire?' Sergeant Harvey asked, attempting to be humourous. He had been on the phone to the ambulances and fire appliances, but they were only half-way from Aboyne.

'Right here,' James snapped.

Kitty was already out of the jeep and running up the steps. Rebecca stood there. 'I don't think you'll really be very welcome in here,' she remarked.

'Listen,' Kitty said. 'That fire on Gannan Hill. It's spreading.'

Rebecca looked past her at the mountains. 'I don't see anything.'

'It's under the ground. Gannan Hill is on fire, inside. And the various gas vents, which spread under the earth in this direction, are also igniting.'

'Oh, don't talk rot.' Tara had come outside to join the conversation. 'You'll be telling us next that the castle is in danger.'

'That is just what I'm telling you!' Kitty shouted. 'You are sitting on top of a reservoir of burning gas. Now, it may burn itself out. But if it doesn't...' she paused, because her imagination couldn't cope.

'Oh, you...you cretin!' Tara snapped, and went back into the hall.

'I must speak with your mother and father,' Kitty told Rebecca.

'I'm afraid they don't want to speak with you,' Rebecca pointed out.

But now Kitty had been joined by the men. 'This is a very serious matter, Rebecca,' Gus said.

'Oh. Well, as it's you...'

'Where's the laird?' MacPhail demanded. 'He's sitting on a powder keg, all right.'

'You'd better come in,' Rebecca decided, and led them into the hall.

Gus and MacPhail made for the office. Kitty and James went through the baize door to the utility room, where the injured men were having their burns soaked in cold water by Mary and Margaret; Buckston was sitting in a chair having his arm tended by Ethel and Coultrain. Rebecca began handing round cups of tea, assisted by Guthrie, reverting to his butlering duties even if officially fired, and Mrs MacBain carried the teapot round for refills. There was no sign of Niall or Beatrice.

'What are you doing here?' Margaret snapped when she saw Kitty. 'Haven't you caused enough trouble already?'

'Listen,' Kitty said. 'You must evacuate the castle immediately.'

'Are you out of your tiny mind?'

'Did you see what happened to the drilling rig? No, you didn't, I suppose. The earth beneath it was on fire, and it just caved in and disappeared. That is what could happen here. You must get out, and get these people out, while you can.'

Margaret looked from her to James. 'I'm afraid that could happen, Mrs Morris,' James said.

'You'll have to talk to my husband,' Margaret decided.

'MacPhail!' Bernard exclaimed as the drilling-engineer entered the office without knocking. 'Just what the devil is going on?' He scowled at Gus. 'And what the hell do you want?'

'We are here to tell you, Mr Morris, that it is almost certain that there is an underground fire now burning beneath this castle, and that the premises should be evacuated immediately,' Gus said.

Bernard looked at MacPhail in consternation. 'You seriously expect me to believe that?'

'Aye, well, it's happening, man. Seems the little girl was right all along, and there's a lot more of that gas just under the surface than we thought possible. It's alight, man. Can ye no feel the heat?'

'Holy Jesus Christ!' Crowther remarked. 'I'm getting the hell out of here.' He ran for the door.

'Evacuate the castle?' Bernard asked. 'Am I covered for such a thing?'

'Now, that I canna say,' MacPhail said. 'Ye'll have to look up your policy.'

'For God's sake,' Gus shouted. 'This land could cave in any moment, and you're worrying about your damned insurance policy? We're talking about lives, man. Lives!' He followed Crowther through the door. The accountant had gone up the stairs to fetch his overnight bag. Gus stood in the drawing-room doorway. 'Everyone out!' he called. 'Hurry now. Everyone out.'

'Thank God for that,' Kitty said.

'Oh, not you as well,' Margaret complained.

Inspector Campbell stamped in. 'Those bloody ambulances are taking a hell of a long time,' he complained. 'And that courtyard is damned hot. How do you explain that, Professor?'

'It's on fire underneath,' Gus told him. 'Inspector, I can't get any sense out of these people. You must take charge. Call those ambulances and tell them not to come any closer to Abergannan. Tell them you are coming to them. And then get these people out of here, by force if you have to.'

Campbell looked at James. 'I'm afraid the Prof is right, Campbell,' James said. 'And you don't have a moment to lose.'

'Aaaagh!' Tara's scream shook the rafters.

'Oh, for God's sake,' Rebecca snapped.

Margaret came to life. 'Girls, go upstairs and get packed. Guthrie, I don't know what's happened to Mr Niall, but he must be found.'

'Me?' Guthrie demanded.

'I'll find hiın,' James said.

'James! ' Kitty snapped. But he was already at the door, where he was joined by the two young women who hurried past him up the stairs. 'There's no time for packing!' Kitty shouted. 'No time.' But no one was taking any notice of her. She ran behind James.

Bernard strode out of the study, followed by MacPhail. 'This idiot seems to think we're about to go up in smoke,' Bernard said.

'That's right, Mr Morris,' Campbell said. 'We're evacuating. Sergeant, you and your men take these injured people out, put them in the trucks, and drive like hell. As for you, Mr and Mrs Morris, I want this castle abandoned, now.'

There was a moment of total consternation. Then the policemen started lifting the groaning fire victims back out of the castle.

Immediately the entire household was seized with panic. Mrs MacBain ran for the kitchen. Mary ran for the pantry. Margaret ran for the stairs. Bernard stood still, opening and shutting his mouth, glaring around him in impotent fury. Ethel and Coultrain between them lifted Buckston to his feet and started to help him towards the door.

Gus looked left and right. 'Kitty? Kitty, where are you?'

MacPhail hurried for the door behind his people. As he did so there was a dull roar from beneath them.

'Oh, Master Niall,' Beatrice said, wriggling ecstatically against the bottle rack while Niall surged into her. She'd never done it standing up before. 'Oh...Niall!' She'd never called him Niall before, either. But now there could be no doubt that he loved her.

Niall gasped for breath as his movements stopped. God, he was hot. Something must have gone desperately wrong with the thermostat. He stepped away from her, pulled up his pants. 'We'd better get back upstairs.'

Beatrice was still holding a bottle of brandy in each hand. 'When will ye speak with your father?' she asked.

'What about?'

'Oh, Niall...us, of course.'

'Oh, Dad knows about us.' Niall stooped to peer at the bottles of red wine. There was some awfully good stuff down here, but if something wasn't done about the temperature it was all going to spoil.

'Does he?' Beatrice squealed. 'Oh, lord!'

'Don't worry, he isn't going to fire you.' Niall went to the door.

'Fire me? It's marrying I'm talking about!'

Niall turned in consternation. 'Marry you? You have to be joking. You're a housemaid.'

'And who the hell are ye?' Beatrice demanded. 'Lord muck!'

'Why, you impudent...'

'I'll have ye in court for rape,' Beatrice declared. 'That'll wipe the smirk off your face.'

'You little bitch. As if you weren't crying out for it.'

'That's not what I'll say in court,' Beatrice told him.

'You...' Niall turned for the door, angrily, and watched it coming towards him, blown clear off its hinges by the explosion in the boiler room. The blast reached him before he could say anything, hurled him back into the cellar, where he fell to the floor in the midst of a cascade of shattered bottles and spurting wine.

Behind him, Beatrice also had her words smothered by the force of the blast, which drove her back against the wall; she dropped the brandy bottles to smash at her feet. Blood dripped from her nose and mouth, but she got her breath back to utter a ringing scream, as she saw, filling the doorway, a huge plume of flame.

Niall reached his knees, his clothes torn to rags by the force of the explosion. He couldn't speak, only point; the cellar was only half underground, and at the far end there was a window, high in the wall. It had been a barred window, but that too had been blown open by the force of the blast. Panting, gasping, feeling the flames already clawing at his back, Niall grasped the young maid by the shoulders and dragged her towards the opening.

James had just started down the cellar stairs when the oil tank exploded. He was hurled back up by the blast into the lobby, cannoning into Kitty as she ran along the servants' hallway. They fell together, rolling against the wall.

Kitty sat up, staring at the stairwell, which was an inferno. 'What happened?'

'The tank blew up!' James shouted. 'Too much heat. And if that opens up any vents down there...' he grabbed her hand and pulled her to her feet. But already the hall leading to the front of the house was sagging.

James turned, threw Kitty over his shoulder, and ran into the pantry. Mary had fallen to her hands and knees when the castle had shaken to the explosion. Now she peered at the intruders with an almost comical expression of dismay. 'Out!' James shouted. 'Get out!'

He ran at the back door, hurled it open, checked as he saw that one of the crenellated battlements from the rear tower had been dislodged and come crashing down. But those were risks he had to take: there were flames issuing from the cracks in the stone patio, and the smell of gas was very strong. He ran down the steps, Kitty hugged against his chest.

Mary staggered to her feet, looking around her like a trapped wild animal. She couldn't believe that this was happening to the house in which she had worked, and lived, all of her adult life. And where was Mr Guthrie, her mentor for most of those years?

The kitchen was along a short passageway to the right of the pantry, and she stumbled down this, to find Mrs MacBain fallen behind the table, thrown off her feet by the blast; blood was dribbling from a cut on her forehead. The kitchen was like an oven, but there were no flames to be seen as yet.

'Mrs MacBain!' Mary shouted. 'Mrs MacBain!'

She knelt beside the unconscious cook, and lifted her head, but Mrs MacBain didn't make a sound. Mary laid her down again, and ran to the sink to draw some water, stared at the steaming liquid in horror: it was all but boiling. 'Mrs MacBain!' she screamed, returning to the cook. 'Ye have to wake up.'

But Mrs MacBain didn't move. Desperately Mary grasped her shoulders and attempted to drag her to the door, but the cook was extremely heavy and Mary could only shift her a few inches. Panting, she collapsed back to her hands and knees, and gazed in horror as the floor seemed to be parting before her eyes, allowing little darts of flame to spurt upwards. 'Oh, Mrs MacBain!' she screamed, as she got up and ran through the doorway.

When the oil tank exploded, the burned men had already been taken out of the house and were being loaded on to the trucks and into the police van. Every head turned towards the castle, but from outside it was impossible to determine whether anything very serious had happened, save that several panes of glass had been shattered.

'Get moving!' Campbell snapped. 'Drive, drive, drive. You're in charge, Sergeant.'

'But what about you, sir?' Harvey asked.

'I'd better find out what's happening in there,' Campbell said. The sergeant hesitated only a moment. Ethel Yardley and Coultrain were already driving out of the yard with the injured Buckston. He signalled his men to move. Campbell ran across the yard and up the steps, paused in the front doorway in consternation. Twenty feet in from the door, the entire hallway was a mass of flame, seeping up from the cellars, and enveloping the great staircase.

Crowther stood at the top of the stairs holding his overnight bag, screaming. 'Help me!' he bawled, voice high and shaking with terror.

Campbell gulped, looked right and left. The study door was open, and Morris stood there, staring at the destruction of his dream. Guthrie stood in the drawing-room doorway, also staring at the flames; like Mary, he had lived and worked in this house all of his life.

'Help me!' Crowther screamed, and now was joined by Margaret, standing behind him.

'Windows!' Morris shouted, holding his hands in front of his face to shield himself from the heat. 'Make for the windows.' And then added, 'Oh, Christ, the windows are barred!'

Campbell swallowed; the underside of the first floor landing was on fire. 'Get away from there,' he bawled. 'Get to the servants' staircase. Hurry!'

Margaret disappeared as she ran along the corridor. Crowther hesitated for a last moment, looking down—and the landing gave way. With an unearthly scream he dropped straight down into the inferno below.

'Oh, God!' Morris was shouting. 'Oh, God!'

'Everyone out, whatever way you can,' Campbell yelled.

'My daughters!' Morris screamed. 'My daughters!'

'They'll have to use the servants'

staircase too,' Campbell said, and ran into the yard, wishing he hadn't sent all his policemen away, and giving a sigh of relief as he saw that MacPhail, having despatched his own people to safety, had returned.

Guthrie heard a roaring sound behind him, and turning, saw that flames had come up into the fireplace, and were already licking at the drapes at the far end of the room. He stood as if mesmerized for several seconds as he watched the twin elephants literally melting in the intense heat, then he ran behind the other men, out of the building.

Tara had run up the stairs so fast she was completely out of breath as she stumbled into her bedroom. Her life had never been in danger before. Well, she supposed it had, when careering from party to party in a car driven by drunken friends, but she had never supposed anything would happen. Now... And to think of the castle, so safe and solid...why, it had stood for several hundred years. Not that it had anything going for it; it was a dreadful bore. But she didn't want it to go up with her still in it.

She stopped panting, went into her bathroom and threw her toiletries into a washbag. This she then threw on the bed while she opened her wardrobe and surveyed her clothes. She wanted to take them all, but... The explosion sent her staggering and she fell over a chair. Oh, my God! she thought. But what could it be?

She pushed herself up, scooped golden hair from her face, and ran to the wardrobe. She seized an armful of clothes and threw them on the bed, standing on tiptoe to drag down her suitcase. Why was there no one here to help her? Beatrice the housemaid normally did all of this.

Her door crashed open. 'What are you *doing?*' Rebecca shouted.

'Packing,' Tara said crossly. 'What was that bang?'

'I don't know. But the house is on fire. We have to get out.'

'What about our things?' Tara demanded. Rebecca, she observed, was not carrying anything.

'There's no time for that. Hurry.'

Tara continued to stare at her, and Rebecca ran into the room, seized her sister's wrist, and dragged her to the door. 'My clothes! That was a new...'

'Fuck your clothes. Claim on the insurance.'

The sisters stumbled into the corridor together, looked along its length at the stairhead, where Crowther and their mother were standing, shouting. As they watched, Margaret turned and ran back towards them. And Crowther...they saw the floor give way and the accountant just disappear in a sea of seething red.

'Aaagh!' Tara screamed, paralysed. 'Aaaagh!'

'For God's sake!' Rebecca tugged at her.

'The back stairs!' Margaret yelled, running past them. 'The back stairs.'

'We're going to die,' Tara moaned. 'We're going to die.' She sank to her knees, despite Rebecca's attempt to hold her up.

'Of course we're not going to die!' Rebecca shouted. 'Get up, you great lump.'

She heaved Tara to her feet, and heard her mother scream. Half dragging Tara she hurried along the corridor to the far end, where the servants' staircase descended to just outside the pantry—and looked down at a sea of flame, already consuming the steps and bannisters and carpeting.

'Oh, my God!' Margaret was panting. 'Oh, my God! We're trapped.'

'The windows!' Rebecca snapped, and began dragging the screaming Tara back again, to the nearest guest bedroom. She hurled the door inwards, terribly aware of the roaring heat attacking her from behind, and threw her sister across the bed while she ran to the window. But the windows at Abergannan Castle were barred, as they had been since the days of Highland feuds. Rebecca remembered there had been much discussion as to whether the bars should be removed when they had bought the house, and Mummy had opted against it, because, she had felt, it would spoil the original look of the place. Now... She slid the double-glazed panels aside. 'Help us!' she screamed. 'Help us!'

Behind her Margaret stumbled into the room, tripping and falling to her hands and knees. With her came a plume of smoke. 'Shut the door!' Rebecca screamed. 'Help us!' she shrieked through the window.

And now the floor was heaving beneath her feet.

James continued to run for some seconds, carrying Kitty in his arms, until he tripped and they both fell heavily. Here they were some hundred yards from the castle, and to their relief the ground was reasonably cool. Then they sat up to gaze back at the huge building, to watch the flames issuing from the back door and the kitchen windows. There was surprisingly little smoke, but then, burning gas does not give off smoke, and the furnishings inside the house were being consumed so rapidly they had no time to smoke, either. But even as they watched, flames shot from the first-floor window above the back staircase.

'Mary,' Kitty said. 'She was right behind us.'

'Listen,' James said. 'Keep going, down the valley.'

Kitty caught his arm. 'What are you going to do?'

'Look for Mary. And there may be people still in the house.'

'James, Mary is dead, if she's still in there.'

'There may be others. I have to go, Kitty. I'll get back to you.' He got up and ran towards the burning castle.

A hundred yards from the rear of the building, James found Mary lying on the grass, panting. He knelt beside her. 'Are you all right?'

'Mrs MacBain,' Mary moaned. 'Oh, Mrs MacBain.'

James straightened. But the kitchen and pantry were a mass of flame; there could be no one alive in there, 'Listen,' he said. 'Get on out of the valley. You'll be safe there. Look for Miss Cochrane.'

He ran on, heard a shout. 'Help us, for God's sake, help us!'

In a gully he saw Niall and Beatrice, huddled together, clothes half blown off their bodies, cut and bleeding. 'Can you move?' he snapped.

Niall nodded feebly. 'But we're hurt. We need help...'

'Help yourselves,' James recommended, and ran on.

Campbell, MacPhail and Gus ran round the building to be at the back door when the Morris women emerged, checked in consternation as they gazed at the flames.

'The windows,' Campbell snapped. As they turned again, they heard Rebecca's scream.

They ran back round the front of the building and looked up at the white face at the window. 'Fucking bars!' MacPhail cried.

'Jesus!' James panted up to them. 'Ladder. In the shed. And a hacksaw.' He and MacPhail ran to the shed, while Campbell and Gus continued to look up at the window.

'Hold on!' the policeman called. 'We're going to get you.'

MacPhail and James ran back with the ladder, set it against the wall. Now the entire castle was alight and flames and smoke were rising into the air above them. The courtyard was almost too hot to walk on, and it would clearly soon burst into flames itself. Even more ominous were the cracks appearing in the paving, and the terrifying groans coming from the building as the foundations began to collapse into the fiery pit beneath the building.

'I'll go!' James had the hacksaw in one hand as he went up the ladder, reached the window, only some fifteen feet from the ground.

'Please! Hurry!' Rebecca gasped.

James looked past her into the room. Tara lay on her back on the bed, screaming continuously. Margaret knelt on the floor just inside the door; she might have been praying. And Rebecca clung to the bars, although they were almost red hot; her face was only inches from James as he started to saw. Behind the women, smoke was starting to seep through the closed door.

Desperately James sawed to and fro, using all his great strength. He got through the bottom of the first bar, seized it to bend it up. But he would need to cut at least three. 'Please hurry,' Rebecca said. 'Oh, please, James!'

Something fell past him and struck the ground with a crash; he looked down, and saw that it was another dislodged segment of battlement. The men beneath him had seen it coming and scattered, but it had struck Gus and sent him sprawling.

James sawed again, bent up the second bar. Now Tara was sitting up, still screaming, and Margaret was on her feet. James almost tore the third bar out of its socket in his haste, leaned in, grasped Rebecca by the shoulders, and virtually threw her past him. She gave a despairing scream as the jagged metal of the bars cut her clothes and her flesh. James turned back to reach for Tara, and the bedroom door burst open, to admit a huge tongue of flame and smoke.

'Help me!' Tara screamed, but it was too late. MacPhail and Campbell had seen what had happened, and jerked the ladder again from the wall before James could be burned. He fell through the air and landed with a thump which knocked all the breath from his body. Gasping, he scrambled back to his feet as the policeman and the engineer came back to him. The face at the window had been replaced by the gush of flame.

The three men were too horrified to move for some seconds. But then they had to, as the intense heat reached out from the burning windows, and they saw cracks appearing in the walls. While Gus was groaning and pawing at his leg, Rebecca was lying beside him; she did not appear to have broken anything in her fall, but was too dazed and shocked to speak.

James knelt beside them, examined Gus's

twisted leg. 'It's broken,' he told the others, sweeping the little scientist over his shoulder.

'We have to get out of here. All of us,' MacPhail said.

'I'll bring the lass,' Campbell volunteered, and lifted Rebecca, with some effort.

'Help Mummy and Tara,' she whispered. 'Oh, please help!'

They hurried round to the front of the building and found Guthrie and Morris on the lawn, staring up at the flames. 'My castle,' Morris muttered. 'My gas! My God!'

'Mr Morris,' Campbell said. 'I'm afraid that your wife and younger daughter were in there. There was nothing we could do.'

James thought grimly: Mammon is your god and it has destroyed you. But he didn't say it.

Morris's eyes were wide, vacant. 'I would have been a billionaire,' he said, his head turning from side to side.

Campbell looked at the other men. 'I think we had better put these people in a car,' he said, 'and get the hell out of here.'

Kitty ran straight down over the hillside, twice stumbling on the slippery grass, until she reached the stone wall beside the road. Breathless, she paused, leaned against the lichen covered stones and turned back to look at the castle. It was burning like a giant bonfire, huge gushes of flame spurting up out of the roof, or what was left of it. The outbuildings were blazing too and, like the castle, surrounded by a carpet of flame, as fissures opened in the courtyards and lawns allowing the burning gas to escape.

As her breathing returned to normal and her brain cleared, she became aware that the air was cooler. And so was the ground. The grey stones under her hand were chill. She had reached beyond the end of the subterranean reservoir.

Away to her left she saw someone crawling painfully out of danger. Mary! Thank heavens for that. Closer at hand were two more people, clinging to each other as they staggered towards safety. Niall and the chambermaid! She felt that should be significant, but couldn't decide why.

Away to her right, perhaps half a mile distant, those protesters who had escaped without injury were gathered. They were shouting at her, but her gaze was drawn back to the castle, and her heart seemed to skip a beat as she saw that huge, ancient edifice crumble, from the inside. The roof fell in while the walls still stood, as the floors collapsed into the disintegrating gas furnace. Then the walls also caved in, and the flames were almost obscured by a huge cloud of dust.

She fell to her knees, weighed down by the extent of the catastrophe. Then she saw the Land Rover coming down the road. It was scorched and blackened but it was moving, and there were people inside. She clambered over the wall and ran on to the road, waving her arms. The vehicle braked beside her, and James jumped down to take her in his arms. She looked past him in consternation at the five men. 'But...'

'We'll pick those three up,' James said. 'Then we have to get Gus and Rebecca to hospital.'

'Still raining,' Kitty said. 'That's forty-eight straight hours.'

Gus moved, restlessly. He was under slight sedation and his leg, broken in three places, was totally encased in plaster and suspended from a derrick contraption attached to his bed. But it was his mind which was uncomfortable. He glanced at Gillian, seated on his other side. She got the message, and stood up. 'Chemist-speak,' she remarked and left the ward.

'I wanted to apologize,' Gus said.

'I didn't know what was really going to

happen,' Kitty said.

'Your estimate was much more accurate than mine. What's it like up there?'

'Just a great scar,' Kitty said. 'The castle has collapsed, and so has most of Gannan Hill. The environmentalists are going mad.'

'But the rain has put the fires out?'

'Nobody knows. The surface fires are out, and the rain has obviously raised the water level underground sufficiently to cut off any vents. What's actually happening down there is anybody's guess.' She wrinkled her nose. 'I don't think anyone is going to find out, for a while.'

'Not even Morris?'

'Not even Morris,' Kitty said, definitely, and stood up. 'My time is up. I'll pop in again some time.'

'They tell me I'll be able to go home in another few days. Till then, you're in charge of the lab.'

Kitty raised her eyebrows. 'You mean I still have a job?'

'Well, of course you do, Kitty. Ben's orders. You were right and I was wrong.'

'Hm,' she commented. 'Take care.'

She paused outside the next ward. But she wouldn't know what to say to Rebecca. Rebecca was apparently quite recovered, physically; remarkably, she had not broken anything in her fall. But psychologically she apparently had big problems. Well, that presumably went for her father and brother as well.

Inspector Campbell was waiting for her downstairs, with James. 'What do you wish to do about Morris, Miss Cochrane?' the policeman asked.

'What do you mean? The attempt on my life? I thought we didn't have sufficient evidence?'

'We don't. But frankly, he is in such a distraught state, what with losing his wife and daughter, not to mention his castle and his gas, and being a bankrupt, and he seems to be in fear of his life from some Arabs he swindled. Also of course there is the inquiry into his responsibility for what happened, in view of your professional advice to him not to drill...and now his son committed to marrying Beatrice Farquharson... I mean, I've nothing against the girl, but Morris wouldn't think she was in his class, well... I think that if you brought a face to face accusation against him, he might well confess.'

Kitty looked at James, who raised his eyebrows. 'I don't think I want to accuse Morris of anything, any more,' Kitty said. 'He seems to have enough problems to fill his time for the next few years.'

Campbell nodded. 'Very civilized of ye,

to be sure. Ye'll be needed to give evidence at the inquiry, ye understand.'

'She'll be here,' James promised.

'Will I?' Kitty asked. 'Seems to me that now you're out of a job and I've just been told I still have one, that makes me the breadwinner. In Oxford.'

'We'll talk about it over tea at the cottage,' James decided. 'The animals need to be fed.'

This Large Print Book for the Partially sighted, who cannot read normal print, is published under the auspices of

THE ULVERSCROFT FOUNDATION